PENGUIN BOOKS

TAKE A GIRL LIKE YOU

Kingsley Amis, who was born at Clapham in 1922, was educated at the City of London School and St John's College, Oxford. At the age of eleven he embarked on a blank-verse miniature epic at the instigation of a preparatory school master, and he has been writing verse ever since. Until the age of twenty-four, however, he remarks: 'I was in all departments of writing *abnormally unpromising*.' With James Michie he edited *Oxford Poetry 1949*. Until 1963 he was a university teacher of English; he is a keen science-fiction addict, an admirer of 'white jazz' of the thirties, and the author of frequent articles and reviews in most of the leading papers and periodicals. His novels are *Lucky Jim* (1954), *That Uncertain Feeling* (1955), *I Like It Here* (1958), *Take a Girl Like You* (1960), *One Fat Englishman* (1963), *The Anti-Death League* (1966) and *I Want It Now* (1968). Of his other fiction, *My Enemy's Enemy* (1962) was a book of short stories, he wrote *The Egyptologists* (1965) with Robert Conquest, and *Colonel Sun* (1968) was published under a pseudonym. *A Frame of Mind* (1953), *A Case of Samples* (1956) and *A Look Round the Estate* (1967) are the titles of his books of poetry, and he is also the author of *New Maps of Hell* (1960 – a survey of science fiction) and *The James Bond Dossier* (1965), which he terms 'belles lettres'. His latest publications are *The Green Man* (1969), and *Girl, 20* (1971). Kingsley Amis is married and has two sons and a daughter.

Take a Girl Like You

KINGSLEY AMIS

PENGUIN BOOKS

Penguin Books Ltd, Harmondsworth, Middlesex, England
Penguin Books Australia Ltd, Ringwood, Victoria, Australia

—

First published by Gollancz 1960
Published in Penguin Books 1962
Reprinted 1964, 1965, 1966, 1967, 1968, 1970, 1971, 1972

—

Copyright © Kingsley Amis, 1960

—

Made and printed in Great Britain
by Hazell Watson & Viney Ltd,
Aylesbury, Bucks
Set in Linotype Granjon

Where shall I go when I go where I go?

Go, gentle maid, go lead the apes in hell.

TO
MAVIS AND GEOFF NICHOLSON

Chapter One

'HALLO, Miss Bunn,' Dick Thompson said on a note of celebration. 'Do come in, that's right. Here, let me take that for you. I expect you'd like to go straight up, wouldn't you?'

Jenny Bunn, a slender girl of twenty with very dark colouring, watched him turn and cross the square hall. His body was tilted forward and to the right, probably with the weight of her zip bag. He moved with short quick steps that were also somehow uncertain, as if he was going down a hill. With her music case in one hand and her tangerine-coloured topcoat thrown over the other arm she followed him up the stairs. These had rubber strips along the edge of each one, like stairs in a café.

On the landing a door opened and a rather plump girl came out. She was wearing a white blouse with a velvet bow, a very full skirt, and navy-blue knee socks. The most noticeable thing about her face was a pair of large brown eyes. Fixing these on Jenny, she said with a foreign accent: 'I shan't be in to supper, Dick.' With that she went past and began going down the stairs.

Dick Thompson wheeled round and called: 'Oh, Anna, this is –,' but the girl could not have heard, because she went on going down the stairs. 'That was Anna le Page,' he explained to Jenny. 'A grand girl. You'll like her very much, that I can guarantee. Everybody does. She's French, you see.'

'She looked nice.'

'Oh, she's a grand girl. Anything you want to know, Anna'll tell you. Here we are, then. I think you'll find there's plenty of room if you plan properly. Supper won't be ready for a minute or two, so you've timed it quite nicely. Now you've got all this cupboard, you see, but not this bottom drawer here, I'm afraid. The wife likes to keep spare bedding and so on in there. I say, is this all the stuff you've brought? It doesn't seem very ...'

'My mother's sending the rest of my things on next week,'

Jenny said defensively. 'They weren't all quite back from the cleaners.' When she said this she stuttered a little.

'I see, yes. I hope you like these curtains; we didn't feel really sure about them.'

'Oh, I think they're lovely. I love those big –'

'We weren't really sure they went with the room. Don't you think they're a bit on the heavy side?'

'Oh, no, it's the kind of material that –'

'Good, good. We've never felt really happy about them. Well, before I leave you to yourself I'll just show you the geography, shall I?'

'Thank you very much.' Jenny wondered what he could mean.

'Come along then. I expect you'll want a wash, won't you? Now this is ...' – he pushed open a door and showed a rather old-looking water-closet hissing quietly to itself – 'there, and over here we've got the bathroom. We'll have to arrange a time-table for that for the mornings but we needn't worry about that just now. Have a bath whenever you want one, of course. Except in the mornings, if you don't mind. That's the geyser here,' he went on to point out. 'I'll just show you how it works while I'm about it. Oh, and before I forget: I know you won't mind my saying this, but do try if you will to remember not to wash your, you know, your stuff in running hot water. It wastes fuel, you see. We had a lot of trouble like that with the girl who had your room before, quite apart from her habit of ... Now personally I can't bear a house with notices up all over the place, do this and don't do that and keep off the grass and thank you very much, so I'm just going to ask you to try and remember. Is that all right?'

'Yes of course, Mr Thompson.'

'It's common sense really, isn't it? Now this thing's perfectly simple when you understand it. This affair here turns until it's against this red mark – mind you don't go beyond it – then ...' He put a metal flint-scratcher into the mouth of the geyser and went clicking away. A jet of blue flame appeared, roaring feebly. 'Now the water; here we go. Hallo, that's funny. The whole issue should light up now.'

He tried the flint again. After a while there was a puffing explosion. It was fairly loud, and to go with it there was a jagged flame that came billowing out some way from the mouth of the geyser, which was where it had started.

Dick Thompson jerked himself upright, overdoing it so that he danced for a moment on the linoleum. He said: 'It shouldn't do that. I expect the water-pressure's a bit down. It sometimes is round here. Not usually at this time of the evening, though. It should be all right normally. You'll soon get used to it.'

Jenny looked up at the geyser and swallowed. It towered over her and seemed very fat, many sizes larger than herself and capable of behaving in almost any way.

The rumbling and splashing stopped. 'If the flame should suddenly take it into its head to go out, don't try to relight it with the flint thing whatever you do. Turn the whole issue off and start again. And if it starts to spit, then turn it off double-quick. It's quite a reliable old contraption.' He gave the geyser a familiar and affectionate slap on its smooth white flank, making a loud booming noise which sounded somehow sad. 'Should be, anyway, considering what I had to pay for it. The price things are these days, if you let yourself brood on it it'd turn your hair grey. That's our precious Tory government for you. We never had it so good, eh? Well, this won't do. See you downstairs in seven or eight minutes, Miss Bunn, but don't hurry yourself unduly.'

'I'll be very quick.'

'Good, good. Well, I hope you'll be happy here. Things are pretty informal round here, you'll find, we don't stand much on ceremony. We're all friends in this house. I think you'll like it.' He gazed at her for a moment, tilting his head on its long neck and smiling, then made a little noise like someone settling down to their favourite meal. 'I hope so, anyway, Miss Bunn. See you soon, then.'

He went away quickly, and although he now carried no zip bag his gait was just as easy to notice. In fact he seemed to be doing it more than before.

As Jenny bustled about having a very quick wash in cold water and brushing her hair, she gradually forgot about the geyser. But the ordeal of coming into a strange house still weighed upon her, especially since she was tired after travelling:

seven and a half hours it had been, from door to door. And in the morning there was the appointment with the Head, Miss Sinclair, who was going to show her round the school and explain her duties to her.

Miss Sinclair had been very kind to her when she came down for the interview. She had not asked Jenny any questions about why she proposed coming all this way south for her first job, which was just as well, because the true answer was too embarrassing to give – how could she have explained in public that she wanted to get as far away from her home town as possible so as to forget how she had been hurt? Miss Sinclair was not inquisitive, and her manner had shown that she was not going to keep reminding Jenny of her youth and inexperience. But she was the sort of career woman who expected efficiency from her staff and was not going to put up with anything less: her grey tailored suit, square-cut unpolished fingernails, and tightly packed naturally wavy grey hair had managed between them to make this plain. And the day after tomorrow all those children were going to come trooping in, laughing, squealing, crying, making faces, punching one another, falling over, and she was going to have to do something about every bit of that. Her teaching-practice report had said that she was inclined to be too lenient – could she stop herself being it? The school was huge and there were all those other staff all of them older than she. Where's that disgusting noise coming from, Miss Smith? – I think it must be Miss Bunn's as usual, Miss Brown.

Then there was the coming to a strange part of the world. It was not only a matter of this being a country town, even though it did seem to be very near London, instead of its being the large manufacturing city she had lived in all her life. What had made her feel nervous, in the bus coming up from the station, was thinking of the enormous number of total strangers there were about. Just a glance out of the window now showed house after house full of them.

That was no way for a sensible girl to go on. Deliberately, as she put on fresh lipstick, she set herself to think about Mr Thompson. He was obviously a nice enough man, if only because it had been Miss Sinclair who had fixed up for her to have digs in his house. But she did wish she understood more about him and about how he had come to be as he was. He was too kind and cheerful, and not badly dressed enough (he was wearing a collar and a self-colour tie even though his trousers were that very dark grey flannel kind), and not really old enough either, to be the kind of man to take in lodgers. He had treated her almost like a guest, or at least a relation. And how was it that he was an auctioneer, as Miss Sinclair had written to her? Chalking or sticking the numbers on, reading out about dinner services, and getting through the going-going-gone part was not enough to count as a full-time job for a grown man, a man past thirty. And why did the rims of his glasses not go all the way round the lenses? Perhaps time would show.

Before going down she looked round her room, which she knew she could brighten up in no time, and felt happy again. It was her base for a new life, one she could tackle all right and in which she was not going to be hurt. Coming here really had been the right thing.

Shutting her door behind her, she just had time to notice that it had a little brass knocker on it, in the form of a terrestrial globe wearing a straw hat and carrying a cane, before the sound of the front door being violently opened made her jump. A tall young man with curly brown hair and a sunburnt face was coming in. He caught sight of her when she got to the half-landing and she had to go down the whole bottom flight with him staring at her. The look on his face was one which she had got used to seeing on men's faces – some of them quite old men – when they first saw her, and sometimes when they had seen her before. Usually they seemed not to know they were giving her any particular kind of look, but this one did seem to know, and not to care much. He was handsome in a rather sissy way, and was pretending to have forgotten he still had his hand on the open door. She could tell that if he had been smoking a cigarette he would have taken it out of his mouth and thrown it away without taking his eyes off her. As was her habit in this situation, she stared right back at him as blankly as she could.

'Hallo,' he said when she reached him. 'Are you a friend of Anna's?' He had a deep voice with a slight London accent.

'Anna's? Oh, the French girl. No. At least, not yet. I've only just arrived. I've just come to live here.'

'Oh, you have, have you? How funny, though. I could have sworn you were French. It's the way you look.'

'Well, I'm not,' Jenny said positively, 'I'm English.' She said it positively because thinking she was French (or Italian, or Spanish, or – once each – Greek or Portuguese) on the evidence of the way she looked had evidently been enough to get quite a number of new acquaintances to start trying it on with her straight away. There had even been that time in Market Square at home when a man had accosted her and, on finding she was not a tart after all, had apologized by saying: 'I'm awfully sorry, I thought you were French.' What could it be like to actually live in France?

'Then you must be the young lady who's come to teach at Albert Road,' the man was saying. 'Well, I never did. French or not, you certainly don't look like a schoolmistress.'

To take the lead off him, Jenny said: 'If you're looking for Miss le Page I'm afraid she's gone out.'

'Oh? Are you sure?'

'Oh yes, I saw her go out about ten minutes ago. She said she wouldn't be in for supper.'

'That's funny. She told me . . .' He blinked and pursed his lips, still looking at her closely. 'I wonder what's best to do.'

'I could give her a message for you if you like.'

'That might be a good idea. Let's see . . .'

He had still not composed his message when a door opened at the end of the short passage that led rearwards from the hall. A voice easily recognizable as Dick Thompson's called out: 'Hallo, Patrick, come on in. Thought I heard you.'

A spasm of pain or something crossed the man's face and he whispered a word or two to himself. Then with great warmth he said: 'Hallo there, Dick, how are you? I think I'd really better be off, thanks all the same. Got a lot to do. First night back, you know.'

'Oh, come on, don't be mouldy. Stay and be introduced to our new member.'

The man gave Jenny an extra look. 'Well, I suppose I could do that, couldn't I, now you come to mention it? Just a few minutes, then.'

'That's my boy.' Dick Thompson introduced the man as Patrick Standish and took them into what would have had to be the kitchen. Its door had another little brass knocker on it, this time representing a religious-looking person on a donkey. The room was a long narrow one that ended with a further door and a large, oblong, buff-coloured stove. A medium-sized woman with reddish hair and a purple dress was doing something to the stove, but stopped when they came in. She had a snouty kind of face which was not completely unpretty. It broke into a smile at the sight of Patrick Standish, then went ordinary again at the sight of Jenny.

'Hallo, Martha,' Patrick Standish said. He was wearing a stone-coloured corduroy jacket with a navy-blue scarf knotted round his neck. Both of them helped considerably to give him his sissy look, without hiding the fact that he was older than she had thought at first, round about thirty.

'Hallo. I'm afraid Anna's gone out.'

'So I've just been hearing. Never mind, she'll have to come back some time, won't she?'

'Pretty late, if her recent behaviour's any guide.'

'Ah, these continentals. They live life to the full in a way that we can only –'

'A *rakish* sports car seems to have got into the habit of picking her up here.'

'Hope it's a nice chap driving. Hope it's a chap, in fact.'

'Oh, it's a chap all right.'

'This is Miss Bunn, dear,' Dick Thompson broke in in a slightly ticking-off tone.

'I rather thought it might be. How do you do? You found us all right, then. I expect you're hungry, aren't you? We might as well get on with it, I suppose. Dick, get the cruet, will you, and the sauce?' Mrs Thompson spoke quickly turning her face to and fro without looking at Jenny, and blinking a good deal. Over her shoulder she said: 'Have you eaten, Patrick? Sure? Well, you won't mind watching us eat, will you?'

'Watching the animals feeding,' her husband corrected her, showing Jenny her place at the table. This piece of furniture was covered with a plastic cloth in large red-and-white check, which did not stop it being like the water-closet upstairs in looking old:

not antique, just old. The armchairs, one of which was a rocker with a long round cushion on it, had the same old look. But the hard chairs were the newlywed-suite kind often on show in the windows of shops. They had semicircular backs.

Mrs Thompson put a plate of fish and potatoes in front of Jenny. The fish was probably haddock, with a horny, pimply skin. There were a lot of potatoes, with some unexpected colours to be seen among them here and there. They were steaming briskly. So was the fish.

Dick Thompson sat down with emphasis, moving his shoulders about a lot so that his flimsy dark hair fell forward. Very genially, he said: 'Well, I suppose I'd better put you in the picture about our Miss Bunn, Patrick. It appears she's come down to infant-teach at Albert Road, the renown of which must have spread far and wide, because her home is located as far away as –'

'I knew that,' Patrick Standish managed to interrupt. 'The Albert Road thing, I mean.'

'You knew? But it hasn't been fixed longer than –'

'Ah, but you forget Patrick had already had speech with Miss Bunn before coming out here' – this was Mrs Thompson, who had become very lively – 'and that was quite long enough at the rate he –'

'My godfather, yes.' Dick Thompson gave a laugh like the cawing of a rook. 'Second to none in the speedy acquisition of vital information. A powerful man in the intelligence network, our friend Patrick.'

'If you must know, I happened to run into –'

'Ooh, now I do declare we've got him rattled. Look, Martha, here's something to tell the grandchildren if you like: Patrick Standish, Esquire, Master of Arts, engaged in the act of blushing. I never thought I'd live to see the day.'

'Just shows you it doesn't pay to be too sure about people.'

'Think you've got them taped and then you get this kind of thing.'

Jenny had been smiling at the way everyone seemed so jolly, but something in Patrick Standish's manner made her turn serious again when he said to her: 'I don't know whether I shall get a chance of finishing this sentence, but anyway I'll start telling you that I'm in the teaching business, too, so you and I are colleagues in a sense.'

'In a *sense*,' Mrs Thompson said, drawing one corner of her mouth over to the side.

'Yes, that's what I said, in a sense. I'm at the College here.'

'Oh, that big school up on the hill, with the tower?' Jenny asked.

'That's the one.'

This surprised Jenny, in much the same way as she had been surprised by the notion of Dick Thompson being a man who took in lodgers. When the talk moved to what somebody called Graham might now be up to, then to the funny way he always carried on, she thought over the new fact that dressing like a person away on holiday, and having a sort of free-and-easy manner, were apparently no bar to being a teacher at what was very likely a public school. It had looked like one anyway, she remembered thinking as she explored the town after her interview, with all that ivy, what must have been a private chapel, and boys all wearing the same kind of suit. She would have expected teachers at such a place to be like teachers at the Grammar at home, only more so. It was plain that her new life was going to be full of what she would not have expected.

Dick Thompson leaned back in his chair and, having cleared up his fish and potatoes in a workmanlike manner, lit a cigarette and made absolutely no bones whatsoever about how much he was enjoying it. All Jenny had been able to manage in that time was sucking at a few mouthfuls of fish as if they were toffees, until they were small enough to swallow. She looked down at her plate. On it was a lot of fish, haddock actually, almost as much as had been there when she began. In fact – although this could not be right – there seemed to be slightly more. She had at last identified the taste of it as that of the lionhouse at Southport Zoo, where she had once gone with her parents and been sick over somebody else's coat. At least when she now breathed out through her nose while chewing there was a kind of smell of lionhouse. Why was that?

In the intervals of talking about this Graham, who it appeared had been getting on less than well with a girl who worked at a local barber's, Patrick Standish had been giving Jenny some more looks. Often the men who gave her the kind of look he had given her to start with made a point of suddenly turning their attention somewhere else after a few seconds, as if they wanted to show that they had seen as much as they cared to see, thank you, but that had not happened with him. This additional run of looks he was giving her was of the kind that had been known to lead straight on to an invitation out. Jenny quite hoped that this was going to happen. It was true that he was rather old for her, probably a bit older than would have been allowed by the sort of sliding scale her father used for helping him to make up his mind who could and who could not take her out: nobody over sixteen when she was fifteen, nobody over eighteen when she was sixteen, and nobody over twenty-one when she was seventeen. But for somebody of twenty, and a wage-earner, and standing on her own feet away from home, the time for the sliding scale had surely gone by. Leaving age out of it, then: now that she was more used to Patrick Standish's appearance and manner they seemed quite attractive, and intellectual rather than sissy – the two were sometimes hard to tell apart. Also, he was funny, or so it could be gathered from the cawing laugh with which Dick Thompson was greeting most of the things he said. She had thought earlier on that Patrick Standish must be going round with the Anna le Page girl, but she now decided that that idea only went to show how immature and unsophisticated she was. Probably he was just trying to get hold of her to arrange some French conversation classes at the College, or something like that.

'I'll make some coffee,' Mrs Thompson said, gathering the plates together. Jenny got up to give her a hand, but Dick Thompson would not allow this.

'No, no, you've been travelling,' he said considerately; then he glanced round at them all and added: 'Well, this is very pleasant, I must say. What about popping down to the George for a couple in a few minutes? We could give Graham a ring later to see if he's turned up yet.'

'I ought to unpack and so on,' Patrick Standish said.

'You can do that tomorrow.'

'All right then.'

'Talked you into it, have I? What about you, Miss Bunn?

I'm sure you'd like to see our local. Nothing very much in the amenities line, but you see some very interesting types. We've had some pretty good discussions down there in the past. I'm sure you'd enjoy it, really I am.'

'That's very kind of you,' Jenny said, 'but I don't think I will if you don't mind, not tonight. I've got one or two things to do and I'm rather tired. But thank you for asking me, Mr Thompson.'

'Are you sure?'

'Yes, honestly, thank you.' Jenny saw Patrick Standish shut his eyes and pass his hand over his brow as if a bad headache had suddenly got him.

'What's happened to the coffee, Dick?' Mrs Thompson called from what must have been the scullery. Her husband rose to his feet in a disordered way and hurried out. Patrick Standish leant forward in his chair and fixed Jenny with his eye.

'Please come,' he said in a pleading half-whisper.

'No really, I'd be sat there falling asleep if I did come. I'd like to, but I'm not up to it this evening. I'm not being a spoil-sport, honestly.'

'If I'd known I wouldn't have ... Look, can I give you a ring some time? Would that be a good idea?'

'Well, I don't know ...'

'Ah, come on, a phone call won't hurt you.'

'Yes, all right.'

Coming back into the room to fetch a tray from the plastic-topped sideboard, Mrs Thompson heard the last part of this. She gave Jenny a look that she had already treated her to a couple of samples of, a kind of look Jenny had got to know well. Usually the women who turned it on her were older than Mrs Thompson. A pair of them would watch her coming down the street or across a teashop, give her the look as if they had been rehearsing together for it, and then lean over to mutter to each other as she went by; she had often wondered what about exactly. This present look of Mrs Thompson's had an extra bit to it. It was broken up by a sideways look at Patrick Standish, not going on so long but just as hard. One way and another Jenny felt she had had enough of looks for the time being.

She still felt this to some extent when, twenty minutes or so

later, she began moving round her bedroom arranging her be-
longings. But the last look of the evening had been worth all
the others. Patrick Standish had given her it as he said good
night and added in sort of capital letters: 'See you again.'
Before and after this he had nodded his head once. She made up
her mind not to think about any of this – not too much, anyway
– until she had found out whether he meant it.

On the mantelpiece she lined up her photographs: the one of
her father in his sergeant's uniform with her mother in a floral
dress hanging on to his arm and laughing; the family group,
taken about the same time, with her sister Trixie in plaits, herself showing enormous knees under a tartan frock and Robbie
looking frightened and blowing out his cheeks; the Redcar one
with them all in bathing suits – Jenny thought she looked nice
in it, but it was not really vain to put it up, because it was good
of all the others, especially Trixie; a snap of some of her Training College friends she had taken herself; and one of Uncle Reg
and Auntie Kitty and her cousins. It was the same collection as
she had had for years at home, except that there was not one of
Fred. When she had been packing she had almost slipped in the
studio portrait he had had done specially for her – but what
would have been the point of reminding herself of something
that was over and done with? She told herself to forget Fred
had ever existed, and tried to hope that he was enjoying himself
with that Madge Bennett. But it was hard to feel in that way
when Fred had been Jenny's Fred for so long.

With her mouth firmly set she took her pyjamas and dressing-
gown, walked into the bathroom and faced the geyser. It looked
bigger than ever, but if she did not try it tonight she never
would. The flint-scratcher worked all right, but after that it
came down to two choices: she could have either a thick stream
of tepid water, or a weak trickle of scalding water plus a fog of
steam and a huge panting in march rhythm from inside the
geyser. Working out that she had better wait until her newness
in the house had worn off a bit before setting about blowing up
its bathroom, she made do with a quick thorough wash standing
on a towel in front of the wash-basin. On her way back she
noticed that on the French girl's door there was a third little
brass knocker. This one was of a man with knee-breeches, staff

and lantern who, to judge by the state of the metal of which he was made, had just been given a burst from a larger-than-usual machine-gun. How old the house was.

One thing about the bathroom had depressed her slightly. The absence there, now established for certain, of any rubber animals, boats, small shoes, or breakages put it beyond argument that the Thompsons had no baby. Although in the nature of things it was unlikely that any other baby could have been as sweet as little Stephen, Trixie's second baby, who had gone to Jenny of his own free will after tea the previous day, any baby at all would have been better than none. She wished again that she could have brought Mac with her; he was marvellous company. Mac was the Bunns' Scottie, or rather the curious tiny huge-eared animal that had been sold to Jenny and Robbie as a pedigree Scotch terrier puppy. Anyway, Robbie was taking good care of him, and she would see him when she went home for the holidays. When she knew Mr and Mrs Thompson better she might ask them if she could keep a kitten in her room. She could easily buy a tray from Woolworth's and put earth from the garden on it to make an earth-tray. They had forbidden pets at the Training College (though that was understandable and quite fair). Things were bound to be different here.

Everything was done now. She arranged her hairbrush and pot of cream on the dressing-table, which had a miniature railing round it as if it had come from on board ship, and rolled in between the sheets. The rolling was easier than it might have been because of the way the bed sloped in towards the middle. But the mattress was a decent one and the pillows were soft. Lying back on them she read the rest of the *Woman's Domain* she had bought for the journey, first finding out about ways of increasing her self-confidence, then about ways of making fruit pies. This made her feel very hungry, and it was a good thing that she had thought to save the chocolate biscuit and apple from her sandwich-parcel. After eating these and glancing through the horoscopes – her own promised her a quiet week with an opportunity for travel at the end of it, her father's warned him to beware of a masterful, selfish person who might put temptation in his way – she got out of bed again and turned off the light. String on the switch tomorrow.

A street-lamp threw a triangle of light across the ceiling. Staring up at this she thought again about Mrs Thompson's look. Perhaps there was something she ought to have apologized for, or had she not thanked her heartily enough for the meal and for agreeing to put her up? Well, it simply meant that she would have to work extra hard to convince Mrs Thompson that her new lodger was a quiet, responsible girl, helpful and easy to get on with. And she would do that gladly, because of the way Patrick had looked at her when he said good night. How incredibly lucky she was to have met someone as nice as that within a few minutes, really, of arriving in a strange town.

Except for the odd car, the road on to which her bedroom faced was a quiet one. Once a group of people passed up the hill, talking and laughing noisily; then silence. Some time later a loud harsh male voice came into range, singing a short piece of tune.

'*Father's got 'em,*' it sang several times over; '*father's got 'em.*' When the owner of the voice had drawn level with her window, was perhaps standing under the street-lamp, he started talking instead.

'Father's got 'em, father's got 'em. And what about mother? She just don't know what she's up against, poor bitch. Father's got 'em. And by Christ no wonder. Being sane and of sound mind he couldn't do nothing else. Father's got 'em. You know why? Because he knows what he's bloody up against, that's why. Suburbia. That's the enemy. That's the deadly mortal foe. *Morning, portah, she going to be on time this morning?* Oh yes sir, wouldn't keep you waiting sir. *Air, jawly good, portah, and how's the waif?* Nicely thank you sir. Nicely's right. Mind you, in a way it's the poor bloody wives I'm sorry for. Five years trying to land yourself a man and the rest of your life wishing you hadn't. Not a man really, of course. Corpse, more like. There's the money, though. Legalized bloody prostitution, that's what it is. Look at their faces, that'll tell you all right. This is the news and this is Able Seaman Arthur Jackson reading it. Ever-loving wives? Don't make me laugh.'

But the speaker did laugh, so much so that he broke into a fit of phlegmy coughing. Well before it was over he was on his way again.

Jenny lay curled into a tight ball. The address she had heard had succeeded in reminding her of how far she was from her family and friends and any scenes that were familiar to her. What was going to start happening to her in the morning seemed impossible to imagine, and the new place she had come to was enormous and foreign. For the moment, its silence was complete. Then she heard a train whistling in the distance and, immediately afterwards, quick steps coming towards the house. The front door shut loudly; someone ran up the stairs; the bedroom door next to her own banged, so that she caught the tiny tinkle of its brass knocker: the French girl, Anna le Page. There was somebody she would surely be able to talk to.

Jenny turned over on her side and slowly let her feet push down the bed, put her hand under the pillow and spread the fingers as she always did. She relaxed. She was asleep.

Chapter Two

'Miss, they're all fighting in the passage. They're breaking the milk-bottles and all.'

'Who are? Where?' Jenny had been picking up some of the worst of the mess left by Class 1a at the end of the day – it was the cleaners' job really, of course, but she disliked the thought of Miss Bunn's lot being judged by anybody as the piggiest. Now she got up from a crouching position in the centre aisle, where a bag of peanuts had emptied itself, and went over to the two little girls at the door. 'What's happening, Ava?'

'They're all fighting, Miss Bunn.' Ava's manner showed satisfaction at not being fighting herself, and also that she was very interested in seeing how the new teacher would handle a proper row.

'Who? How many of them?'

'A lot of them, Miss Bunn,' the other little girl said, fingering her mauve suède belt. 'Boys mostly. That Donald Rayner.'

Jenny hurried out. She already knew that Donald Rayner by sight and reputation – he was not one of hers – as a character who was going to cause a lot of relief when he went off to the

Junior School at the end of the year. Downstairs, as she went along the gloomy corridor towards the centre of the noise, she found she was panting and took some deep breaths. It was a tip which had stood her in good stead at her interview. She could not afford to stutter in a situation like this.

About twenty children had clustered together just inside the exit to the playground. Here there was a small alcove where the metal crates of empty milk-bottles were always stacked. It made a handy rallying-point for those who thought they were too re-fined to chase one another about in the open air. The noise was quite loud in the alcove; it got less when the nearer children noticed that Jenny had arrived and turned round to face her. They all had the same expression of being proud of being serious, like some famous author photographed in the *Radio Times*. As she had expected, those actually doing the fighting were few: Donald Rayner and two other boys. A fourth boy, Michael Primrose, who was a member of Jenny's class, was standing in the doorway, no doubt on guard, but when she gave him a glare he began to behave like someone who has worked out the best place to stand and can see no reason for shifting.

'Stop it,' Jenny shouted. 'Stop it at once. What do you think you're doing? Let him go.'

Their eyes fixed on hers, their faces perfectly blank, the three fought on, but at a slower rhythm, as if they were under water. Although Donald Rayner still clasped his fat enemy round the waist and tried to kick his shins while having his own head forced back, although his friend, a small dark creature with the face of a man of forty, went on punching the fat boy on the bottom, it was obvious that by now they were only putting on a demonstration. The idea behind it came out when Donald Rayner said clearly and dangerously: 'You bugger off, miss.'

All the little girls present gasped with indignation and shock. Somebody on the fringes gave a short laugh, a cracked, crazy one.

'Don't you swear at me,' Jenny said, and parted the two who were wrestling. To do so she had to pull Donald's hair, but she felt she could stand that. He backed away, showing his teeth; then, with everyone suddenly quiet, he rushed at her and threw a punch which she took easily on her forearm. Although quite a hefty punch for a child of six and a half, it was not the hardest he could have managed, and Jenny could tell that the worst was over. Before he could get away she caught his wrist with her left hand. Remembering in a flash a torture that she and Robbie used to practise on each other, she put the back of her right hand against the back of Donald's and pinched him with the second joints of her first two fingers. This hurt much more, she and Robbie had proved, than the ordinary thumb-and-first-finger pinch, but like all pinches it left no wound and so was good for staff-parent relations. She held him at arm's length to prevent him from closing with her, and said in a coaxing voice: 'Now, Donald, I'm sure you don't really want to fight. Let's just forget about it, shall we?' She stepped up the pressure a bit. 'Let's all be friends, Donald, eh?'

He relaxed and she let him go. After a moment's thought he picked up his satchel from the nearby stairs, jerked his head at his mate, who had been watching with bright rabbity eyes, and lumbered away, saying conversationally as he went out: 'Silly bitch.' The others started talking it over loudly.

'Are you all right?' Jenny asked the fatty buster. 'Of course you are. Run along now, all of you. Your mothers'll be waiting. Thank you for fetching me, Ava. Off you go, there's a good girl.'

'What's going on here?' another woman's voice asked. 'Oh, I beg your pardon, Miss Bunn, I didn't see you. Really, the light in this passage is appalling. Why the whole place wasn't pulled down long ago I can't think. Has there been trouble of some kind?'

'Why no, Miss Sinclair, nothing much, just a little wrestling-match or something.'

'Come out into the light; it depresses me to talk in here.'

They emerged into dull sunshine among the last of the rioters. Miss Sinclair put her hands on her hips as she watched them. 'Well, whatever it was you seem to have broken it up quite effectively.' She was wearing her grey tailored suit with a tiny watch at the lapel and had an off-white hat on her head. This hat, which was smart in a way that Jenny had never taken into consideration before, managed to add to the effect of the slightly scaring things about her. But Jenny was too delighted at the compliment just paid, and too grateful for the way Miss Sinclair had not taken any of the credit for restoring order, to feel scared, or anyway to mind feeling slightly scared. Then she caught sight of a half-rolled-up oblong of American cloth on the floor of the alcove. 'Oh, they've knocked down that chart thing from off the wall. I'll just put it up again.'

'Never mind about that for now, Miss Bunn. I'm afraid we haven't managed to have a proper talk since term began. It's my fault – the start of the year's always rather a busy time for me. How do you like your first taste of teaching?'

'I like it very much, Miss Sinclair, thank you.'

'Good. Of course, it's still rather soon to tell. But they're a pretty decent sort of children, the ones we get here, I think. You haven't had any serious disciplinary trouble?'

'None at all, thank goodness.'

'You shouldn't in fact. But be sure to let me know if you ever do. And please regard yourself as at liberty to consult me about anything else that ... may strike you. After all, you are a long way from home. Will you do that, Miss Bunn?'

'Yes, that's very kind of you.'

They had been walking slowly over to the corner of the playground, where a church of no particular coloured stone was to be seen on the far side of the road. The sight of it depressed Jenny. There was a lot about it that reminded her of what it had been like to go out for walks with her parents when she was a child. These walks now seemed to have always taken place on cloudy Sunday evenings at about this time of year, they had always gone through a street where, so it was said (and she could well believe it), a famous mass murderer had done his stuff, and they had always ended up at her grandma's, where in semi-darkness – the old lady had not much cared for switching on what she called the electric – Jenny had had to keep Robbie quiet while hymns of the sort that made you want to do away with yourself had been sung: *The King of Love My Shepherd Is* and *There Is a Green Hill Far Away*. Over the road now an elaborately got up notice-board advertised forthcoming attractions in gilt on black, and a wayside-pulpit placard told her that there would not always be a tomorrow on which to do better than yesterday. A draught of cold air – the evenings were turning chilly about now – passed up her spine. She longed for the sight of cheerful modern colours, the cover of a new copy of *Woman's Domain*, the yellow or blue label of a record on the top twenty, somebody passing in scarlet jeans and luminous socks.

Miss Sinclair turned back when they reached the railings. She said in a sharp tone: 'I hope you'll do as you say. I want you to feel that you have somebody to turn to if you need anything. These days I never seem to get as much contact with junior staff as I should like. I hardly even know what their problems are any more.'

Jenny found this hard to answer. Having remembered after a gap of almost twenty minutes that Patrick was taking her out that evening, she felt much too happy to imagine herself needing anything from Miss Sinclair. And she knew that if ever she did find herself in real trouble she could never ask someone over twenty years older for advice or help, even when the someone was as kind as this. To suggest the opposite, she said: 'I'll just come to your room, shall I, and see if you're free?'

Miss Sinclair gave her a brilliant smile, showing white teeth that were obviously her own. She must have been very good-looking once, Jenny thought. 'Oh, will you? I should be so happy to think you would.'

'Of course I will.'

'I should like to talk to you longer now, but you want to get away and I've got to talk to that frightful new caretaker. He still can't understand about the boilers, curse him. Tell me, Miss Bunn, how are things with Mr and Mrs Thompson? Is it a pleasant sort of household, do you find?'

'Oh yes, very matey and nice.'

'I've no direct knowledge of it myself, but one of your predecessors was there for a short time a couple of years ago and reported favourably. Mr Thompson's an auctioneer, I believe.'

'That's right.'

'I never remember seeing his name on hoardings but no doubt he has his own modes of operation.'

'Good afternoon, Miss Sinclair. Thank you for a very nice afternoon at school.' This speech, pronounced in the style of a child doing a television commercial about how much he liked somebody's sausages, was made by a pale small boy who had sneaked up on them unnoticed. He had a tiny full-lipped mouth, narrow eyes and pouchy cheeks, and only needed a wig and a royal-blue dress to look like a lady in a historical portrait. On his head was a huge new-looking cap, which he raised with a movement that reminded Jenny of the examples of poor physical co-ordination she had seen in instructional films. There was a touch of Dick Thompson about it, too.

'That's quite all right, Elias. Good-bye. Dreadful little creature, that,' Miss Sinclair added to Jenny after a moment. 'And it's no real excuse to say he only behaves like that because his parents tell him to. A child should show some independence. Elias, indeed. Well, Miss Bunn, you must come and have a cup of tea with me when things have eased up. Would you like that?'

'That would be lovely. Good-bye, Miss Sinclair.'

When Jenny had hung the chart thing up on the wall again (it gave an account, hard to believe, of how they did tree-felling and such things in Canada), put a single chipped milk-bottle back in its crate, fetched her music case, with books and not music in, from the classroom and finally got out to the street, she found three children still waiting for her. One of them was Michael Primrose, the boy who had acted as sentry during the fight. He gave her an apple-cheeked grin and said: 'Ooh, Miss Bunn, it was smashing, the way you beat up old Donald Rayner just now. How did you do it?'

'I didn't beat him up, it was all will-power.'

'Yeah, I bet.'

Close by, a small group of mothers were waiting for the last of the children, some of them clutching the hand of a toddler, others rocking a pram. Although she was ashamed of doing so, Jenny took a great interest in these and other mothers. As regards about two out of three of them there was a terrific difficulty in imagining them taking part in the act that, seven or five or even three or fewer years ago, had ended up in the children they had come to meet or brought along. They looked – the thing had got to be faced – much too horrible. Not only that, but the kind of man who thought they were not horrible, or not horrible enough to make much odds, must himself be more horrible still. To really let the fact that these mothers were mothers sink in meant completely changing all sorts of ideas about what went on in marriage. Jenny hoped that it was just that all those husbands were drunk, blind drunk, all the hours there were, and in some cases, since people did not get worse as quickly as all that, had been drunk for twenty years. At the end of the line today was a creature looking like a giant mad sheep that had just been bundled into a coat of the colour Jenny called depressing red. It was clasping in its front legs a tightly wrapped-up baby that was a little lamb to more of an extent than most. Poor wee thing, Jenny thought as she led her trio past; then she brightened up again. If that was a mother, nobody ever needed lose hope of anything.

All the way down to the bottom of the hill where the disused remnants of part of the pickle factory were still to be seen, there were groups of children in various formations, running round one another, in rough circles all facing inwards but still on the move, walking in a polite way with their mothers. Quite a large car slid past, carrying one of the rare fathers and his two sons. On a brick gate-pillar outside the Junior School somebody had chalked ALL THE BOYS WE KNOW A NASTY AND UGLY. Underneath were a few signatures. Ordinary passers-by started being noticeable, mixing with the stream of school.

'What sort of box can't you get into?' Michael asked suddenly.

'Boxing-match,' Diane Coade said.

'That's not a sort of box, that's a sort of match.'

'Pillar-box, then.'

'No.'

'But you can't get into a pillar-box.'

'But that's not the answer.'

'But it must be : you can't get into it.'

'But you can. Postmen do, so as to get out the letters and all those things.' Michael was speaking in a hard abrupt way, as if he looked down on his audience.

'They don't, they just put their hands in.'

'They don't, they get into it, the big ones, I've seen them.'

'Ooh, you are a liar.'

'Well, what is the answer, Michael?' Jenny asked trying to think of a kind of box you could get into. In a fortnight of knowing him she had found out so much about him that it seemed impossible there should be any more to find out. First there was his way of carrying on conversations. He very quickly got over the gaps between the things he wanted to say, and he very easily avoided subjects his hearers might know something about. Even people twelve times his age would have had their work cut out to beat him there; even Mr Burrage, the retired florist who lived next door to the Bunns at home, even Jenny's grandfather himself, hard to beat as he was when it came to spreading a conversation out thin, would have had few tips to give young Michael.

Then there was his naughtiness. Jenny felt she could have written a long English composition on this theme. At the cry 'All get out your reading-books' which she gave about twelve times a day, Michael's book was sure to be the last to be got out, but never quite long enough after the others to count. In asking 'What time's playtime, Miss Bunn?', though, he was always first, and the stock reply, 'When you've done all your sums,' never satisfied him. Later he would get round her ban on mentioning playtime by calling it the interval and so on, or by shouting out about how well he was getting on with his sums. He was a fine judge of all sorts of limit, and when he yelled 'I'm the boss of the sums,' as he was always doing, the yell was never quite too loud, or quite an interruption, or quite too soon after a warning. And his interest in himself and what he could do was too natural and too full of joy to be worth cracking down on.

Jenny thought what a handsome little boy he was as he reeled along in front of her now, his neat dark fully moulded face permanently over his shoulder to give out his speeches or quizzes. It was hard not to be charmed by his looks and his smile, by his clear pronunciation, or by the way that when he thought of it he asked to carry her books for her, like a schoolchild in a story, but nicer. Diane Coade gave no sign of giving in to all these charms except by having at once admitted, when challenged by Jenny, that she was Michael's girl-friend. He would be a terrible one for the women when he grew up, Jenny thought, being not only lively and able to show he knew he was wicked, but also simply incapable of noticing opposition. There seemed to be nothing to be done about it.

But the one who needed something being done about him, far more than Michael was ever likely to, was tiny silent open-mouthed John Whittaker who walked along holding her hand. His face was flat, so that he had no proper eye-sockets, and his nose and mouth were reddish and rubbery. Except for a pair of rather pathetic pink legs, there was nothing anywhere near attractive about him. It was already as certain as it could be that he was not going to be a terrible one for anything most people would want or be interested in, above all not for the women. Apart from howling like a monster in the playground and muttering the word *toilet* once or twice in class, he had never uttered a sound in front of Jenny. With people like Michael so ready to pounce on anybody less quick than themselves, it was better not to do any coaxing. But that so easily turned into an excuse for not noticing people like John. She had already asked a colleague casually if anyone knew anything about him. It seemed that no one did. Jenny looked down at the strands of dry colourless hair that ran lengthways along the top of his head, and made up her mind.

Michael had long ago given the answer to his riddle in a jeering tone of voice and was now telling them at top volume about the dense jungle, infested by sharks and octopuses, which his mother had to cut her way through with a cutlass every morning to do the shopping. It lasted them till the High Street, where the yawning, stubbled face of some lorry-driver or other, unnoticed by any of them, peered glumly out from the window table of the Gourmet Café. On seeing Jenny the eyes lit up briefly, then seemed to fade in despair or apathy. Across the road by the antique shop, in which there were some copper candlesticks Jenny would have liked to have for her mantelpiece, the four of them parted. Michael shouted 'See you in the morning, Miss Bunn' and flashed his best smile. Diane shouted 'So long', and ran away after him. Keeping hold of John's hand to prevent him joining in, Jenny stooped down and said to him: 'Would you like to come and have tea with me on Monday, John?'

His eyes, which had been staring over her shoulder, focused on her for a moment and he nodded. She told him to ask his mummy if he could come and, if he could, to be sure to wait for her after school on that day. He gave another nod, less definite than before. With no more sign he put his head down and ran after the others. From behind he had a square look, like a little robot. He was well enough fed and dressed, anyway, and no dirtier than the average. Perhaps he just hated school.

After a couple of minutes' climb between bungalows on one side and three storeyed houses, all very different in colour and shape, on the other, Jenny turned in through the gate of Carshalton Beeches, the Thompsons' house, and nowadays, of course, her own home. In front of the big window at the side of the house and partly hidden from the road by a bunch of pampas grasses, were the chicken run and the chickens she had heard so much about recently from Dick Thompson. She was bang up to date on the laying figures of the *birds*, as he called them, and on what good management it showed that they were still completely free of the fowl-pest that was going on in the district. She went up the crazy-paved path and over to the wire.

The chickens, which had been moving about as if they were very excited about something but knew how to keep it under control, came crowding over to her. They seemed to be expecting her and at the same time inquisitive about who she was. Jenny apologized to them for not having brought any goodies with her, but added that she would do what she could to see that their tea was sent out in decent time. On hearing this, the cock turned aside and strolled like a military policeman towards the drinking-trough, crowing off-handedly as he went. Jenny knew all about that crow. Every other morning at about four o'clock she would find herself wondering who the cock thought he was helping when he did it. On the other hand she sympathized with him because she knew Mrs Thompson disliked him, complaining of the noise he made and his savage pecking attacks on anybody who entered the run. To be disliked by Martha Thompson must be nasty and, if you happened to be a cock, dangerous as well. Any day Jenny half-expected a bowl of soup, garnished in all probability with a bit of chalky, underdone rice and a piece of string or two, to turn up as evidence of the cock's death. It was a good job for all concerned that he was thought to be too old to be eatable in any form, even in a place like . . . Jenny gave up this unkind line of reflection and looked round for her favourite hen.

Before she could pick her out from the crowd, which was now melting away with a good deal of dissatisfied muttering, some-one began crossing the gravelled area in front of the house. It was Anna le Page. The size and shininess of her eyes were strik-ing even at this distance and in the poor light under the trees (perhaps they really were beeches) near the entrance. Jenny smiled and waved, calling 'Hallo'. The other girl shook her head slightly and swept on into the porch, swinging her legs from the hips in an active way. Under her arm was what looked like a framed picture done up in brown paper.

Jenny felt downcast for a moment. Then she remembered that Anna le Page was probably shy, and after all this was a foreign country to her. Jenny had done her best, whenever they ran into each other round the house, to show that she felt friendly to-wards Anna, but was glad now that she had not yielded to her impulse to ask her into her room for a chat. It might only have embarrassed Anna, and in any case it was her privilege, as the one who had been living in the house longer, to ask Jenny in if she wanted to be friends. The girl kept rather away from the household in general, not turning up very often for the com-munal evening meal and not having much to say for herself when she did. And what she did say was usually so complicated, or about something so out of the way, that Jenny's readiness for friendship was lessened by the fear that the French girl would think her stupid.

Jenny waited, rather guiltily, until the cock had let go of a hen on whose back he had jumped, then she went thoughtfully indoors. She was trying to make up her mind whether to go into the kitchen or not. Most weekday afternoons so far Dick Thompson had come and knocked on her door (using the brass knocker) soon after four, just when she had got back from school, and had asked her to come on down to the kitchen for a cup of tea and a biscuit. He had added each time that the next afternoon she must come down without waiting to be asked. So far she had not dared to do this. But now it had got to the point where she would have to, if she did not want to appear snooty and stand-offish. Right, then. She put her music case on the enormous polished table by the stairs, took a quick peep in the hallstand mirror, went past the oriental yellow brocade curtain that hung half across the passage, knocked at the kitchen door (using the brass knocker, in case her landlord had some sort of thing about knuckles on wood) and entered.

'Hallo, Jenny,' Dick said, leaning over to see her better. He said it on a note of more than just celebration, having known her for a couple of weeks. 'So you managed to find your way all right at last.'

'Oh yes,' she said, laughing. 'I'll be in here all the time now.'

'Good, good. Well, I'll just pour you some tea. No, you sit down, Jenny. You've done a day's work.'

He said this on every weekday occasion – at week-ends he changed it to 'You're a working girl' – when she tried to do something about her natural feeling that men should not do things like seeing to the tea when there was a woman at hand to do it. She had already been twice gone for by Mrs Thompson for trying to make herself useful, once when she offered to cook the Sunday dinner to give the other a rest ('It would take me just as long showing you where we keep things'), and the other time when she asked for a dustpan and brush to do her room out ('I'd as soon you left that to the char, if you don't mind'). Washing-up, plus a bit of ironing one evening, was the most she had been allowed to do.

'Here you are, Jenny. I don't know whether it's up to the wife's standard. It's one of her bridge afternoons today.'

Jenny heard this with definite relief. Most of the time Mrs Thompson was quite cheerful and talkative, and would even ask her about her family, but every now and then she went quiet in a meaning way or said something which made Jenny feel vaguely that she was being got at. One evening Martha Thompson had given her a booster shot of the unfriendly-look treatment she had handed out that first supper-time. Why? What had she done?

Dick had left her again: his heels could be heard clacking about on the tiled floor of the scullery. She wondered what he was going to be doing this time, in the sense that at most of these tea-sessions he would be busy round the place in some way or other, pasting down loose corners of wallpaper, going to and fro for nails and other things that would help him to overhaul the chicken run, or pouring curry-powder from one half-empty glass jar into another. Sometimes he managed to make these things seem urgent by drinking his tea standing up during them. But today, it turned out, he was doing no more than fetching a plate of biscuits, and after offering them to Jenny he sat down in the rocking-chair, ready to talk.

'What about you coming along to the Film Society on Friday with me and Martha?' he asked.

'What's that exactly?'

'They're showing one of those damn good Italian neo-realist efforts, you know, *Bicycle Thieves*.'

'It's gangster, is it?'

'No, just poor people in Italy. Shows you what lies behind this Americanized façade we all take for granted these days.'

'It sounds lovely, I'd love to come, thank you very much. But what's the Society exactly?'

'They run it at the College, at the theatre there. It was really Patrick who got it going, as you might expect. I don't know what this town would do without that lad, I really don't.'

Neither did Jenny, though from a different point of view. She tried to sound casual when she asked: 'Does he do a lot of things, then, in the town?'

'I should say he does. He's a grand lad, old Patrick. The wife and I are very fond of him, you know. We see quite a lot of him.'

'How did you –?'

'You see, in a town this size the number of people who take any interest in intellectual pursuits, politics and the arts and that, they're pretty few and far between. So if you're that way inclined you tend to keep running across the same crowd. Now both Patrick and myself have a good bit to do with the Labour Party here. That's a small enough group if ever there was one, seeing that the place is turning more and more into a London dormitory, which means there's a pretty small progressive element that's at all active, if you follow me.'

'You mean the people who –'

'Of course we have our differences of opinion, it wouldn't be healthy if we didn't I think you'll agree, although I think I can say Patrick and I see pretty well eye to eye on most things, this Nyasaland fandango for an example, but anyway we like to get our official business out of the way, and pretty dull most of it is, but there, someone's got to do it, and then we like to all get together over a pint at the George and we thrash matters out like that, which is a sight more pleasant in my opinion than the atmosphere of an official discussion, and some damn heated to-and-fros we have too, I can tell you. You ought to hear us at it – well, you already have, haven't you?'

'Yes, I –'

'All in good part, naturally. But talk about dry humour – my godfather, old Patrick's the boy for that. Well, for an example, whenever I drop in at his place, as I quite often have occasion to do, with something or other to do with the Labour Party, a meeting to fix up or something, if Patrick's there, mind you he's often out chasing the girls, not that there's much harm in that I suppose, anyway if he's there, as soon as he sees me coming in, do you know what he says? Oh, he's a boy.'

'How does he mean?' What was it to her, Jenny asked herself, if Patrick did go in for girl-chasing? She had known before-hand, too.

'No, sorry, I mean Patrick's a boy, sorry. Do you know what he comes out with, though, as soon as he sees me coming in? Regular as flipping clockwork, never varies. As soon as he sees it's me he comes out with *Oh Christ, you here again?*' Dick made a noise like a whole rookery disturbed by a gun. 'Same thing every ruddy time. *Oh Christ* – hope you don't mind, Jenny – *oh Christ, you here again?* And not a smile on his face.'

Jenny stirred her tea vigorously. After that last bit there was a very good chance that Dick was a stooge, as she had suspected some afternoons ago when the job he was doing was putting his back numbers of the *New Statesman* into chronological order. She must watch to find out whether he kept his change in a purse and how he carried a suitcase.

Dick got up now and she noticed without surprise how short and wide his trousers were. 'Well, Jenny, I'm afraid I shall have to love you and leave you. Something rather urgent's come up at the office' – he said this clearly and proudly – 'and I'll have to be getting down there, I'm afraid. See you at supper.'

'Oh, Mr Thompson, I meant to tell you, I shan't be in for supper, I'm going out.'

'Painting the town red, eh? Who's the lucky man? I mean you're not going on your own, are you?'

'No, well, as a matter of fact it's Patrick.'

'Patrick. Mm.' Suddenly looking like a probation officer, Dick sat down nearer her on the table and watched his foot swinging. 'I see. Well, I just hope you know your way around, that's all.'

'How do you mean?'

'I hope you know how to take care of yourself, that's all.'

'Yes I do, thank you very much.'

'Mm, I wonder. You know, Patrick's a pretty wild sort of character in some ways. He's rather one who's out for a good time, old Patrick, and not much care for other people's feelings. You don't want to let yourself get talked into anything, well, anything you might regret. I shouldn't have thought he was your sort at all, not Patrick. I hope you know what you're doing, that's all.'

Jenny had been struggling against her stutter to interrupt this. Now she said: 'I'd like to know what business it is of yours.'

'Here, now, you mustn't be offended. I'm only after your good. And it is a little bit my business, because a young girl like you away from home, I'd be failing in my duty if I didn't keep a weather eye on your welfare.'

'That's nice of you, but believe me I can look after myself.'

'All right, Jenny, but I had to say something for my own peace of mind, you see. Now let's forget it and you enjoy yourself, eh? Now I really must be going.' He slid off the table. 'Oh dear, oh dear, got to feed those perishing birds first.'

'Oh, could I feed them for you, do you think?'

'Do you really want to? Won't take me five minutes, you know.'

'Oh yes, I love hens.'

He gave another rookery imitation, then put his hands on his hips and stared at her. He smiled in a way that showed off how big his lips were. With his long head on one side and nodding up and down slightly, he said: 'Well well, Miss Jenny Bunn.'

'What?' she asked, hastily picking up her cup of tea.

'You are a funny little thing, Jenny,' Dick said.

Chapter Three

'It's nothing urgent, I hope?'

'Good God no, it'd keep for a quarter of a century as far as I'm concerned. She just wants to be sure I'm in good condition, or at least not got any worse since the last time. And she needs to hear her loving son's voice to be sure of that, you see. I might be lying if I just wrote and said. Not but what being rung up isn't a good deal less horrible than having to write a letter, I'm clear on that.' Patrick made a signal to the dignified foreign-accented waiter who was standing by the buffet table and looking as though he was keeping guard over the remains of the huge pink fish that was lying there. 'But it's a bloody nuisance all the same, isn't it? – having to dash back to the flat like this just when we're ... in the middle of things. Of course, she's not on the phone at home, so she has to ring me. I can't ring her.'

'I don't see anything funny in her wanting to keep in touch with you, though, do you?'

'Not a thing, I wish I could. But there's no danger of me slipping out of her ken, what with her only about thirty miles away and me going there every holidays for a bit and a week-end every term. We're right bang in touch, believe me.'

'But it's only natural, you being the only one and everything.' Jenny's voice had softened. It was common knowledge that only children had a difficult time of it and were liable to be immature. Not that Patrick had shown himself all that immature yet awhile.

'It's natural all right, yeah. So's dysentery.'

'I don't think you ought to speak of your own mother like that.'

'Why not? I know her better than anyone else does, don't I? All right, as they say, I'm sorry. I suppose you get on pretty well with your parents. You look as though you do. In some ways, at least. In other ways you look as though you don't. It's something to do with up north, I expect – I wouldn't know. Never been there.'

'What ways don't I look as though I get on with my parents?'

'Oh, I didn't mean anything. Don't you have rows with them occasionally because of staying out late, and that kind of thing? What I really meant was, you look like someone that people are always trying to persuade to stay out late. And that kind of thing.'

'Well, yes, a bit, I mean there is the odd row, but nothing out of the way. They give me a lot of freedom.'

'There's nothing like a lot of that, is there, for a growing lass? You'll have another of those, won't you?'

'No thanks, I'm half tipsy already.'

'Well, get two-thirds tipsy, then.'

'No really thanks, I've had enough.'

'Let's hope so. I wonder if I have. Ah, another large green chartreuse, please. And the bill. We've got plenty of time but I don't want to rush. Not too much. Well, this is going to be a great success, I can feel it already. Can't you?'

The look he threw in with this was fine in a way – he had his face tilted down towards his glass and his eyes coming up at her from under his eyebrows – but there was perhaps rather a lot of it. Jenny smiled at him to show she had noticed it, then said: 'When was it you lost your father, Patrick? Or don't you want to talk about it?'

'Not much, no, but not because it distresses me or anything like that. My father was a bit of a ... funny chap, really. He went off when I was ten. There was a stepfather too at one stage, but he didn't stay around long either, I'm happy to say. He didn't die, he just cleared off. He was supposed to be coming back any day, but that didn't fool me. And then there was a top sergeant from Urbana, Ill., who gave me a wad of gum and a can of pineapple juice every time he caught sight of me. I didn't mind him. Anyway, don't let's talk family history tonight, we've got more important things in front of us. My God, you look tremendous, Jenny. How did the industrial north ever manage to come up with something like you? And what the hell were they all thinking about up there when they let you come down here? It's a facer, isn't it, boys? You're absolutely wonderful. Every bit of you goes so well with all the other bits, and the bits are all so good in themselves, that's the extraordinary thing.

39

Look, I know you're not going to believe this, but you really are the best of the lot. Literally, not just sort of vaguely and because I feel like it and what the hell why shouldn't I say it. I mean *the* ... *best*. Of the *lot*. The best-looking character I've ever been out with. Christ, ever met. Honestly.'

'Well, it's lovely to hear that said.'

'But you don't believe me. I knew you wouldn't. Too many of those northern chums have said it already. Not so well as I say it, though. That's right, isn't it?'

'Just listen to him, he sure does hate himself.'

'Oh, like a bastard. But I'm serious underneath it all, you see.'

'Yes, you look it. Solemn as an owl, that's you.'

'I didn't say that, I said serious. I mean every word I say. Not always, perhaps, but tonight I do. Not that there's much credit in that, admitted, it's too easy. I don't have to try to be original or ingenious, I just tell you what you look like and the job's done. Nothing to it.'

'Do you write all this stuff out beforehand and learn it off, or does it just come naturally and you make it up as you go along?'

'You see what it is, don't you?' Patrick said to an invisible third person at their table. 'These bloody girls, the ones of this sort of standing, naturally they're getting the old line shot at them every day and twice on Sundays. So what happens? Of all classes in the community they least believe what they're told, so when a poor sod comes along and tells them the truth, the whole truth, and nothing but the truth he just doesn't get anywhere at all with them. The market's been spoilt.'

Jenny had been thinking that if the chap talked at all there was really no way of not having this sort of conversation. And although some of the things that got said might be pretty embarrassing if you remembered them the next morning (like finding on the other person's mantelpiece a letter you had written a couple of days earlier, postmarked now and with the envelope torn open) two people could not go on all the evening just repeating (chap) *I like you and* and (girl) *I like you but*. And Patrick was cleverer than most in being able to use the idea that they were playing a game as an extra way of playing the game. Jenny said : 'You ought to go out with my grandma, you'd be happier with her, wouldn't you?'

'There you are, you see, that's what you've got to put up with. Ah, I feel wonderful tonight. Somebody at Bastards' HQ's slipped up, you know, letting anything as nice as this happen. I've been waiting for years for something as nice as this and now here it is.'

'Yes, I can tell you haven't been out much. As soon as I saw you I said to myself, there's a lad who spends every evening curled up with a good book.'

'Let me tell you quite straight, I don't think you ought to be allowed to go round loose, not if you're going to insist on looking like that. A danger to public order. Mmmmm. I'm afraid you're not going to stay a schoolteacher very long, Miss Bunn.'

During this last bit he brought his hand down on hers, the first time he had touched her apart from a certain amount of elbow-work involved in getting her in and out of the car and in and out of the bar and up here to the restaurant. Besides her pleasure at what he had been saying, which stood up jolly well even when you took off the 95 per cent for the game, she liked his hand: it was broad and thick, lovely clean nails, not too hairy and he-mannish without at the same time being at all clawy, as Fred's hands – she could admit it frankly to herself now – had tended to be, especially in cold weather. The fact had got to be faced, though, that Patrick's hand had a ring, gold or getting on that way, on its little finger, and rings on men had something flashy and foreign and common about them. Or so she had thought in the past; but Patrick himself was obviously none of these things, and here most likely was another of those rather young and narrow-minded ideas of hers which more experience of the world and meeting all these new people were going to teach her to do away with.

Just as she was wondering whether it would be all right for her to look up and meet his eyes, or whether she might feel too awful and corny if she did, one of his knees touched hers and, after wiggling to and fro for a moment, started trying to push itself in between her own two. This, even while she went smoothly into action and took her knees away under cover of just happening to be generally rearranging her position in her chair, threw her off. Knee stuff, plus the various stuff it could lead to, was easy enough to deal with on her own home ground, but here in this swagger restaurant, with little black iron fences with curlicues running here and there (there was even a sort of iron cage over the nearby radiator) and dinner-mats with old-master pictures on them and a menu the size of the *Daily Mirror* each, her usual defence system might have to be altered at short notice. Luckily the waiter came up with the bill just then and the situation was saved, but while Patrick was looking through his money she could not help hoping that he was not going to turn out to be a wolf, as his self-assured manner and his knee made it possible to think. It would be such a pity if he was. Anyway, she would know for certain fairly soon, while they were waiting in his flat for this phone call.

'Well, I'll just get rid of this rocket-fuel and we'll be on our way,' he said, drinking.

'That was a lovely meal, Patrick, thank you very much.'

'Oh, just a sample of what'll be coming your way if you *aaaahhh*.'

Startled, Jenny looked round to follow his eyes and saw Dick and Martha Thompson standing in the doorway of the restaurant. Near them there was a funny-looking man with a sad expression on his face. Dick swung his head about for a few seconds before the dignified waiter went up and led them away to the far side. Dick went last, in a hurry and yet seeming to take a long time. His way of managing both at once reminded Jenny of how he had come into the kitchen the previous evening. The lionhouse haddock itself had not been dished up again at the Thompsons', but she had not been able to help thinking of it again because of the beef Mrs Thompson had given her. It had tasted of damp tea-towel. By the look on Dick's face as he came tottering in and saw her trying to eat her supper, she had thought he might be going to apologize to her about it, but he had said 'Hallo, Jenny' loudly and sincerely instead and started rubbing his hands together.

'I thought it couldn't last,' Patrick said. 'They must have repaired that fault at Bastards' HQ. Did you tell him we were coming here?'

'Well, I couldn't have, could I? I didn't know.'

'Sorry, of course not. Look, we want to dodge them, don't we?'

'Well, if you don't think it'll look rude ...'

'With luck it will, but they probably won't see us. Anyway, you go first. I'll see you downstairs in the hall place.'

Jenny picked up her bag and started off, but before she could reach the door the waiter had evidently changed his plan for the Thompsons and their friend and brought them back again directly into her path. 'Hallo, Jenny,' Dick said, sincerely and loudly again, but with so much more of both that some people eating near by all stopped eating. 'Well, if this isn't the most extraordinary thing,' Martha Thompson said with a very wide grin and almost as loudly; 'whoever would have thought of running into our little Miss *Bunn* in a place like *this*? And looking so charmingly *soignée*, too.' 'How nice this is – you must stay and have a drink with us, Jenny. Is Patrick –?' 'That's very kind of you, but he said we had to be on our way. He wants to –' 'Oh, rubbish, just five minutes can't make any difference.' 'I'm sure the dear lad can curb his natural impatience long enough to give his *other* obsession a turn.' 'Well, I don't know, it's very –' 'You sit yourself down here, Jenny.' 'Where you can watch all these nice, interesting people, dear.'

By the time Patrick arrived, with a serious expression, Jenny had had to sit down opposite the funny-looking man. The others were taking hardly any notice of him. Perhaps he was not really with them after all. Jenny made a shrugging face at Patrick. Dick said: 'Hallo, Patrick, how are you?' He said it differently from the way he had said 'Hallo, Jenny' either of the two times; he made it sound as if Patrick had just come out of hospital after an internal operation. Then he started arranging chairs so that Patrick could sit down.

Patrick had nodded, still seriously, at Jenny's shrugging face. He said: 'I thought we were going to be safe from you in here. Thought it wasn't working-class enough for you. And who's paying for the dinner you're no doubt going to eat?'

Dick gave one of his longer caws, varying the pitch more than he usually did. Jenny realized that he made them by breathing in, not out. He did not answer Patrick's question; instead, he asked them what they were all going to have. Patrick watched him with what looked like amazement, as if Dick had a joke hat and false nose on.

43

Just then the funny-looking man twitched his nose a couple of times, which gave him a livelier appearance, and said in a high Scottish voice: 'Good evening. I think you must be Miss Bunn.' Then he slowed down to dictation speed and said: 'My name's Graham McClintoch,' afterwards spelling out his surname and explaining which of the letters in it were capitals.

'Oh, yes, I know who you are. Don't you share with Patrick?'

'I most certainly do.' He laughed briefly. He was a good deal funnier-looking close to than at a distance. His head was large and unevenly covered with short, not quite sandy hair, and his face was the kind that Jenny was well used to seeing on her parents' television-screen, often with a sentence like *Eh, it's a hard life being a married man* coming out of its mouth. This man, though, would not have said anything like that. The imposing way he spoke fitted in nicely with the old-fashioned neatness of his clothes (the folded white handkerchief sticking out of the top pocket, for example, in amongst the blue serge suit) and also, somehow or other, with the funniness of his face. After saying that he had heard of her too, he was going on: 'Of course, a place like this flourishes mainly on snob appeal. It has no authenticity whatever, and so we find these various attempts to give it a traditional look – not tradition in particular, just traditional*ness*, if you follow. Hence all these curious ...'

Oh dear, Jenny thought to herself; she had guesssed he was the sort who told you things. She felt useless and as if she had no special reason for being where she was. Then, while the man went on talking to her about commercialism and something called mass media, and an unkind-looking waiter stood over Dick to take the order for drinks, and Martha Thompson said quite a lot to Patrick without him saying much back, Jenny realized that a tall well-dressed man at the entrance was watching her closely. At first she thought he must be the manager wondering whether he ought to have her thrown out, but she soon saw that that was wrong. What he was doing was giving her the look. He went one better than Patrick had done that first time in not simply not caring much that he was giving her the look, but actually glorying in it. She drew the corners of her mouth inwards in the way her mother used when her father said

44

he was thinking of asking a couple of the boys in after supper for an hour or two. When the man's look went on exactly as before she pushed her pupils as far up under her eyelids as possible in the way her mother used when her father went on to say that he personally intended to have a few drinks and a few laughs that evening and other people could make their bloody arrangements to fit in with him for once. This failed. So did the heavy-sigh-cum-closed-eyes that came when the first of the boys was heard being let in and laughing in the passage, and so did the loony open-mouthed headshaking goggling that Jenny had learnt from Trixie. One or other of this selection always worked with the fellows at home, making them shrug their shoulders jerkily or shout furtively to their mates. But this man was obviously well over forty. Jenny fixed her glance on the stained-glass window of the Queen's face that somebody had thought worth putting in over the entrance, then woke up suddenly when Dick asked her what she was having. 'Oh. Oh, nothing, thank you.'

'Come along now, Jenny,' Martha said, 'you've got to remember your obligations, you know. I'm sure Patrick would like you to have something. It'll do you good – that's right, isn't it, Patrick? She adores crème de menthe, I can tell. Yes, and a crème de menthe, please.'

'Ah, there's Julian at last,' Dick said. He leaned a long way over past the waiter and waved. The beaky-nosed staring man waved back and came towards them. 'This is a grand chap,' Dick added. 'You'll love him, that I can guarantee. Julian, I want you to meet some friends of mine. This is Jenny Bunn ... Patrick Standish ... Julian Ormerod. Oh, and Graham McClintoch.'

The man said 'Hallo indeed' to Jenny, taking longer over it than the total time he took over saying 'It's an honour, sir' to each of the two men, and nearly as long as it took him to say 'Gin and dubonnet, Gilbert, please' to the waiter (who went away quickly) and 'I see our little party has expanded somewhat' to all the rest of them. He had a deep, very confident voice with a B.B.C. accent.

'Only for the moment, Julian,' Martha said, smiling at Jenny with her eyes nearly shut. (To do this she only had to move her

45

eyelids a comparatively short distance.) 'Mr Standish and Miss Bunn are *dashing off* soon. They have another engagement, as it were.'

'Very jolly,' the Ormerod man murmured, also looking at Jenny, which he seemed unlikely to ever stop doing. 'Oh woman, in our hours of luck.' Jenny thought he was an unusual sort of friend for Dick to have, and from the expression on Patrick's face she could tell that he thought the same, or something very like it.

Graham McClintoch said: 'We'd better be ordering. We don't want to find we can only get the cold supper.'

'Nonsense, dear boy,' Julian Ormerod said. He raised his chin in a sudden way, evidently trying to pull some more of his neck out from inside his collar. 'I practically own this place, unless I'm mixing it up with the Three Crowns along the road. Anybody under my protection gets nothing but the best, as they come to realize in the fullness of time. A significant proportion of them, anyway.' He paused and stared hard across the room to where a woman with heavy make-up and fierce blonde hair was drinking an elaborately decorated drink, her nose buried in a little clump of mint. 'Well, there's something admirably suited for a spot of hoo-ha, I should have thought. Now what about the old faggeroo? Eh? Let's try the old fag-o'-my-firkin.' With this he brought out cigarettes and offered them round. In the hand that Dick did not use to take a fresh cigarette he had another one, already burning and a good deal shorter. Graham McClintoch took out a box of matches and lit one carefully at one end of the strip of sandpaper. Jenny could see that he had lit all the previous matches at that same spot. Why had he done that?

Dick was moving his head about on its flexible neck, giving quite a different effect from the way Julian Ormerod had moved his. For the past minute, too, he had been pouting and repouting in quick time as if he was trying to pull something off his front teeth. Now he said: 'How did things go this afternoon, Julian?'

'Oh, mustn't grumble, thanks. Spot of window-cleaner trouble early on, actually, but I managed to convince the girl that there was nothing to get worried about. After all, if a window-cleaner isn't a man of the world ... Sorry, mind wandering again. See what you mean now. Well, Dickon, things went reasonably well. Date isn't set yet, but there's no particular hurry, is there? Bad thing if there were, what?'

'Did you see the fellow himself?'

'No, but there was another fellow exactly like him I did see.'

'Fine, we'll talk about it later, I just wanted to get that bit straight.' Dick turned round to them all and said like somebody on a public platform: 'Julian and I are doing a little bit of business together.'

'Oh, so that's what you're doing?' Patrick said. 'Well I never. I wondered what could have brought you here, right in the middle of expense-account subtopia. And what about you, Graham? Are you doing some of the business too? You know, I do love this. It sounds a welcome note of novelty.'

'To hell, Standish, I just happened to drop by on Thompson and he very kindly asked me along.'

'That was kind, yes. And so here we are, the whole bunch. If I'd known I'd have given you all a lift.'

'Lift? What have you got?' Julian Ormerod asked sharply.

'Graham and I share it. One of those old 110s, I don't know whether you know them.'

'Not really? I should just think I do know them. Drove one myself until ten years ago. Marvellous old crates. The sweetest road-holder you ever saw. Delicious creature. How extraordinary. Brings it all back. You must let me ... Ah, splendid.'

While the drinks were being given out Dick leaned across to Jenny and said in a special tone: 'Well, how's it going, Jenny? Been having fun with young Lochinvar?'

'Yes, it's been very nice, thank you. We had a lovely dinner.'

'Which is more than she ever gets at that bloody Dothegirls Hall of yours, I bet. Cheers, everyone. Well, that's that. Thank you for the party.' Patrick put down his empty glass and stood up.

'Here now, hold it a second, chaps, the young lady still has a drink to dispose of. No huge rush, is there?'

'It's all right, Mr Ormerod, I couldn't drink it, thank you. And Patrick has to be back for a –'

'I'll give the old 110 a kiss on the bonnet from you.' Patrick

47

took Jenny's arm and drew her clear of the table. 'We'll leave you to your business conference.'

The Ormerod man pressed his lips together and opened his eyes very wide. The whites were clear and bright, which was unexpected in view of nearly everything else about him. 'Then this is what they call a pleasure deferred, eh?'

'Something like that,' Patrick said. 'See you around.'

Jenny got a different kind of look from each of them as she said good night: a sad nose-twitch from Graham McClintoch, a repeat of his earlier performance from Julian Ormerod, a sarcastic beam from Martha, a warning frown, meant to remind her of his take-care-of-yourself line, from Dick. She thought these over in the Ladies, which was called the Powder Room and had a woman in a white overall supervising it. Jenny decided that, in spite of the rather funny atmosphere of the last ten minutes, things had gone pretty well up to now.

A peep in the glass showed her that the red wool sheath dress, though not new, was doing its job, making the best of her bust without being too ostentatious, and the backswept hair with medium earrings gave the right sort of grown-up look. And she had got through the restaurant part quite decently, asking Patrick to do the choosing for her – a good tip from *Woman's Domain* – and getting rid of nearly all the raw fish and sort of meat fritter and rather sharp wine without hankering much after a gravy dinner and a cider. She had managed the cutlery all right, too, by just keeping her head and working inwards from the outside. And it was so smashing here: not only the curly iron fences but the bar downstairs, with the waiter coming over specially to light her cigarette and emptying the ashtray every few minutes; and then all the business in the restaurant, with the foreign-accented waiter bringing the bottle of wine to show Patrick (who had said approvingly 'Nice and full') before it was opened. No doubt there was a ballroom somewhere in the building, where they had big dances at the weekends, probably with bands like Johnny Dankworth's or Humphrey Lyttelton's. The whole thing made her feel treasured and – something she would have died rather than admit to anyone but Trixie – like a starlet or a singer.

Outside in the yard of the roadhouse it was fairly dark, dark enough, evidently, for Patrick to see nothing against putting his arm carelessly round her waist and pulling her half towards him as they stopped by his car.

'You and I are going to get along just fine,' he said, all on one low note.

Chapter Four

WITH his hand still at her waist, or perhaps her hip, Patrick got her into the car, which had looked big and dignified at first glance, but had turned out to be big and lively. As well as being called a 110 and being pre-war, he had said that they did not make them any more. That seemed reasonable on several grounds. The heavy door creaked and bonked shut. It was rather like being shut up inside Dick Thompson's geyser.

As they backed round, the headlights picked out, apart from a great many other cars, some brick walls topped by more curly-iron railings and an occasional elaborate plaster vase affair with a weedy plant in it. The shadows of these slipped sideways excitingly, like something out of a film. Then, with a sound like a felled tree beginning to topple, Patrick put the car in gear and almost at once started going very fast. Jenny thought she enjoyed going very fast in cars, even though on the way out she had had to close her eyes once and had reopened them to find something worse than before going on. She felt like a starlet again, and sat there for some time in this role, wishing there could be some conversation to give it more room. But there could not be much: the engine made a lot of noise when Patrick was accelerating, and that was what he was usually doing. You could not shout and be sophisticated at the same time, not when there was just the two of you.

Anyhow: being a starlet going very fast in a car came close, perhaps too close, to being *speed mad*, which was a thing her father often said – he often said most of what he said – the whole modern generation was. Jenny hoped she was never going to suddenly find out one day that she was any of the other things he said the modern generation was: *money mad*, or *pleasure mad*,

49

or *only interested in what they could get out of life*. She thought not, with luck, feeling that she was the steady type who got married and had babies. But the starlet thing did put a tiny doubt in her mind – just occasionally, like now – whether the steady type might not be missing some of the fun. At the time she had meant what she said about being given a lot of freedom at home, but the unbreakable midnight curfew her father had put on her evenings out till she was turned eighteen might strike some of her new friends as rather Victorian, or at least pre-war. And even marriage itself, coming back to that, could have its less ideal side, as she had heard at first hand (reading it was different) from the married woman on the staff at Albert Road. Mrs Carter seemed to divide her time between school, trying to get her husband to *leave her alone*, and baking steak-and-kidney pies for him.

The starlet idea and what went with it, interrupted by a few shouts from Patrick about the badness of other drivers, kept her going until the car began to slow down. Jenny found that they were crossing a hump-back bridge over the local canal, in which there were some very clear reflections of bright yellow lights. On one side was a low flat-topped hill with many more lights: Patrick's school was somewhere up there. As they turned into the High Street and passed the slightly worse of the town's two cinemas, Jenny felt a comforting sense of familiarity creep over her. Another turn, and the noise of the car rang hollowly against a row of houses that had once or twice already reminded her of where one of her aunts lived – not Auntie Kitty, who was very modern, but Auntie Minnie, who doled out brick-red tea and pliable ginger-biscuits at any hour of the day – then the noise rang flatly across a sports ground where the moon shone on a hut with a tin roof. The place looked deserted, but cheerful too. She could no longer remember what it had looked like when the strangeness of the town had chilled her, when she knew nobody in it. She knew somebody in it now all right: although this was the first time they had been out together, she had met Patrick twice in the George, and after one of the times had spent the equivalent of about a working afternoon chatting to him at the Thompsons'.

They stopped by another row of Auntie Minnie houses, and

got out. Jenny did that on her own before Patrick could work up to half-carrying her wherever they might go. But in no time at all here he was again with his arm diagonally across her back, as if they were in a crowd coming out of a soccer match, and was pressing and nudging her into a gateway. In the small front garden she could make out a fair number of artificial rabbits, toads and such among the imitation crazy paving and the rock plants, looking rather grand and interesting in the bright moonlight.

'Sorry about those,' Patrick said, indicating them with one hand while he found his key with the other. This meant that he had no hand free to touch Jenny with, which made a change. He was looking at her frequently, perhaps to make sure of catching her if she decided to make a break for it. The ride had sobered her up after the three gins and tonics and the wine and the cherry brandy, and that was probably just as well, but now that it was coming to the point she felt a little uneasy and had some trouble dismissing Dick's warning from her mind. It came back some of the distance because of the way in which Patrick drove her over the threshold (there was a sort of *he knew she was his woman* feel to it), and further still at the sight of the hall inside, which with its bare floorboards and peeling wallpaper was very much the kind that belonged to houses they had gangsters-and-police sieges in on the films. But seeing a pram stuck halfway under the stairs helped a bit.

They went up the stairs and Patrick opened a door and put on the light. Jenny just had time to notice that the room they entered held far more than its fair share of books before being grabbed by Patrick, right on the nail, and passionately kissed. That was all right, in fact very much better than all right, but it did not go on being all right for very long. The greedy way he murmured, 'Ooh, aren't you lovely? Ooh, aren't you beautiful? Ooh' into her ear was not quite so all right as the kiss itself, and the confident suddenness with which he put his hand on her breast was not at all all right.

She gripped his wrist. 'Don't do that, there's a good boy,' she said as soon as she could, and leaned back away from him.

He evidently did not hear, going on with his 'Ooh, aren't you lovely?' line, certain that she was enjoying it all as much as he, peering at her with his eyes almost shut, then pulling her against him harder than ever, trying to open her mouth with his own, forcing his thigh between hers, finally starting to push his fingers down under the neckline of her dress. What was the matter with him? It was difficult to stand there and think things over, about how soon to start trying to slap his face and so on. Her shoulders went thudding against the wall. When she felt his hand at the zip of her dress, when it appeared she could neither get free nor disengage her mouth to protest, she took hold of his back hair and tugged hard. He winced and let her go at once. With a heavy, angry expression on his face, made less impressive by the lipstick that covered most of the lower half of it, he said: 'That was a bit unnecessary, wasn't it?' He was rubbing his head energetically.

'It seemed pretty necessary to me.'

'Nobody's ever done that kind of thing to me before.'

'In that case you've been damn lucky, my lad, if that's the way you usually carry on.'

After wiping his mouth on his handkerchief, he said quietly: 'I'm sorry, I made a mistake. I thought you were ... I'm sorry, Jenny.'

She had been thinking how little she knew him; now he was familiar again and she was no longer sure she had tried hard enough to break out of his embrace without causing a fuss. 'I didn't really mean to hurt you,' she said. 'I got scared.'

'Actually you needn't have been, I can assure you, but I can quite see how you were. Very understandable, I must admit. I'm afraid I just got carried away. But I'd soon have realized how you were reacting, I was beginning to anyway. I wouldn't have gone on much longer in that strain even if you hadn't ... taken action. Bad thing to get carried away, of course, but people do, you know.'

He was over it now; he was giving reasons, having a discussion with her. She looked at him sadly. 'Yes, I know.'

'You were quite justified. I deserved it. Jenny, don't be angry. Don't go. I promise I'll behave myself.'

Jenny thought that she should go. But it would look so silly, so high-and-mighty. And she could not bear to go, not now, not when she had only just got to know him, not when she looked at his hair and the shape of his head and the nice position it had on his neck, not after the way he had talked to her earlier in the evening at the roadhouse, before they started playing the game, lively and straightforward and really interested as well as putting over a bit of a line – which they all did. And after all, what was she committing herself to merely by staying? – she could walk out any time she felt like it. Over his shoulder she saw a poster with a queer-looking church on it and the letters *S.N.C.F.* underneath. The room, which up to now had just been a big box, empty except for the two of them, was starting to be a real room full of things. It was all different from what she knew, and nobody ought to go on leading a life where everything was the same. Nobody could, not these days. 'All right,' she said to Patrick, 'but mind you do, now.'

He grinned and stepped actively forward and took her hands. To recoil now would be ridiculous and young. 'That's my girl. And a great relief too, by God.' He sighed comically, blowing out his cheeks and dilating his eyes. 'I really thought I'd had it for good then, honestly. What an idiot I was. Well now, what about ... just to show there's no ill-feeling ... ?'

He kissed her again, but it was quite different: calm and gentle and without him having to shove his teeth against hers to show how keen he was. It was really much nicer like this, if only they knew. All that tongue work was very overrated and, when you came to think about it, rather rude as well. Probably it was a thing people went in for because it was the fashion, not so much because anybody was meant to like it, the same as with those short haircuts for girls which seemed to be going out now that everyone had had a turn at them. Perhaps the tongue thing would too. Anyway, Patrick's mouth was curved just the right amount, and soft without being squashy, with a good sort of washed smell. The kiss started going on and on rather, but he was the one who finally stepped back, saying: 'That was more like it, eh?'

'Mm.' She nodded, smiling.

He breathed in deeply through his nose, dilating his eyes again but in a different way. 'You know, you really are the most ... but we've been into all that, haven't we? Now I know what you'd like now. Bet you. A nice cup of tea.'

'Ooh lovely, yes please.'

'There you are, always trust a Standish hunch.'

'Could I go to the bathroom?'

'Well, yes, if you insist. I'm afraid you won't think it's a very nice bathroom.'

It wasn't. Not nearly everything, in the way of pipes, etc., that in most houses was covered up was covered up, and you would have been doing pretty well to get out of that bath much cleaner than you had got into it. And that was only the start of it. The other stuff was too bad even to have been allowed to be featured in one of those advertisements that showed what not to have (with a big cross over it to emphasize that it was wrong) and threatened those who did have it with being talked about in the neighbourhood for it and losing all their friends. She imagined that Patrick and the Scotsman shared the facilities with another pair, and so it was no particular person's responsibility more than another's, and nobody's job got done by nobody, as her father often said. She repaired her mouth, using a mirror that gave everything a thick brown look like under water in the river at home (the one that ran past the chemical works), and joined Patrick in the kitchen.

This was less bad, but then it had less scope. At any rate, it was as if the two men had got it up specially to look like a bachelor kitchen. It had a sink full of dishes (of course), a wooden draining-board that was at least crumby and probably more, and a horrible rag on the crook of the waste-pipe underneath. There was a rubbish-bin of the kind, she could tell, where treading on the button failed to budge the lid, which did not fit properly anyhow, and with streaks of congealed gravy down the outside and bits of tomato round about on the lino. But the best was the gas stove: Jenny had seen smarter ones on dumps. On the plate-rack above it (no newspaper) were three socks. The attitude that let it all go on was beyond her. How she wished she could give the whole place a thorough clean-out; but that would look organizing or even possessive. In people's kitchens at home it was natural to empty a teapot or dry up a few cups more or less in the course of conversation; down here they evidently liked to keep things to themselves, at any rate if Martha Thompson was any guide, and went off into their kitchen as if it was the bathroom. They were friendly enough in their own style, but they were a funny lot, there was no getting away from it. She got a tray ready, keeping her eyes off a furry marmalade-pot that the sugar had been next to in the open wooden cabinet, and when the time came carried it into the sitting-room. As she did so the telephone rang.

'That'll be your mother,' Jenny said.

'What? Oh yes, I suppose it must be.' He had not spoken much in the kitchen, though he had not avoided looking at her. Frowning now, he picked up the phone. 'Hallo? Yes. No, I'm afraid not. Definitely not, I'm sorry. Well, you know how it is, I just can't. I've got other ... Yes, I know, but ... Look ... Look, there's no point in ... I thought we'd settled all that. No. I can't. All right, I won't, then. No.'

The pauses in between were very long and filled with an excited female chattering from the other end. During them Patrick twisted and coiled himself into all sorts of different positions, once laying his face down with the receiver next to it on the sideboard where the phone was and shaking his fists above his head. It was an odd way for a man to go on with his mother. But that was no business of hers.

Jenny started looking round the room, noticing how few things there were in it apart from the actual furniture. It would be no use trying to play I-Spy for long in here, unless you were allowed to count the titles of the books. There was no doubt that there were a great many books, twice as many as a couple of schoolmasters (the Graham man was one too) would need just to hold their own. Two of the nearest ones seemed to be called *Q. Horatii Flacci Carmina IV* and *Substituted Dihydroresorcinols*. Two others were called *The Faber Book of Modern Verse* and *The Organization Man*, whoever he was. The books on her own shelf, when they were not called things like *God's Little Acre* or *The Robe,* were called things like *First Steps with Figures* or *Claws, Paws, and Hooves.* This helped to show the great difference between masters – or mistresses – and teachers.

Some of the other things in the room were easy to understand, for instance the roll-top desk streaked with red ink, the two easy and four or five hard chairs, the wooden holder full of unillustrated magazines. Other things were less straightforward, like the open tin of metal polish on the side table, and the cake-stand with no plates in it. And beside her flat on the floor there was a round picture of a Spanish galleon sailing away like mad; it was buff-coloured, went in and out like a sculpture, and had a chain fastened to it. It must be there to cover a tear in the lino. But there were two things she both understood and was glad to see: the TV set on legs and the auto-change record-player with an LP on the turntable. She would have liked to see what was on the television, but as well as it being rude to go and turn it on without being asked and while the phone was going there was also the point that a lot of people were getting much too attached to television and reaching the stage where they could not do without it. There had been a big article about this in a recent *Woman's Domain* by the man who usually wrote about his daffodils or the charming young married couple he had just been dining with in a restaurant hardly anybody besides himself even knew existed. This meant that the television business must be pretty important. Of course too much viewing was bad, if only for the eyesight. But nobody who was not absolutely old ever said that records were bad.

She finished her tea. Crouching down a little so as not to disturb Patrick on the phone – he had almost given up trying to say anything now – she moved over and squatted down by the untidy pile of long-players. But again, rather in the same way as the books, instead of being called things like *Julie London Sings with Strings* or *Songs for Swinging Lovers*, they were called things like *Thelonius Monk and Cannonball Adderley at Newport* or *Symphony No. 1 in C minor*. For a moment, she felt irritated with the records for not being any good when it was so easy for them to be.

Behind her, Patrick said: 'I shouldn't think so. Ever. Cheero.' He put the phone down and came over to her. 'We don't get on too well, I'm afraid. It's a pity but there you are. Sorry to have taken all that time.' He sounded as though he was reading to her out of a book.

'Oh, that's all right. Shall we have another cup of tea?'

He looked down at her, slowly combing his hair with his fingers. Then he smiled suddenly. 'Why not? My God, it's freezing in here. I'll do something about that. Let's try and get comfortable.'

In a couple of minutes they were sitting by the gas-fire drinking tea and listening to a Mel Tormé Patrick had found among the records he kept on a shelf between two big dictionaries. In between the singing there were long bits where the sax or the vibes made it up as he went along and played as many notes as he could in the time – the sort of thing that Jenny's father said reminded him of a crowd of cannibals dancing round a pot of human remains – but the singing itself was quite good. Jenny was sitting on the rug with, after about half-way through the first track, Patrick's arm round her shoulders. It showed no tendency to move. A conversation about jazz slowly got going. Jenny found that nearly all of what she had thought of as jazz was really called pop, and was not as good as what was called jazz by the people who knew. When she said she liked Dave Brubeck, though, she was obviously starting to do better, and spent a few happy minutes being told about him. There was always something they liked telling you about.

After Dave Brubeck had been sorted out and pieces from a couple of his records played as examples, Patrick left the gramophone alone. It was just about time for kissing to come round again, and very soon, after he had bent slowly downwards and sideways from his chair, it did. It was gentle and smashing. Jenny began to feel warm and dreamy. Then Patrick said: 'I'm sorry, this is hellish uncomfortable. We used to have a couch, but it was like sitting in a hammock and then the back fell off. I wonder ... I can't really reach you there. Do you think you could come and sit on my lap?'

This was a bit of the old cleft-stick method, where they asked you to commit yourself without committing themselves to asking you to commit yourself. In its different forms it seemed to cover almost the whole field of male approaches, all the way up from the first only-being-friendly (ha ha ha) offer of a cigarette in a cinema. 'I don't know,' Jenny said. 'I'm not much of a one for sitting on men's laps.'

'I'm not men, you silly little thing. Come on, it'll be all right. Honestly. Just you see.'

If Jenny had not had at the back of her mind the feeling that a man who had bought her a dinner on tonight's scale was entitled to some return, and a bit further back still the fear of being thought high-and-mighty, she would not have hoisted and edged her way, with the awkwardness of someone mounting a camel, on to Patrick's lap. But she did.

About five years seemed to go by. As well as the actual kissings there were the strokings, mainly neck and ears, which were very well done. Jenny felt dreamier than ever. At the start of the second five years he took his mouth away, but not far, and said in a blurry voice: 'Oh, darling Jenny, you're so sweet and beautiful.' It did not sound altogether natural, but then that kind of thing never did, and this was not done in a heavy, grand way.

She rubbed her cheek against his. 'You're a nice kisser,' she said. 'That's what the girls at home say. *Eh, he kisses smashing,* they say.'

He evidently did not hear this. At any rate he made no reply, just said 'Darling' with a breathy sigh and started kissing her again. She could have told to a second the time for his hand to slide round under her armpit and climb on to her left breast. This time she let it stay there. It was her rule to do this with boys she liked, provided there had been a decent build-up first. There had to be rules, which was a pity when being kissed and fondled made you feel so cosy all over, but you could not do without them.

Before long Patrick slipped his left hand under her dress in the non-important places: back, shoulders, upper arms. It was rather like one of the kids at school getting out of his seat to borrow a pencil-sharpener or pick up a writing-book when you knew that what he really wanted to do was run round the room yelling. Soon Patrick's hand, moving sort of sleepily, began trying it on at the front. She took a sleepy grip of his wrist.

'Jenny, I want to tell you how much I like you,' he said as if he had suddenly been reminded of it. 'You are a sweet little thing. You've got a lovely face and a lovely figure. And beautiful colouring. You're an absolute little smasher.'

'Thank you,' Jenny said in the voice of a bus-conductor going round for the fares.

'No, honestly. I do love being with you, darling. Did you know you've got a very attractive way of talking? The way you form your words and the way you think over what you're going to say. Your mouth turns down a bit at the corners when you do that. It gives you a wonderful wary sort of puzzled look. I want you to talk all the time so I can watch. You've got the most wonderful mouth I've ever seen, I just can't keep my eyes off it. You're as nice as I want, anyway. Oh Jenny . . .'

He took hold of her again and in less than a minute was back at the stage where she had taken his wrist. He seemed to think that by saying what he had just said, or even by going on talking as long as that, he had altered everything, he had shown that what he was trying to do now was much more harmless, much more important in one way and much less in another, than what he had been trying to do before. She took his wrist again. 'I think we came round this way about an hour ago,' she said.

'Oh please . . .'

'No please.' She shifted her position to a more upright one.

'Oh, but please . . . Honestly, I won't do anything . . .'

'I know all about you and your won't do anything. I've read about you in books.'

'Oh, Jenny . . .'

She said in a coughy bass voice: 'When I say no I mean no.'

After that they went the rounds again from scratch, this time with Patrick trying slightly less routine things like ear-nibbling and neck-nuzzling and small-of-the-back massage, evidently in the hope of suddenly finding something that would make her leap to her feet and drag him off to wherever he kept his bedroom. But in a shorter time than before they were back at the stage of *oh please* and *no please* and then *oh* and *no*.

He sat up with his arm still round her, but differently. 'Are we going to go on like this all night?' he asked in a conversational voice.

'I don't know about all night, I'll have to be getting back soon. School in the morning.'

'Hell, it's not much after ten, you've got lots of time. But look, Jenny. Why wouldn't you let me do what I was trying to do

59

just then? It wasn't anything very serious, was it? Not as if I was asking you to strip, was it?'

'Of course not, but you know how one thing leads to another.'

'But there wasn't going to be another, I told you that.'

'There always is another. And with this kind of thing it gets harder and harder as you go on, to tell where one leaves off and the next begins.'

'But I've just said I'd made up my mind to stop after that.'

'There's no game to beat this for changing minds.'

'A fine piece of salty northern wisdom, that.'

'Call it what you like.'

He gave a laugh and patted her shoulder. 'All right, hold it. But do you mean you think I was just trying to fool you, leading you on and not meaning it when I said I'd stop?'

'Oh, I don't know, pet, don't let's go into that. This business of why shouldn't we do *this*, and we do it, and so then why shouldn't we do *this*, and we do that, because it's only a tiny bit more than the one before, and it would be so nice – it's leading on and it's not leading on, it's like with a bag of sweets, just one more and we'll put them away, except one more's only just the one more, isn't it? And they are nice, so there's never anything against ... Oh, all I mean is people forget things and lose their heads. You know how they do.'

'And you're making bloody sure you don't lose yours, eh?'

'That's it.'

'Why?'

'*Why?* Because I don't want to do anything I'd be sorry for afterwards. That's pretty obvious, isn't it?' She had not expected him to be a question-asker.

'Oh, abundantly.' He gave another laugh, staring at her. 'You made that plain all right. But I don't quite get this. I should have thought a girl like you would be more up with things. You see, I could understand it if you had a moustache and spots, or if you liked sewing meetings and what?, I don't know, things you have to like because you've got a moustache and spots – oh, nature walks and choral festivals and what-have-you. Instead of which, here you are looking like something out of Françoise Sagan and keen on clothes and skiffle and pop and dancing and the pictures and going out with blokes. And then you come out with a lot of stuff about codes of honour and a girl's most precious treasure and lead us not into temptation. It beats me.'

'I didn't mention any of that.'

'But you were going to. It's that gradely northern upbringing coming out. Dogged as does it, eh, lass?'

She got off his lap. 'Very funny, aren't you?'

'Oh, I'm sorry, baby,' he said, but like a grown-up who knows that a child's trouble is not as bad as it thinks. He kissed her as if he was being very decent to. 'I didn't mean it, really I didn't. Now come on, let's have a chat about this, what do you say?'

'All right, I'll make some fresh tea.' She did not want any more chat, but could not think how to say so without running the risk of sounding both stagey and toffee-nosed, without falling into the style of *I don't wish to discuss it further* or even *I'll thank you to take your hands off me* (next stage) in a world of *Ah, come on, relax, will you?* and *You don't know what you do to me when you do that.* To lighten things up a bit, she said: 'You put another lovely record on. I liked that last one.'

When she came back with the tea he was pretending he was playing the double-bass in a happy, quite-forgotten-her way. She was careful not to let him see she had caught him. They got back in their old position by the gas-fire.

'There's one thing I've thought of,' he said, smoothing his hair back. 'It wasn't that you ... I hope you didn't think that this was all sordid, did you?'

'Of course not, silly.'

'Are you sure? I know things aren't too ...'

'Oh, Patrick, if I was going to let you make love to me I wouldn't care where it was, or when.'

He drank some tea. 'But you're not going to, are you?'

'No, I'm not. Sorry, pet. We do seem to have got on to this a bit quick, don't we?'

'You know, Jenny, I just can't see how anybody can be so sure about that kind of thing. After all, we are – well, this is all to do with emotion, isn't it? Behaving naturally, not according to any ideas you may have got worked out. Human beings aren't ... Weren't you enjoying yourself?'

'You could tell I was, surely.'

'You can't really have been or you wouldn't have wanted to stop.'

'That's a ridiculous argument; that can't be what you think.'

'Don't you like me?'

'Darling, if you think I don't like you you must be crackers.'

'I can't see it, Jenny, honestly. Why wouldn't you go on? I wouldn't have shocked you or anything, would I? And I'd have – you know, taken care of . . . You'd have had a lovely time.'

'Yes, I know I would. It's not that I wasn't tempted.'

'Then . . . what the hell is it? You religious or something?'

'Patrick, please don't say it in that sneering way. No, I'm not particularly religious, if you want to know; in fact I haven't been near a church for months. It's just that I don't believe in this – whatever you call it – this free-and-easy way of going on. It –'

'Anticipation of marriage is probably how they put it in your – in the advice columns. It isn't something in itself, you see; oh no, it's an anticipation of something else. In fact of promising to work for another person for the rest of your life, in return for which you receive the privilege of promising not to go to bed with anyone else for the rest of your life. Oh, and the perks, of course, like getting the food you've paid for cooked on the stove you've paid for in the saucepan you've paid for with the gas you've paid for and dished up on the plate you've paid for on the table –'

'Eh, you've left me way behind. I didn't know this was a debate on marriage, I thought we were just on about, well, heavy necking.'

'It's all part of the same issue, can't you see that?' Patrick spoke with a seriousness he had not shown at any earlier time. 'It's all part of this bloody mess we've got ourselves into, treating two things as one when they've got nothing to do with each other. Or only a bit to do with each other. Why should two people like you and me have to get mixed up with all that when what we both want, what we *basically* want, is . . . ?' He stopped, and Jenny could have sworn he was weighing up whether to say

'Oh, what's the use?', so she broke in before he could get round to it.

'I've heard about basically before,' she said, thinking of Fred. 'I'm not too happy with basically. Aren't there other things just as –?'

He tore open a packet of cigarettes, which seemed to slow him down a little. 'Look, Jenny. You're not the sort for – fooling around, are you? You know what I mean.'

'Yes. No, I'm not.'

'Right, now shall I tell you why you feel like that? I'm not being sneering now, I promise you. It's because you've had the kind of upbringing – very excellent in its way, I'm not saying anything against it – but it's the kind with the old idea of girls being virgins when they get married behind it. Well, that was perfectly sensible in the days when there wasn't any birth control and they thought they could tell when a girl wasn't a virgin. Nowadays they know they can't and so everything's changed. You're not running any risk at all. But you've had that kind of upbringing and that's why you feel like this. Do you see? It's just your training.'

'Maybe it is, but that doesn't make any odds to me. I just don't care why I think what I do, it doesn't change anything. What about why you think what you do? There must be reasons for that too.'

'The difference is that I haven't got my ideas from anyone else, I've thought them out for myself.'

'So have lots of other people who don't think the same as you. Wherever you get your ideas from it doesn't make them any better.'

'At least mine work. Because they fit in with the way life's lived, which is more than yours do.'

'That remains to be seen. And fitting in's not the only thing. Patrick, don't let's argue, darling. Give me a kiss and let's be friends.'

'Friends is about it, isn't it?'

'I hope not.'

'No, of course it isn't, how could it be? I don't know why I said that. I was just being beastly.'

He kissed her again, in a style about half-way between the

63

getting-going-again one and the child-soothing one from just before she made the fresh tea. So where were they now? She felt she would sooner not find out exactly, not just yet, and said: 'I really think I'd better be getting back, sweet.'

'All right, I'll take you along. We've both had about enough for one night.'

As they left and got into the car – no pulling and pushing to and fro this time – Jenny felt depressed enough to admit to herself that she had realized something she had been pretending not to have realized: the phone call had not been from his mother and there never had been going to be one, not from his mother. It had all been just so as to ... But what had given him the idea that she would ...? Perhaps it was this French-looking thing of hers again. Or perhaps there really had been something in the complaint of an ex-boy-friend of hers – he had had nice ears but was otherwise rather hopeless and inclined to talk about his mother – when he said that everything Jenny did was purposely designed to excite him. She hoped very much that was not the impression she gave. She must watch herself next time to make sure she did not wriggle or run about too much or anything. Her depression was deepening into a real grump: the lights along the High Street, the crowd in front of the Town Hall where buses were waited for and probably pick-ups made, the old cottage with the stone that had *The guift of Thomas Nailor Esqr 1678* on in old-fashioned lettering – all of it just seemed pleased with itself for being there and proud of being as it was. And seeing an aeroplane at night generally made Jenny think in an excited way about people being up there going off to distant places, but the one low down over the common now was only a way of showing off.

They eventually drew up outside Carshalton Beeches. Also drawn up outside it was a newer and much more expensive-looking car than the 110. Patrick looked at it with interest. 'The Thompsons are moving up in the social scale,' he said. 'I didn't know they knew anyone with a Jaguar. Oh, of course, it must be that Ormerod fellow's.' Then he turned to Jenny, frightening her by using the manner of someone getting ready to say something nasty but thought-out. 'Jenny, I don't quite know how to say this, but it'd be hellish difficult for me, going round with you without being able to touch you. You're far too attractive to me, I should keep wanting to take hold of you and kiss you.'

'Well, I can't see anything against that, so long as no one's watching and everything.'

'But then I couldn't be satisfied with just kissing. Like tonight. I should keep wanting to go further with it, and trying to. And you not letting me. It would just be like tonight over again.'

'Would it have to be?'

'I think it just would be, that's all.'

'Yes. So you don't want to see me again?'

'It sounds so awful, put like that. And it isn't true, either : of course I want to see you again. Oh, it's all so bloody complicated. I know I'll find anything's better than not seeing you. I'm all confused tonight. I'll give you a shout soon.'

'Aren't you coming in for a minute?'

'I don't think I will, thanks, despite the huge attraction of Martha and Mr Martha. Got to look at some stuff for those needle-sharp scholars tomorrow. *Nil admirari prope res est una, Numici* ... Ah, why couldn't they write in English like everyone else?'

Enough of his friendly niceness had shown then to pull her up out of fright, grump and depression. 'Then you'd be out of a job, wouldn't you?' she said, and kissed him on the cheek. 'Good night, pet. Thank you for a lovely evening.'

She darted out of the car and gave him a wave from the path as he drove deafeningly away. Ready for bed but anxious to show she was not too late back and in good order, she made her way to the kitchen. As she appeared Dick flashed his glasses in a questioning way, Martha gave another of her sarcastic beams, the Ormerod man leaned forward on the couch as if he was waiting for the start of a stage turn which he knew was going to make him laugh a lot, and the Scotsman twitched his nose and said : 'But my main complaint is the utter unreality of the thing. It's the same with all these British script-writers, they never –'

Dick said : 'Ah, Jenny, all alone? We weren't expecting you back yet awhile.' He said it seriously and gave her a ten-out-often look while his wife gave a quiet laugh and said something in the background. 'Is there a drop more milk, dear?' he asked.

Martha wrinkled up her nose and mouth, probably working out about the milk, but the way she glanced at Jenny during it gave the impression that she was making a piggy-face before putting out her tongue or blowing a raspberry or both. When it was over she went out into the scullery.

Julian Ormerod said: 'Come and sit by me, pigeon. Just for you I sacrificed a session at a rather splendid country club I'm almost certain I belong to where you and I must have luncheon some day soon. Would you like some scotch? There's nothing to put in it, I'm afraid, except water or more scotch. Or try it in your coffee. Bucks a cup of Thompson brew up no end, you'll find. All right, well what about the old fragrant weed?'

Jenny took a cigarette out of the big silver case that he offered her, feeling she might need to have something to do on her own. When she joined him on the couch he had not shifted up to make room for her nearly as much as might have been expected, so that the leg nearest her, crossed over the other one at the ankle, was practically lying on her lap. 'Don't blow, angel, suck,' he said as he gave her a light, an action which he milked of all its coming-closer value.

'Nobody in real life was ever faced with a choice like that,' the Graham man was going on, rocking slightly in the rocking-chair and showing off the little black shiners and grey ribbed socks that went so well with the rest of him, face included. 'May I ask you, Miss Bunn, what would somebody like yourself do in a case of that kind? Surely it's quite simple?'

'I'm afraid I didn't –'

'Your only concern would be to hold on to your agh . . . agh . . . *agh* . . .' After a moment's utter silence he sucked in his breath with a gobble and began to sneeze. Jenny watched him anxiously as he shifted his shoulders about like someone having things thrown at him from different positions, rocking much more than before in the rocking-chair and making a string of short tearing screeching noises. Each one of these whipped a new and surprising expression on to the face he already had and prevented him from getting any further with finding his hand-kerchief. His eyes, whenever she could see them, were fixed on

66

hers as if he hoped she knew he was doing it all for her. The whole thing had a very important feel to it.

'There's probably an old Hebridean superstition about this, meaning that one of us is going to be terribly lucky,' Julian Ormerod said, his bright dark eyes on Jenny. 'I wonder if I can possibly guess which one.'

Chapter Five

'I'll *patres conscripti* you,' Patrick Standish said. 'I'll give you *ut ita dicam*. And what makes you so proud of *esse videatur*, eh? Shakespeare had your number all right, you ponce.'

He was talking to the shade of Cicero, or alternatively to himself, as he moved from the entrance-hall of the College across the main court towards the Chemistry Laboratory. The buildings, made out of some yellowish stone that might or might not be local, had an air of calm antiquity in the autumn sunlight. They should not have done, having been there for less than eighty years and owing their existence to the endowments of a Methodist pickle manufacturer, the only really successful citizen the town had ever produced. Patrick was in his usual twelve-thirty state of being a little dazed with work. The last forty minutes had been spent in taking, or rather hauling, the Junior Sixth through not nearly enough of *In Marcum Antonium II*. For a man so long and thoroughly dead it was remarkable how much boredom, and also how precise an image of nasty silliness, Cicero could generate. 'Antony was worth twenty of you, you bastard,' Patrick said.

Then he slowed in his walk. He had that moment entered unfavourable conjunction with the stocky blue-serged figure of a certain F. B. Charlton, the College secretary, who was nastier than Cicero and alive to prove it. Unless Patrick did something about it, he would soon be coming face to face with Charlton just by the Library. He decided to do something about it and entered one of the bicycle-sheds. Here a boy of seventeen with a face like a horse, who was pumping up a tyre, turned round and saw him. 'Hallo, Mr Standish,' he said.

'Hallo, Horse, what's new?'

'Oh, nothing much,' Horse said, grinning. 'Look, Mr Standish, about next term's play.'

'What about it?'

'We'd better have the first meeting soon if we're going to choose the play and get the books in decent time for the casting meeting.'

'That's nothing to do with me, thank God.'

'Mr Gammon told us you were producing again like last year.'

'Tell Mr Gammon to . . . No, I'll tell him myself. Look, Horse. Last year was last year. It's this year now. Two years ago, after *A Phoenix Too Frequent* as may be readily understood, I said no more plays. This time I mean it. Hard. No more plays. Not produced by me, anyway. Right?'

'But if –'

'No.'

'If you don't do it there's nobody. I've asked everyone.'

'Ask your grandmother, Horse,' Patrick said wearily. 'Oh, why can't you get yourself expelled? You're the only chap in this entire school who wants to have plays. So that you can impress your girl-friends with your genius in the role of Thomas à Becket or Harry Monchensey or what-not. And about thirty other people have got to rush about helping you to indulge your ego. All right, curse you, come and see me on Monday round about two o'clock. But none of your Eliot or Fry this time. Let's make it *Hamlet*. I'll ask Mr Charlton if he'll play Yorick.'

Patrick went out, telling himself he must be mad. Mad with good-nature and keenness. That pleasant self-admiring glow of beneficence, plus the agreeable prospect of messing about with the stage and the production, would all fade when the time came to get to work, but he was always bad at believing this at the outset. Work was like cats were supposed to be: if you disliked and feared it and tried to keep out of its way, it knew at once and sought you out and jumped on your lap and climbed all over you to show you how much it loved you. Please God, he thought, don't let me die in harness. When he did die he would find St Peter at the Pearly Gates looking at his watch and saying: 'Oh, Standish, you're just in time to ref that Colts match with Lucifer's. I'm afraid nobody else seems to be free just now. You don't mind, do you? Here's the whistle – catch.'

While he was picturing this, his heart vibrated in the way it had recently started to do and he had the familiar, but never at other times imaginable, feeling of being outside himself, as if his brain had suddenly frozen, become a fixed camera, while his body continued to breathe and walk and turn its head about in a simulacrum of attention. Terror made him catch his breath; pins and needles surged in his fingers; he stopped and looked up at the sky, but that was worse and he shifted his gaze to an evergreen shrub in a raised oval bed nearby. Some configuration of the leaves under the slight breeze formed, as he watched, a shifting face in profile, the eye blinking slowly with idiotic humour, the mouth gaping as if in the painful enunciation of heavy and foreign syllables. He shut his eyes. Then it passed and he was only retrospectively frightened, soon not even that. Just nerves, he said to himself. Nothing to do with dying, And anyway, men must endure their going hence even as their coming hither, mustn't they? Ah, but then men weren't given the tip in advance about their coming hither, were they? Anyway, nothing to do with dying. Perhaps a little bit to do with going mad. That would be unusual, because he was pretty sound these days on the bonkers question. Meditations on the old last end were giving him a good deal more trouble. Well, thinking about sex as much as possible was the only way to lick that.

Charlton, at any rate, was no longer about. He had done his job by driving Patrick into the bike-shed and on to Horse's bayonet. Patrick went under an archway littered with planking and raw window frames, then entered the Chemistry Lab and found Graham McClintoch, late as always, just packing up. Formulae and molecular diagrams, disposed with chilling neatness, covered the blackboard behind him. Patrick nosed into the dark and decaying workshop by the door while he waited. There were things in there which seemed of no possible terrestrial use, and he said as much to Graham as they walked over to where their joint car was parked in a corner of the side court. They were destined to drive through the town and have a fairly alcoholic lunch at that place that was trying so hard to be a roadhouse, a thing they did most Fridays in term.

Patrick's remark was taken with a sigh and a resigned nodding of the head. 'It's a beautiful day. I wish I was doing something more appropriate to it this afternoon. It seems such a waste to be working and nothing more.'

'That's true. But then it's always true, not just this afternoon.'

'You know quite well you enjoy your job here, Standish. Don't pretend you don't agree that this is a decent well-run school with a lot to offer its staff.'

'I suppose it isn't a bad school really. Bloody sight better now than it was when I came, anyhow. But it isn't the job I mind, nothing much wrong with that. It's having it, and having to have it. It's coming here so often and staying here so long that I don't like. Having to come here and having to stay here. So often and for so long each time. After you've started wishing you could stop. And coming back here again so soon after you have stopped. When you don't want to.'

'You'd die rather than admit you're contented in your work, would you not? I've noticed it's the fashion nowadays.'

'I like things that are the fashion,' Patrick said, almost at random. 'Except for those kind of liquorice-allsort women's hats you see in the advertisements – good job nobody wears them in real life. And those bathing suits that cover them up, of course. Oh, and flamenco records and Indian films.'

He had achieved his object: Graham was not now going to couple his lament about having to work this afternoon with a lament about not being able to take a young woman out instead, this or any very readily foreseeable afternoon. The frequency and intensity of this second order of complaint was one reason why, in the past year or so, Patrick had put in some serious though intermittent work with Graham in an important field. The field was a double one. It consisted at once of trying to get hold of a girl for Graham and of unobtrusively coaching him in the kind of behaviour appropriate to such girls as might be got hold of. One minor success had been scored in the early summer of that year. The long-nosed girl who took the money (often giving wrong change) and sold the razor-blades at the barber's near the College had been induced to go three times to the pictures with Graham and to submit, once, to being repeatedly kissed by him.

After that he had declared an aversion from the long-nosed girl, complaining that she appeared unresponsive and had tried to call him *Gray*. For a chap who ate as he did and dressed as he did – his obdurate resistance to the notion of that cavalry-twill sports jacket, a snip at a local January sale, still rankled – he was too fastidious, Patrick thought. But a chap so clearly constructed for the Glasgow music-halls, a chap whose whole frame cried out so audibly for a glengarry, a kilt, and a curly walking-stick, was the sort of chap who deserved all the help he could get.

They reached their car. Graham sighed again, his glance seeming to fall on a drift or two of dead leaves over by the wall. Patrick could not stand the thought of an ode-to-autumn sexual lament, having currently every reason to deliver one himself. He opened his mouth to start further diversionary moves, such as a discussion of petrol additives. Then he caught sight of Charlton standing quite near, being squat and horrible, in fact, in the patchy shade of one of the laburnums that bordered the open side of the court. He was watching Patrick, who shut his mouth again and made for the driving-seat. Graham had the key. Before he could hand it over Charlton had abandoned immobility and begun to demonstrate how much more horrible he looked when he was walking. The direction of his walk was towards the car. He had a piece of paper in his hand.

Ceasing to fumble in his clothing, Graham said: 'Hang on a minute, will you, Standish? I must have left my watch on the bench.'

So Graham and Charlton were in this together, were they? Patrick draped himself against the car like a rally winner having his picture taken.

Charlton came up. He was wearing a green knitted cardigan under his jacket and there were any number of pens and propelling pencils in his top pocket. He asked Patrick how many times he had told him not to park his car in that particular spot.

'I can't remember off-hand,' Patrick said. 'But there's nothing in the rules about it.'

'Masters don't have rules,' Charlton said efficiently, in his champing way. 'They're expected to behave like gentlemen without having to have rules. See?'

'Is the car causing any obstruction, do you think?'

'It obstructs the exit of that bicycle-shed, for one thing.'

'Only if they come riding out four abreast. And there's a rule about that, I'm sure.'

'And there's the vans driving up to deliver to the kitchens.'

'That might make it tricky for me to drive out, but I'll take a chance on that. It can't interfere with them.'

'Now I'm not going to argue with you, young fellow. I'm telling you. In future you park your car in the place provided, behind the Masters' Lodge. See?'

'Charlton, what is it that makes you behave as if you're the College adjutant or something? You have no jurisdiction whatever over what I do. Don't you know that? You're a secretary in the scribe sense. You're just the man who writes Mr Torkington's letters. You're not like the Foreign Secretary. Well, wait a minute, perhaps you are rather, now I come to think of it.'

'Don't you try and take that line with me, my lad. You're getting too big for your boots, talking to me in that tone, and I'm not having it.' Charlton stood gazing at Patrick, moving his mouth about slowly, wrinkling his woolly-caterpillar eyebrows, and in general looking like the kind of bus-company official who is kept in reserve to announce delays, changes of boarding-point, and suspension of services. After an interval which he used to scratch what there was of his neck, he added: 'So don't you try and take that line with me.'

'Why not?'

'Now just you listen to me, Standish. There are too many of your kind about these days. When I was a young man, the position of schoolmaster carried with it a sense of responsibility. A teacher was supposed to set an example to the community. He was expected to show he knew the right way to carry on, and if he didn't, he went *out*. Right away. That's what's going to happen to you if you don't start pulling yourself together. You'll find yourself *out*.'

'But I thought things were supposed to have changed since you were a young man. They've had plenty of time, God knows.'

'You know what I mean. Some things haven't changed. There are still a few people about who care for decency and the old ways, people who haven't forgotten the difference between right and wrong, never mind what you think. I don't know who the hell you think you are, tearing around in that damned car and drinking yourself silly and running after the women. I know all about how you carry on and you needn't think I don't. I know your sort. And I'm warning you that I've got my eye on you. The Head would take a serious view if he heard about some of the games you get up to, that I do know.' Glancing at the piece of paper he held, as if prompting himself, he changed his manner from the minatory to the reproving. 'You're a good teacher and I've nothing to say against you on that score. Why can't you try and grow up a bit, eh?'

'How?'

'If you don't know there's no use me telling you.'

'So you only tell people things they know already, do you? It seems a curious system.'

'That's enough of that, my lad. I'm warning you seriously now. You're a bigger fool than I take you for if you can't see I mean what I say. You're heading for serious trouble if you go on carrying on like you do. I've got my eye on you.'

'Now let's get this straight, Charlton. Must I get better or must I just not get any worse? Which is it?'

'You know what I mean.'

'Well, say what you mean, just in case.'

'Oh, good morning, Mr McClintoch.'

'Morning, Mr Charlton. Sorry I was so long, Standish. It was in my inside pocket all the while.'

While Charlton, immobile again, watched them they got into the car. As was their practice, Patrick took the wheel so as to give Graham, who considered he drank less or at least held it better, his turn on the way back. Before and after engaging gear Patrick revved up a great deal for Charlton's benefit. Had he meant by all that that he had heard about Sheila? And if he had, just how much had he heard? Hardly anything more than nothing at all was liable to be too much. Patrick looked back before turning into the roadway. Charlton was still standing there. At that distance his piece of paper might have passed for a Roman orator's scroll. Patrick marvelled anew at the clairvoyance shown when the infant Charlton had been allotted his initials.

They moved down the hill along a street lined with small terraced houses, tenanted by workers on the railway or at the glass factory beyond the station. The slope was steep enough to enable the car to coast and so make conversation possible for its occupants. There was much to be said for a noisy car, in that it gave an air of dash and confidence valuable in dealing with girls, but it could not be denied that the occasional halt by the roadside, so necessary to such dealings, had perforce to be made either without verbal lead-in altogether, or after a ferocious, take-it-or-leave-it bawl. That was a pity, but until he could afford to increase his financial holding in the present car to something much nearer fifty per cent – which would mean cutting down on clothes and records – Patrick felt he could hardly press for a quieter replacement.

Graham said: 'What was the matter with you this morning? I couldn't get a word out of you.'

'Depression. The angel of death had me by the throat.'

'Did you drink a great amount, then?'

'No, it's these bloody Gauloises. Too much for me first thing.'

'How did it go last night?'

'Oh, much as expected. Or much as I saw afterwards I should have expected.'

'Mm.' Graham twitched his nose. 'Where did you get to later on?'

'Nowhere really. I just dropped Jenny and cleared off. It would have been awkward at the Thompsons' with Anna there. I'm keeping clear of the place for a bit.'

'But she wasn't there; she was at that Art Club thing she does. We heard her come in pretty late and go straight up to bed. By the way, you were going to –'

'Overtime on the culture, eh?' Patrick said quickly. 'Still, I didn't know that, did I?'

'I could see the Thompsons wondering why you hadn't come in. Dick was quite concerned.'

'Was he, now? Funny thing, isn't it, the way Dick thinks he's a friend of ours? I wonder where he could have got hold of an idea like that. Of course, you dropping in on them and going out to dinner with them helps him to think so, there is that.'

'To hell, Standish, you drop in on them too.'

74

'Into their house, not in on them.'

'And then you do this Labour Party thing with Dick.'

'In spite of him, not with him. You know, there must be something basically unsound about any political organization that can command the allegiance of a sod like that. I shall have to go Tory. But then Charlton's on the Association committee, isn't he? Just nowhere for the progressive intellectual to turn.'

As he pronounced this judgement Patrick trod on the accelerator to carry the car over the canal bridge. They passed a cobbled yard where a great collapsing pile of rotting and peeling cardboard boxes was permanently on view. Today a bald man in grey overalls was bending down studying one of them closely. It seemed an appropriate activity in a town that, so far from addressing itself to any industrial effort of the meanest significance (even the glass factory only turned out the more rudimentary forms of chemical container, plus a few jars and bottles for the rump of the pickle king's empire), was evidently quite set against keeping itself tidied up. Admittedly, much of its population, especially the many London-employed post-war arrivals, would not notice any of that. They were too busy telling one another they lived in a market town as they rushed by – Patrick imagined – on their way to the golf club or the flying club or the country club, not to golf or fly or be rustic, but to drink. Ah well, their system of moral priorities was not altogether an invalid one.

There was a long queue at the High Street traffic lights, mainly composed of westbound lorries detouring a more severe bottleneck nearer London. The halt gave an opportunity for further speech which Patrick, being Patrick, felt he could not afford to pass over. He said: 'You know, we really must start insulting Dick more, seriously. Things have gone far enough.'

'We've tried it quite seriously in the past. He thinks we're just pulling his leg.'

'To show how much we like him. I've got dry cockney humour and you've got pawky Scottish humour.'

'I shall never forget the time I offered him a packet with two in it and he took one between his ring and little fingers because he'd got a pork pie in that hand and a pint I'd bought him in the other.'

'Or the time he borrowed that quarter of tea and never did anything about paying it back because the next day he found that for once he couldn't get out of buying a round and had to go before I could buy him one back.'

'Stern action is required,' Graham said. He had an expression of happiness on his face.

'I'll line something up for him, don't you worry. One of these days I'll do him proper. For Christ's sake take your finger out, you vile fool.'

This last was meant for the driver at the head of the line of traffic, who was evidently not availing himself of his chance to proceed. Immobility in front of a red light was bad enough, but immobility in front of a green one affected Patrick like the sight and sound of Charlton. He blew his horn. To calm himself, he did a little more talking: 'How does Dick manage for drinks when he's not with us?'

'He didn't offer his cigarettes round once last night. Not once. I watched particularly.'

'God, that doesn't surprise me. I bet he let that Ormerod fellow pay for the whole meal plus all the drinks, didn't he? Ah, here we go at last.'

They crept forward towards the lights, but when these changed back to red there still intervened between the 110 and freedom a large furniture pantechnicon with a notice across its back saying that the removal company, or perhaps the driver and his mate, wished to extend to them the courtesy of the road, and requesting them to sound their horn. Patrick obeyed to the full, yelling loudly the while.

'I tried to pay my share,' Graham resumed, 'but Ormerod wouldn't hear of it. We had a very nice moselle – two bottles. And liqueurs. Thompson took him for two large V.O. brandies.'

'Thorough as ever. I should think he's on to a good thing there, whatever he's after. Oh yes, did they have that business conference they were going to have?'

'I think so, but I didn't get much of it. I was off buying drinks and so forth. And what I did hear I couldn't make out. Something to do with some estate that Ormerod could arrange to have put into Thompson's hands for disposal.'

'For a consideration, no doubt. I wish I knew more about that sort of thing. Curious chap, that Ormerod. I wonder where he gets his money from. The Dicks of this world wouldn't keep him in moselle, I bet.'

'Says he's a company director.'

'I thought you only got that in the *News of the World* with chaps up for going to bed with girls of fourteen. Sort of corresponding to scoutmaster.'

Just as the lights changed to amber Graham, who had been half looking at Patrick with an expression he knew well, said: 'You were going to tell me why it was you and Anna came to break it up.'

The lights went green, but still nothing stirred. Patrick concentrated on the task of getting the pantechnicon to move by the unaided force of his will. For once this proved effective: motion was achieved. 'I'll tell you about it later,' he said; then, just before turning left by the chain chemist's, leaned outwards in order to lay upon the man at the wheel of a still-becalmed car the obligation of learning to drive. This action toned him up slightly. He would in the end have to tell Graham enough about the last stages of the Anna business to keep him quiet, but he now had time to nerve himself for that minor ordeal. To give inscrutability a run instead would be unkind, and anyway inscrutability had been abandoned too long ago and too thoroughly to make its resumption plausible. He accelerated decisively towards London, past the municipal offices, in front of which stood a horse-trough newly painted green and overflowing with litter. It had an inscription on its side saying what it was and why it had been put there.

Something irreducibly unwelcome, Patrick reflected, attached itself to all Graham's frequent requests for sexual reports. It had only the most distant connexions with prurience – and who said prurience was a bad thing anyway? – but one was bound to have trouble in expelling the idea that there could be nothing merciful in acquainting a man like Graham with a situation involving another's amatory success, however flawed, partial, precarious, minor, brief, and rare such success might be. On the other hand, any dispatches at all from that firing-line, so far removed from Graham's daily and even yearly life, might easily prove useful to him at such time as he might arrive there on active duty. And talking about the old nonsense, while nothing like as good as performing it, was better than just thinking about it.

These and derived meditations, together with the unreasoned but vital task of getting them to their destination in eighteen and a half minutes, occupied him while he took them there in just under eighteen minutes. As had been feared, Graham soon returned to the charge, before in fact they had finished approaching the bank-like façade, festooned with wrought-iron nastiness, of the aspirant roadhouse. 'I should imagine there were no tears shed on either side,' he said authoritatively, wrinkling his nose and sniffing, 'at the recent sundering of relations between yourself and the wee girl.'

'Very few. We never saw eye to eye particularly.'

'What was the actual cause of dissension?'

'Well, it was all that talk, you see. I don't mind the girls having ideas of their own, but I do like being allowed to keep mine. She's reasonably attractive, of course, and she's got a good line on that – no nonsense about getting rid of unsightly fuzz on her legs the way the beauty pages are constantly on about, doesn't add twenty years to her age by getting her hair set for that vital date, she's about a stone too heavy according to protocol so she's about the right weight, that kind of thing; never bothers with all that rubbish. But it's the way she doesn't bother that I can't stand, the way she goes on about it, not just being French, though that's part of it, but being so bloody keen on being a woman. Never got over finding out she was a woman. Only real advantage she's got, she isn't interested in marriage. Morning, Mr Crosland. Two amontillados, please.'

Chapter Six

FIRST detaching with his little finger the ash of the cigar he was smoking in an amber holder, the landlord strolled to the shelves behind the counter. His face, reflected in two or three among many mirrors, exhibited more shades of blue than even an advanced portrait-painter might care to render, striving against one another rather than harmonizing. He was more frequently on hand than most licensees at his comparatively exalted level, because he considered it more important and rewarding to be a bastard out in the body of the hotel where it really counted, than to just sit in his office minding his own business and being a bastard all by himself – so, at any rate, it appeared to Patrick. Mr Crosland charged by the nip for all bottles of spirits bought for consumption off the premises, and nobody had ever worked out how the hell he made up his mind about the late drinkers and their division into the sheep, or goats, allowed to continue their revelry disguised as 'residents', and the goats, or sheep, propelled into the great outdoors at ten-thirty. It often seemed to have something to do with how he was feeling at the time about his wife, a woman with a baby's figure-of-eight mouth and low-slung breasts, but here again the investigator had to fall back in the end, baffled. Despite these defects, and the fearful crappiness of mind evidenced in the choice of furnishings and the coaching of the waiters, Mr Crosland's establishment appealed strongly to Patrick: unattached, or lightly attached, young ladies were sometimes to be found in it, the food was good, and at least the place was doing its best to be flash.

At this thought Patrick felt a violent pang of embarrassment about Jenny and the events of the previous evening. She was the only girl he had ever brought here to whom it had simply never occurred to conceal her delight at the presumptive flashiness of her surroundings. That ought to have been enough to tip him off, actually: he was now in a position to codify as an axiom the fact that willingness to be impressed was inversely correlated with willingness to be assaulted. Another such axiom, perhaps axiom 1, said that to have frank lechery inspired in oneself bore no correlation whatever to the lechery coefficient, frank or other, of the inspirer. He fancied he could detect, lurking somewhere behind his anger at having bungled things from start to finish, a tiny wisp of remorse at having so rudely turfed Jenny out of her early mood of pleasure and trust. Being in this bloody bar again had done that. But no thinking now, for Christ's sake. Talk was the stuff.

'God, that being-a-woman line,' he resumed vehemently. 'A lot of men are unpunctual, for instance, all right, but the consensus is to treat it as a bad thing, flaw in character if it's habitual, and needs apologizing for seriously, i.e. not as a mere way of being charming, and it isn't a claim to bloody distinction, the being late, I mean. And then being lazy. It looks random but you always find they do the precise minimum, when they're like that. And being hysterical and unreliable. You know, creatures of mood, not coldly rational and impersonal and predictable like the other sex, the one that earns all the money. Men would be just as hysterical if society encouraged them to be, like it does with women, instead of having to discourage them so that the work gets done, that's true. But why aren't they ever interested in anything? – I know, they're interested in *people*, as if nobody else ever was. You know, Graham, I sometimes think I'll marry the first woman I meet who can sit through three minutes of a gramophone record and listen to it. One that's any good, I mean. Some of them can manage about thirty seconds of Harry Belafonte or the Sugar-Plum sodding Fairy before they say *That's nice* and get down to the chatting or ask to have Radio Luxemburg on or want to dance or need a light, but ... Look, what is this mental block they've all got about having their own bloody matches?'

Graham laughed appreciatively. 'For a man who hates women as much as you seem to do, you spend a good deal of time in their company. I must say I can't help wondering just why.'

'Ah, now that's a very good question, a most interesting question, I'm glad you asked that question. Because I want to ...'

His voice tailed off as a jet of flame crepitated into being an inch or two in front of the cigarette he had just put in his mouth. The flame was the product of a big cubical lighter held in a hand with strong hairs on the back of it, and the hand belonged to a man who had approached unseen at his right rear.

'Morning, Mr Ormerod,' the landlord said, a tiny decaying remnant of what could be thought of as the pristine mine-host tone entering his glutinous voice.

'Morning, Charlie-boy. You characters live here, or what? It was here we met last night, wasn't it? Good, thought it must have been. All right, Charlie, take your time, I don't want anything to drink, I'm just standing here for a bet. After all, I'm only a country member. Yes, I can see you do. What are these, sherries? Similar, please, Charles, and a large pink gin for me with some gin in the pink. Well now friends, extraordinarily nice to see you. Spotted that perfect old darling of a 110 just inside the drawbridge here, thought there couldn't be two of these around these parts, and here I am turning out to be right again, which causes me no surprise at all, let it be said.'

'That was most observant of you,' Graham said with approval.

'No more than the norm, I assure you, no more than the norm. That was a merry little gathering at Dick Thompson's last night, what? What? You weren't there,' he informed Patrick.

'No, I wasn't, was I? I was somewhere else instead.'

'I should have been too, really. Can't quite think now what could have stopped me going off to that club of mine instead. At least there'd have been something on offer there, rather than coffee and bridge rolls. Thought those things went out with plus fours and musical evenings. Still, there were compensations. That little Jane Bum, for instance. Pretty little thing, eh?'

'Jenny Bunn,' Graham said, with severity this time.

Patrick felt like vaulting the counter, sending its ice-pot and shakers of bitters and plates of olives and onions and nuts flying over Mr Crosland's green corduroy suit, and emptying at a draught the bottle of Pernod that had been filed among the liqueurs. Doing that, or something on that scale, might at least blur the image of Jenny that had ignited itself in his mind at the mention of her name. That long shining stream of dead straight dead black hair, that smooth almost dusky skin, that tough/tender mouth, those small but high and noticeable breasts, those delicate oblong wrists, and above all, worse than anything else for some unfathomable reason, those quick nervous movements plus that steady gaze : never having all that to himself would be, was going to be, would be very horrible. He wanted more than his share of her before anybody else had any. And here he was, perhaps slightly ahead of Graham in the running, slightly behind Mr Crosland on present form.

'Very jolly,' Ormerod was saying reflectively. 'Knows how to get herself up at inconsiderable outlay. Not very communicative, on the other hand, and went off to bed after about twenty minutes. I must be losing my touch. Ah, thank you, Charles. Well, here we go then, chaps. All the breast.'

Graham's high thin laugh sounded. 'And the same to you, sir,' he said epigrammatically.

Patrick's spirits had lifted directly Julian Ormerod manifested himself. They rose again, past their earlier level, at the revelation that the other had not done as well with Jenny as he evidently thought was his due, even though, should he really decide to put his mind to it, there was no doubt whatever that he would prove a formidable competitor in that or any field, talking for instance. Not that talking was much of a field at all: on his own view, Patrick only talked as much as he did, which was not as much as all that, to keep the ball in the air while slower-witted persons whittled away at preparing their own contributions.

The drinks were paid for and carried to an adjacent table, the cigarette-lighting and ashtray-emptying waiter being held in reserve until the evenings. The table, a too-high affair with bas-reliefs of W. G. Grace's face all over the supporting framework, was presumably there not out of any devotion to King Willow, but because everything except its top was of wrought iron. Patrick remembered the close interest, combined with total lack of admiration, with which Jenny had examined the table, or one identical with it a few feet away. Her concentration had caused her to turn her lips slightly outward. Oh, why had he let himself remember that tremendous mouth, so vividly that by olfactory hallucination its odour seemed to be with him still? He strode out to the Gents.

No, he would not under the most extreme pressure give Graham a rundown on last night's Jenny-dealings, nor on future ones, if any. Anna-dealings, perhaps spun out into a saga or series, would have to do instead. God knew there was plenty of material. For a moment he marvelled sincerely at the size, number, variety, and outlandishness of the hoops through which Anna made her men jump. Or this man jump; had they, he wondered, been specially put up, specially hand-done, for him? Certainly that final hoop, the one to do with him having to recite by rote all the ways in which she was more mature than he was, the one which, that afternoon last week, he had irreversibly baulked at – that hoop had looked horribly *ad hoc*, or *ad hominem*. And if that one, why not the others? This odiously familiar query, coupled with the image of Julian Ormerod, ordering a drink and not recognizing a hoop if one were brought to him on a plate, ought to be depressing. The fact that it was not showed something or other, and not simply that here was a counter-irritant to Graham. Perhaps the fellow was going to convert him to Catholicism, or make an extravagant offer for the 110. He combed his hair, a towel thrown round his shoulders to catch falling debris, and returned to the others. Anyway, here was luck. He downed his first sherry.

'We've just been having a chin-wag about your chum Dick Thompson,' Ormerod said. 'Funny sort of chap. Have you known him long?'

'Long enough. I met him quite soon after I came here.'

'When was that?'

'1857. I mean 1957.'

'I expect you gathered last night I've got a deal of sorts on hand which I might use him for.'

'He could do with one,' Patrick said. 'He's only in business in a small way and it seems to be getting smaller. Mind you, he keeps his end up by economizing on paying his round. Penny wise and pound wise as well.'

'But as far as is known he's quite sound and reliable,' Graham said. 'One hears nothing against him professionally.'

'One doesn't bloody listen if one's got any sense.'

'Cigarette to smoke,' Ormerod said, handing them round. He seemed to have lost interest in the question of Dick. 'You heroes lunching here? I thought I might grab a crafty bite.'

'Grab one with us,' Patrick said.

'Do by all means,' Graham said.

'I'll do that small thing if I may. Shouldn't be too alcoholic, though. Got to keep hand and eye steady for the old shoot-bang-fire. Not feeling too good already, as a matter of fact. My back's getting bent with carrying my money-bags.'

'Shoot-bang-fire?'

'Yes, the old blaze-away. Thought I'd take a couple of guns down to those marshes on the far side of the reservoir. Some duck there I felt I might call on. Care to join me?'

'I'm afraid we'll have to be getting back,' Patrick said regretfully. He was pretty sure he liked the idea of guns. 'In fact we ought to be thinking about eating fairly soon.'

'Let it be so. I think perhaps a little cold salmon today, accompanied by a bottle of what they call French dinner-wine. And postluded by a little of that Hine I seem to remember them getting in for me here, if I'm not mixing it up with that sort of municipal brothel place at the other end of the by-pass. Yes, there may not be much to be said for Charlie-boy here, indeed I rather tend to associate him with the Shropshire and Herefordshire Infantry Training School, but he can throw up a decent meal.'

Patrick assimilated this, running his eye over the well-finished figure of the man before him. This fellow was clearly an excellent example of whatever he might in the fullness of time turn out to be an example of, and with his tan-coloured suede shoes, his charcoal-grey suit and his narrow, horizontally-striped bow tie (duly noted), not to mention his frowning but just-smiling expression, cold rather than crafty but crafty as well, he resembled the kind of British-film villain who ought by rights to be allowed to make a fool of the hero. Patrick said: 'You're lucky to be able to take the afternoon off whenever you feel like it.'

'How true. Freedom is the greatest human good.'

'I suppose your office can get along without you for a bit.'

'To the extent that I have an office, it can.'

'I thought companies went quite a way with having offices.'

'So I have often been told.'

'What exactly do you do?'

'That would be telling.'

'Naturally.'

'And telling involves deciding.'

'So it does.'

'I'm lost, I must confess,' Graham broke in. 'You fellows have left me right behind.'

Elegantly ignoring this, Ormerod clenched his fist and swung it to and fro without menace, a gesture Patrick had already seen him use more than once. 'In point of fact, it's the old hoo-ha that absorbs most of my energies these days. Don't want to give you the wrong impression, of course. It's not that I'm in operation all that much, it's all the chatting and the feeding and the old squiring and the toing and froing that runs away with the time, don't you agree? Not often you can just pop in for one like getting your hair cut, eh? Though I am hoping to work in a quickie after the duck session, that's if my calculations are right and the husband's on nights this week. May have made a non-sense of the schedule, on the other hand. Never was much of a one for paper work.'

'I'll go and get the menu,' Graham said without tone. 'We can't afford to sit around here the whole afternoon.' He gave a sniff or two. Although notoriously hard to deflect from sexual debate carried on in what he regarded as adequately earnest and emotional terms, he was in the habit of rebuking any reference to the subject which seemed to him to fall even a little short of these standards, especially when it was a question of somebody getting his way without much trouble. Watching his retreating back in its indefensible ginger-coloured suit, Patrick felt nettled. He considered that he had his work cut out behaving reasonably himself, or reasonably reasonably, without having to make allowances for others.

'I suppose you're pretty well fixed up with that little Bunn creature, are you? Very jolly . . .'

'I wouldn't put it quite like that.' The truly bad thing, he now saw without difficulty, had been not so much the hilariously inept grab as the long display of fluctuating babe-in-arms bad temper which had followed the perfectly reasonable rejection of the said grab. And all the histrionics. And all the avuncular stuff. And the lecture on sex and society. And every detail of his performance (especially the curtain-speech in the car – oh Christ, especially *that*) as a sort of sexual Charlton. And it was hardly worth pleading to himself that the phone-call from Ruth had thrown him off, even it had been mildly annoying to have on hand at the same time somebody who wanted him but whom he did not want and somebody whom he wanted but who did not want him. And surely Jenny had rumbled the whole thing? She had given no sign, but she was sharp. Anyhow, he had done less than nothing to earn being called *darling* and *sweet* by her, and had not begun to pay it back by his loftily generous revela-tion, as he dropped her outside the Thompsons', that he would be getting in touch with her soon. On grounds of sentiment, justice, and humanity, *soon* ought to mean today. It really was a pity that, on grounds of reason and strategy, *soon* was going to mean next week or later.

'. . . I must say,' Ormerod was going on in his reflective tone. 'Looks as if she'd been so grateful for it. I'm rather fond of those docile ones. Not that she's the type to stay docile very long, I'd have thought.' He pointed his nose probingly at Patrick. 'You're quite a lad for the old hoo-ha, I should imagine.'

'In intention rather than execution,' Patrick said clearly, trying not to think of all the ones he had missed through lack of opportunity, lack of means (though not lack of motive), lack of forethought, lack of sobriety, lack of unscrupulousness. Well anyway, the one he seemed to remember missing through that last lack.

'Aren't we all? But seriously, I'd have marked you down as a veritable king of shaft. What appears to be the trouble?'

'Well, for one thing I tend to go for the pretty ones.'

'A great mistake, I agree. Two mistakes, in fact, if you put it in that form. The waiting game is the answer there, clearly. Got to show a bit of self-command, after all. Strict discipline is your only man, soldier. Why not sign up for a course of instruction? Visual aids. Qualified staff. Your money refunded if not satisfied. Simply fill out and mail the enclosed order blank.'

Patrick caught sight, for the first time, of a great raw chunk of the Western European cultural tradition which Mr Crosland had had put on the wall of the bar: the reproduction, in full colour, of some vast open sewer in the Venice of a fortunately bygone age, fairly crawling with gondolas and alive with nothing-better-to-do characters who were making an honest effort to get a bit of conviction into the way they were milling around on landing-stages and hanging out of windows waving. There was an electric light shining straight on to all this so that it could be seen better. Next thing you knew there would be originals round the place, hot from the brushes of living artists. Was nowhere safe? Patrick tore his glance away and fixed it on Ormerod, who was grinning now. He said abruptly: 'What exactly do you mean?'

'It just occurred to me that one of these evenings you might feel slightly surfeited with pictures in the fire and relish the notion of a foray into the smoke. Soho and so forth. That kind of thing. I can't believe I haven't a contact or two still bravely hanging on, waiting for the nod. You never know what you may run into, what? London, city of contrasts. If nothing more we could probably contrive to raise some adequate din.'

'Kick up a row, you mean?'

'Din-din. The old scoff. Bevvy too, naturally.' He leaned forward across the great horizontal chevron of his leg to light Patrick's cigarette with the big cubical lighter, cupping his large hand round its flame as if he was showing him an indecent miniature, an action which might not have seemed at all out of character. 'Let's just hypothesize that I give you a ring, shall we? You're in the book, eh?'

'Yes. I'm all for it.'

'I suggest we start with potted shrimps,' Graham said, returning to the oversized menu. He added with an emphasis Patrick found vaguely sinister: 'They're pretty reliable here, I find.'

'The very thing,' Ormerod said. 'Put me in trim for later. Now I feel it's the will of God that I should have another jolt. Same for you two? Oysters is amorous ...' As he got up slowly from the table, his voice began to thin and blur. 'Lobsters is lecherous ... but shy-rimps,' he droned, turning somnambulistically away, 'shy-rimps,' on the move now towards the counter with its skied row of tankards that nobody had even been seen drinking out of, towards the woaded, cigar-puffing landlord, but more directly towards the newly arrived barmaid with tight white sweater, charm-bracelet and fringe, 'shy-rimps will do at a pinch.'

Chapter Seven

'WELL, what do you think of it? You must say frankly.'

Jenny looked up at the great whirling picture on the wall of Anna le Page's room. There was a lot of red and green and yellow and blue and orange in it, and the artist had evidently had plenty of colour to spare, for as Jenny saw when she went closer there were big flakes and ridges of paint standing out from the canvas. That made it certain that here was a real picture, not a copy or anything. But what it was a picture of was less certain. Some parts of it seemed to be of a forest during a hurricane, only most of the things that might have been trees were too simple to be really trees; they were more like those shiny weeds that grew on lawns. And here and there there were ones that were apparently growing in the sky. Jenny said 'Mm' once or twice, finishing up with: 'I'm afraid I don't know anything much about pictures.'

Anna le Page tossed back her funnily shaped mop of brownish hair, keeping her eyes shut. 'Oh, you English girls,' she said. 'There's nothing to be known about pictures. You must simply respond to them with your whole being. With your eyes, your heart, your soul' – her own eyes came open and gazed at Jenny – 'and your body. Now say something, say at once what you feel.'

'I don't know,' Jenny said. 'I think it makes me feel puzzled.' But without minding much one way or the other, she wanted to add.

'Good, it's intended to do this, to challenge you and shake you out of your complacency. To make you feel free, even if only for a moment. Today none of us is free. Don't you feel this, Jenny?'

'I hadn't noticed it,' Jenny said, 'Anna.'

'Of course you hadn't noticed it. That's the power of this thing, that most of the time we don't notice it. But when we think about it we can see we're not free. We're all being made the same, very very quickly. Your glorious Welfare State exists to do this, to turn us all into little cogs in the machine. What is it you call it – individuality? We're all losing our individuality. Soon they'll be breeding us from test-tubes.'

'Er ... who painted the picture? Do you know the artist?'

'*Know* him isn't quite right, perhaps. He's a young man who calls sometimes at the shop where I work. I expect you knew that I work in the so-called art shop in the High Street?'

'Mr Thompson told me. What's he like, the young man?'

'Oh, he's a crazy person. But I think he has talent. He's serious about his work if not about anything else. He has no money and never thinks of it. That's good. People should learn to be independent of money.'

'What's he like to look at?'

'He dresses up a little as an artist. Like all of you, he's on the defensive about questions of art; he can't quite be natural, he can't regard art as a normal thing, as a mode of life like any other, no more curious than being a roadmender or a worker in the drains. It's strange that he paints so well.'

'Is he good-looking?'

'He's got a sensual face. But he doesn't know much about women, I think. He talks all the time, and this isn't necessary, as we women soon learn.'

Resigning herself to not finding out so much as the colour of the young man's hair, Jenny sat down on an unpainted wooden stool near the centre of the room. Perhaps if she just hung on, the conversation would turn of its own accord into the good gossip she was beginning to hope for. She had been too thunderstruck to hope for anything in particular when Anna, speaking to her directly for almost the first time after nearly four weeks, and calling her *Jenny dear*, had invited her up to her bedroom to be shown something. The picture was the something. In itself it was probably not enough to fill up a whole Sunday morning, but never mind; early days yet. Her eye fell on a bottle of pretty turquoise glass on the mantelpiece; it must be a French wine bottle, there to remind Anna of home. On the top of it was resting something that looked exactly like, but surely could not actually be, a red tennis ball. Jenny stared at it in amazement.

Anna had meanwhile put her hands behind her head and was stretching in a way that people like the author of *God's Little Acre* probably had in mind when they wrote about animal grace. The movement showed off the largeness of her bust beneath the sleeveless black sweater – Jenny, thinking of her own mere thirty-four inches (to be honest, thirty-three and a bit) felt a twinge of envy – as well as revealing a thick growth of dark hair under each armpit. Was that right? Jenny's training had been quite clear on it not being, saying that it was careless and lazy and the sign of someone who did not bother, but that it was also not right in some altogether different way over and above the carelessness, the kind of way that would make her mother lower her voice and narrow her eyes if she could bring herself to mention it at all. But you had to keep an open mind if you wanted to benefit from new experiences, and Anna certainly looked as if she had a whole set of original ideas about, well, life in general.

As she was thinking this, the other girl flashed a smile at her and said: 'Mm, I feel sexy today, don't you?'

'Not particularly, I don't think. I hadn't really thought about it, I'm afraid.'

'For myself, it doesn't take much to make me feel like this. The young man who painted that picture, he told me that my eyes show I'm always thinking of bed. Bedroom eyes, he called them. He meant he wanted me to think of him in that way, but I couldn't, I'm too busy thinking of ... someone else. I told him this, but he wouldn't take no for an answer – that's what you say, isn't it? He insisted that I should accept this picture as a gift – I said I'd take it gratefully, provided he understood the answer's still no. He pretended he didn't see what I mean. Oh, he's very young. Would you like a chocolate?'

'Thank you very much. What a pretty box.' How could it be any concern of hers, Jenny asked herself angrily, if Patrick Standish was Anna's *someone else*? She, Jenny, was not involved with him in any way at all. (And obviously he was not involved with her, either, after not trying to see her in the ten days since the hair-pulling time.) Then why did she feel frightened of Anna, as if the other was going to start tearing a strip off Jenny's family?

'They're from home,' Anna explained. 'And how do you find the men in this town? Aren't they a hopeless collection?'

'I've no idea, I haven't been here a month yet. I haven't really met more than two or three.'

'It's enough to be sure. They've no sex, most of them. They've no energy left after making money and driving their cars and their silly politics and their amateur dramatics. And their gardens – why are they so often in their gardens? They have this thing about the country, you see: they fill their ground with vegetables they could buy much more easily, and they learn to ride horses – for what? And their boats on this revolting smelly canal. Where will they go in their boats? They seem to be trying to escape from something. I think they find the grown-up world too much for them. And they've nothing to say to you. You speak to them about art and life and sex and civilized things and

90

they stare at you as if you're quite mad. Ah, they're impossible. Give me a girl any day.'

Anna stopped talking with her eyes on Jenny, who had nothing much to say but felt the conversation would have to be kept up. 'A girl? You mean they're more fun to chat to.'

'Of course. Girls understand each other.'

'But they wouldn't be much good for ... the other things that make going out with men fun, would they?'

'Wouldn't they? A girl knows what pleases a girl.'

'Sorry, I meant ... kissing and things like that.'

Anna's eyes went enormous. 'So did I,' she said as if she was indignant about something.

'What, girls kissing? But that's not –'

'What's wrong with it, if it gives them pleasure.'

'Well, nothing, I suppose.' Jenny did not feel they had known each other quite long enough for her to explain that she had been talking about sexy kissing, not just affectionate hugs that girls might give each other. 'Let's get back to men.'

'Oh, you're still in that stage, I suppose.'

'I hope so, I've got a bit longer time to run yet.'

Anna sighed, 'Very well, let it be men.' This time she sounded as if she was giving in about something important. 'Patrick, then. What do you think of him?'

'I hardly know. I only went out with him once.'

'Something went wrong? He tried to work too fast with you, perhaps?' A careful look went with this. 'Am I right?'

'Well he ... we sort of got off on the wrong foot together.'

'I'm sorry. But he'll come back to see you again, of this I'm quite sure. You want him to come back, don't you?'

'Oh yes. He's terribly nice. Or he can be.'

'Yes? What did he do that wasn't so terribly nice?'

Jenny hesitated; then the desire to talk overcame her. 'He just rushed at me. You know. We'd had this marvellous supper, and he'd been so nice and terribly funny, and then we went back to his flat to wait for a phone-call from his mother he *said*, and as soon as we got inside the door, he well, he just rushed at me, that's all.'

'And you didn't want him to?'

'He seemed to think I was all ready to do anything he wanted.

91

He didn't give me a chance. And I got all flustered and lost my head in a big way and gave his hair a terrific pulling. It all sounds so silly now. And then later on he tried the same kind of thing again only going at it easy this time, and when that didn't work he told me my upbringing was all wrong. And being hurt. You know.'

'Yes. I've seen a lot of this thing in Patrick.'

'Oh, Oh, you mean you've . . . Sorry, I just . . .'

'Go on. Or shall I go on? There's nothing to tell. I knew him a little at one time. It wasn't important and it was soon finished. But I remember that often he'll behave as you say when someone disagrees with him or he thinks they've been rude to him. He's a bit spoilt, I think.'

'Oh, I see. Yes. Yes, he is, isn't he?'

'We can find you a better one than that. How old are you, Jenny darling?'

'Twenty,' Jenny said, beginning to blush.

'And you're virgin still, aren't you?'

'Yes.' Jenny felt she must be blushing down to her belly-button.

'I suppose you've been living with your mother and father. It can be difficult like this, with no place to be free.'

'Yes, it can, but it isn't that. The reason I'm still a – it's just that I don't believe in any of that kind of thing before I'm married. It doesn't work.'

'No? And how do you know this?'

'I know it wouldn't work for me, that's all I mean.'

'No doubt you feel you'd be making yourself cheap.'

'No, that's nothing to do with it. It's because I don't believe in it, I've got different ideas, that's all. I don't want to be like that. It's not the kind of life I want. I shouldn't enjoy it, I know. What I'm after is find one chap and stick to him right from the start. See, I'm just not cut out for – going to bed with people.'

'Ah, poor Jenny, you're all confused.'

'I'm not a bit' – she tried again – 'not a bit' – still no luck – 'mixed up. It's perfectly straightforward.'

'Has nobody ever tried to take you to bed with him?'

'Yes.'

'Not very hard, perhaps?'

'Oh yes, quite hard.'

'Not hard enough, then. Or didn't you want to go to bed with him? Was he wrong for you? Is that it?'

'No, it isn't that. I did want to, a lot, but I wanted not to as well, and that's the part that won. I made it win, I had to.'

'It'll be different, you'll find, when you fall in love.'

'I was in love.'

'No, no. If you'd really been in love you wouldn't have been able to stop yourself in your cold way.'

Jenny, who had got to know this line of argument much better than she needed to in the days of Fred, jumped smartly to her feet. 'Now look, there was nothing cold about it. Anyway I was no colder than he was with his trying to blackmail me into it all the time, if I didn't he didn't see how we could carry on and why had I let him start if I was going to keep frustrating him and in the end it even got so that not doing it was bad for his *health*. I wasn't being cold. The cold thing would have been to let him and then I'd have been able to make him marry me. You just don't . . .' She wanted to finish up with 'know what you're talking about', but felt she could not manage it.

Anna had got up too and now put her arm round Jenny's shoulders. 'I'm sorry, Jenny dear, I've upset you. I didn't mean to. You're far too nice to be upset.' She shifted her hold to Jenny's waist, standing rather close so that one of her breasts pressed against Jenny's arm. 'Will you forgive me?'

'Of course I will. Nothing to forgive.'

Anna kissed her low down on the cheek. 'You know, darling, you've a very sweet nature.' Jenny tried to draw away, but Anna held on. 'And you're very beautiful. You can have any man you want, so stop worrying. You have a charming sensual face and good hands and your figure is lovely.'

'That it isn't, it's like a schoolgirl's.'

'I tell you it's beautiful.'

'That's nice of you, but it isn't as good as yours.'

'Nonsense, I'm too full, I know. Yours is just right.'

'You don't think I'm flat chested? I've tried all sorts of exercises and things but none of them seem to work.'

'You don't need them.'

'Ooh, I am glad to hear that said. But I still think you're lucky to be like you are.'

'You're perfect for your type, the slim and graceful.' Anna put her hand on Jenny's collarbone, then moved it down a short way. 'You're well shaped.'

Disengaging herself this time, Jenny went back to her perch on the stool. 'Can I have another of these chocolates? They're ever so good.' She was a little ashamed of being embarrassed by Anna's kiss and the rest of it. Everyone knew that the French were meant to be terribly emotional, and frank as well.

'Of course. Jenny, tell me about your family. I think they're very stern people, aren't they?'

'Oh no, not a bit, they're terrifically free and easy. My father puts on a great business about being strict, but we can easily get round him, all of us, for any special things. I remember once one Christmas time –'

'What's his trade, his profession, your father?'

It always came sooner or later. The thing was to say it very offhand and carelessly, as if half the people you met were it. 'Oh, he's a hearse-driver.'

'A hers? A *her* . . . ?'

'He drives a hearse, a funeral car. For when people are being buried. He works for a very big firm in . . .'

With a peal of foreign laughter Anna collapsed on the striped travelling-rug that covered her bed and drew up her slightly bulky knees. Jenny watched her with a half-smile. If it took them like this all that could be done was to wait until they got over it. For a moment she thought back to what Anna had said about modes of life and artists, and wondered why hearse-drivers were not normal when artists were. Then she told herself that that was tetchy and silly. Her smile broadened. Actually you had to admit that a hearse-driver was rather a funny thing to be, although, as her father was fond of saying, no funnier than being a schoolteacher.

Gasping and shaking her hair back, Anna got over it. 'I'm sorry, darling, but I have such an odd sense of humour. Do go on. Tell me all the other things. How old is he, this father?'

'I never really thought to ask him. I suppose he must be getting on for fifty-five. He was in the war. He was in the army in the desert and in France. He was a sergeant in the Royal Artillery, the gunners. He was –'

'My father is a most magnificent man, very handsome and young. All the women in the village at home are crazy about him, but he's – what's the expression? – he's choosy. He'll only take the best-looking girls.'

There was a pause. Feeling she ought to, Jenny asked: 'Take them? Take them out, you mean?'

'No, no, take them, make love to them.'

'Oh. Doesn't your mother mind?'

'My mother knows nothing of this.'

'Why not?'

'She's dead.'

'Oh, I'm awfully sorry, Anna, I didn't know.'

'You needn't be sorry. I'm not sorry. She was a bitch.'

'Was she?'

'I'm glad that she's gone.'

Jenny felt embarrassed in several ways. The most unusual way came from sensing dimly that she and Anna, but especially Anna, seemed as if they were taking part in a TV play (the sort where the announcer said beforehand that he and his friends did not consider it suitable for children) going on in some hot dry place on the Continent, with wine and goats. If Anna had so much as added 'Yes, glad, do you hear?' to her last statement, it would have been a devil of a job not to expect a man with thin lips and tight trousers to come strolling in, starting to play a guitar with ribbons on it. 'What does your father do?' Jenny finally asked.

'Please?'

'What does he do for a living?'

'He's a peasant.'

There was not much you could say about that sort of fate. Jenny was wondering whether they might not now go on to show each other their clothes to really get the friendship settled, when Anna, who had tucked one leg up under her on the bed, stuck out the other in a pin-up girl pose. Dreamily, but with a side glance at Jenny, she said: 'Of course, he's mad about me.'

'Who is?'

'My father.'

'Mad about you?'

'That's what I said.'

'You mean he's very fond of you?'

'No no no no *no*. He – is – mad – about – me. Don't you understand? And I'm the same way about him.'

Jenny snorted. 'What nonsense, you can't be. Your own father.'

Her eyes dilated with anger, her bottom lip stuck out, Anna leapt to her feet. 'How horrible you are. Stupid and horrible. I hate you. There's something terrible wrong with your mind. You absolutely revolt me. I can't stand you.'

Jenny stood up too. 'I think I'll be going.'

'How can you say such things. You're so ignorant I simply can't believe it. You know nothing and you've no sensitivity.'

'I don't know why you're so angry, but I'm sorry I've offended you, I didn't mean to.'

'But you have, very much.'

'I can't think what to say.'

'You go rushing into things you don't understand and then you're surprised when I'm angry.'

'Yes, I am. I mean –'

'You're a very silly little girl. You've a lot to learn.'

'I know that.'

'I think perhaps you didn't know what you were saying.'

'No, I don't think I did. I am sorry, Anna, honestly.'

'Perhaps I'm too unkind to you. I'm afraid I lost my temper. I shouldn't have done this.'

'It was my fault in the first place.'

'Let's forget it.' Anna advanced on Jenny and kissed her firmly on the mouth. 'We're friends, eh?'

'Oh yes.'

'Together we'll face them all, no?'

'That's right.'

'Ah, what shall we do today?'

'There isn't much, is there?'

Cheery almost to the point of hysteria, Dick Thompson's voice reached them from below. 'Girls? Coffee up, you girls. Jenny and Anna. Coffee. Chop-chop, now.'

Anna lifted her hands in a real French person's way and laughed. 'You see? Our problem's solved. There's this to do. The morning coffee. Hurrah.'

Jenny laughed too. 'It'll be smashing, just you see. Bet you there's chocolate biscuits. Come on, let's go down.'

'Ah, such enthusiasm. You're young still.'

On the way out, Jenny noticed a big poster drawing-pinned to the wall by the door. On it was a picture of a man on a blinkered horse pushing a lance into a bull's neck. There was lettering that said GRAN CORRIDA DE TOROS Y MAGNÍFICAS NOVELLADAS, and a lady down in one corner with a man and a fan and a mantilla. She looked a very jolly lady, but foreign. Well, there was nothing wrong with that (though the bull part was horrid); foreigners were colourful and good luck to them.

While she was following Anna downstairs, Jenny was going over the nice things Anna had said to her about her looks and the bit at the end about the two of them facing things together. That much more than cancelled out the scaring way Anna had jumped down her throat about the father business, which all still seemed very odd. Jenny suddenly realized she knew the exact word for Anna and the way she went on: *mercurial*. In other words there was not a hope in hell of guessing how things would go from one minute to the next. Of course, people with that temperament needed much more tact and understanding than everyone else. Jenny hoped she had enough. The great thing was that she and Anna were friends, in spite of the one or two awkward moments. They had not had a clothes-showing session as had been hoped, but they had had a short bust discussion, which was just as good. Jenny still felt a tiny discomfort over that last kiss, which she had not liked to dodge. She had thought that the French tended to kiss people on both cheeks rather than on the mouth, but perhaps that was only generals giving away medals. Things were always less simple than they seemed at first.

Chapter Eight

Dick was sitting reading the Sunday papers in what he called the parlour. He pointed out the coffee and biscuits standing on a low polished table that had not always been low, for he had spent quite a bit of the previous week sawing the bottom eighteen inches or so off the legs. Beyond asking them to help themselves he did not say anything. Reading his way through the two papers he had by him – each of them had just one small photograph on its front page – was about the most serious thing he did in the entire week. He kept up his pouting and repouting trick the whole way, a sure sign that he was concentrating, and he would not let up until he turned to the *Pictorial*, which he would look through very quickly, laughing shortly at about every other page. Jenny passed a cup of coffee to Anna and took one herself. The two girls settled down on the sofa, Jenny with the *Pictorial*, which Dick would not be wanting yet and Anna never seemed to want at all. Jenny tucked her feet under her and felt contented.

'Oh, these Sunday mornings in England,' Anna said, doing another gesture with her hands: 'really, they're endless, endless. Everything becomes completely grey, both inside and outside.'

'I don't know, it does give you a chance to take things easy.'

'But do you want this, this taking things easy? I don't. I want someone marvellous to come along and sweep me away, give me champagne and make me laugh and drive me at a hundred miles an hour to anywhere, anywhere far away and new and alive and full of colour.'

'It would be rather nice, I must say.'

'And we'd never come back, never.'

'Trouble is I've got school tomorrow morning.'

'Ah, this tomorrow morning, it's your whole existence, you're thinking about it all the time and you're missing all the movement and colour that's around you today.' Anna lowered her thick eyebrows as if she had not said quite what she intended to say, but went on cheerfully enough – she really was being a chatterbox this morning: 'Now perhaps, when we've read the newspapers and drunk the coffee, we'll become dissipated and drink a glass of beer at the pub before lunch.'

'That sounds a pretty good programme to me. And a little nap this afternoon.'

Anna laughed, giving her eye-opening muscles more work to do at the same time. 'Jenny, you're quite incorrigible. You love your slow old routine of stay in the same place, don't you? Here, you must have another biscuit.'

She passed Jenny a tin made in the form of half a dozen elaborately bound tin books held together by a tin strap. It reminded Jenny of the tin out of which her Auntie Minnie had so frequently offered her pliable ginger-biscuits (to go with the brick-red tea) in the past – in fact, this lot was a kind of companion volumes. Today's tin fitted in well with the furnishings of the room they were sitting in. The chairs and things had a fair amount of green plush on them, the pictures – a cornfield with poppies, a ship in full sail without anything else going on, a cavalier who was doing a lot of laughing with being, Jenny was nearly sure, the Laughing Cavalier – were the sort that nobody would look at except just to see that they were there, the corner cupboard thing had on its glass shelves a miniature cow and calf in real hide that she would have liked, but surely no living person could take any interest in the china castle, which was far too simple compared with actual castles, the ebony elephants, and so on. Apart from the yellow distemper, which had probably been put straight on top of wallpaper, and a pigmy knight in armour that no doubt had poker, tongs and hearth-brush inside it, there was hardly anything here which could not have been taken over as it stood from Mr Thompson the elder, who had been described by Patrick as an important figure in the town twenty or more years ago–'so they say, anyway. I wouldn't know, thank God. Before my time, all that.'

Seen against this background, Mr Thompson the younger looked almost dignified, or at any rate as if he had been in the same place as long as people could remember. He sat in a chair with big sides as well as a back, across the room from the two girls. Every now and then he read a couple of sentences aloud from his paper and/or threw in something of his own. 'I see the

Yanks are doing their best to stir up trouble in the Middle East again,' he had already said, and 'So *the motives of those agitating for Britain's renunciation of nuclear weapons require careful scrutiny*, do they? I suppose it hasn't occurred to anyone that they might just not like the idea of them and their families being blown up,' and '*He went on to claim that the British people were now enjoying a standard of living unparalleled in their history.* I'd like to see him stand up and say that in Lancashire,' and 'My godfather, another royal tour. It's enough to drive you round the bend.'

Jenny did not care for that last one: everybody knew that the Queen and the Duke of Edinburgh had a very difficult job that they had not asked for, and that they did it well. She had not been all that interested in Dick's previous ones, come to that, so that when a stepping-up in the pouting and repouting and a very short outbreak of cawing meant that another quote was coming on, she picked up the *Pictorial*, folded it in a way that showed up the photograph of a man that the article underneath said was an evil schoolmaster, and passed it to Anna. 'That's your one,' she said, giggling. 'You've *got* to marry him.'

'But who is this? I don't understand.'

'Only a terrible man. You're meant to have to marry him.'

'Why? Is this a game?'

'Then it's your turn. You pick the one I've got to marry.'

'Really, Jenny, you mystify me with your games. I can't see where you learn them. But this one's better than the game the other evening when you pretended to be an old woman. What is it you say? – *I'm eighty years old . . .*'

'I'm eighty years of age and I can eat an apple and crack a nut,' Jenny said with her lips stretched over her teeth.

'If I'm to have any more of this I'll have to be strengthened. I must have fresh coffee. I'll make some in the French way.'

'Don't bother for me.'

'Of course you must have some. I'll only be a few minutes.'

It was a bit of a nuisance, Anna going out. Jenny would have liked to go to the kitchen too, but if she did Martha Thompson might easily tick her off for hanging round on the off-chance of an odd job. (There would be a smile with this, but not a very jolly one.) Jenny felt that if she was going to be allowed to help with the vegetables, as she hoped, then she had better do nothing that might irritate anyone. These days, actually, there was more to it than just wanting to play her part in the household. Doing the potatoes herself would mean that she could get rid of the eyes in them at the sink rather than at the table. Eyeless potatoes would go some way to cancel out whatever was going to be next on the list after the lionhouse haddock, the tea-towel beef, and the rusty-knives steak pie (which had turned up a few days previously). So she had better not go out to the kitchen just yet.

On the other hand, there was something to be said against staying where she was. Although Dick was always cheery and thoughtful, she had not felt absolutely at ease with him since the time he had called her a funny little thing for wanting to feed the hens. It was no use telling herself not to be vain: the fact had to be faced that he was getting ideas about her.

Ideas about her, she had had to learn, were liable to be got by any man she might nowadays meet. She considered she had led a fairly normal life until she was fifteen or so. She had had friends who were girls and friends who were boys, and she had known quite a few older, married people of both sexes, most of whom were nice to her in the ordinary way. And then quite suddenly, just over the weekend as it were, the whole set-up had changed. All at once there were men everywhere. Men turned up in large numbers on public transport, especially after dark – there were always more of them then; they fairly thronged the streets; they served and waited to be served in shops; the cinemas were packed out with them; they came to the front door selling brushes and encyclopedias; some of them had even penetrated into the Training College. Men had begun not only to get ideas about her in passing, but in a fair number of cases to stay on the spot and get going on putting those ideas into practice. A fair number of the fair number of cases had been rather surprising ones by reason of the age, married status, or general dignity of the man concerned. At least they had surprised Jenny to start with.

A good example of it all had been when she was coming home from school one day and the bus-conductor had tried hard to hold her hand instead of giving her her change. This man, who looked very like a psychologist she had once admired on TV, she had often seen smiling in a fatherly way as he swung toddlers off the platform (when the bus had stopped), and he had been known to stop the bus between proper stops so as to oblige old people and expectant mothers. It was almost incredible – or, again, it had seemed so at the time – that such a polite and stately kind of person should suddenly start behaving like a prowler in a pin-table saloon. It was like being casually told that Mr Burrage next door at home was a famous author or a Russian agent.

When she stole a glance at Dick, though, she forgot about the getting-ideas business for the moment. He had put his papers down and was evidently repairing a cigarette, one of the small sort, with a piece of stamp-paper. This put it absolutely beyond all possible doubt that he was a stooge, even though she had still not had a chance (since the first minute of their first meeting, and she had had too many other things to think about then) to notice whether or not he carried a suitcase with his forefinger crooked over the lid to stop it flying open if the catches both snapped at once. Earlier, there had been valuable clues in the way he held his cigarette in his first two fingers as well as in his mouth when it was being lit for him, and in the way he sometimes wore a white shirt with an open neck.

Stooges were easiest to pick out as children, of course, when they had clean navy macs and big, old, meaty faces (ones like Elias at school were so obvious that it was almost a shame to take the money, spotting them), but Jenny had got so good at recognizing the grown-up ones that just catching sight of them at a distance was sometimes all she needed. They had to be walking then, because apart from things like their always having the latest bus-timetable and writing in their personal memoranda on the page for it in diaries and looking at times a little like a lady, the most reliable way of telling one was if he had one of the two kinds of stooge walk: one with the knees loose and the head turning to and fro to look at everything, the other with the eyes fixed in front and the hands closed up with the thumbs forward, rather like the way of soldiers marching that her father had several times shown them all at home. Dick had managed to fool her for a time only by having a third kind of walk and talking a lot. It was a pity he was a stooge, because nobody could have been kinder. But in another way it was a good thing, because so far she had never run into a stooge with ideas about her who had started anything. They just looked, in a sad, fixed way, like someone watching after a street accident.

Still, you could never be sure. She found it hard to believe that Dick was going to run over and grab her hand when he had finished with the stamp-paper. But that was part of the trouble. She could remember as if it was yesterday how seriously the bus-conductor – admittedly not a stooge – had set his ticket-machine before making his grab. Jenny had never found too much difficulty in convincing even the more active kind of man that she was not the kind of girl he hoped she was or, as in Patrick's case, could not believe at first she was not. It was just that there were situations where having ideas about her could lead to awkwardness. This would be that kind of situation if it arose. Something in the set of Dick's long-jawed head, in the upward tilt of his elbows as he smoothed the stamp-paper down, made Jenny feel uneasy.

Now that the repairs were complete he put the cigarette into his mouth and lit it in a way that said he had smoked thousands of the things in his time. He sat for a moment as if he was arranging a lot of facts in his mind. Then he said: 'Things are very difficult.'

'Are they?'

'Running a house this size is no picnic these days, believe me.'

'I wish you'd let me help. I get plenty of free time, you know.'

'You do more than your share as it is. After all, you are supposed to be a guest here, even if it's only a paying guest.' He gave one of the short caws. The longer caws had been changing recently; they had in them a bit of the sound Patrick produced when he put the 110 into bottom gear. But the short ones were still more or less the same. 'But that's the way we see it,' he was going on. 'We don't feel it's up to us to charge the earth off two young girls who've only just started earning. That's how we look at it, me and Martha. Now from what I've seen of you I'd say you were probably by no means ignorant of what running a house means.'

'Well, I have –'

'So you'll have seen we're hardly in the idle-rich class. What we get from you and Anna just about takes care of the rates and general upkeep, which are pretty wicked in a house this size, I don't mind telling you. But there, we like it the way it is.'

Jenny had been starting to say that that was right; she did know a bit about housekeeping, having had to take charge at home for a couple of months while her mother was in hospital with that internal thing and complications. Her father always said that the modern girl was a fool in a home compared with her mother's generation, but unless Jenny had stayed out too late the evening before or come down to breakfast wearing too much make-up he always made an exception of her. Not being a fool in a home, then, she was in a good position to weigh up the economies Dick went in for so as to make things less difficult for himself.

There was not much to be said for the electricity-saving drive which every night made the hall and the stairs a death-trap. About the cheap toilet-paper you could go further and say that there were some things where economy was out of place. This was another motto of her father's, and oddly enough he always picked on toilet-paper as an example. His mother (the hymn-singing grandmother) had had the habit of putting greaseproof wrapping from the groceries and old sweet-bags out in the lavatory, and one dark morning, evidently, her father had had trouble as a result of half a stray acid-drop. Not only out-of-place economy and lavatories, but dark mornings, paper bags, and even sweets were subjects which could remind him of, and so naturally made him tell, this story. He always laughed a great deal before, during and after telling it, especially after, and Jenny's mother always looked at him as if he had said he had another wife and family on the far side of town. Jenny herself could not help laughing now at the memory of it all, snoring a little in the act as she usually did.

It was a mistake. Dick said at once 'What's so funny?' and shot up from his chair. 'Let's share the joke.'

'It's too silly, honestly. It's not funny at all, really.'

'Oh, come on, don't be mean.'

'It'd take too long to explain.'

'We've got all the morning.'

'No, please, it's not worth it.'

He came nearer, looking down at her. 'You're a mysterious little person. I don't know what makes you tick at all.'

'I'm just the same as everyone else.'

'Oh, far from it, Miss Bunn, far from it.'

'I think I am.'

'Well, you think wrong in that case. You're hellish pretty, for one thing. Far too pretty for my peace of mind.' With this he sat down on the arm of the sofa and, glancing over at the door, put his hand on her shoulder.

People down here bothered less about there being a time and place for everything than people at home. Anna, with her midnight baths, dressing-gown at tea-time, and chocolates after breakfast, was in the lead on this, but Martha kept it up with coffee in the afternoons and hanging out the washing when she came back from the pub. And here was the master of the house doing his bit. Jenny moved sideways and reached for the *Pictorial*. 'You should see me when I've got my make-up off.'

'It wouldn't make any odds, not with your skin.' He touched her cheek. 'Schoolgirl complexion right enough. All over and all, I shouldn't wonder.'

'I'll thank you to keep your hands to yourself, mister,' Jenny said, twisting round in the nick of time as his hand began to descend. She want on instantly: 'Do you think this chap did it? It says here he made a confession and then withdrew it. Nasty-looking bit of work, isn't he? Awful sort of squirrelly eyes.'

'Here, now, don't change the subject.'

'We weren't on any subject.'

'Well, I certainly was.'

'That's as may be, I don't remember being.'

'Here, there's no need to get all hoity-toity, you know.'

'Oh, I'm that glad.'

'Little terror, you are.'

'That's me.'

'Little smasher too. And you needn't think you can get rid of me like this. I'll be back, that I can guarantee.'

'Do you want to see the *Pictorial*, Mr Thompson?'

Almost joyfully, Dick said: 'Now then, young lady, you can just cut out this *Mr Thompson* lark, I've been meaning to mention it to you before. We're all christian names in this house. Now I'm Dick and you're Jenny, right?'

'Yes, of course.'

'Come on, let's have it properly to break the ice.'

His eagerness had made him shoot one of his legs out straight, so that his trouser-cuff rode up and a piece of bony, geometrical-looking shin came into view. Men's legs always made Jenny want to laugh, and it might have been her struggle not to as much as anything which made her stutter come on in the way it had and completely prevent her from getting the name out.

'All right then, we won't insist on it this time. But you'll have to remember in future, mind. No, I don't want the *Pictorial*; got more important things on hand. Bills to be paid, much as it goes against the grain.'

Admiring the way he had got out of trouble, and reckoning that that was probably going to be that, Jenny caught sight of a headline on one of Dick's papers. It said *Cambodia: U.N. Debate Likely*. The *Pictorial*'s said *Autumn Isn't Here, Say These Bikini Belles*. And *this* was the paper Dick had no time for.

A great noise from outside, like an airliner in difficulties, made them both turn towards the window. Dick, who was tall enough to see over the net curtains, flashed his glasses and said: 'Ah, I thought I recognized the hunting-cry of Boanerges.'

'Who?'

'That's what I call Patrick's and Graham's car. Yes, here they are, the pair of them. Not often they come dropping in at this time of a Sunday. I wonder what they're after.'

'I've no idea,' Jenny said, feeling she might go bobbing against the ceiling if she was not careful.

'I'll go and admit them,' Dick almost yelled. He just missed a corner of the tray of coffee Anna was carrying in.

'Well, and what's all this excitement?'

'Patrick and Graham have turned up.'

'But how magnificent, and after so long. This is nice for you.'

'Yes.'

'You see, Jenny my darling, here's the someone who'll drive us away at a hundred miles an hour.'

'At least that, if Patrick's anything to do with it.'

There were sounds of arrival from the hall. They included Dick's voice saying 'Ah, hallo, you old monsters' and Patrick's saying 'Hallo, you bastard.' 'Come on in.' 'I swore I never would again but I suppose once more can't hurt.' 'You old monster.' 'Where is everybody?' 'In the parlour; you're just in time for a cup of coffee.' 'What, one each?' 'Here they are, the old monsters.'

Patrick was wearing this time a moss-green suedette jacket and a pair of khaki-drill trousers. He looked friendly enough, but a bit uneasy. Jenny just had time to notice these four facts before Anna ran past her and gave him a big but short kiss on the mouth. Graham McClintoch said good morning to the two girls without catching the attention of either. When Patrick could be seen again his face looked a bit more uneasy. He said hallo to Jenny as well as he could. The way Anna was holding his hand, with her arm straight and swinging to and fro, and the way her knee-stockinged legs were dancing slightly made it seem as if she had pulled him in through a french window at the back of a theatre stage and was on the point of announcing their engagement. But all she said was: 'How lovely of you to come and see me, darling. I was getting so bored.'

All this struck Jenny as odd. Why was Anna behaving and talking like this when not half an hour ago she had been giving a fairly unflattering opinion of Patrick in a very unflattering tone? *Mercurial* hardly covered it.

'Hey now, you two, break it up, chop-chop, general conversation if you please. I'll go and get another couple of cups. Sit yourselves down.'

'Listen, Jenny, what about –?'

'Darling Patrick, how providential that you should bring your car now. Jenny and I have been saying that what we most want is to be driven a long way very fast. You're the very one to do it for us. Where shall we go?'

'Well, I hadn't thought exactly. We just wondered –'

'We'll decide after we've started. That'll be better. Must you wait for this coffee? I'm restless to be away.'

'If we're all to go, as it seems, perhaps we should ask Dick if he might like to –'

'Shut up, Graham. Oh, hallo, Martha.'

'I thought I'd come and see what all the uproar was about. Hallo, Patrick. Quite a stranger.'

'Well, you know how it is, what with work and all the –'

'Yes, I know how it is all right.'

After that, which was said with the same quick blinking that Jenny remembered from her first meeting with Martha, things slowed down to some extent. But it was really not very long before the four of them – Martha said she had to get the lunch ready, and after a glance from her Dick said he had to give her a hand – began to drift one at a time out of the house. Patrick went to turn the car round. Graham followed Martha about, talking to her. Anna ran up to her bedroom for the third time, the last trip having had no more result than a tartan stole to keep her warm during the drive. It looked very weird with the new striped Italian cardigan she had put on the first time up. Jenny got permission from Dick to help with the vegetables another time, then wandered outside.

Patrick was strolling across to the hen run. 'Ah, less of it for Christ's sake,' Jenny heard him say. 'Ger, piss off, you bloody fools, I'm not Thompson. Go on, get out of it.' He picked up a handful of gravel and drew back his arm to throw.

'Stop it Patrick,' Jenny called. 'What do you think you're doing? For shame. Leave them alone.'

'I was only going to wake 'em up a bit, it'll do 'em good.'

'You're not to, it's cruel. They haven't done anything to you.'

'Something in that, I suppose.' He dropped the gravel and wiped his hands on his trousers. With his eyes fixed on her, he ran his fingers through his hair and said: 'Jenny, I'm sorry about that evening. I behaved badly. Not just in ... leaping on you like that, but in being so bloody afterwards. I was nasty to you. That was really worse than the other.'

'That's all right, I was to blame as well. I was silly.'

'Before you say any more just listen. That phone call wasn't from my mother, it was just coincidence it came then. It was from a girl I used to know. My mother wasn't ever going to ring. That was a lie. I made it up to get you back to my flat so that I could ... you know. It was just a sordid bloody little bit of scheming. I was completely wrong about the sort of girl you are. It was idiotic. And then I took it out of you for not doing what I wanted. And why I had to go and start on all that up-bringing stuff … I'm not a very nice sort of chap, I'm afraid. You tumbled to it about the phone call, didn't you?'

'Well, I did sort of half guess, I suppose.'

'Of course you did, you're not a fool. I had it all worked out in about two minutes: back to the flat, a couple of kisses and straight up to bed, pretty well. That's how I wanted it and so it was going to have to be like that, and so the phone-call thing was obviously going to be completely convincing, because it had to be. God, it's as if I was tight – you know, I haven't got the car so I want to be driven home, and that chap's got a car, hasn't he? so he'll drive me home, won't he? He happens to live in the other direction, but that doesn't matter, does it? because he won't mind, will he? because he's got to do it, hasn't he? And if he says he doesn't want to, then it's *You bloody drive me home, Jack, and like it, because I want it, see?* Oh Christ. Terrifying. I don't know. Let's wait by the car. Look, Jenny, can we just scrub out the other night, pretend it didn't happen?'

'I'll forget all about it if you will. And never mind the scheming part, it was quite flattering in a way.'

'Especially the things I said, I want you to forget all about those. Do you think you could?'

'Nothing to it. I couldn't follow half of it, anyway.'

'I bet. But … Listen, are you doing anything in particular this afternoon? Well then, let's drive out and have tea somewhere. Graham won't be wanting the car – a gripping book-length yarn about dehydrated sodium bicarbonate or whatever it is arrived for him yesterday and he hasn't had time to get into the full swing of the narrative yet. And I kept the *Observer* away from him all morning on purpose so he couldn't start the Ximenes crossword – competition puzzle, too; that always gets him. He'll be as happy as a pig in … a pig-sty. Well, what do you think? We could even have a drink on the way back. At least you could; I'm sticking to dandelion and burdock for a bit.'

While he was talking, Jenny glanced over his shoulder up the hill. At its crest the road forked, one branch, as she knew from her exploring walks, passing the cottage hospital and making straight for the next town (which she had never visited but whose Roman remains she had read about), the other twisting around through a thick wood with ivy on the trees and brambles and nettles. Last Sunday up there a tall man with a gun under his arm and a beautiful golden labrador trotting behind him had been crossing the road as she came along and had smiled and wished her good afternoon, as country folk did. The trees – she visualized them now – had been bare and the ground covered with fallen leaves and the light all murky, but when the summer came everything would be fresh and bright. And what a summer it was going to be. After Patrick's first couple of sentences she hardly noticed what he said, because she was too busy seeing in her mind's eye, like a terrifically speeded-up film, the fields full of crops, the herds of cows being driven along the lanes, the little lakes with ducks on the ripply water, the grey stone churches all cool inside, the foals cantering about with their mothers, the Saturday lunches of bread and cheese and pickled onions and scrumpy cider out in the garden of the country pub. 'Oh, Patrick, I'd love to,' she said.

They looked at each other and Jenny felt a thrill that was almost a shiver. Her body tensed. She noticed that Patrick's eyes were wider than usual, as though he was surprised about something. Then there were footsteps and voices on the path and she relaxed.

'It's lovely to see you, Jenny,' Patrick said.

'It's lovely to see you.' She beamed at him. It would have been nice, no getting away from it, if Patrick had brought her two dozen roses, knelt down and kissed her hand, read out to her from a parchment a sonnet he had written about her eyes with a quill pen, sung to her in the voice of Nat King Cole (*Dorling – it's increddabull – that you should be so – unforgeddabull*), but what she had was enough.

Chapter Nine

ANNA had pencil slacks and sandals now with the cardigan and stole. Jenny found herself in the back seat of the car with her, which seemed to irritate Patrick rather. Graham drove, using up every bit of his attention on it. You could have told he was driving simply from the look of the back of his neck, and the fat cap he wore made it more important, reminding you of hill-climbs, rallies, endurance tests, or stock-car racing, at least in back view. From the front it was more as if he had decided to chuck everything up and go on the halls while the market lasted. After a time they got a view of the canal which suggested, falsely, that it was nice down close to it. Then they came to a part with streams and woods, a quarry, platforms for milk to be loaded, telegraph poles with little fences round them. The sun came out and at once things looked full of rich growth. Patrick turned round and called to the girls: 'Shall we stop and get a breath of air?'

By the time Graham had found a good place to park at the roadside, the woods had petered out and the streams fined down to form a long marshy strip with clumps of bushes. They all got out. Nobody had much to say until Graham and Anna went on with an obscure argument about the Americans that they had begun back at the house as a result, probably, of some remark or other from Dick, who had been having an extra thin time that day putting up with the Middle East situation and whatever the Americans were supposed to be doing to make it worse or better or keep it the same.

Anna said the Americans were arrogant. Graham asked which ones she meant. Then Anna said the American language was arrogant. Graham pointed out that Americans spoke, not American, but a variant of English. He added that of course American expressions would not sound the same to non-Americans as they did to Americans. As the four of them lined the grass verge, rather as if they were waiting for the start of some sporting event, a satisfied look came over Graham's face at having thought to say *non-American* and so not having had to remind everyone that Anna was non-British. The satisfied look altered him enough to do away with some of the music-hall idea about his cap and instead give the feeling that he might be an evil organist on holiday.

Anna said aggressively: 'The way they always talk of the places in America, this shows their arrogance.'

'It seems to me hardly very arrogant to mention features of one's native country.'

'You don't see what I mean. I'm talking about the actual words they use. It's always New York *Siddy*, as if it were the only city in the world. As if London and Paris and Berlin weren't cities too.'

'Ah, but the point of that is to distinguish the city of New York from the state of New York, which is an immense area stretching up to the Great Lakes. You wouldn't expect –'

'It's the same.'

'Excuse me, Anna, but you must see it isn't at all the same.'

Before Anna could go on about the sameness of the two New Yorks, there was a rushing, fizzing noise in the air a dozen feet above their heads and at the same moment a sound like a sharp knock from somewhere in the marshes. Patrick said 'Christ, someone's shooting at us' and threw himself down full length on the muddy verge. Jenny took Anna's hand and looked round for somewhere to run to. Graham, however, got clumsily but quickly over the low wire fence and began advancing towards two people who must have just come out from behind a clump of bushes about a hundred yards away. One was a girl with a scarf round her head. The other was a man about whom Jenny thought there was something familiar. He had a gun in his hands and another apparently slung over his shoulder.

'What do you think you're doing?' Graham was shouting angrily. 'You're acting in the most irresponsible way, sir. You might have killed someone.'

The man waved cheerily in reply and moved forward to meet him. The girl came too. 'Good Lord, it's that Ormerod man,' Jenny said. 'You've met him, Anna, haven't you?'

'Not that I know of. Well, this is a new way to introduce oneself, isn't it?'

Jenny laughed. She went on doing so when Patrick got up slowly from the ground and looked down at his clothes. There were plenty of mud-stains on his drill trousers and the moss-green jacket looked as if it had some actual moss on it. 'You dived down there a bit too sharp, didn't you?' she said.

He gave her a glare that made her feel cold all over for a second, then smiled reluctantly. 'Better to be safe than sorry,' he said. 'That mad sod.' He took out a rather battered packet of cigarettes. 'I suppose we can still smoke these.' Jenny took one;

she was up to nearly ten a day now. When he lit it, Patrick gave her one of his best smiles and said in his warm tone: 'You know, this chap Ormerod is the most fantastic character you ever met. What the hell does he do? He's up to some deal with Dick but I can't make out quite what. He's bright too, you know; don't let all that Raf-and-Jaguar dialect stuff fool you. Graham and I ran into him the other day at the – tell you later.'

'No, actually there wasn't the slightest danger,' Julian Ormerod was saying confidently as he came up. 'In fact I could have put one between you if I'd cared to, but I thought that might be carrying the invigoration lark a bit far.'

'You might easily have got one of us with a stray pellet,' Graham said. He was still pretty angry.

'Ball, man, ball. By which I mean that I fired ball cartridge, not shot. This is a rifle, in case you hadn't noticed. Of course it's not often in the nature of things that I find a job for the joker, but I like to feel I have it with me. You never know when you might need it.'

Patrick said: 'What, you mean if you met a rattlesnake, or a –'

'Surely you'd be better off with a shot-gun against a snake,' Graham said. He made it clear that his indignation had only gone down just enough for him to say it. 'At short range, anyway.'

'Or a homicidal maniac,' Patrick went on, raising his voice. Jenny saw him glance over at Julian's girl.

So did Julian. 'That's the ticket, Pat, or some humorist trying to remove my lady-friend. Which brings up a point, as you might say. Friends, this is Wendy.' He introduced her round the circle, starting with Jenny, at whom he dilated his eyes and waggled the pupils to and fro at a terrifying rate. She wondered how he could not mind the Wendy girl, and the others too, seeing him do this. The Wendy girl did not seem to be noticing anything much, though, including being introduced. Her face was too chubby to be really pretty, but she had a startling figure. The position of her light tweed coat – thrown over her shoulders – made it possible to think just at first that she had her arm in a sling across her chest instead of only having a chest. Jenny thought rather fretfully that it was a bit thick, the way there seemed to be so many enormous busts about, more down here, she was sure, than up home. There was no doubt that a big bust gave a girl an advantage, though Jenny had never been clear on how or why. What did a big bust *prove*? Of course flat-chested was bad, fair enough, but what did the fellows hope to get out of a girl's having a big bust? What was it *for*? She noticed that Wendy's waist was not far off as small as her own, but her hips were not.

'And this is Anna le Page,' Graham said after a short silence, this time using his tone of voice to suggest that he was not really the one to do this introduction, but that since others had not bothered to, he had had to. Like most of the people down here he was good at using his voice to suggest things like that. She saw Julian give Anna a very quick but thorough run-over with his eye, like an experienced dealer pricing a horse; it was not possible to guess his verdict.

'Fine day for a shoot,' Patrick said.

'Better than pork, isn't it?' Julian mysteriously answered, then said to them all: 'Well, this is well met, what? It was the old horseless carriage that gave me the clue, by the way, as once before. Know that 110 anywhere. Now ... eleven-fifty. Just nice time for a couple of bangs, as the b said to the a, and then we can depart for a swallow, eh?'

'You mean the old blaze-away, do you?'

'That's right, Patty. We'll each have a go with this faggot.' He tapped the butt of the gun he had slung over his shoulder. 'Doesn't seem to be much wild life about today, just a moose or two and a caribou and a bison cow or so, so we'll have to have an artificial target. What about that cap of yours?'

'I'd like to retain it if it's all the same to you,' Graham said.

'By all means. Each to his taste, what? Here, this'll do. I'll just prop it up. You three'll have to get over this fence, I fear, we can't do much while we're standing here like a frontier pow-wow. Come on, get moving, soldier. My, what a state you're in. I declare you aren't fit to be seen, indeed. Careful, precious, give me your hand. I'll let you have it back.'

Although Graham was ready to help, Anna got over on her own, showing less animal grace than usual, probably because the ground was muddy and she had new sandals on. It crossed Jenny's mind that it was funny how Anna never used any French words mixed in with her conversation in the way that French people were meant to: Professor Lumière in the Garth strip in the *Mirror*, for instance, was on all the time with *sacré bleu* and *mon vieux* and *mon Dieu*. It must just go to show how long Anna had been living over here.

Patrick seemed even keener than Julian on the idea of a shooting competition. He held out his hand for the gun, which was unslung and passed to him, and looked it over. 'Mm, fascinating. What is it, a twelve-bore or something?'

'Twenty, boy, twenty. Twelves are for people who can't shoot.'

'Who says I can shoot?'

'Old Sigmund's got a line on that somewhere, I'm sure. And it's gauge, not bore. Are you going first?'

'Is this a repeater? Or aren't there repeating shot-guns?'

'Oh yes indeed there are, and very popular they are too with game-wholesalers, I can tell you. This is not a repeater. Here we go, then. Imagine it's your very-near-future father-in-law at the other end and Graham's the justice of the peace. Last chance you'll have before they start tying that fatal knot. Right, everybody behind the line of fire.'

There was a tremendous explosion, a lot of smoke, and a muffled 'Christ' from Patrick. But the piece of slate that Julian had propped up on one of the posts of the fence stayed where it was. 'Spread too much, I expect,' Patrick said.

'Nonsense, dear boy, it wouldn't spread appreciably at this range. Thing works like a hose, do you follow? – not a power-assisted watering-can. You were waving it around like a parasol. All right, Graham, your turn.'

'I'm not satisfied this is very safe, Ormerod. What if somebody should come by?'

'Then you don't shoot, do you? Or do you? Suit yourself. Here.'

Graham took a long time aiming, but when at last he did fire the slate jumped off the post into the road.

'That's more like it. Dead centre, I should say,' Julian said, going over to the fence. 'Yes. Nice shot. Good job I didn't put any money on this, isn't it? Ah, me now. It means another walk to put the thing up again, though. You can do it this time, Patrick.'

As Julian brought the gun up to his shoulder, Jenny could tell that Patrick was hoping he would miss. He did not miss. Patrick looked at his watch. The way he walked to the fence showed he was thinking that shooting was silly, perhaps even that it was a bad thing to be good at it.

Anna turned her head away when she fired and Jenny looked anxiously over at the car. Anna explained that in her part of France it was considered *not correct* for women to do any shooting. Then it was Jenny's turn. Her ears were singing already and she badly wanted to shut both eyes, not just the one, but she forced herself to look at the slate as she pulled the trigger. The slate vanished.

There was a little round of applause, led by Graham. 'Well done now, Jenny. Excellent shot. Ah, it's pretty plain that you and I have got an aptitude for this kind of thing.' The look he gave her under the peak of the cap hinted that he was wondering whether this aptitude he said they both had had any chance of being worked up into something else. The cap made that idea harder to face.

Wendy said, or rather showed by signs and grunts, that she did not want her turn, and the group began to break up. Julian's car was parked off the road a couple of hundred yards from where they were standing. 'We'll go to my house,' he said. 'Don't think I could face Charlie Crosland this morning, somehow. Order of march, now. Wendy, will you go with the visitors and show them the way? Jenny can come with me.'

'So can I,' Graham said, and did. 'Very interesting, Ormerod. I must say I was most impressed by Jenny's performance. You can't beat a steady hand, eh, Jenny?' He seemed to think that he had found a good line and should stick to it.

Julian at once said: 'Well, precious, that's a pretty stirring outfit you're wearing, and no mistake. Never realized how much I adored polo sweaters until this instant.' He laid his arm lightly along Jenny's shoulders, which took a bit of doing with his two guns to carry. 'Some very special bone-work here, I can tell. Which makes me sorrier than ever that you weren't able to see your way to entertaining that notion of mine I brought up the other day. No end of fun we'd have had.'

Julian had brought up his notion to her over the phone, but she had cut him short with a polite refusal before he had had time to explain it in full. It would not have been fair to go out with him while there was still a good chance that Patrick was going to get in touch with her, and it would not have been wise under any circumstances. The hair-pulling incident was enough of a reminder that when you have been nearly hauled into the river by a pike you are best advised not to go after sharks. This had somehow been rubbed in by the hundred-per-cent pleasantness with which Julian had said 'Some other time then, I hope, my poppet' before ringing off. The whole thing had jumped up again in Jenny's mind on recognizing Julian that morning, but since then there had been too much going on for her to think about it. Now, after some fishing about, she came up with a useful standby: 'Well, I'm sure you understood it would have been rather awkward.'

'Never was much of a hand at understanding that kind of thing, but we won't go into it now. A wise general always selects . . .' His voice turned into the talking-to-himself mutter she had heard him do once or twice before.

All this time, Graham had been moving his head about jerkily and in an offended, incredulous way, but he said nothing until they had reached the car and hardly anything then. The three of them sat in a row in the front seat. Although it was a thrill to be going to ride in a Jaguar, and it was quite soothing to hear Julian explaining to Graham about automatic gear-changing and something called anti-creep, Jenny could not help wishing she had Patrick beside her. On both sides of her would have been better still, for the pressure of Graham's thigh against her left one and of Julian's against her right one were equally disconcerting, in two quite different ways. As well as this, there was the thought of that Wendy girl riding with Patrick. It was true that Anna was there as well, but Jenny felt, without being able to explain why, that Anna being there in that situation managed to count for less than anybody else being there. And in the last couple of minutes before they all parted she had seen that Wendy creature beginning to return Patrick's glances.

Jenny felt ashamed of her own jealousy, but a fat lot of help that was.

Without very much having happened to notice it by, life had suddenly turned out to be a complicated and mysterious business, like a new card game with two packs and counters and special scoring explained by a person who was bad at explaining, especially *why* you did things. Instead of the ordinary one-at-a-time system that was probably still chugging along up home, everybody down here seemed to be interested in everybody else at once, though on the other hand perhaps that was quite wrong, and they were all just being friendly to one another, and there was no one not in it for her to ask. Was Julian really having a thing – never mind what sort of a thing now, just a thing – with Wendy and still trying to, well, have a thing with her, and what about Dick, and how could it possibly have entered her head that Martha was keen on Patrick, and what was Patrick up to if not *everything*? All she was certain of was that Wendy had not fallen in love with Graham, and given two or three gin and tonics and a French dinner and a cherry brandy at the road-house, even *that* might not be too hard to . . .

Chapter Ten

JULIAN'S house was so large and had so much land surrounding it that at first Jenny thought it must be a school or a nursing home. In the place corresponding to where Dick had his chicken-run there was a cobbled yard, perhaps with old stables, and further back a stone outbuilding which looked about as big as the Bunns' house at home. The front porch was of the miniature-Greek-temple sort that she had only seen in the middle of cities before, and was big enough for quite a crowd of people to stand under it at once. Inside, the hall had the staircase running round some of it instead of just leading up out of it, so that it was really two storeys high. Up in a recess there was a statue of a naked man with his hair close to his head, very wide lips, and a leg or so missing – Greek again, Jenny guessed – and opposite that a picture of art-gallery size that showed a crowd of girls with fat calves dancing about holding little curvy harps. A sinking feeling to do with butlers came over Jenny, but none appeared while Graham hung up his cap, Julian dumped his guns and haversack, and the three of them went into a room reached by a passage that turned corners. The whole of its floor was covered with mushroom-coloured carpet and a lot of its dark-red walls with small pictures.

'I'll go and get the drinks,' Julian said. 'I can't help feeling there must be some.'

'Do you live here on your own?' Jenny asked.

'Well, the statistical norm is that the Foots run the show, but they're off this weekend.'

'The foots?'

'Married couple who look after me. Invaluable pair.'

'You mean like servants, sort of?'

'A bit like that, yes. Shan't be long.'

'Well, Jenny,' Graham said the instant they were alone. He had a lively expression, so much so that if it could have been moved with his face to Jenny's parents' television screen, nothing about the married man's hard life would have been called for, but instead something on the lines of *So I gives her a look, and she gives me a look, and I thinks to meself 'Ay-ay'*. In fact, though, he said nothing more.

Jenny was in a bit of a difficulty. To answer 'Well, Graham' would have given her the TV feeling again, and she had had enough of that recently to last her. But to leap right out of the way would have been unkind. So she settled for 'What an amazing house this is, isn't it?'

'Isn't it now?' he agreed eagerly. 'The money that must have gone into all this. And the upkeep must be something quite staggering. I'd like a wee glance at the details of Mr Ormerod's monthly income, I must say. Where it all derives from, in particular.' Then he quietened down, like somebody who knows he has let on to being a bit too interested in how they manage the floggings in prisons. He dropped his voice almost to a mutter: 'Jenny, I'd like to ask you something. I know that you've been – how shall I put it? – *seeing a bit of* Patrick. I recognize that this isn't the ideal time to ask you, but it may be the only chance I'll be getting. Could you . . . do you think you could come out with me some evening? I'd like it very much if you would. Would you, Jenny?'

This put Jenny in a bit more of a difficulty. *Come out with* was like *sleep with* in meaning a lot more than it said. The evening with Graham, if it ever came off, would probably have one physical pass in it and probably several. Neither would be fun. Although – despite the cap – Graham was not a stooge, being too slow in his movements and not looking anxious enough, he was certainly a dud, and she had found out very early on that it was a mistake to imagine that duds like Graham were any slower off the mark in sex things than smashers like Patrick. To get out of the proposed evening without hurting Graham's feelings was going to be tricky. It was a pity she had already used the rather-awkward routine in his hearing, and also a pity she had no really solid rather-awkward argument, like her being engaged to Fred or Graham having a wife and seven children; he seemed to have already got round her thing with Patrick. Well, she would put it back in front of him again. 'It would be nice,' she said after a slight delay, 'but there is Patrick, you see. I wouldn't feel quite easy in my mind.'

'Ah, but you mustn't think . . . I'd come to an understanding with Patrick, of course. There wouldn't be any question of . . .'

Then Jenny had an inspiration – Trixie again. What would she have done without her? 'All right, Graham, let's go out, then. But on condition that I pay for myself for everything. That would make it all all right, wouldn't it?'

Graham looked disappointed. (*Why*, if she mustn't think and there wouldn't be any question of?) 'When can you come?'

'I shall have to work it out. Can you give me a ring?'

'Can't we fix it now? I don't want to have to – I don't like bothering the Thompsons on the phone.'

'If you don't mind I'd sooner we did leave it.'

'All right then.' He smiled, not at all a bad smile considering. 'I'll be looking forward to it very much. It's sweet of you.'

Jenny smiled back, holding it as long as she could, or thought she should, before turning aside and staring hard at the nearest picture. In it a number of very ugly men in old-fashioned clothes were capering to and fro with long speeches in copper-plate handwriting coming out of their mouths. Of course, they went

120

in more for the art of conversation in the old days. One of the speeches began: *Now am I in a Fair Way to show this Son of a W—e my BREECH.* 'What's this about?' she asked Graham.

'Ah, they're cartoons. Originals, I shouldn't be surprised. Must be worth quite a packet.'

'I can't make out what they're about.'

'It's all political.' He started getting himself into position for something mild, like arm round shoulders, but still something: he was shuffling his feet a little and glancing back and forth between himself and her like a golfer preparing for a tricky shot. When she gave a slow-motion shimmy that took her out of range without looking too much like a sidestep, he ended up disappointedly: 'Controversies and so on.'

'I see.'

He looked as if he was limbering himself up to chassé in pursuit, but before the two of them could get properly started on circling the room Julian came in with a tray of drinks. It was funny to see him with something in his hands that was for other people. Jenny accepted a gin and tonic. She would have preferred plain tonic for the taste, but she could tell by the feeling in her stomach that things were very soon going to start happening that would be better coped with after a strong drink or two. (Oh, where had Patrick got to?) For the same kind of reason she took a cigarette when Julian offered them. She had finished it and had stubbed it out in an ashtray that had a coloured picture of a vintage car on it before the other three arrived.

'Sorry about this,' Patrick said. He was speaking and moving quickly and seemed to be trying not to laugh. 'Anna wanted to pick some buttercups or something, didn't you, Anna? But there weren't any, or perhaps they got lost.' Just then, with timing Jenny could see no reason for, Wendy burst out into giggles, a surprisingly girlish sound to go with such a womanly frame. 'Anyway, we haven't got the bloody buttercups. What's the matter with you?' he asked Wendy, grinning. 'That's right, isn't it? Anna, isn't that right? Nobody believes me.' His glance flickered as it passed Jenny.

'Oh, absolutely right, there were no flowers worth picking,' Anna said with what struck Jenny as exaggerated innocence. In anyone else this would have been suspicious, but Anna was not much of a one for underplaying, and had been known to get what was probably most of what was probably the way great foreign actresses went on (especially, probably, in plays where one great foreign actress was acting the part of another great foreign actress from years ago) into things like passing the sugar or picking up a newspaper. 'Thank you, Julian,' she went on in a stately tone; 'just plain dubonnet for me. None of your un-civilized gin.'

'Gin for me,' Patrick said. 'Some of the uncivilized, if you can spare it,' and they all became just some people having drinks. In a minute or two Jenny asked Wendy if she knew where the bathroom was and was taken outside.

As soon as they had left the room Wendy spoke for the first time in Jenny's hearing. 'Who's that extraordinary man Patrick something and what does he do? Who is he?' She had a sort of squealing, whimpering voice and used a lot of emphasis.

'Patrick Standish, he's a schoolmaster at —'

'I mean who is he? Most amazing person I've ever met in my life. How old is he? I mean he looks about thirty but from the way he goes on you'd think he was about fourteen. Do you know him? Is he pissed or something? Honestly, I've never known anybody go on like that in my whole life. He's absolutely stark raving mad. Darling, what happened to him to make him be-have like that, do you suppose? Do you think he was brought up in the most weird morbid sort of way by some ghastly old maiden aunt or something, you know with all harmoniums and aspidistras and antimacassars and things? Sort of vicar's son going to the dogs thing? That's the way it's supposed to take them isn't it?'

'Do you mean . . . ? What happened?'

'Darling, you're not to be nasty to her. Nothing actually happened at all. I mean how could it? I'm only talking about what a mad sod he is, and he is you know. Is he a terrific chum of yours or something? Honestly I don't know how you can possibly manage to put up with him for a single second. I know he's rather a sweetie-pie and all that but just look at him. And the way he drives that car. Now, darling, you mustn't be so stuffy, there's no need to go tearing off like that. Why don't you stay and chat to me? After all we're all girls together aren't we?'

Jenny came back in again from the doorway of the bathroom, having retreated as far as there when Wendy, still talking, had gone in and set about plonking herself down. Dully, not wanting to, Jenny asked: 'You and Patrick went for a walk, did you?' She stared out of the window into the cobbled yard. It looked neglected, with moss growing between the cobbles and orange lichen on one of the roofs. In one corner she noticed a tap with boarding round it that was certain not to be in working order.

'Nothing like that, you silly little thing. We had that fat Frenchwoman or whatever she is. Of course I'm a bit on the podgy side myself these days, admitted, but I've got it distributed better than she has. I haven't got that enormous bum and legs like her. I wouldn't wear those ridiculous slacks if I was her. But I do keep putting it on with all these disgusting cream cakes and chocolates and marshmallows and waffles and syrup and things. It quite worries me the way I keep at them, I just don't seem to be able to stop myself, it's probably some revolting sex thing really. How do you manage to keep so lovely and slim? You're like an absolute wand. You can't eat enough to keep a flea alive. Of course all these shortages with the war and everything, that was really my best time, I was quite thin then the rest of me but with the most gigantic chest still, I used to look quite deformed, darling but they all seemed to like it. They are horrible aren't they? Darling, you're sure you can cope are you? – because I can always beat a gentlemanly retreat if you really want me to. Who is that Frenchwoman? Is she a great chum of yours or something?'

'She lives in the same digs with me. I've only –'

'Where do you dig up all these mad people from? Of course old Julian's absolutely bonkers too you know.' Wendy, arranging her surprisingly long blondeish hair at the mirror, broke off to sing a few bars from one of the *My Fair Lady* hits in a loud screaming wail that still managed to be impressively rhythmic and in tune, then went on: 'Do you know he wouldn't give me an atom of peace until four o'clock this morning? Not what you're thinking, darling – helping him to make his sodding cartridges for this shoot of his. You wouldn't know I don't suppose but there's this little doofer that sort of hoicks out the old cap and pushes a new one in you see. Then you have the gunpowder – he wouldn't let me go near that of course. Then there's the little bloody cardboard washer arrangement and then there's the wad. It looked like a cork to me but it's a wad. He says it's a wad. Then the shot – he wouldn't let me touch that either but Christ knows why not, it can't blow up can it? Then another bloody little cardboard washer. And then another doofer which turns the end of the cartridge inwards or something. And then – do you know what? – I had to write *8* on the end in pencil if you please. What do you know about that?'

'What for? What does it mean?'

'Oh Christ knows, darling, he got angry when I kept asking. You know honestly they are all the same aren't they?'

They got back to the room downstairs without Jenny having been able to notice much about the house apart from the number of pictures along the passages and the size of everything. It was not just that there were lots of rooms, but the rooms themselves seemed to have been made for very big people: high ceiling in the bathroom, four-foot wash-basin, eight-foot bath, ten-inch nailbrush, cakes of soap like little rugger balls. Even the staircase was like a sort of stepped living-room.

Jenny was feeling happier now, and had time to reflect on how hard it was to finish a sentence in these parts. Everybody seemed to be putting too much energy into being themselves to listen to others. She had known that as people got older – Mr Burrage was a good example – they wanted less and less to hear what you had to say, but round here they evidently reached that stage almost as soon as they left school. To be a good listener, as *Woman's Domain* was constantly nagging away at her to be, was a much easier job than was usually made out. Being with the other person was enough.

'It's obviously a most mistaken policy,' Graham was saying as they went in. Patrick had one elbow on the mantelpiece and was looking through a book; he glanced up only for a second. Anna was gazing out of the window and slowly scratching her thigh. Julian was stirring a jug of drink and ice. 'They won't get the technicians they want by putting quantity first,' Graham went on.

'Another drink for her please, darling,' Wendy said to Julian.

'On the way up, my queen. Now I think there's a lot to be said for us all having lunch here, don't you? I think there might be one or two scraps still just about fit for human consumption if I can contrive to locate them, and even the odd dreg here and there that might not have gone off yet and perhaps won't be totally inferior to red ink when it comes to washing down the old scoff.'

'That is kind of you,' Jenny said, 'but I don't want to be a spoil-sport but Anna and I really ought to be getting back. We'll have dinner waiting for us at home, won't we, Anna?'

'Calm down, darling, we can miss it for once.'

'But Mrs Thompson'll have prepared it all. It'll practically be on the table by now.'

'Then she must take it off the table. We can eat it some time, it makes no difference.'

'But it seems so –'

'Get hold of her on the far-speaker, my love.'

'Beg your pardon?'

'There's a telephone in the hall.'

'Wouldn't you like to talk to them, Anna? You're better at that sort of thing than I am.'

'I deny this. And it's you who are so anxious for them. For myself I couldn't care less.'

'Oh, all right, then.'

Jenny hoped she would get Dick, but knew she would get Martha. She got Martha. 'Hallo, yes?'

'It's Jenny here. Look, I'm afraid we –'

'Who?'

'Jenny Bunn. I'm speaking from Mr Ormerod's house. We're all there now. I'm awfully sorry, but Mr Ormerod's asked us to stay to dinner, and the others want to, and I don't think we're on a bus route, and I can't really –'

'Stay to dinner? Oh, you mean lunch, I suppose.'

'Yes, lunch, sorry. I can't really make all the others come, and we can't really get back without –'

'It's a bit thick this, you know, really it is. I was just about ready to dish up.'

'I know, I'm sorry, I told them you would be, but I'm afraid I c –, I c –' Jenny tried to put into practice what the lady at the speech-therapy place had taught her about relaxation, and tapped her foot on the ground, which sometimes helped. 'I c–'

'What? Are you still there? Hallo?'

'S-sorry, I got a bit mixed up. I was going to say I didn't see how we could get back now, because Patrick wants to stay.'

'Oh, he does, does he? Who talked him into that, I wonder? Who's there, anyway? Just the four of you and Julian?'

'There's a girl-friend of his here too.'

'You mean of Julian's?'

'Yes, that's right. Well, apparently, anyway.'

'I see. You might have given me a bit of warning.'

'I didn't know till just now. I'm terribly sorry.'

'Well, not much I can do about it, I suppose.'

'We can have the stuff for supper,' Jenny started to say, but the other had rung off. Biting her lip, she made her way back through the open door of the drawing-room. On the far side of it a french window was standing ajar, and beyond that she could see the figure of Graham stooping down as he examined some shrub, with Anna, her back towards the house, holding her tartan stole round her and evidently gazing into the distance, as before. Nearer at hand, Patrick and Wendy were kissing each other on the chintz-covered window seat. Their bodies were tightly pressed together and Jenny could hear the faint rustling as he stroked her hip. The sound of Jenny's approach had been muffled by the thick carpets. Even now, while she stood there for a moment unable to stir, the two did not notice her. At the exact moment when she pulled herself together and began to move again, Wendy's eyes opened and saw her over Patrick's shoulder. Jenny reached the threshold of the french window to the sound of a loud wheedling noise, like someone encouraging a dog, made by the separating mouths of the two of them. 'Sorry about that,' she heard Wendy say, but without working out whether it was meant for herself or Patrick.

'Successful?' Graham asked as she came up.

'Jenny, what is it? You're trembling, darling. Was it so bad?'

'It was all right. I'm all right. I just had a little turn.' She realized too late that it had been wrong to come barging in on other people. 'It'll go off. I'm all right.'

'You don't look all right.' Anna's glance switched to the

window where Patrick and Wendy had been sitting, and her expression went hard. 'My poor Jenny. But he's not worth it.'

'What's all this about? Are you ill, Jenny? Like to go and sit down, maybe? Can I fetch you something?'

'No, please, I'm all right, honestly.' The pain in Jenny's throat was being made worse by the concern in both their faces. 'I think I'll just go and give Mr Ormerod a hand with the dinner. The lunch I mean. See you later.'

She found a way to the kitchen that did not go through the drawing-room. Rubbing away a couple of tears with her knuckles, she told herself fiercely not to be a silly fool, not to be inconsiderate and start embarrassing people and spoiling their enjoyment, not to worry anyway because what a blessing it was that she had found out before she had got really involved. Well, at least before she had done anything she would regret.

'Ah, there you are, my poppet. Might have guessed you'd be the one to reach out the helping hand. Actually there isn't a great deal that needs doing, it's all prefabricated as you might say. I thought we might kick off with some of this melon thing if anyone can stand it, and for those who can't there seems to be some kind of paté stuff, and then I suppose this bit of cold pheasant or whatever it is'll keep the wolf from the door, with possibly a mouthful of salad – if you could get going on that it'd be very bounteous of you, and after that I'm afraid I can't really think of anything, except just conceivably you might be able to force a peach or so down if you gritted your teeth, oh, and a bite of cheese. Drink: morsel of serious thought called for there, I fear. We can start the ball rolling with shampers readily enough, but what then? What? I'll have to rout around.'

Routing around took only as long as it took Jenny, who kept her mind hard on what she was doing, to get a couple of cos lettuces ready and slice up some tomatoes. One of the three bottles that Julian brought back with him was very dirty and had printed on its label a year slightly earlier than that of Jenny's birth, no doubt to show how long ago the firm had been established. Drawing the corks, he said: 'Do you think I ought to decant these? Don't want to finish up munching grape soup. Still, it is a chore.'

'Oh, I shouldn't bother.'

'We can go easy on the last half-inch, as the a said to the b. I must say dear old Patty-boy does seem to be going in for some pretty dedicated haymaking while the sun shines. Only snag is there's going to be a spot of rain spreading from the west before very long. Anyway. Well, you've done extraordinarily well on this salad joke, adorable. I'll make the dressing, eh?'

When he paused, Jenny looked up at him. They were standing close together at a white-topped table next to the large and impressive sink. At the sight of him concentrating on her, a kind of warm and soundless rustle played over her skin, as if she was going to be tickled. But Julian showed that tickling was far from his mind by the decided way he now put his arms round her. He did this very well, not pouncing, nor so slowly as to seem to be asking a question, but at just the right speed to give her time to step back out of range if she had wanted to. She saw no reason why she should want to. While her arms were going round his neck, she found time for the thought that the nervous ones gave themselves away by talking first and measuring the distance, like Graham just now; the experienced ones just went ahead at their own pace, making it no more than the thing they happened to be doing next. He kissed her very thoroughly, without trying to do anything else, and indeed without any of the toiling and moiling, let alone the moaning and groaning, gone in for by the too-serious ones and/or the ones that put up a show of being serious.

'Very jolly,' he said after a time, then: 'You know, lover, in so many ways you're exactly the right kind of girl for some figure like me to set up in a handy maisonette somewhere in the wen.'

'When what? It'll be a good long time before –'

'The great wen, flower. The old shocking city, at least in aspiration, London. But then of course, as you were about to remark with such truth, there are so many other ways in which you're exactly the wrong kind of girl for that particular craft. Tragic loss to mankind. Means among other things I'll have to dismiss from consideration all those frightfully exciting plans I drew up when I first saw you. Came to me in a *flash*. Saw the whole thing at a glance, like Newton or Einstein or one of those sparks.'

'Are these still the plans? What sort of plans?'

'Ah, you'll know what sort of plans, even though you aren't the type the plans were designed for. Always been my trouble, plans. Lecherous to a fault, I'm afraid. Such a pity. Oh well. And your Gallic pal wouldn't quite suit my book either; too much like hard work. Incidentally, don't forget your old chum if you ever do move into the maisonette racket, will you?'

'No. No, I won't forget.'

'Because it would be a very splendid thing.'

He said this well too, especially not with a burn from the eyes like somebody saying he was going to knock somebody else's block off. When he left her to fetch the others to lunch another thought, the first for a couple of minutes, entered Jenny's head: how you could never tell when people were going to move up from one rating to another as you got to know them. That first time when Julian had stared at her in the roadhouse she had thought him definitely not a dud, but at the most no higher than middle maybe. Now there was no doubt he was top maybe and perhaps even getting in sight of smasher. Then she remembered his haymaking remark. If he knew what was going on between Patrick and that Wendy creature, why did he not do something about it, or at least appear worried? He might be pretty modern, perhaps, even as modern as Anna or Wendy, but this was surely the kind of situation in which people forgot about being modern. Well, then, why?

She got her answer quite soon. Patrick, flushed and wondering, was led in by Wendy after Graham and Anna had appeared: not long after. With a very friendly look on his face, Julian said: 'Yes, you'd better get your skates on, hadn't you?'

'How long have I got, darling?' Wendy asked. 'I warn you I'm not going to tear off in a frightful rush. Darling, you know I can't bear melon.'

'Where are you going?' Patrick said to her.

'Oh, she didn't tell you? Very jolly, that, and no error. She's catching a heavier-than-air machine at five o'clock. For Wellington. I'm driving her to the airport.'

'Wellington, Salop?' Patrick asked, drawing everyone in this time. His glance flicked to Jenny for a moment. 'You don't need a plane for there, surely to God.'

'Wellington, New Zealand, actually,' Julian said, scratching his chin. 'Where the lamb comes from. She's going out to join her husband. He's got a job with the agronomical-research boys there, pretty keen on it too. Appears they're conspicuously high-powered in that part of the world when it comes to animal husbandry. I like the sound of that myself. Takes a bit of guts to disappear down under for good like that, but old Tony was itching to get away for years. Delightful character. Knew him in the old Battle of Britain days down in Kent. Best Spitfire pilot I ever saw. Mad as a hatter, of course. Now, I must see if I can't unearth a spot of something Spanish to go with that melon. Excuse me a minute, eh?'

Patrick, suddenly looking a stone or two lighter, combed his hair with his fingers. Jenny burst out laughing. So, a second later, did Anna, but it was on Jenny that he turned his freezing look for the second time that day. In this case it did not stop her laughing.

Chapter Eleven

'WHAT sort of animal would it be?' Graham asked.

'Well, it'd have to look very horrible, glaring red eyes and sodding great teeth and all that stuff.'

'We must be careful about those teeth. They mustn't be too formidable or the laddie would perish at once, and that would put paid to the whole scheme.'

'That's true,' Patrick went on paring his nails for a moment. 'Well then, the Dick-hound has very short teeth which hold on firmly but don't penetrate the skin. Or not too far. They'd have to be specially bred. What about the hunters, the huntsmen rather? On horses, do you think?'

'That might be uncomfortable. In jeeps, perhaps, or land-rovers.'

'Half-tracks would do it, better for working away from the roads. Like those Bren-carrier things, open so as to get a good field of fire. Now . . . ideal weapons would be long-range syringes filled with acid or a solution of itching-powder.'

'He'd best be naked, then.'

'Nasty thought that, I agree. But I don't see why not. He'd be able to move more quickly and so prolong the thing. The kill comes when he's too exhausted to move. That'd be the end of that hunt. We don't want to do him too much damage at any one time, got to keep him in trim for every Wednesday and Saturday afternoon in the Dick-hunting season.'

'Suppose he just refused to move, refused to set out, even?' Graham, cigarette in mouth, waited with poised match.

'Oh, no trouble there, we just stipulate that for every minute he's not on the move he buys a round of drinks for all the huntsmen, and that goes on until the umpires decide it'd endanger the future interests of the hunt if he was allowed to continue.'

'Who would they be, the umpires?'

'Us two, but it wouldn't stop us taking our full part in everything. We'd have bearers, of course, or gillies if they're what I think they are, keeping the syringes filled.'

'Gillies is correct, yes: attendants upon sportsmen.'

He gave Patrick one of his rare charming smiles. As usual, while it lasted there was no difficulty in taking his face seriously for a change, and for some period after it was over there was none in taking Graham himself seriously. At such times Patrick would decide that there was still hope of Graham breaking his duck with the women if he could contrive to use the smile on them with reasonable frequency. But to tell him about it would surely vitiate it. Meanwhile, just what the hell did Graham think he was playing at, having as much hair as that? Round his forehead it ran with never a millimetre of recession, an irregularly flattened mound of sandy-and-mouse moss, unedifying but irreducibly there, while he, Patrick, a man if ever there was one who could put a decent head of hair to some use, found dandruff snowing down on to his shoulders whenever he so much as scratched his scalp, had to disentangle a luxuriant skein of fallen strands from his comb every time he used it, saw each day more clearly revealed the two bald re-entrants either side of the central salient of hair. And what about that new threat at the crown? Mm? The opening line of a talk recently published in the *Listener* came slouching into his mind: *Why do organisms even-*

tually decline and die? The study of senescence has failed to reveal . . . Ah, screw that. Screw that like mad. Screw that up hill and down dale, what? He got to his feet. 'I must be off,' he said.

'Are you going for a drink?'

'Later, but I must try and get hold of Thackeray first. He's got the number of *Greece and Rome* I always do my background bit on the Gracchi out of. You know, Roman chaps.'

'Bring him along to the George for a beer.'

'Well, I don't know if I can make that. I thought of looking in on Jenny eventually.'

'I see. She's . . . I asked her to come out with me tomorrow night, did I say?'

'Yes, you did.'

'I thought something to eat at the Toll Bridge and then a flick.'

'Sounds admirable. Mind you get her into the back row.'

Lasciviousness battled with reproof in Graham's expression. This was spectacular, the addition of conflict to a face that was well worth looking at when a single question, or none, was dominant. He said: 'She's a decent wee girl, Standish, and that's her attraction for me. She's the steady kind, not flighty or feather-brained like so many of them today.'

'She's probably got some chap at home who's just as steady as she is, waiting to marry her.'

'No, do you think so?'

'Go on, I'm pulling your leg.'

'I shouldn't want to break into any long-standing engagement.'

God, what forbearance, Patrick thought. He said: 'Don't you worry about that; leave it to her. Cheers, then.'

Driving the 110 out of its garbaged alley, he thought some more about Graham. Clothes, to start with. It had taken him a full week, Saturday to Saturday, to persuade Graham that those oyster-coloured corduroy trousers in Dowsett's window were neither overpriced nor reprehensively sportive. And here he was, wearing them not only with *black shoes* but with *a grey herring-bone jacket* and *a silk tie* that had *stripes* on it. Patrick shook his head. He knew now how the Americans felt when they

132

signed a Sabre-jet over to Chiang Kai-shek. Then, deportment. Patrick wondered idly which of the Old Toll Bridge Café's dishes Graham would in twenty-four hours' time be throwing fast and hard in the general direction of his mouth. Not the favoured spaghetti, he hoped, for Graham was in the habit of using on it in all seriousness a technique normally only resorted to as a bottom-of-the-barrel laugh-raiser : that of sucking furiously at any strands found to be left hanging from the mouth, thus producing a slight form of self-flagellation and veining the eater's cheeks and chin with tomato sauce. (He had been known to go into his all-out sneezing routine *during* this.) Egg on chips would be better, even though Graham, an opponent of waste in any form, regularly ate his yolks whole, putting them into his mouth on the blade of his knife for maximum security.

Finally, and most important, there was what you might call the general strategy. The position there had been neatly summed up one evening last term when Graham had refused to take the long-nosed girl to one of the weekly jazz sessions held in the upstairs room of a neighbouring pub. The drummer was too loud, admitted, and the trumpet man rarely blew a phrase without at least one fluff, but the tenor sax was excellent and the baritone had clearly listened with profit to a few Mulligan LPs. Anyway, what had held Graham back was not musical perfectionism. His real case against the Ivy Bush set-up was that persons of inferior education and breeding were to be found there, many of them engaged in contemporary-style dancing and calling out to one another in unpolished accents. Graham had not gone into any of that part of it, adducing only the fact that the Ivy Bush sold no draught bitter. But Patrick was not deceived. It was clear to him that Graham would have been more eager to take the long-nosed girl to the kind of dance where there were suits and long dresses, where you gave your partner a box of chocolates and a bunch of bloody flowers, where the band concentrated on section work and never really wailed all evening. But the world had moved on and left all that type of stuff high and dry. Or something had.

What had seemed in the opening stages to be a dead certainty had lured Patrick, earlier in the year, to a rugger club dance. As it turned out he had suddenly found himself one of a *party* (horrible men in crested blazers passing round crested cigarette-cases), and not until after ditching the whole bunch, an exercise that had demanded all his virtuosity, had he discovered that the dead certainty was just a naughty little tease after all. Honestly, the way they ... But that was beside the point. The evening had not been entirely wasted, in that it had confirmed an existing suspicion of his: organized dances were attended by the plain, the attached, the enthusiastic (about dancing), and above all the kind of wide-eyed, censoriously inquisitive, *my bag's in the car get it for me will you* mean little schoolgirl of hell that had put the cigarette-case-wielders through it so. Yes. The real stuff was to be found elsewhere, if anywhere.

The notion of driving out somewhere and finding some of the real stuff was so attractive, and so utterly *right*, that for a moment or two he devoted serious thought to the related notion of giving the go-by to Jenny, Thackeray, *Greece and Rome*, and the Gracchi. But no. To do that would be to go against his dogged convictions that he was conscientious about (*a*) being nice to women, and (*b*) work and duty. And, far more important, he knew that if he did manage to find a specimen of the real stuff – a gigantic proviso – he would in all probability be nervous of it. Irritating, that. What was it that had long ago set his taste at variance with his temperament, with the result that the ones he liked were never the real stuff and, in cases where their transmutation into something nearer the real stuff became possible, he was apt to find himself confronted with something other than what he had originally liked? A bit more irritating, that. There was also the point that to keep on transmuting non-real into quasi-real stuff was a procedure of dubious moral tendency. But screw all that from here to eternity. Trying not to be a bad man took up far more energy than he could, or was prepared to, spare from trying not to be a nasty man, a far more pressing task, especially this last year or two. Not only that: all this moral business was poor equipment for one barely into his stride on the huge trek to satiety.

Putting it in this way delivered the salutary reminder that to think of himself as a lamb-gobbling wolf, capable of leaping into any fold that took his fancy, hardly squared with the facts. He was not attractive enough for that mode of life, especially this last year or two. (Comparable with the bad-man/nasty-man shift had been this other one whereby pessimistic speculation about whether he was attractive had given place, after a medial period of calm lasting about ninety-six hours, to pessimistic speculation about whether he was still attractive.) He was not rich enough, either. That was a less unwelcome thought, just about, but he reckoned he liked women too much to get any real comfort out of it. If only they'd just . . . If only you could just . . . Never mind that thing a moment ago about not liking non-real stuff – what was wanted was the sort that laughed and lay down. He could make them laugh. Some of them, a bit, now and then.

That Wendy piece had laughed all right. Oh Christ, why bring that up? The deflationary aspect of the episode had pretty well spent its force by now, and jokes against yourself, while it was probably a bad sign if you enjoyed them, conceivably did you good. However that might be, any rebuke that might be read into this one was more than deserved. The initial encounter in his car on the way to Ormerod's place had been fairly harmless, though it had proved to have its odd side. He had been too excited to feel puzzled when Anna asked him to stop the car so that she could look for some – what? bluebells, dandelions, wild garlic? too active in the front seat with Wendy to feel anything in particular, and too astonished to feel embarrassed at first when the odd side had manifested itself in the shape of Anna leaning gracefully on the bonnet of the car and taking a good look at the excerpt from the *Ars Amatoria* he and Wendy were then enacting. Things had luckily not gone so far that they could not be retrieved without total loss of composure, but it had been a near thing. Anna had been being lesbian again or perhaps merely French (unshockable, uninhibitedly curious, after all, my dear, you must admit it's a subject of great interest to us all, etc., etc.) as usual, he had supposed, but he had not had the leisure to do much supposing for the rest of that lunch-time, nor did he feel, by and large, that he had enough such leisure now, as far as anything to do with Anna was concerned.

Anyway, none of that early part of it had been inordinately discreditable. Where he had gone wrong, in all senses, had been in touching Wendy up again on that flaming window seat. On any view it had been pointless: to get the whole thing done that afternoon had clearly been out of the question, and it was just as clearly going to get done as soon as they were properly alone (so he had had every reason to think at that stage hagh hagh hagh), and it would merely get them wrought up to no end if he started again. After working all this out in such fine style he had started again. And then – Jenny coming in, and her look of pain and incomprehension, and his own look of fury when she laughed at him, as she had had every reason and right to. How could he have done that to a humble, defenceless little thing like Jenny? With the same lack of effort, presumably, as when he had been peevish with her for resisting his grab, and the same lack of compunction as when he had decided to call round at the Thompsons' to give both her and Anna a look-over. He was now fairly sure that his interest in Jenny, plus his mistaken estimate of her chastity, had had a lot to do with his decision to ditch Anna.

He had turned up in a finely impartial frame of mind: if Jenny seemed worth another try – and he had not been able to drive out the image of her giving him a slow burn from those slightly slanting dark eyes and telling him he could do whatever he liked with her – then that would have been fine, and if not, then it was pretty certain that he had been over-hasty in having given up Anna for a scruple. Graham's role had been to dilute the party if the decision had gone Jenny's way, and to pay some attention to Jenny (up to and including that invitation out which Graham had been nervously but vocally contemplating for some days) if quick returns from the Anna direction had appeared preferable, or obtainable. And then there was Martha – just the flattery of her interest, naturally. Although the bedding of Dick Thompson's wife was a duty amounting to a categorical imperative, it would have to be evaded until such time as he was too drunk to see or hear.

As Patrick parked the 110 outside the College and got out, a thin rain was falling. The sight of the clouds of it swirling softly under a street lamp, with the vague glimpse beyond this of the High Street traffic and the rounded hill above, where chains of lights stretched upward until they were lost in the woods, made a picture sugary enough to remind him of how appealing the town had looked when it was new to him, how certain to offer up someone he would fall authentically in love with. The most that could rationally be said for the dump now was that it was not the London suburb where his mother ran her dress-shop. And yet, well, there was something about the look of the train beginning to move out of the station above the canal bend, the way a line of young trees in a nearby front garden caught the light from the uncurtained windows, the sound of the church clock striking the half-hour through the noise of vehicles, something which made it not impossible to believe that even here and any time now that simple and final encounter might take place – to believe it for a moment, before the image was blurred and fouled by the inevitable debris of obligation and deceit and money and boredom and jobs and egotism and disappointment and habit and parents and inconvenience and homes and custom and fatigue: the whole gigantic moral and social flux which would wash away in the first few minutes any conceivable actualization of that image. Was it really he who had spent a whole string of autumn evenings fifteen or sixteen years ago in the front room just off the London-Croydon road, playing his Debussy and Delius records by the open windows, in the hope that the girl who lived at the end of the street, and whom he had never dared speak to, would pass by, hear the music, look in and see him? Well, it was a good thing, and impressive too, that he could still feel a twinge of that uncomplicated and ignorant melancholy.

Thackeray was most likely to be found in a sort of common room in a building called the Masters' Lodge that dated from about 1930. The College had expanded since then, and there was now no longer enough accommodation in the Lodge for all the unmarried masters. A cash grant – not big enough – was paid to those choosing to live in the town for reasons involving sex (Patrick), sexual aspiration (Graham), or misanthropy (a sodding old fool called Meaker who reputedly had tried to get the two local hotels put out of bounds to the GIs from the war-time camp), as also to those excluded willy-nilly out of insufficient spirit to protest and/or recency of arrival. It was a mournful place, heavy with the despondency of, among others, the hundreds of boys who had at one time or another been invited to tea in it.

Patrick entered it in a foreboding spirit. This was Charlton country, in fact the very heart thereof. In spite of being neither unmarried nor a master he had somehow managed to invade and hold almost the entire top floor for himself and his family, and there was now no hope at all of ejecting him. Torkington, who had only been Head for two years, was believed to have attempted Charlton's dislodgement, but to have been unable to breach the main defence, that of *having to be on the spot*. Yeah. So as to get as near as possible to prohibiting, rather in the spirit of martial law, all gatherings of more than three persons, virtually ban gramophones and wirelesses, oppose reform in the nasty little cafeteria, and screen visitors – Mrs Charlton had an observation-post on the first-floor landing, a linen-cupboard which she put and took towels and sheets into and out of for several hours a day, according to Thackeray, who whenever they met would look at Patrick with the pleading defensiveness of a scholarship boy in a mining town encountering a contemporary in his pit-dirt. Not only females from about menarche to long after menopause, but – *post* and theoretically *propter* a scandal of 1948 or so – unengagingly engaging boys could alert Mrs Charlton's defence system and send her bursting into victims' rooms on various synthetic errands. It must be like living at home, Patrick thought passionately.

The hall and passage were certainly home-like in seeming to contain no object that could ever have been new. Somebody, either a Charlton or some *âme damnée* among the household staff, had managed to impose on the place an Edwardian hopelessness that contradicted the rather cheery vulgarity, as of a hugely swollen suburban villa, which it must once have had and which was now only to be seen upon its tile-encrusted, pebble-dashed, bow-windowed exterior. What was that bloody barrel-shaped vase, a cloudy and uneven purple in colour, doing on the fat newel-post at the foot of the stairs? Who the hell was that mutton-chopped bastard photographed in the act of delivering a warning about self-abuse? – not the pickle-manufacturing founder, Patrick was nearly sure. And what about that sofa with the tasselled cushions, at right angles to the empty fireplace? To provide rest for those whose stamina had failed after bringing them thus far, or simply to make it harder to get into the passage? Patrick added his raincoat to the dozen hanging from the sort of science-fiction tree that served as a hallstand, and put his head into the common room.

He started to withdraw it on seeing that not only was Thackeray not there, but Charlton was. Sitting next to him was the lean tweed-suited figure of Torkington smoking a pipe, which he snatched from his mouth to call across the room: 'Hallo, Patrick, what on earth brings you here?' When Patrick came over to explain what as shortly as possible, Torkington adopted his greeting expression, one suggesting that, after taking the Holy Name, he would plunge into an account for his reasons, long noted and now at last found unanswerable, for resigning the headship. The upward nod he gave did most of it.

'Good evening, Mr Charlton,' Patrick said. Seeing the other two together made him feel frightened.

Charlton looked up at him, his face heavy with menace, or possibly just with being Charlton. 'Quite a surprise to see you here,' he said, doing a pretty good job of ironical silent apology for the absence of naked women and tanks of gin from the amenities on offer.

'So it seems. It's duty, that's all.'

'You didn't turn up to hear Horse on Friday,' Torkington said.

'No, I felt I knew all I wanted to know about the development of Eliot's verse technique.'

'I fell asleep in the middle of it and woke up with the most tremendous kicking and thrashing. A pity you missed it. Did you think people noticed, Charlton?'

'Oh, I don't think so, Headmaster. You weren't very loud.'

'How extraordinary; I had the feeling I stopped the show. That is most odd. It just makes you realize how widely people can differ when they're reporting the same event. Amazing.'

'Horse is a menace,' Patrick said. 'He keeps on at me about that play he wants to appear in.'

'You'll have to do it. Gammon's too excited about that new wife of his, and I must say ... There aren't so many Horses round the place that we can afford not to give this one a bit of support. I'll take you off the prize-day committee if that's any help.'

'That's okay, I don't mind that.'

'All right, fine. Oh yes. Charlton, where's that thing from that fellow who's just back from wherever it was?'

Charlton had a buff folder on his lap, or rather in the cleft between his belly and thighs. He drew out and passed to Torkington, who passed it to Patrick, a sheet hastily torn from a pad bearing a few ill-written lines in green ink. Without formality the writer announced that he had recently returned from an academic appointment in the Argentine, had been preparing a talk on the educational institutions of that region, and would be available for its delivery 'in due course'. He would be writing again 'before very long' and signed himself 'L. S. Caton'.

'No, you think?' Torkington asked Patrick.

'Yes, no.'

Torkington wrote *No* on the sheet and gave it back to Charlton. 'No,' he said. 'Oh, and what about the draft report to the governors? Did you bring that?'

'It's over in the office, Headmaster. I'd be very happy to go and get it, but it would be easier if you'd –'

'No time like the present.' After Charlton, his creep-speak effectively silenced, had departed in protest-march style, Torkington waved Patrick to the vacated chair. 'I can't stand that office,' he said. 'Especially when ... Look, I'd like to have a chat with you some time. I've got something on my mind.'

Alarm went up a couple of notches in Patrick. 'Oh yes?'

'I'm not happy about Sheila.'

Patrick had seated himself on the orange ape-chair next to the blue version inhabited by Torkington. These articles, of which the yellow, green and rust-coloured fellows were currently supporting a trio of resident bachelors some yards away (Thackeray had broken the scarlet one after a session with Patrick and Graham at the George), perhaps represented an attempt by Mrs Charlton at practical criticism of the kind of master living in the Lodge, and certainly they would have accommodated to perfection any of the larger non-human buttockless primates, having great broad high backs and tiny shallow seats some nine inches from the floor. Patrick leaned across, carefully so as not to over-balance sideways, and said: 'What seems to be the trouble?'

'Everything. School work. All that interests her about school is leaving it. Tastes. Little worms who wear jeans and caterwaul and play those damn fool guitar affairs. Er ... male companions. The qualification there is they must be nitwits. The girl hates intelligence in any form. I loathe it.'

Patrick understood that what Torkington loathed was not intelligence itself but his daughter's hatred of it. Differing from his headmaster here, he prized this hatred highly as one of the girl's two sincerities. He hoped very much that the conversation would not turn to the other one. 'Quite natural at her age,' he said. 'She'll grow out of it.'

'There's trouble on the way, I'm certain. I can feel it. You see, I wouldn't mind even, if I thought she was interested in the type of boy we have here, but no. Calls them soft, or – what is it? – square or some idiot jargon. Meaning they get their hair cut occasionally and can read and write. But lads of her own age or a bit older, that's reasonable. It's these older men I'm scared of. She admits quite frankly that some of them appeal to her. Poise, you know. After all, she's still not quite seventeen, and there was that business ... There's one in the background now, I can tell – if I catch him ... I don't know who he is yet. She was in a funny sort of mood tonight. It's very worrying, you know, Patrick. Where is she, anyway?'

He looked accusingly at Patrick, who resisted the temptation to offer an exuberant denial that he had had Sheila secreted somewhere for an impending bout of profligacy. Instead of that, he said: 'I don't know.'

'Still putting the heavy roller on her complexion, no doubt. She was supposed to pick me up here and take me to the cinema to see some piece of trash with one of these yelling, capering imbeciles in it. As if she didn't get enough of them on television. I'm showing her I'm not a *square*, you see. Wonderful evening. Dinner with the Charltons and then this.' He turned towards the three bachelors, who although out of earshot had been attentively watching the free play of his gestures, and gave them a collective glare likely to send them straight to the Appointments Vacant section of *The Times Educational Supplement*. 'Her mother takes her side, if you can believe it. It's the trend of youth. I'll trend her.'

'I saw her at a dance a couple of weeks ago,' Patrick ventured. Torkington's face, which had begun to relax after the glare, at once became like that of an actor of the old school turning from Dr Jekyll into Mr Hyde. (This would have appealed strongly to Patrick in another mood, considering as he did that Hyde, not least in that striking scene where the small child gets trampled underfoot, was one of the best adjusted and most sympathetic characters in literature.) 'Where?' Torkington asked in a voice to match. 'Who was she with? Had she been drinking? Did you speak to her? When was this, did you say?'

'Oh, a fortnight or so ago, in that place behind the Three Crowns. Territorials do, very respectable. She seemed all right, I thought. I only just caught a glimpse of her, couldn't see who she was with.' All this was true, except the final detail. Sheila had been with a thin-moustached man who looked like an off-duty, or perhaps out-of-work, waiter. The fact that she was not on her own caused Patrick simultaneous annoyance and relief, in the way that things involving Sheila usually did when they failed to cause him simultaneous lust and terror.

'I shouldn't bore you with all this, I'm sorry. What can be keeping that girl? I must get away soon; I can't take much more of . . . The way things were shaping earlier on there's sure to be a row if I go over there.'

Patrick knew what was going to happen now. Torkers would ask him to nip across to the house in the opposite corner of the court and fetch Sheila for him, thus avoiding familial abrasion. The rest would follow inevitably: he even knew how he would feel as he stood at the tall olive-green front door (intrepid, like private eye still on case after warning from Mr Big), how he would feel on encountering an irresistibly attractive and welcoming Sheila (disturbed, like incipient psychotic about to be pushed over brink by enactment of central fantasy in real life), and how he would feel as they agreed that ten minutes would be safe (tranquil, like tank general at start of battle realizing fate now in charge and further worry useless). Further than that he could not see clearly, except to predict that relief at having got on with it at last after all these months of advance and retreat was going to be slightly eroded by other factors, notably the memory of Torkington's matter-of-fact tones as he said 'It's very worrying, Patrick.' But the earlier stuff was not a mere matter of prediction: he knew.

He was thus a good deal thrown off (like incipient psychotic frog-marched away from brink) to see Charlton tramping towards them across the room and hear Torkers say: 'Agh, here we go again. No need for you to stay. Look, come to the house for a drink some time. I'll ring you up.'

Patrick took his leave, acting his head off in a bid to convince Charlton that the just-ended Torkington-Standish conversation had been all about him and gravely damaging. Thackeray was in his room putting new plaster on a boil under his arm. He removed his attention far enough towards the external world to find the needed *Greece and Rome* and hand it over with an intensified, more abject version of his scholarship-boy look. Patrick's mind had moved on with sufficient speed for him to feel quite surprised when, outside the Lodge, he nearly knocked into someone and found it was Sheila. There was plenty of light to explode another area of his recent vision of the future by showing him that this Sheila was not by any means an irresistibly attractive Sheila, but just a run-of-the-mill, everyday Sheila, in other words a Sheila who was an oversized girl with oversized hips and an oversized face that had an oversized chin on it. She was backing all this up by looking roughly two and a half times her actual age.

'Why, hallo there, Patrick,' she bawled. 'What's your hurry?'

'Good evening, sir. Good evening, sir,' came at almost the same moment from two boys who were crossing from the Library.

'Good evening, good evening, good evening,' Patrick babbled.

Chapter Twelve

ABOUT five seconds later Patrick found, as an experienced infantryman will move into cover when fired upon without consciously looking for it, that he and Sheila were standing in one of the murkier regions of the court, partly sheltered alike from rain and prying eyes. It was not murky enough, however, to hide her similarity to her father, whose image was still fresh in Patrick's mind. This overdone family likeness, so extreme in

143

general physical outline as to permit of either fitting snugly into a suit of armour built for the other, extended under better optical conditions to points of detail: the thinning of the hair, for example. This was eerie, no other word for it. Once, just after she had had a shorter cut than usual, she had been sitting on his knee in the back of the parked 110 when a passing headlight had revealed just the right amount of her to suggest to him that he had been spending the last twenty minutes or so in kissing his headmaster, something which, although the latter was by no means a repulsive man, Patrick had on the whole no desire to do. After that he had had a sudden attack of conscience about keeping her out so late, which had later broadened into a resolve not to have any share in the further corruption of this semi- or pre- or would-be delinquent. But at their next meeting a month or so later, during a punch party held in a half-heartedly converted barn, this firm moral front had collapsed. Stare at her chin as he might, her evident enthusiasm had swept him first into the dance, later out of it completely and into the handiest little nook you ever saw, well away from the lanterns, where only his own singular lack of provision had saved them from the ultimate indecorum. But from this he considered he had small prospect of final escape: that neat quadrilateral of forces, in which his susceptibility and her assiduity were lined up against his prudence and her chin, was not going to remain indefinitely in equilibrium. The same was true of the temporarily equal and opposite action and reaction set up by the fact that she would not be seventeen until after Christmas. Oh well, he had often thought that the fatalist boys were on to something.

These thoughts went through his head, in the crisply efficient way such thoughts regularly had with him, while for another five seconds or so they peered at each other and Sheila said this was a surprise and so forth. Then she seemed to get into her firing cycle: 'Where've you been all this time? I just don't ever get to see you. And I thought we were going so great.'

Real affection came over Patrick. The unreserved devotion of her self-Americanization (to the point where *been* had definitely become *bin*, even) commanded respect, the straight tweed coat he had caught sight of just now was a great advance on the pink nylon froth affair of memory, and it had always been hard not to respond to the intensity, candour, and disinterest of her liking for him – just as hard as it was to remember that anything in trousers, or rather divested of its trousers, would have suited her equally well. 'Oh, I've *been* around, you know,' he said jocularly. 'Where have you *been*, come to that?'

'I'm just bored to hell with this god-awful town. Are they all trying to drive each other into the nuthouse, or what? And whatever happened to that call you were going to give me, remember?'

'Look, I can't ring you up, if that's what you mean, not with all those extensions and things at your end, and anyway I thought you told me not to with your mother about. If anyone's going to ring anyone up it's got to be you ringing me. Did I say I'd ring you up? Was I tight at the time?'

'We just have to get together,' Sheila said, coming closer, and he recognized her mention of the *call* as purely emotional, not factual, recognized this with some alarm – was he never going to understand them? His alarm sharpened, changed direction, when she came closer and said in her full-throated dance-hall yell: 'We'd be so fine together, I just know it.'

'Ssshh,' he said warmly, quite scared now, his mind rehearsing formulas of conscience and discretion while his hands got ready to fend her off if she reached the stage of getting together with him here and now, closing with him, wrapping herself round him. This he felt she was very capable of doing: he had never heard a reliable account of the *business* alluded to earlier by Torkington, but it had most probably involved advanced sexual play with some drunk in a shop-front opposite a well-attended bus stop, and had certainly threatened a scandal which it had taken all her father's influence and ingenuity to avert. 'Don't shout,' he added.

'I'd come around to your apartment but I just don't care to when I never know if your room-mate'll be there or not. Listen, will you be at the Ivy Bush Wednesday night?'

Patrick hesitated. The factors making for restraint were grouped about him on various levels of immediacy: Torkington, Charlton, the public nature of the Ivy Bush set-up, Sheila's chin. He might have said yes even so if the latest of his many glances over his shoulder had not revealed to him a figure apparently watching them from a peculiarly relevant upper window – Charlton's. He knew it was Charlton's because, not long after breaking the scarlet ape-chair, Thackeray had pointed it out to him in the hope of getting him to throw an unopened bottle of Guinness through it. 'I'll see,' he jabbered. 'Don't go there specially on my account. Got to be off now. Nice to see you.'

He minced away, hunching himself into a scholarly stoop, making his head vibrate on its neck, clasping his hands behind him in token of senile harmlessness. He felt more frightened at this sudden glimpse of his own powers of indiscretion than at the situation thus engendered, but not by much.

A little later, standing solo at the counter of the George with a justifiably large pink gin before him, he did some pondering. The watcher in the court could have been none other than undergrown and round-shouldered Horace, the Charlton's sixteen-year-old son, a detestation for whom was almost the sole point of agreement between Horse and the captain of the First Fifteen. Much hereby became clear, especially the basis of Charlton senior's cryptic threats in the court ten days earlier. Patrick now remembered, belatedly enough, that when Sheila in her bragging mood had once listed some of the *squares* in the school who had tried unsuccessfully to persuade her to go out with them, the name of Horace Charlton had come along somewhere towards the end of the second dozen. Most boys of sixteen would have had no difficulty, Patrick considered, in turning their attention elsewhere when thus rebuffed, but it made sense for Horace to have kept at it, at least in aspiration, with the same stoical obduracy that led him, after innumerable corrections, to go on larding his proses with the perfect passive participle used in an active sense and spelling Catiline *Cataline*. There were few things more dangerous than the jealousy of the unsuccessful; once roused, Horace would have had little trouble in identifying some of the people to be seen in his love's company, and none whatever in handing on to his father the more interesting names.

Passing to beer and a sandwich, Patrick reviewed means of defence. The danger of an immediate leak about tonight's encounter via Charlton senior could be met – since there had been no actual grapple to witness, and Horace could have heard

146

hardly anything – by an act of pretended contrition for having *gone too far* by giving Sheila *a few words of advice.* (He could hear it already: 'Well, actually I do feel a bit repentant.' 'What? What for? What did you do?' 'After what you'd been telling me, running into her like that, I'm afraid I rather … let her have it,' no, 'blurted out a lot of rubbish about duty and so on.' Torkers was shrewd in his way, but that should hold him.) In the longer run, the most promising factor seemed at the moment to be Horace's desire – his father no doubt goading him on with threats and obloquy – to sit for a university scholarship the following year. The time would soon come round when Patrick, in consultation with Purdy, the senior classics master, would have to deliver favourable or adverse recommendations on boys in Horace's position. Since Horace was genuinely on the borderline, and since Purdy would have been best pleased if no boy was ever allowed to sit, Patrick felt that an unveiled threat to Charlton along these lines might be most effective.

As he left the George and crossed the road in front of that item of cultural light industry in decline, the art shop where Anna worked, he felt momentarily depressed. The possibility of having to engage in direct deception of Torkington was not altogether a pleasant one, and he suspected vaguely that there was some flaw in his long-term anti-Charlton scheme. But it was not in his nature to stay depressed for long, and he got back to normal on receiving a brief but definite eyeing from a girl in a black mackintosh and hood who was waiting at the Green Line stop, perked up further on savouring the slight but perceptible romanticness of his encounter with Sheila in the College court (he blessed sweet Night for having cast her mantle between him and the girl's chin), and for the first time got the full benefit of that shot in the moral arm derived from his virtual turning-down of Sheila's invitation. He had not been consciously thinking of Jenny at the time, but of course that was where a good part of his motive must have lain.

Getting into the 110, he noticed that the various lights of the High Street were reflected on the wet pavements in not too bad a way at all. The rain had almost stopped. Life was all right really. In fact this was one of those evenings when the thought of death seemed intrinsically uninteresting, like the doings of the Queen and her consort or the history of banking. He drove off past the lighted shop windows, full of television sets and bottles of intoxicating liquors and other selections from the good things in life, and felt there was quite a good chance of his never actually being called upon to die at all. Those medicos would probably come up with something in the next decade or so; they were getting as wily as hell these days. Short of that, it had incontrovertibly been an outstanding day in the good old cancer research laboratories. The ones in England would presumably have packed up by now, but the Yanks would still be hard at it, and if his figures were correct the fellows in Japan would fairly soon be slipping into their white coats and making with the microscopes. Only an idiot would fail to chain-smoke his way through the evening after that. Nevertheless he hoped that, if and when dying should finally be required of him, the death-wish everybody was supposed to have would be getting going in him at a really helpful pitch.

Turning off at the electricty showroom, he was lucky enough to send the greater part of a puddle over a sod in ragged clothes who was doing his level best to blow his nose into the gutter. Patrick wondered what he could possibly devise to say to Jenny. It would have to be good. Was the whole thing hopeless, was she simply the wrong sort for his purposes? Despite the wealth of evidence in this direction, he had not been altogether mistaken, he was prepared to bet, in his early assumption that the Great Sculptor and Colourist, particularly in his latter capacity, had fashioned her primarily as a bedroom amenity. Where he had gone off the rails had been in thinking that she must already be acquainted with this fact, which, it was now clear, would have to be explained to her carefully, sympathetically, and at length. How the hell he was ever going to get into position to deliver this explanation was beyond him at the moment, but get there he must. A death-bed roll-call that did not include Jenny's name would be hardly worth reciting: to allow her to pass on in maiden meditation, fancy free, would be to acquiesce in the vital primacy of Charlton, Mrs Charlton, Horace Charlton, Charlie Crosland, Cicero, Dick, *et al*. As against this, the existence of Jenny threatened that whole happy system of his whereby four or so women could be taken on at once without violence, or too much violence, to emotional integrity, No. 1 being (say) someone whom your mind had taught itself to forget but whom your body would always remember, No. 2 someone between whom and yourself an unnameable spark had leapt, No. 3 someone towards union with whom your whole life had been tending, and No. 4 someone apparently unimportant whom you could not do your heart the injury of parting from. What would happen if a No. 5 were to blow all that sky high?

Patrick pulled up outside the Thompsons' house and got out in a hurry, slamming the door viciously behind him. He had felt the wing of the angel of marriage brush his cheek, and was afraid. This passed off smoothly enough when he realized that, for the second time in an hour, he was of his own free will approaching bastard territory. Life was full of surprises, no doubt about that. The front door would not be locked, a useful factor during the days of Anna and eventually, he hoped, destined to become similarly useful again. The thing now was to burst in and scuttle at silent-cinema speed up those stairs, the ones on which Jenny had made her first vividly remembered appearance. The bursting-in part went off all right, but the scuttling sequence had perforce to be abandoned, for coming down the stairs before him he saw, instead of Jenny, Martha with about a bushel of dirty washing in her arms. 'Oh, hallo,' he said. 'Is –?'

She cut in with prompt efficiency. 'The young lady of whom you are presumably in quest doesn't happen to be in at the moment, I'm sorry to have to tell you.' Plenty of tone and face went with this.

'It is a pity, isn't it? When will she be back, do you know?"

'Well, she told us that she was going to see her friend Mrs Carter, but she wouldn't be very long, she said, because she wanted to wash her hair and iron her suit and so on. She always fills us in on what her programme is. I don't know whether we're supposed to be taking notes for her biography or what. Come in here for a bit. I think there's about two-thirds of a flagon of mild under the stairs still, if Dick hasn't drunk it.'

'Where's he tonight?' Patrick asked, confident now of the total absence of the other, whom the sound of voices in the hall normally brought tottering into view within ten seconds.

'Seeing a man about an auction, if you ever heard of such a thing. You've turned up to make reparation for your little misdeed on Sunday, I presume.'

'Who told you about that?'

'Oh, Anna gave us a blow-by-blow account. In front of Jenny.'

'Christ, what a bitch that woman is.'

'Ah, I can see it's off with the old and on with the new as far as you're concerned. Here.'

Patrick sipped at his beer. It was flat and tepid, but the thought that Thompson had paid for it imparted all the savour of a 1949 Eitelsbacher Karthauserhofberg Kronenberg feinste Auslese. He said nothing.

'And I hear you've got a rival in the field.'

Patrick took out his cigarettes and lit one.

'Passing the young lady down the line, I see. McClintoch takes a hand. I didn't think any of them were too tough nuts for you to crack. I should hate to think you were losing your grip.'

'So should I.'

'Haven't touched you on the raw, I hope. Well, I suppose it's early days yet. Let's hope this evening gives cause for a favourable prognosis. You'll have your work cut out, though, I imagine. She's a reet champion lass with her head screwed on and her legs together, is our Jenny. Still, never say die, eh?'

'No, don't let's ever say that.'

Martha sat down and screwed up her face in speculation. 'I wonder what Graham thinks he's going to get out of it. Just the being seen with her, perhaps. Difficult to fathom. You know, his real trouble is he doesn't laugh enough. Too ... solid, even for Jenny.'

'Oh, lots of nice girls like men who don't laugh.'

'None of the ones Graham likes do.'

'I think he thinks the whole thing's immoral anyway.'

'Well, at least you don't suffer from that, do you?'

'Not all the time.'

'Oh, lucky you.' Martha did some more speculation. 'I know what you mean about Graham, though. Going out with girls is a thing one does, so he has to try and do it. But he doesn't really like it, don't you agree?'

Patrick spoke to this question for some time, accommodating

various points raised by Martha. He admitted to himself that for this kind of semi-malicious discussion she was one of the best partners currently available. This admission, however, threw into unwelcome prominence the notion that he must be more like her than he realized, a notion given support by the disloyalty aspect of his part in the chat. It would be nice to even things up a little by indicating to Martha that her assumption of equality with him in sexual status was unfounded, and that in fact her level was to be distinguished from Graham's only with difficulty. He was still contemplating this when the front door opened and shut and someone ran lightly up the stairs.

'There she is,' Martha stage-whispered. 'Don't let me keep you.'

'Well, thanks for the beer.'

'Try not to take it too hard if you don't get anywhere. After all, there are plenty of fish in the sea, aren't there? That's the main thing. There's always whatshername, the headmaster's daughter – dear Sheila: I thought she looked rather like a policewoman the time I saw her, or perhaps a police*man*, but there, the time comes when you've got to take what you can get, right? How is she these days? Flourishing as ever?'

Patrick felt his cheeks going hot. With his teeth clenched he said in an undertone: 'Listen, doll, quit riding me, will you? Suppose you just keep your bloody little witty comments to yourself and stop shoving your nose into my affairs? How about that, now? How about trying that, eh? How about giving that a whirl for a change? Mm?'

Her face twitched and she got clumsily to her feet and walked out into the scullery. Patrick stood still for a moment, then went off upstairs. By the time he reached the door that must be Jenny's he was repenting slightly of what he had said, but having no time for that just now he knocked and entered.

Chapter Thirteen

JENNY sprang up from the bed and faced him, demonstrating her ability to look even better than he remembered her each time he saw her. 'Oh ... hallo,' she said without confidence.

'I've come to apologize for my behaviour on Sunday.'

'Oh. Oh, you shouldn't have bothered.' She was wearing a dress of some soft dark green material which he had not seen on her before. It suited her, but then so would a fireman's uniform or a 1910 bathing suit, complete with cap. She kept her eyes on the floor, where a going-thin-on-top rug crossed the chequered lino.

'Yes I should. I'm sorry. I've no excuse. I behaved like an utter fool, I know.'

'Yes, you did, didn't you? And all to no purpose, too.'

'Do you think you'll ever be able to forgive me, Jenny?'

'Oh, I shouldn't wonder, but you're not to think that means I'm coming out with you again or anything like that, because I'm not. You might as well know that straight away.'

Well, this was getting down to business and no mistake, wasn't it? And that was right, wasn't it? 'I must have hurt you a lot.'

'Yes, you did, but that's not really the point. You see, Patrick, if you can be so nice to me, the way you can be when you want to be, like you were outside the house before the others came out, and you give me a terrific boost doing that, and I don't say you don't mean it at the time, and then you start this snogging with someone else with me there . . . well, surely you can see? How can I have anything more to do with you after that?'

Oh lordy lordy lordy, how lovely she was, with all that thick inky-black hair and the slightly hollow cheeks and the faint blue veins at the temples and the very definite natural line surrounding the lips and the lips themselves and and and and and and. And, to select almost at random, the permanent faint Disney look, for some reason slightly accentuated this evening. 'I suppose it wouldn't make any difference at all if I promised not to do it again?'

'No, none at all. I don't think for a moment you would do it again, not exactly what you did, but that wouldn't change anything. It's too late to start promising. I don't believe in promising.'

'I can see it was one of the cruellest things anyone could do. You must have thought I didn't care for you at all, just been fooling. But I do care for you, Jenny. You know I do.'

'Oh, anyone can care for someone. In their own way – that's how it goes, isn't it? It's too easy. But I still haven't explained properly what I mean. It wasn't just that you were unkind to me; it's no problem getting over that and it wasn't as if you'd been telling me you were in love with me or anything. No, what it was, you showed me the sort of person you are, that's to say someone who can't even wait for one to be safe out of the way before you start making up to another one. The stage you and I were at, I'd not got any rights over what you did when you weren't with me, but when you started –'

'You mean if I'd done the same thing when you weren't there you wouldn't have minded?'

'Of course I'd have minded if I'd found out about it, I couldn't help it, but that would have been different. I'm not going to ask a man to swear off other women from the first moment he gets talking to me, that'd just be plain silly. If I'd happened to see you out with someone else some evening I wouldn't have liked it, but it wouldn't *surprise* me, I'd think it was quite natural and fair, I wouldn't go thinking it was, you know, irresponsible.'

'Oh God, I am bloody irresponsible, you're not telling me anything new there.' Patrick dropped into a lumpy armchair that had a large-pattern chintz cover and put his head in his hands, an action that was no mere piece of stage business. Things were going far from well. Anger or tears or head-tossing disdain he felt he could have dealt with, but this tone of reasoned explication was in the wrong area for his repertoire of flank-turning procedures. 'But I wish you didn't sound so sort of clinical about everything, as if I was just an interesting case-history or something.'

'Sorry, I didn't mean to sound like that. But it's no use getting all into a tizzy about it, is it? No sense in that.'

'I don't want to be irresponsible,' he said, still through his fingers. 'It isn't a thing you just decide you'll be. I do try not to be. But it's so difficult.'

'Yes, I can see how it must be, changing yourself about. Now, if you'll excuse me, I'm going to wash my hair.'

He heard her moving round the room. 'Don't go. Wait till I've gone. Your hair doesn't need washing.'

'Oh, that it does, you'd be surprised how soon it gets greasy.'

'Well, I shall always be sorry it ended like that.' He sat back and watched her shut a drawer and come away with a clean white towel.

She still refused to look at him. 'How do you mean?'

'Me behaving like an idiot without even thinking what I was doing and then finding it's all over.'

'All what's over? Nothing very much had gone on, had it?' For the first time there was a note of strain in her voice. 'You make it sound as though there'd been some great grand-passion thing. This is only about the sixth time we've met and we only went out together once.'

'That's enough to be able to tell, though, isn't it? It was enough for me and I'm pretty sure it was enough for you.'

'Tell? Tell what?'

'Now come on, Jenny, don't play it dumb, there's a good girl. This is too important for any of that debating stuff.'

'I'm not playing in any way.'

'Yes you are. Not consciously perhaps, all right, but you don't really believe half of what you've been saying. You're angry with me for the way I behaved with that woman – what the hell was her name? – and my God you've every right to be, but you don't mean all that line about –'

'You're a great one for knowing what people mean better than they do themselves, aren't you? Why can't you let them mean what they say? And do you always mean what you say? And you needn't think you're impressing me or fooling me when you pretend you can't remember Wendy's name, because you're not.'

'There you are, you see, it is just the Wendy part of it, just the personal thing, bloody important I agree, but –'

'Will you listen? I brought that up because I wanted to let you know that for once one of your clever little bits of tactics didn't go down and didn't register, that's all, one little detail that didn't do what it was meant to do. You're a bright lad, Patrick, really bright, and you can beat me in argument any day of the week on almost any mortal thing, but you're a fool if you think you can talk me or argue me or persuade me or wheedle me off this one, because you c-c-c –, you c –'

She swung away towards the window, still holding the towel, her head bent. The slenderness of her shoulders and arms nearly overwhelmed him, nearly made him speak and behave without forethought, nearly drove from his mind the purpose that had brought him here. He waited until he was in full control of things again, then said violently: 'Now just you listen to me.' She turned round and looked at him in the way she had, with more alertness in her face and body than he had ever before seen in anyone, the Disney look intensified to the point where she became a small deer in *Bambi* scenting danger by the stream. 'What?'

'I want you to forget everything I've said so far. Except that I'm sorry for what happened. Now let's get down to brass tacks. From what I did you deduced, correctly, that I'm irresponsible. Fine. I'm more irresponsible than you could even guess. Perhaps I can grow up some time, especially if you give me a hand. Perhaps I never will whatever happens. But all that side of it, none of it really matters. I'm involved with you now. I realized it during that ghastly lunch at Ormerod's place and that even more ghastly drive back. I'd have felt bad anyway, naturally, whoever it had been; who wouldn't? But this wasn't just remorse and so on. It was myself I'd hurt as well as you – I was worrying about myself too. I'd damaged myself; I'd thrown away something valuable and found out too late how valuable it was. I was so sick about that, I pretty well forgot what I'd done to you.' Conscientiousness inspired him to leaf rapidly through his memory: he had felt very much like that at the time, hadn't he? Check. He gazed at her and she looked away. 'Are you with me so far?'

'Oh yes, I'm sure it can't be much fun for you to be like you are. You're far from being a pig in a lot of things and so you're bound to get hurt yourself now and then. What I'm against is the way you seem to think it's me who's the one who ought to join in and get hurt with you.'

'But you've already joined in, you see. That's the other half of it. I'm involved, which means you'll never get rid of me. I'll be ringing you up and coming round to see you and crashing in when you're with other people so it'll be too embarrassing for you to try and chuck me out – oh, I'm going to be a proper bastard, I'm going to pile on every bit of pressure I can to get you to change your mind. But I don't think I'm going to have to try very hard or for very long, do you? Because you're involved too, aren't you? You've joined in, Jenny. You might as well admit it. It'll save a lot of time and trouble. Come on, now.' She had turned away again and he went gently up to her and put his hands on her upper arms. 'It's going to hurt too much to get rid of me, isn't it? I know, because I know how I'd feel if you did.'

She stood there stiffly, clutching the towel, evidently staring at the drawn curtains. 'You're making it just as hard as you know how, aren't you?'

'You bet I am. No holds barred on this one.'

'I ought to have chucked you out before you'd said a word.'

'You couldn't have, any more than you can now. Too painful.'

She said in a muffled voice: 'Better bad now than worse later.'

'That's just a motto.' He slid his arms round her waist and felt for her hands under the towel. She held herself away from him but did not try to prevent him. One of the hands was tightly clenched around some object and he began prising the fingers loose one by one. While he was doing this a tear splashed on to his wrist. The object in the hand turned out to be a plastic sachet of shampoo with a price-reduction stamped on it by the manufacturer and the honey-coloured liquid showing through the transparency. It succeeded in being more moving than any crucifix or lock of dead sister's hair. 'Darling,' he said, and started to kiss the back of her neck.

The reaction was as for molten lead rather than regular male mouth: she broke free and was over by the door in a flash, making him rotate momentarily on one leg. 'All right, Mr *Big Heart-Throb*,' she said with relish, looking very healthy and not at all tearful. 'You made it, ten out of ten and excellent, very good work, a real scholar. That's all we need, isn't it? Kiss and make up and everything's just great again, and we're all involved and lovely, because who could resist Mr *Teenage Idol*, because he's *so handsome* and *so charming*? Well, it doesn't work with me, *mister*, so just you be out of here by the time I come back. You can pop into the next room and wait for dearest

Miss Anna *Fat-Legs* to show up, or there's always sweet little Mrs Martha *Floppy-Chops* – she's one of yours, isn't she? *Oh, oh, darling Patrick, kiss me again, oh, oh . . .'*

'Martha is not one of mine whatever you mean by that, not in any sense. You don't imagine I'd –'

'Ah, but she *adores* you, doesn't she, *darling*? That's the main thing. So that any day you feel like it you can just *stretch out your hand . . .'*

'Look, it's no fault of mine if for some reason –'

'If you're so *charming* and *handsome* that they won't give you a minute's peace? Of course not. We understand. Tell us, Mr Standish, when did you first realize you were beautiful?'

'Jenny, please . . .'

'Please is good. Please shut the gate. When you go out.'

Left alone, Patrick first expounded to himself the concept of *hysterical*, then the larger one of *women*. He was at the disadvantage that whereas his attacks were planned, or rather under the control of reason, her defences, and even more her counter-attacks, suffered from no such inhibition. He wandered round the room, looking at some of the many things in it: a pile of childish drawings with one showing a dropsical anthropoid creature (caption: *SPAC MAN*), a shallow raffia bag containing reels of cotton and so on, a pair of standing birds of indeterminate species hacked out of the horns of some ruminant or other (Thompsons' choice, he hoped and trusted), a public-library book called *The Lovers of Linda*, a lot of photographs including a sort of nymphomaniacal-angel one of an adolescent Jenny that he brooded over for a time, a penny notebook with *Birthdays* written on the cover, a pot with a plant in it, a pot with ferns in it, a packet of dental floss, a packet of gum stimulators, blue imitation-leather writing-compendium of which the zip was not drawn. He flipped it open and read on the pad: *Dear All,*

So glad to hear every one is thriving. Do not worry about me, I am very fit and happy and you know your strong girl. Of course I am wrapping up warm, but here in the South we do not get it as cold as you, I think. There is one of those big stoves in the kitchen come sitting-room and I can tell it will be all snug in the winter. I have made such a nice friend at the school, she is called Mrs Carter. Of course, I know what you are saying Dad, 'All Southerners are sly and deceitful,' but really I must say I have found them all very

Well, say ninety per cent of us are very, Patrick thought. Some of us are so very we hardly know what to do with it. He shut the compendium and moved over to the electric fire which, with its single bar about the size of a stout lead pencil, was going to keep Jenny snug in the winter when she was not being it in the kitchen come sitting-room. Should he really be up to what he was up to? He told himself afterwards that he had almost decided to go when Jenny herself spoilt things by returning with the towel wrapped round her head like a gigantic turban. Under it she looked eastern rather than northern or southern, its whiteness emphasizing her role as a critique-in-action of human pigmentation at large.

She knelt in front of the fire and rubbed at the black flood of hair. Whoever had put together the nape of her neck, the angle of her jaw, her ears, etc. had taken more trouble over the job and used better materials than usual. 'Still here then, I see,' she said conversationally. 'You must have plenty of time on your hands. I was thinking while I was washing my hair, I've got just the name for you. Georgie Porgie, and you're going to have to watch that in a few years with that pot you're starting. Kiss the girls and make them cry – that's your trade, isn't it? Well, here's one you're not going to get any pudding and pie out of, *wack*. So you can run away now.' She put the towel aside and started with the brush and comb she had brought with her from the bathroom, a sea-girl now with the damp hair swung forward, the eyes bigger and more brilliant than ever with waterdrops on the lashes.

Patrick lit a cigarette. 'You're only torturing yourself,' he suggested, palpating his pot-belly with his free hand.

'Huh. That's a laugh, that is.'

'Isn't all this rather a fuss about nothing?'

'I don't know, is it? You're making it, so you ought to be able to tell.'

'I want you so much, Jenny.'

'What's that to me?'

'This hard-boiled act doesn't suit you, you know.'

She had brought the picture-mirror from her dressing-table, arranged it among the photographs on the mantelpiece, and now turned her back to do her hair. 'Don't care.'

'Why do you think I came round here tonight?'

'Don't know. It's nearer than New Zealand, I suppose.'

'That bloody Wendy again.'

She went on brushing her hair.

He marshalled all his resources – intellect, imagination, histrionics, and such vestigial integrity as he hoped might still be floating around somewhere in mind or heart – for a final effort. 'These ideas of yours. Jolly sound in 1880 and everything. But I went into all that, didn't I? Now. You say you're not going to sleep with anyone until you get married, right? Sounds fine: you decide you're not going to and so you don't. But, you see, you haven't got a hope in hell. Not these days. And not given the sort of girl you are. It isn't just that you're very attractive, so there'll never be any shortage of offers, though that's part of it, of course. The other thing is that you're a sexy girl – it didn't take me two minutes to find that out. You want it. You know you'd enjoy it. That's what'll be your undoing, not just the offers. I give you two years at the outside. I don't say you won't be married by then, too; people would marry you if you were very very nasty instead of very very nice, and glad of the chance. But you won't be a virgin when you marry. Now lots of marriages that start like that, most of them, they're very successful. But there's a chance yours won't be. There's a chance the man you marry'll be just like me in every way, only you won't like him much. Because there's just one thing missing from your scheme of things: the right kind of man. There's the kind that wouldn't dream of laying a finger on you until marriage, and there's the kind you like. What's the use of a chap who's very respectful and decent and all that, oh, he wouldn't dream of offering you any disrespect, sooner die – what's the use of that if you don't want him to? Do you think you could marry Graham, for instance?'

The strokes of her brush had grown more mechanical. Now, her eyes in the mirror half dodging his, she said angrily: 'You're not to say anything against Graham – he's a damn decent fellow and I thought he was meant to be a friend of yours.'

'Honey, this isn't *against* him. Of course Graham's a friend of mine. I'm just asking you to face facts.'

'Oh yes, I know you've got everything weighed up, you and your –'

'Look. All I've got to say is this. There are two sorts of men today, those who do – you know what I mean – and those who don't. All the ones you're ever going to really like are the first sort, and all the ones those ideas of yours tell you you ought to have are the second sort. Oh, there wouldn't be any problem of temptation there. The problem would come on the wedding night. And on all the nights after that. There used to be a third sort, admitted. The sort that could, but didn't – not with the girl he was going to marry, anyway. You'd have liked him all right, though, and he wouldn't have given you any trouble trying to get you into bed before the day. The snag about him is he's dead. He died in 1914 or thereabouts. He isn't ever going to turn up, Jenny, that bloke with the manners and the respect and the honour and the bunches of flowers *and* the attraction. Or if he does he's going to turn out to have a wife in Birmingham or a boy friend in Chelsea or a psychiatrist in . . . wherever psychiatrists live. These days he just –'

'Oh, for heaven's sake shut *up*, Patrick. The way you go *on*. You remind me so much of someone I used to know, except he never had the gift of the gab like you've got. Now clear off, I've got things to do.'

'Just remember he's dead, the man you want.'

'Stop explaining to me what I want, *genius*. Can't you understand? I'm fed up with you. I've had enough. Go away. Now.'

She said this quietly, but the look she sent with it burnt out every valve in the automatic pilot that, with a pause or two for manual resetting, had carried him all the way through until now. His mouth hung open for a moment, then he said without calculation : 'I'm sorry. Forget everything I've said. I'm a pompous oaf. But I am damn keen on you. I'll get in touch with you some time.'

She went on looking at him a little longer with a changed expression, then moved quickly aside. 'Drop me a picture postcard from New Zealand,' she said uninterestedly, opening a cupboard and removing a suit on a hanger, picking at a stain with her fingernail, not noticing him as he went out.

In the car he swung back into action again, casting about for a likely warming-up run. Why was it, he primed himself into asking himself, that it was always girls who looked like Sheila who were ready to behave like Sheila? A good question. What about it? Well then, why could it not have been Jenny, for instance, who was indifferent to outworn conventions? Yes indeed – if she had been ... if she had been, she would presumably have been set up long ago in a smart flat in Park Lane, or even where? Hell, even New York's east side, which was something or other, which was a comforting reflection in a way. In the – go on – in the roughly comparable case of the woman who had lured him to the rugger club dance he ought to have seen at once that she was far too fine a specimen to value sex for its own sake and behind her there stretched a legion or at least a good half-dozen of fine specimens for whom he had sacrificed his principles to no end by sending them flowers writing them notes complimenting them on their wallpaper letting them bore him ringing them up when ...

Chapter Fourteen

'JENNY, I wonder if you'd be an angel and do my dinner supervision for me on Tuesday? Ted's away up north again midweek and I've got to give him his lunch and get him off. He'll leave his lists behind again if I'm not there.'

'Yes, of course,' Jenny said, trying to sound gayer than she felt. Dinner supervision had much less supervision in it than it had helping to get the food from the hatch to the tables and often from the plate to the mouth. Having to see as well that the quicker ones did not manage to get out into the rain without their coats had so confused her the previous Friday that she had mixed up Richard Stacy and Ian Fairley and told Richard, whose parents were very set on him eating his cabbage, that he need not bother with his cabbage, and spent ten minutes forcing cabbage down the throat of poor Ian, who hated cabbage as much as Richard but whose parents were very set on him not being made to eat anything he hated. It was cabbage having to do with both of them that had fooled her.

'Thanks, love, I'll pay it back on the Friday. Ooh, it'll be quite a relief being on my own, I don't mind telling you. I daren't have the Play of the Week on now in case it puts ideas into his head. You should have seen him a little while ago when they were doing one of these Deep South things, you know, when they're all after each other and never mind if it's their own sisters and uncles and things. You should have seen what he got up to after that little lot. Here, let me give you a hand with those. Why can't old Compton ever show up on time when it's her turn to do the tea?'

Elsie Carter, a small thin woman with pretty auburn hair, started arranging the cups and saucers on the staff-room table, half-closing her eyes, which stuck out more than most people's, to protect them from the smoke of her cigarette. Jenny warmed the pot and said: 'I don't think she means to forget. She's a bit vague, is old Compton.'

'Vague my foot,' Elsie said with a snort. 'She's not vague about bringing in those bunches of roses from her garden for Sinclair. She's not vague when it comes to handing out chores for the Christmas party, either. She'll arrange the desks, she says. Stand there and get the big ones on to it, oh, very strenuous. You get the paper tablecloths and cups and I get the jellies and mincepies. Jenny, you make too many excuses for people.'

'She hasn't got any friends.'

'Huh, can you wonder? Oh crikey, handwork this afternoon. You know, I loathe that. I quite see it's good for them expressing themselves and what-not, but I do. Cutting up the paper and mixing the colours and lining up the easels. Get them illustrating a story, I suppose, though half of them don't seem to know what I mean by that. I've a damn good mind to just give them crayons and chalks and let them get on with it. It's lazy, I know, but it does save the mess. I'll be down to the clayboards and plasticine before this term's over. That's what old Compton gives 'em, week in week out. Oh, good morning, Miss Compton. Hallo, Grace. You're just in time for the tea Jenny's been making, Miss Compton.'

'Oh, I'm terribly sorry, Jenny, I did know it was my turn, but one of my young ones had an accident – you know – and I couldn't find the caretaker. Let me pour out, at least. Oh, here are the others, and we've only got ten minutes, everybody seems to be behind this morning. Would you open the milk, Grace, like a lamb?' Miss Compton's loops of barley-sugar beads swayed about over the table as she took her usual age to mix the teas in the right amounts according to her and put the sugars in instead of letting them all help themselves. Her tiny face was creased up in the anxious look it had on her bad days.

Eventually Jenny got her cup and went over to the window, which was not far from the table or from the door either, to chat to Elsie Carter. They lit cigarettes and stared out at the milling mass below them, Jenny mildly surprised as always by how many different really loud yells could be heard at the same moment. It seemed incredible that when playtime ended the yard would not be littered with torn-off arms and legs. Even when children misbehaved in the class-room they were always nearer then to how they ought to behave than to how they behaved naturally. And to think that, well, Miss Sinclair used to be one of those, unless she came from a special sort of children that you never met. It was easy enough to see that Elsie had not come from that sort, if there was one, but from the sort now in the yard. Perhaps that was what made her so all right to talk to.

'You look a bit down in the mouth,' Elsie muttered now round the end of her cigarette. 'Boy friend acting up?'

'In a way. Oh yes, he acts up. See, it's all a performance. He was on at me the night before last about I wouldn't get what I want so I might as well have him, because what I really want is him.'

'Fancies himself, doesn't he? Mind you, they all do.'

'He knows how to be nice all right, only you can feel him being it a bit too much, being nice, still he is, only sometimes he just thinks he is and he's not. He knows best about everything, he thinks, at least that's the way he goes on. But it's all a game with him.'

'I know. Still I often think, where should we be without them? The other ones are worse, the adoration type. It's better when you know they don't mean all of it, isn't it? Still, there are limits. Oh, you can't have everything.'

'Oh, I know. But I wish they didn't think they were getting away with making you take it all as gospel. All that stuff about me never going to get what I want. He plugged that one like mad.'

'He's just out for what he can get, that lad, from what you tell me. Not your style at all, love.'

'He really is nice, though,' Jenny said, thinking of Patrick's eyes and hair and how his mouth stayed attractive even when he was talking rubbish with it. And his funny legs.

'You won't catch him going respectable, not for years anyway, not till he's beginning to be afraid he can't steal the milk through the fence any more. Then he might consider keeping a cow of his own.' Elsie gave her tremendous laugh. 'Wonderful, that, isn't it? Can't think where I heard it. No, you'd be well out of that, believe me. You know what'd happen if he did marry you, don't you? Load you down with about five kids in the first four years, that's the first step.'

'But I shouldn't mind that, Elsie. I want lots of kids.'

'You don't see what I'm getting at. When you're so well weighed down that you can't leave him, because no one'd take on a girl with half a dozen kids, even if she looked like you, that's when our Mr Fancy Pants gets up to his tricks. Round the town and in and out of my lady's chambers, and see if he cares when you rumble him. He's got you, see? Got you where he wants you. You're the beautiful wife and lovely family that *he* can't leave whenever one of his girl-friends starts turning serious on him.'

'Oh, there can't be many that plot things out like that.'

'I've seen it happen, Jenny, honestly. I even think old Ted had the same little plan lined up for me, only I foxed him by only producing Jimmy. The way he kept at me in the hope of ringing the bell again. I reckon it got into a sort of habit with him then. Do you realize he still wants one as soon as he gets in off a trip? Before he's even sat down. I ask you. Mind you, I don't know what he gets up to when he's away, and I don't want to know. As long as it's all out of the way. But I doubt whether there's much. There couldn't be, not with how he goes on at home.

He'd have to be a sort of Mr Universe.' She roared again, nearly spilling her cup. 'And he's such a little weed, isn't he? You'd never think it to look at him. It's often the way, though. Ooh, hell and damnation, PT next. I'd better get that store cupboard sorted out before the bell rings. Then there might be a chance of getting them into the hall in under a quarter of an hour. Look, what about coming round on Tuesday and cheering me up when I'm a grass widow?'

'Yes, I'd love to, thank you very much, Elsie.'

'I'll get a bottle of that Australian port in you liked and we'll put our feet up and have a real good old natter. So long for now, and cheer up, love.'

There were still two or three minutes of playtime left. Jenny sat down in a folding chair by the window and pretended to read a copy of the *National Geographic* for July 1946 that someone had left about. It had native girls with bare busts. (Why did native busts not count?) She was depressed at what Elsie had said about Patrick: some of it sounded pretty right to her. She was also depressed at being reminded of the ordeal of Patrick's visit to her, at Elsie noticing she was depressed, and at realizing how much of her time nowadays was spent in being depressed. And throwing yourself into your work was not the cure everyone made it out to be. She had expected to find the job of teacher using up all her concentration and energy, but there were large parts left over. That was a bit depressing, too. At one time it had seemed that only older pople got depressed, through not having much fun and everything, but down here, at least, they got started on it young, the same as they did with not listening to what was said to them. But what was really depressing her was yesterday's evening-out with Graham.

Everything had gone well, or anyway much as expected, until the drive home in that noisy old car. She had only felt uncomfortable a couple of times, both of them in the café where they had supper. She had been a little disconcerted right at the start by the way he lit her cigarettes for her, shaking the match about in the air until it had stopped fizzing before he held it out to her, but then she had realized that this was a way of being polite: the match fizzed faster when it was shaken about like that, and so the length of time she had to spend waiting for it to stop fizzing was cut down a bit. (Not much, though.) Afterwards he put the matchstick back in the box. She was just getting used to this when, after the chicken noodle soup, Graham suddenly started singing her a Scottish song: *ah that and ah that* or something kept coming into it. She had not asked him to do this, and she could not remember now what had led up to it. The song had a lot of verses, and after each one there was the chorus, which was almost all *ah that*, and after each chorus Jenny had said 'Jolly good, Graham' in a that-*was*-nice-thank-you tone of voice, but he had held up his finger each time and charged on with more stuff about *raptures sweet* and *ah that*. What made it worse was the way he changed key about once a line without noticing. But it had not been very loud, and there were not very many other people in the café, and of these only a few turned round to watch for long. She was just about over *that* when the spaghetti came and he at once started eating it in a funny sucking manner that got a good deal of the sauce on to his face. It was not bad manners, though; it was just that, as with the singing, he was eccentric, which was not surprising after he knew so much about chemistry. (Some of what he knew he had found time to pass on to her later.) All that had bothered her, apart from beginning to feel sick with the effort of not laughing, was the fear that he might suddenly realize other people might not like him sucking the spaghetti, and feel embarrassed. But he had not done so. And the film was very interesting, all about a poor Indian family. Half-way through the father died and the mother and son went to live somewhere else. It had been silly to expect there to be any love in it. And Graham had enjoyed himself during the early and middle parts of the evening: he had done quite a lot of laughing, which Jenny liked to see, feeling rather as she felt when her father laughed, that it was doing him good. Then came the moment when, on the slightly round-about drive home, Graham had stopped the car, saying that it was a fine night and what about a breath of fresh air?

Without actually saying anything, she had done her utmost earlier on to remind him of the conditions agreed on when he asked her out, insisting on paying her share and backing this up by having dressed as hard not to kill as she could, short of frumpishness: a loose high-necked blouse, a skirt she had never felt nice in, flatties, and her hair done in what Fred had called housekeeper style, parted in the middle and drawn back across the ears. She had also been careful about things like her topcoat, retreating from him when she put it on and tearing it off as if she had been getting ready to jump off a bridge to rescue a person from drowning. And now here she was, faced with a breath of fresh air which she could see no polite way of avoiding.

She scrambled out of the car before he could come round and get to work on helping her out, then led off, doing a sort of Girl Guide march in her flatties, towards a lodge and a stone gateway on which a light was burning nice and brightly. Beyond it she could see the start of an avenue lined with trees.

'Shall we walk along here a wee way?' Graham asked.

A wee way was just what it was going to be, in fact a teeny-weeny way. 'Won't anybody mind?'

'There's nobody living in the lodge as far as I know.'

'Who lives in the big house? I can see it up at the end there. A lord or something? Won't he have footmen and things about?'

'Och, no.' (She had never believed before that Scotsmen really said *Och*. Perhaps singing the song had brought it on.) 'It's a nurses' home now.'

'It must have been marvellous to live here before it was a nurses' home, mustn't it?'

'Why do you say that?' He was near her in his shapeless overcoat.

'Well, you know. All those servants, and the suits of armour, and the swords on the wall, and the paintings. Rather like Julian Ormerod's house, only much more –'

'None of that kind of stuff would have done you much good if you were one of those servants with half an attic and your keep and a housekeeper driving you to and fro fifteen hours in the day.'

She glanced at him, surprised by his sharp tone but not by what he had said. She had noticed recently that there was always another point of view about things she had thought quite straightforward and obvious, a more mature point of view, obviously, than her own, because it took hers into account and hers did not take it. This did not disturb her; what did, as they stood on the grass verge of the avenue looking at each other, was the nerviness in his manner that she had felt ever since leaving the cinema. It was like someone getting up courage to make a grab, but she thought somehow it was more than that. She said: 'I hadn't thought of that part. I was just thinking of the lovely gardens, and the lily-ponds with goldfish in them. And the stables. And the roaring log fires in the winter with all the dogs sitting round. Just think of the Christmas dinners they must have had.'

'If you were on top it was an excellent system, no doubt. The whole thing was organized for you to enjoy yourself.' More gently, he added: 'I wouldn't mind one of those Christmas dinners right now. That spaghetti doesn't stay with you very long.'

Jenny laughed. 'You poor thing, why don't you take me back to Dick and Martha's and we'll have some bread and cheese and cocoa?'

'Don't let's go yet.'

Keeping an eye open for him, she looked out over the fields. A view like this as near the middle of her own town would have shown her, if not rows of small neat houses or a scatter of prefabs, then chimneys and shops and administration buildings with bright lighting on their outsides. Here there was nothing but country, with just a few yellow glimmerings that she supposed might be farms – did they still use candles there? And instead of the sound of machinery in the distance, things being shifted about, men working together, there was only the drone of a car and the sound of a branch moving in the wind, a sound that reminded her of the opening of doors in creepy films.

This corresponded quite nicely with Graham's next move, which was the grab she had been expecting but which had more than she had expected in the way of silence, abruptness and even efficiency. He got her firmly enough in a sort of diagonal lock, hanging on to one shoulder and bringing her round by pulling politely at a bit of the other hip. The kiss itself was not too bad as regards mouth and skin and so on; they seldom were in that way; that was not really how they differed. In that case it seemed only decent to carry on now for a bit. But one thing had the habit of leading to another, and often before you knew where you were too, and although she could put up with this thing all right she knew she would not like the other much, and the one after that would have nothing to be said for it at all. And this would be so whichever branch the things took, whether he got more amorous or more sentimental, and one of the two he was soon going to get or she was a Dutchman, and she had never been a Dutchman yet, anywhere near. Added to all this (which she had come to know so well that it went through her mind in one go, like seeing a picture you saw every day), he was shaking a little, holding her too tight, muttering endearments too fast, kissing her greedily, as if he was making the most of something he was sure would not last. Well, he was right there. As a start, she let her mouth go completely dead instead of half dead, and that turned out to be enough by itself: he let her go. 'I'm sorry,' he said. 'I'm sorry.'

'Sorry? Whatever is there to be sorry about?'

'But I had to do it. Just the once I had to do it. Not to have done it ever would have been too much. You beautiful creature.'

'Graham, I can't have you apologizing for kissing me, there's no sense in it.'

'I'm apologizing for kissing you when you didn't want me to.'

'But I did want you to.'

'You're making it worse, I could tell you didn't. Oh, you were very good, you did your best, but I always know. I've had many opportunities to acquire the knowledge, as you may well guess. It's a long time since I could fool myself over that. I know I'm unattractive. Not just not attractive. Unattractive. A positive quality.'

'Please don't say any more, let's go back.'

'A great British prime minister once remarked that the people were divided into two nations, the rich and the poor, and in effect that these had no knowledge of each other. One might say the same, perhaps, of those who live in parts of the world where segregation by races is practised. But these barriers, or the reasons for them, belong to a part of our history which is fortunately passing away. There is one barrier, however, which no amount of progress or tolerance or legislation can ever diminish. I'm talking about the barrier between the attractive and the unattractive, and if you think I sound as if I've got this learned off, so I have, pretty well. As I said, I've had plenty of time to think about it.

'Unless you sit down and do have a real good think about it, you can have no conception of the difference between the lives of those who look like you and those who look like me. No doubt you and I are extreme examples. But, you see, the whole pattern of our thinking and feeling is just miles apart. Our hopes and our ambitions and the chance we have of making them come true – that's the important one – well, they move on totally different levels, they almost go in opposite directions altogether. You think I'm talking about sex, don't you? Well, so I am, but we'll get on to that properly in a minute. I just want to say first that it applies to friendship as well. Haven't you ever noticed that groups of friends and associates tend to, I'm not saying always, but there is a distinct tendency for the attractive to congregate and the unattractive likewise, wouldn't you say? Why do you think I see so much of the Thompsons, for instance, so much more than Patrick does? It's not that I like them any better. Look round any community like a masters' common room where the association isn't purely voluntary, and you'll see the duffers marking one another out. Like very small men getting together, a mutual defence system. Or any minority. That's what we really are, the duffers, a minority, nothing so grand as a nation. Most people are passable, after all. But it isn't all that easy, is my point, for a duffer to make a friend of an attractive person. There's me and Patrick. We're friends. And you're maybe going to mention those mixed pairs of girls you see going round together, one pretty and the other ugly. But does that really happen often? Don't we notice it because it is so rare? And I'd suppose it was often a kind of manhunting tactic when it does occur; you may know. I'm not saying it may not be a genuine friendship in many cases. After all, friendship includes charity. But there's no charity in sex.'

'Do stop, Graham, don't tell me any more, there's a dear.'

'I won't say anything that may shock you, rest assured of that.'

'It's not that, I just don't want you to upset yourself.'

'Upset you, you mean, by showing you something you'd prefer not to think about. No, that's not fair to you. And why should you think about it? It can't ever concern you. Let's say, then, that I won't be upsetting myself if I merely say out loud what I've already put into words for my own benefit hundreds of times. I never have said it before, but I'm going to finish it now, and I'll apologize later for keeping you standing here in the dark listening to it. There's not much more.

'You can't imagine what it's like not to know what it is to meet an attractive person who's also attracted to you, can you? Because unattractive men don't want unattractive girls, you see. They want attractive girls. They merely *get* unattractive girls. I think a lot of people feel vaguely when they see two duffers marrying that the duffers must prefer it that way. Which is rather like saying that slum-dwellers would rather live in the slums than anywhere else – there they are *in* the slums, aren't they? A great German thinker once said that character is destiny. Appearance is character and destiny would have been better, and truer. What use is your character to you if you can't turn it into your destiny? When I see someone as pretty as you I always start off by thinking that it's going to be different this time, this time she'll have to want me a little because I want her so much. That's the bit I always do fool myself about, at first. Perhaps it isn't normal, all this wanting. But I wouldn't know, would I? I haven't any way of knowing. What's sex all about? How would I know? And not knowing that means not knowing a lot of other things, too. For instance, literature. I used to be a great reader at one time, but not any more. *Eternity was in our lips and eyes, bliss in our brows' bent.* It's not envy. Simpler than that. What's he talking about?'

'Oh, Graham, for God's sake don't go on. I can't stand it.'

'I've finished. There isn't any more.'

'You mustn't think those things.' She went up to him and put her arms round his bulky shoulders and laid her cheek against his. 'It won't always be like that; you see.'

'I have upset you. I didn't mean to.'

'There's bound to be someone for someone as nice as you.'

'Someone, oh yes, there'll be someone.'

'Someone nice.'

'Yes, someone nice, that's it.'

But there had not been anyone at all, let alone someone nice, for Miss Compton, who as Jenny sat over the *National Geo-*

graphic was giving Grace a tremendous amount of information about what the recent frosts had done to her rose-bushes. True, old Compton was not really very nice herself: her constant buttering-up of Miss Sinclair, her just as constant stream of complaint, cancelled out most of her genuine kindness. She might have been nicer once, though, before she realized that there was not going to be anyone at all for her. The sound of the school bell made Jenny jump; she found that her eyes were full of tears.

Three minutes later she had driven the last of Ia into its room and got all of it seated at its desks. The children looked at her expectantly, including two who were still panting violently after their exertions in the yard, but not including, of course, the rather more than two who were not quite up to looking at anything expectantly.

'All take out your writing books and pencils,' Jenny said. 'All, Michael, that means you as well. And quietly with those lids, now. Are there any broken points? All look and see. Right. Can anybody tell me the date? What's the date today? Hand, Ava. Quite correct.' She wrote it on the board in her neat upright script. 'All write down the date. And remember, a capital letter for the month. Always a capital letter for the days of the week and the months of the year ... All finished? Now, you remember what we had in nature study this morning. About the squirrel and the nuts. Do you remember, John Brewster? Good. Well, I want all of you to try and think of a sentence about the squirrel and the nuts. You remember how the squirrel finds a lot of nuts that have fallen off the trees? And how he makes a hole in the ground and puts the nuts in the hole to eat in the winter when there aren't any nuts on the trees? Now, all of you try and make up a sentence about the squirrel and the nuts. Think carefully. The squirrel ... finds ... Yes, John Whittaker?' It was only the second time that term he had put up his hand, except for toilet requests, so this event would have to be noticed; she reminded herself to ask him to tea some day soon, when she felt on top form again.

His eyes wide, almost circular, he said eagerly: 'Squirrel and the nuts, Miss Bunn.'

Michael Primrose gave a loud snort of contempt. 'That's not a sentence, you soft thing,' he called.

'Not quite right, John. And, Michael, first of all you are not to interrupt, and then you are not to be rude. Say you're sorry now to John. Nicely. That's better. Now you give us a sentence.'

'The squirrel finds many nuts which he puts in a hole in the ground so that when the winter comes he can go to the hole and dig them out and eat them and so, and so, and so, he eats the –'

'Stop, I can't remember all that. Let's go back to the beginning. *The squirrel finds many nuts.* All right. That'll do nicely.'

While she was writing this on the board, there was a tap at the door and a small boy of five came in. He frowned at Jenny, as if he was trying to remember why he had come. After a time he said in a husky voice: 'Miss Bunn.'

'Yes, dear?'

'Miss Bunn, the head teacher wants to see you. She told me to come and tell you. I was down there. In that room down there.'

'Thank you, dear.' Hastily she wrote up another sentence to keep the children busy, then raced down the stairs. What had she done? It must be something pretty serious for Miss Sinclair to call her out of her class about it. Or was it someone ill at home? At the door of the Head's room she straightened her jacket, took a couple of deep breaths, tapped and marched firmly in.

'Ah, Miss Bunn.' Miss Sinclair was standing behind her desk with her hat on, gathering some typewritten lists together. 'Help yourself. I must take these over anyway so you're not driving me out.'

'I'm sorry, Miss Sinclair . . . ?'

'Oh, he didn't tell you. I thought two ideas was rather a lot for Harold to carry in his head at one time. You're wanted on the telephone.' She pointed to a small table at her side.

'Oh, thank you, but you're sure . . . ?'

'Of course, of course, you go ahead.' The door shut.

It must be from home. Making sure that she had plenty of breath, she said: 'Hallo, Jenny Bunn speaking.'

'Hallo, Jenny. Georgie Porgie here.'

Now, what with the surprise and the wanting to laugh, she had no breath at all. 'Oh, Patrick . . .'

173

'Look, please don't ring off until you hear what I have to say. I'm sorry about the other evening, talking that load of ... insolent rubbish about *involved* and the rest of it. Not that I'm withdrawing what I said about me being involved. In fact I think I can prove it if you'll give me the chance. Will you? Don't ring off.'

'I wasn't going to. I don't know. I tell you straight I couldn't do with another of those talks.'

'No talks. Chats instead. You know how you like chats.'

'Well, I don't know. What's this proving thing?'

'It won't be as bad as it sounds. I'm just going to show you I can be the way you want me to be if I put my mind to it.'

Jenny put her tongue out at the phone. This was talk stuff. 'How are you going to do that?'

'I don't know. It'll take me a long time, probably. I don't care, though. Can I come round tonight? I'll be as good as gold. Can I?'

Yeah, Mr Big Heart-Throb, she thought to herself, good as gold as long as it suits you and not a second longer. The anxiety in his voice sounded only partly genuine; he was fairly sure she would do as he wanted. After all, everybody else obviously had, sooner or later. For a moment the temptation to bang the phone down was very strong: he would react hundred-per-cent genuine to that. But not only to things like that, not quite. There had been no acting in his last look at her the other night.

'Hallo, Jenny?'

'All right then ... but you're not to expect anything, mind.'

'Fair enough. You'll never regret it, miss, I promise you. Well, that'll get me through the rest of the day all right. I need it, too. You've no idea how horrible it is here. I had to wait till it got extra horrible so that I had the choice of ringing you up or electrocuting myself in the Physics Lab, otherwise I'd never have had the courage. I thought of getting drunk to do it, but then I dismissed that from my mind. You ought to see them here, you know. Have I ever told you about Meaker? I will. He puts cotton wool in his ears so's he can't hear what people say to him. He's the only man I know who can tread on your foot and then *get away with* glaring at you for having it where he wanted to put his. And guess who's taking the sixth form party to the

Motor Show? That's right. Little old yours bloody truly. I know about cars, you see. I knew about them last year, too. I got rather ... tight then at those lager places they have on the first floor, missed the train and got them back late for chapel.'

By half-way through this Jenny was beaming. She could visualize exactly the expression on his face as he hurried on: energetic, eager, confiding, shrewd, enjoying himself, intimate in the cool scoffing way she loved. If only it was going to turn out that she had judged him too harshly, that he was just weak and had mad impulses and was unsure of himself in spite of seeming so sure and got his way too easily. Her face went stern for a moment when she thought of this, then relaxed again.

She was so absorbed in picturing him and following the run of his voice that she got a great start when Miss Sinclair came back. She said quickly: 'Look, I've got to go now. Keep safe. See you tonight. Good-bye ... I'm sorry, Miss Sinclair. I didn't arrange it or anything, it was a complete surprise.'

Miss Sinclair hung up her hat. 'A pleasant one, I imagine. There was nothing urgent about it, was there?' Her voice was preoccupied.

'No, nothing at all, he shouldn't have –'

'I hate sounding stupidly official, but this is supposed to be my room, heaven help us – I'm sure your caller didn't know that – and of course he was perfectly polite – but if you could just see to it that in future –'

'I'm awfully sorry, Miss Sinclair, I'll t–, I'll t–'

'Any kind of urgent thing is completely different and absolutely all right, naturally. Now that's the end of that. Before you go, how are those little 1a creatures?'

'I've left them, I'd better be getting –'

'Mrs Carter's next door to them, isn't she? They won't tear the place down. Though it might not be such a bad idea. Tell me, how's young Michael Primrose conducting himself, for instance?'

'Oh, wonderfully. He's the brightest of the lot.'

'I don't like that lad, you know. Capable of any iniquity. His mother spoils him in the most damnable fashion. An old-fashioned explanation, but I'm coming to like that sort rather, these days.'

'But he's nice as anything when he remembers to be. I know he can be a perfect little devil, but that sort –'

'He needs watching, I think. Still, you clearly know that. We never had that talk, did we? We will when things quieten down a little. I hope everything's all right, by the way? I thought when you came in here just now you looked somehow ... But it's no business of mine, I suppose.'

'Everything's fine, Miss Sinclair, really it is.'

Chapter Fifteen

AND it turned out to go on being fine for some months. Jenny went round to Patrick's flat so often that she began to notice how the old lady next door, who had a face like a tin box covered with skin, peered at her every time through the net curtain, but she soon cured that by waving and jumping up and down on the path. She was a widow, Patrick said, and Jenny realized that that must account for a lot. Of course, the pair of them did not only meet at the flat. There was the pictures, and the jazz sessions at the Ivy Bush, and a day at a race-track not far away by car where she won ten bob and bought them both champagne cocktails, and a Labour Party meeting with an M.P. down from London to speak on Kenya and Nyasaland and what people could do to help, and the dances (the best was the golf club dance – Patrick brought her a beautiful red rose to go with her slinky white dress and wide gold belt), and a wonderful day in London: they drove up on the Saturday morning and had lunch in the West End, went at her request to the Zoo in the afternoon and saw the new tiger cubs, had dinner at a real Italian restaurant with a marvellous fizzy wine that was *better* than champagne, and then went to a jazz club where the pianist was one of the three best outside the States, Patrick said. They did not get home until gone two.

She was rather nervous about introducing Patrick to her parents when they came down after Easter, but as it turned out things went off splendidly. Her mother quite fell for him, saying that he had lovely manners and a good job and that she could see it was a case. Her father said that he seemed a bit full of himself, but that at any rate he was a sight better than the fancy-necktie brigade at home who sat in his chair and read his evening paper when they called for her to take her jitterbugging till all hours, and that he personally had nothing against Jews, there were good and bad like everyone else. Jenny said that Patrick was not a Jew; her father said: 'You can tell by his name, lass. Schtundisch. German Jew. And you told me his mother's in the clothing business. The Jews run that, it's well known. Not that I'm prejudiced against 'em, mind. But it stands to reason. Schtundisch.' He muttered 'Schtundisch' to himself whenever Patrick was mentioned until about the Saturday evening, and each time Jenny's mother looked at him as if he was picking his nose. Actually it was only one of his ways, and happened with almost every new boy-friend: there had been Veelricht and Ullingheim and Lighlunt and Yohanstein and no doubt there would have been Tawmpzohn too if Dick was single. Jenny could see that her father rather liked Patrick, whom Robbie – and this pleased her as much as anything – said he thought was a smashing chap. Certainly Patrick could not have behaved better, asking about Robbie's school career and prospects, calling her father 'Mr Bunn' and her mother 'Mrs Bunn' a lot, and being interested all through a long monologue from her father about road accidents which he gave on the Saturday evening in the George.

'You wouldn't expect much different, though, these days, would you?' he ended up. 'The age of showing-off, that's what we're in. Most folk are damn fools and never more so when they're on the road, young idiots in silk scarves and suède shoes . . .' He broke off, looking thoughtfully down at the suède shoes Patrick was wearing, and Jenny felt her mother, on her far side, shift in her chair and seem to get bigger.

'Do you do much driving yourself, Mr Bunn?' Dick asked.

Jenny was frightened: this would surely bring up the hearse-driving thing, and while Patrick already knew and she would not have minded Dick knowing (she had told the Thompsons just that her father worked for a car-hire firm), the sight of Martha, who was listening to the talk with her smiling face and her head on one side, gave her a chill. But it was all right: 'I've done a fair amount,' her father said coldly, 'and what I'm saying's obvious whether you drive or not.' He did not much care for Dick, saying that he was up to no good, but not what sort of no good, and that he was the kind of lad who lost the Labour Party votes every time he opened his mouth. Dick had said he thought Jenny's father was a wonderful character, which was not quite right, and the way he called him 'Mr Bunn' which he did at least as often as Patrick, was more the sort of way a lord or lady would show how democratic they were by doing.

Dick went cheerfully on: 'If they weren't so crazy on their H-bomb and missile nonsense perhaps they'd have a –'

'Of course, there's tight-fistedness back of it all,' Jenny's father said. 'They just don't feel like laying out the cash on new road schemes, see? Short-sighted, I reckon. Ah, you can run yourself into a pack of trouble by watching the pennies too close.'

He paused again, staring into his pint, and Jenny was frightened again, this time that he was going to remember, and therefore tell, the acid-drop story, but Dick came in with: 'They don't watch the pennies much when it comes to armaments, I've noticed. This new –'

'And bloody lucky for you and me they don't, my lad. Let me tell you things are bad enough without chaps with beards and silk scarves marching to and fro with their banners and petitions and I don't know what all and showing off. And the women in those tight slacks and not bothering with soap and water. And their hair looking as though they'd been dragged through a hedge backwards. And talking of watching the pennies, you're in the chair, my lad. Patrick and I bought one and now it's your turn. Mine's a pint of the strong. It's not up to what we get up home but it is worth the extra few pence.'

While Dick collected the glasses and Martha went off to the Ladies, Patrick leant over, grinning, and said something to Jenny's father, who grinned back. After that he never again muttered 'Schtundisch' to himself. Jenny's mother said to her in a low voice: 'They get on all right, don't they? It's nice to see it.'

'Oh yes, I knew they would.'

'I can see your father's taken to him. You mark my words, Jennifer.' (The *Jennifer* was to pay Jenny back a little for being called *Popsy* – an old family nickname – by her father in front of Patrick, in spite of all her entreaties beforehand.) 'You'll be at the altar before this year's out; just you see.'

'Ssshh, you're getting ahead of things, Mum, that hasn't come up at all, we've never even mentioned it.'

'You will, though, when the time comes. I said to myself straight away, *That's the one*, I said, as soon as I saw you together.'

'I don't know that he's the marrying kind.'

'What? You should see the way he looks at you. He fair worships you, does that boy. Oh, I've never been proved wrong yet.'

Jenny hoped her mother was right, but made a point of never thinking about marriage, feeling it might be unlucky to do so, and concentrated on enjoying being with Patrick. The weekends were the best, naturally, plus the high-spot on Wednesdays when the pair of them went out to the jazz at the Ivy Bush after a meal at the Old Toll Bridge Café. Patrick often wanted to take her to the roadhouse instead, explaining that his mother's dress shop was doing good trade and she often sent him a bit of cash, but Jenny said he had no need to impress her now. At the Ivy Bush they chatted between numbers to Ron Hammett, who was on tenor sax, and Bill Stokes, who was on bass, and eventually Ron asked her if she would like them to play anything. She requested *Utter Chaos* and this choice went down very well – she still remembered how awkward it had been when she asked if they knew *Jailhouse Rock* her first time there. Ron made a little speech about her over the mike when he announced the number, calling her 'a beautiful young lady' and a lot of silly rot like that. Patrick sat there next to her with a real after-me-with-the-cream look on his face, and some of the fellows stamped so hard on the floor that the landlord of the pub had to come up to complain. And the music, although it did seem to have very little tune to it, was terrifically good; she found that with Patrick to explain it to her she was really starting to like modern.

But the best part, as always, was just sitting there with Patrick on one of the wooden benches, one of her hands in his, the other holding her half of cider – he had packed up trying to make her drink gin long ago. They had a couple of dances, although the floor, which was only bare boards, prevented the actual dancing being much fun, and the main thing, as they admitted to each other, was just the excuse to get into a clinch. Most of the time they sat and listened, or perhaps went down to the bar for a drink in more comfort and to play one of their games. In the smasher-maybe-and-dud one – she had told him how she divided men up, and he had got very interested straight away – she would guess the rating of some girl there or that they knew, and he would say how it stood up to a man's rating, and then he would start with a man. They hardly ever differed more than one point; for instance, Patrick had guessed Julian Ormerod as smasher and Jenny had put him at upper maybe. He had not been seen around for quite a time, and when they rang him up one night there was no reply, so perhaps he had shut his house up and gone to London. The other game they played was the yokel one, in which the idea was to have a conversation where you added nothing to what the other person had said without actually repeating it. If you did either you lost a point.

A boy with a two-tone sweater of which both tones were nasty separately and together, and a beard, came over and asked Jenny for a dance. She refused politely. Then a big girl who looked a little bit like a man came and asked Patrick. The girl had asked him the week before as well, and he had said he had a bad leg. This time he took a pull at his pint of black and tan before answering. 'I've got a bad leg again,' he said. 'Sorry, Sheila.'

The girl gave Jenny a glare. 'It was in great shape just a minute back, in that blues. What happened to it all of a sudden?'

'It wasn't a blues, doll; sixteen-bar chorus. No, I've got to watch the old limb, I'm afraid. I'll let you know when it's better.'

'Well, that's just great. Don't I call you, you'll call me. Okay, I got the message.'

'Who was that?' Jenny asked.

'That was Sheila. She's . . . I've run into her here a couple of times.' He looked as if he had just remembered he had a rich fruit cake at home all ready to eat.

'Is she a dud?'

Meringue and ice-cream and chocolate sauce lined themselves up next to the cake. 'My God, I'll say she is.'

Quite soon the Sheila girl found herself a fellow with a crew-cut and a black leather jacket who first of all threw her around in the dance so hard that their scuffing and panting and crashing pretty well drowned out a solo Bill was taking on *Lullaby of Birdland*, then pulled her into a corner and kissed her so hard that Ron had to come over and tick them off, and to finish up with swept her out of the door so hard that she tripped over the threshold and thumped with him into a door on the opposite side of the stairhead. 'Ar, I likes to see they young folks enjoying theirselves,' Patrick said, quoting from the yokel game.

'Is he going to ... you know ... do you think?'

'He'll be lucky if he escapes with less.'

'But ... you know ... where?'

'Love will find a way. There's the towpath, and the common, and the woods, and the fields. Plenty of room.'

'But it's cold, and everywhere'll be wet.'

'If you really like beer, you don't mind drinking it in a hot smoky crowded bar at the wrong end of town.'

Jenny thought this over. 'You mean it's actually no more important to some people than drinking a glass of beer?'

'Except that this is harder to get and the beer doesn't have to like you and you think about this more and you're proud of it afterwards and you're not supposed to have it, I suppose it is like a glass of beer. To some people. Except that this is much nicer.'

'All right, I didn't say it was like a glass of beer, you did.'

Luckily, the band started playing again then, one of the loud quick dodging-to-and-fro ones. The room was really too small to hold all the music, especially when the drummer got excited, and he easily got that: there was one bash he was particularly fond of, using both hands and both feet, that was like being hit in the face. Everybody roared with delight every time he did it. Patrick, after going downstairs to get more drinks at the hatch, said the whole set up was an interesting sociological pheno-menon 'if that doesn't sound too much like Dick.'

'How do you mean, darling?'

'Well, look at this bunch of louts. And Ron blowing the best tenor I've heard outside London. What do they see in him and what does he think of them? And all this bloody nonsense on the walls.'

The bloody nonsense was paintings, unless they were coloured drawings, done straight on to the dirty yellow plaster. They showed very long thin Negroes, or at least people who were black in the face, at all sorts of angles and playing musical instruments of toy size – what was probably meant to be a trombone looked like a sort of sliding tin whistle. Why was that? Here and there were bushes and trees that reminded you of the jungle, as if the artist thought that jazz came from Nyasaland or one of those places, instead of from New Orleans in America, as Patrick had explained. Jenny was pretty sure that the jungle parts were by the same man that had painted the picture on Anna's wall, and asked who had done all the decorating.

'Oh, craps from that Art Club. Art and jazz are akin, you see. Anna had something to do with it. Stage-managed the whole thing, for all I know.' He lit a cigarette. 'Look, Jenny, I want to tell you about Anna. I can't be straight with you about everything, I don't think there's anybody I could be, I'm not that sort of chap I'm afraid, but I am bloody well going to be as straight with you as I can, straighter than with anyone else.'

And then it all came out: how he had known Anna was not really his sort, but he had made a pass at her when he was feeling low about his work; how they had never got on very well because of her temperament, but he had to admit she had her good points (as Jenny had probably noticed, hadn't she?), though she could be absolutely – well, never mind about that for now; how the business had dragged unhappily on until Jenny turned up, which had put paid to Anna immediately as far as he was concerned; how, anyway, Jenny understood these things; how much better he felt now that it was off his chest, by Christ. Very little of this was news to Jenny, and she was not all that convinced by the bits that were, but the main thing was that he had decided he must tell her. In return she told him a bit about Fred, and he was fascinated and made her promise to go into all the gory details some time.

When the Ivy Bush finished she went up and thanked Ron and Bill and told them how much she enjoyed their playing and how good they were, not that she felt her opinion counted for much but because she was so happy. Then Patrick drove her back to his flat and as usual they went straight up to his bedroom. He drew the curtains, dribbled a dirty shirt under the bed and came and started kissing her. Soon she seemed to be supporting all his eleven and a half stone as well as her own eight, and made the move to the bed. They lay down on top of the new gay bedspread that she had forced him to replace his old tatty tartan blanket with, and went on kissing.

Horizontal lovemaking was a great many things, one of which was its being a question of trust, and she had been very wary of letting it begin, but having done so she had not had to worry. When their kissing reached one of its climaxes she felt, as she often did, like making some little satisfied, appreciative noises, and was only held back by the thought, based on experience, that such noises were liable to act like a red rag, or rather a green light, to a bull. He slipped his hand down the front of her dress. It was odd how you could be so relaxed and yet feel energetic enough to scrub twenty floors one after the other, so far away and yet noticing everything as much as someone with high-powered contact lenses and a deaf-aid in each ear turned right up added on to their normal sight and hearing, and one skin fewer than everyone else and the kind of fingertips a piano-player or a conjurer might have. Lying in his arms, his mouth and hands so gentle now and his clean smell so wonderful, she realized that the things you read about being in love were not exaggerated or silly as she had once suspected, but quite literally true. It could change your whole life, it gave you all sorts of new feelings you would have no idea existed otherwise, about work and other people and the weather and the time of day and the look of the town and the thought of places all over the world you had never been to (they meant more : you could imagine all the foreign-looking buildings and the men and women crowding along the streets) and records and food and drink – stuff not really connected with love at all. She had a sort of permanent two gin and tonics inside her.

The kisses started mounting up again. They filled her with warmth and strength and confidence. Soon this turned into starting to feel like not keeping still and wanting to change over to a different style of breathing. It was always round about now that Patrick's hand made its next move, the one that would take it over the line they had drawn. He was reminding her of how he felt about her, or perhaps giving her the chance of showing if she had changed her mind. She removed his hand, a job that took rather longer than usual, which was natural and corresponded with how, without coming anywhere near altering her policy, she regretted more and more deeply having to draw the line. She knew he could tell how passionately she wanted him to make real love to her, and his never using this to try and persuade her, not really, made him even more marvellous. If this was courting, what would marriage be like? That was not a thought to dwell on. In a moment she whispered: 'Darling, what about me making a cup of tea?'

He sighed, but it was a mild, non-peevish one. 'Okay, beautiful.' She saw his face come back to normal from its heavy, drowsing look, sensing that he had travelled further away from the here and now than she had and so took longer to return. Well, men were meant to be more imaginative.

He grinned at her. 'How you manage to look as fresh as that and yet as if you've just ... got out of bed, it's a mystery to me. You make me feel as if I could edit Sallust and put old Gaiters right about the Labour Party and score a century before lunch for the Gentlemen and show Stan Getz how to blow tenor. Nothing like Jenny for that. Jenny for strength. Every man ought to have a Jenny supplied on his twenty-first birthday. Or perhaps ...' Jenny put her arms round his neck and kissed him. 'Don't do that again until we're downstairs, please.'

While she made the tea and Patrick got the record-player going, she thought about their bedroom sessions and how much rules and routine had entered into them. She knew how bad these were supposed to be, even though probably nobody would think to find fault with a rule that said you could not have more than seven meals a day or a routine that said you had a new dress and pair of shoes given you on the first of every month. But no doubt a rule-and-routine thing with kissing and so on had a lot wrong with it. She knew how much. On the other hand, the non-rule idea seemed by all accounts to have even more wrong with it. She could see the point of sex being *frank*, *free, and open*, as Patrick had unwisely put it to her once and as she had put it back to him again a couple of dozen times since. What was meant by the expression in practice was a frank, free, and open (and immediate and often repeated) scuttle into bed with some man; to tell them all to drop dead, however frankly, freely, and openly, did not count as that. After dwelling on the frank, free, and open enjoyment that would follow arrival in bed the story tended to fade away rather. At any rate, it stopped well short of later possibilities like a wedding followed five months later by a frank, free, and open christening, or a realization that while you were sitting at home knitting a pair of bootees the chap was off somewhere drinking scotch and lecturing some other mug about frankness, freedom, and openness. Patrick had lent her a couple of books that he said explained the thing better than he could, but she had not got much out of them, except that you had no chance at all with any of it unless you were sensitive and warm and proud and naturally aristocratic and heavy and dark (especially that), and not much of a chance even then. They were long books and very hard to find your place in.

Well, all that would come out in the wash or not at all. She warmed the bright blue-and-white-striped pot she had made Patrick buy to replace the old chipped brown horror, and took down the two floral mugs she had bought herself. With fresh paper on the shelves and in the drawers, a new frying-pan and milk-saucepan, and a proper set of rags and cloths for the sink, the kitchen was beginning to look a bit less like a slum. But there was still a way to go yet. It had taken her two whole Sundays to get the ingrained muck off the walls and ceiling and floor, and this had made the woodwork, which had obviously not had a paint-brush near it for years, look worse than ever in contrast. She had doubled the light from the electric bulb by washing it, so that you could now see every smear and smudge in the awful plastic curtains. She had not done too badly, though; even the bathroom was not all that depressing now. And it was like a little bit of setting up home to do it all, to get the sitting-room curtains and cushion-covers out on to the line, to cook Sunday supper for Graham and Patrick – who had put up no opposition when she suggested Graham coming too, or rather being allowed into his own flat – and to be told that her hot-pot and apple pie were the best argument for the north of England they had ever come across, except herself, as Graham was sweet enough to add. They had had a bottle of wine in that time, and the two men went on to some brandy, and Graham got merry and was an absolute scream about his schooldays in Dundee. She had admired him tremendously for the convincing way he said, round about nine o'clock, that he had to go down to the George to meet Thackeray and discuss some important College matters with him. Thackeray was seeing a lot of Graham these days; one Saturday Jenny had stayed so late without Graham appearing that she wondered if he might have a camp bed fixed up in Thackeray's room. The situation bothered her, but what was to be done about it?

She carried the teas into the sitting-room and perched on the arm of Patrick's chair while they listened to some of the new Miles Davis. Patrick did not react when, towards the end of a five-minute trumpet solo, she chipped in with some chatter. He sat there staring into space in a manner that did not suggest he was concentrating on the music. Perhaps he was having one of his depressions that he had explained about; they did not necessarily have anything to do with what was going on, he said. And somebody who was so lively so much of the time was bound to have his off moments. As her father said, you never saw the real man until people started feeling sorry for themselves. Well, nearly as her father said. She knew Patrick was half Irish; perhaps some of that Connell blood was making itself felt. It was well known that the Irish, like the Welsh, were Celtic and so more emotional than ordinary people, though not so mercurial as the French.

Her mind went back to the time she and Patrick, stopping at a pub on one of their Saturday drives, had come across some beer-mats with horoscopes on them. 'Ah, here we are. The Ram, that's me,' he had said emphatically, and read out from the mat: 'UP ONE MINUTE DOWN THE NEXT KIND AND GENEROUS QUICKLY VEXED. Rather good that, don't you think? *Up one minute* ... Pretty fair, you know.' When they went he seemed sorry to leave that mat, and while they stayed he had looked it over every so often, as if it was a letter from the Queen. Of course, astrology was a lot of rubbish – her father was right enough on that one – but there was no denying that that mat had been very interesting.

When the music finally switched itself off she thought she would try to get him out of his mood. 'Who was that girl tonight?' she asked.

'What girl tonight?'

'You know. The one at the Ivy Bush. Stella or something.'

'Sheila. What about her?'

'Who is she?'

'I told you, she's just a girl I've run into a few times round the place. Why? She isn't one of *mine*, if that's what you're getting at.'

This came out with a half smile, the less friendly half. She said quickly : 'I wasn't getting at anything, it's no business of mine. She's got a crush on you, though, hasn't she, teenage idol?'

'I don't know, has she?'

'Of course she has, silly, anybody could spot that a mile off. You've no call to be modest about it. I'll give her this, she's got good taste.' Jenny laid her head on his shoulder for a moment. 'I can see it's going to take me all my time, keeping you out of their clutches. *Dear Evelyn Temple, my boy friend is very susceptible* ...'

'Whose clutches?'

'Well, you know, darling, everybody's, the lasses'.'

'I'm not in anyone's clutches, thanks very much.'

'That you are, Patrick Standish. You're in mine, aren't you?'

'Oh yes, I'm in yours all right.'

'Good, as long as we're clear on that.'

He sat up in the armchair, turning towards her like a schoolmaster very well might, particularly one at a political discussion who has some figures he knows will make mincemeat of the other fellow. 'Look, what makes you think I'm in people's clutches?'

'Oh, for heaven's sake, Patrick, I never said you were.'

'Because if you want a complete account of my dealings with Sheila, such as they are, I'd be happy to give you one.'

'Oh, honestly. What would I want that for?'

'You seem to think . . .'

'What? What do I seem to think?'

'Well . . . that you can sort of run me, decide who I can talk to and who I can't. As soon as I happen to run into a girl I know you start weighing her up.'

'Yes, and I've weighed up Miss Sheila Giant-Chin and I've decided you can talk to her as much as you like. What are you making a fuss about her for? I thought she was meant to be a dud.'

'There's one thing in her favour, anyway.'

'Has she got a bedridden gran she looks after, then?'

Patrick pushed his fingers through his hair. 'She's quite a good sort, that's all, which is something, not much, I suppose, but still, mustn't be too hard on her, poor old Sheila's not too bad in her way, not too good, either, now you come to mention it, but that chap in the leather jacket certainly seemed to . . .' He gave her a startled look. 'Hey what the hell was all that about?'

'No idea, I was just trying to give you a boost. Now just you wrap up. Another boost coming.'

She gave him what was intended as an affectionate kiss, but almost as soon as it landed it turned into a soft deep gently pushing one, and very soon after that her chest went hollow and she started wanting to tremble, as if they were still stretched out on that blessed counterpane. It was quite an effort to keep still. Oh, they were playing with fire all right. Just as well that, while she was feeling like this, they were playing with it down here, instead of in that ruddy gunpowder factory upstairs.

Patrick, at any rate, seemed to notice nothing out of the ordinary. 'My little pep pill,' he said, 'my little bottle of champagne.'

Later, as they sat in the car outside the Thompsons – so late, in fact, that an image came into Jenny's mind of Graham reading Thackeray to sleep with a Noddy book – Patrick said: 'Sorry about all that Sheila nonsense. I just seem to get like that sometimes. Try and put up with me. This business with you and me, it is a bit of a strain sometimes.'

'Oh, darling, don't I know it?'

He went straight on: 'Jenny, I've never said this to anyone before, and I haven't quite worked out what I'm committing myself to, but never mind, I'm going to say it anyway: I love you, I really do, honestly.'

'Oh, I love you, Patrick.'

They had a terrific kiss lasting about ten days. Then Jenny said shakily: 'I must go in now, dearest. Oh, Patrick. Ooh, are we doing anything at the week-end?'

'Hell, I forgot to tell you, I've got to go up and see my mum. But I'll see you before then.'

'Mind you don't get into any mischief up in London.'

'I'd like to see anybody get into mischief where I'm going.'

Chapter Sixteen

'FATHER's got 'em, father's got 'em, and this is Able Seaman Arthur Jackson telling you for why. And nobody better qualified, by Christ. I've given up binding about it for a long time now, of course. Yeah, because it don't do me no bloody good, that's why. Can't think what got into me to make me come out with it. Moment of bleeding truth, I suppose. Nobody more surprised than I was. *Never cared for it much all these years, have you, girl?* Just like that. *No Arthur*, she says, *I'll be straight with you, you've always been straight with me*, she says, *I never have.* What would you do chums? *I put up with it because it's not right I shouldn't, but if you want the truth I've never had a atom of pleasure out of it right from the very first time. Well, where does that put me?* I says. *Well*, she says, *you know a bit more now about asking silly questions, don't you?* she says. Yeah. Mind you, in this life you get plenty of silly answers without asking any questions at all. Some people wouldn't have taken it as calm and gentle as I done. Foundation of married life? Don't make me laugh.'

'You. You over there. That's enough. If you don't shut up right away and clear off I'll call the police. Go on, get moving. Sharp.'

'Ger, who do you think you're ...? Come out here where I can get at you. Ger, if you wasn't such a tich I'd kick your teeth in.'

'If you're not away from here in one minute I'll call the police.'

'Think you own the bloody street, do you? I know your sort. Nothing but ... just because I ... bloke can't ... no wonder they ... bloody whist drives ... same wherever ... modern way of ...'

The voice faded and Jenny heard the slam of a front door across the road from her bedroom. Able Seaman Arthur Jackson had read the news two or three times since she had first heard him on her first night in the house, but never so angrily or so frighteningly, nor so late, as just now. And yet he had not said anything in particular that was frightening, and he had obviously not been going to climb up a drainpipe to her window. What was it, then? And what was she nearly but not quite reminded of? No, better to forget it. She curled herself up more tightly in bed and tried to think about Patrick. Being kissed by him was getting more and more extraordinary all the time. If it got much more extraordinary still, say ten per cent more than it had been an hour or so earlier, then, she said to herself, she would have to make sure he only kissed her with his headmaster and Miss Sinclair watching, otherwise there was no knowing, or rather plenty of knowing, what would happen. But she did not really believe any of this. Then she remembered what she had been half reminded of.

She had been in a bus in the rush hour at home, sitting on the rear seat that faced the nearer pavement. During one of the bus's frequent halts it was slowly overtaken by a big man with white hair and a red face, wearing a shabby ginger-brown topcoat and carrying an American-cloth shopping-bag. He looked hard at every woman who went by, even the older ones, wandering to and fro across the pavement, turning round, sometimes stopping altogether. All the time he whistled *Here Comes the Bride* very loudly, with lots of trills and grace notes and tricks with the time like a gipsy fiddler. He eventually moved out of earshot ahead, then the bus got going and passed him (its engine was too loud for her to hear, but his lips were still pursed for whistling), then at the next halt she heard *Here Comes the Bride* gradually coming into earshot again and approaching, reaching and passing her as before. Then the whole round had been repeated, twice.

She had relaxed during her think about Patrick, but now she curled up into a ball again. She felt completely alone: everything was quiet and there was not even enough breeze to stir the curtains; she could not get out of her head that something was after her, something nasty. When she probed at this with her mind she could find nothing more, just something nasty, after her. What? And how could anything be after her? What sort of thing? Oh, stuff and nonsense, it was time she got over her childish fears.

But in the semi-darkness the furniture of her room, which had such a pleasant welcoming look when she came on it by day, seemed squat and heavy and just dumped down where it was, as if she was in bed in the corner of a warehouse. And however hard she peered at the mantelpiece, where she kept the pot-plant with the yellow berries and the big crayon drawing of the Nativity which Michael Primrose had done her for Christmas and the calendar with a photograph of a different cat for every month of the year, she could make out very little of them beyond where they were. There was a sudden horrible moaning voice in the distance; after a second she recognized it as the hooter of one of the new diesels on the fast London run. What time was it? The house was absolutely still, so much so that when she had slipped her dressing-gown on and sneaked downstairs for a sly cup of cocoa, it came as a great surprise to find Dick sprawled out in the new wine-coloured chair by the kitchen stove, smoking a cigarette in one of the several ways he had, not the almost-unbearable-enjoyment one nor the old-smoking-campaigner one, but the wise, thoughtful one, as if he was the only person in the whole world who understood exactly about cigarettes.

'Well, well, well,' he said heartily. 'Look what the wind's blown in. Miss Bunn in person, eh? And what brings you down here at this advanced hour, might I inquire?'

Jenny tried to get more of herself inside her dressing-gown; she had had it since she was fifteen and nowadays it barely reached to her knees. 'I couldn't sleep. I didn't think anyone would mind if I came and made myself a drink. I didn't know there was anyone still about, I'm sorry.'

He heaved himself out of his chair with a sudden energy that almost drove his pointed chin down on to the hot-plate of the stove. Perhaps he had been drinking. 'I'll get it; you sit yourself down in the warm. It's quite nippy, you know, after all it's only – what are we now? – end of April. And you've hardly got anything on, have you?' He got a lot out of this question, but staying official. 'Now what's it to be, champagne or cocoa?' He laughed so hard at thinking to say this that his face started objecting to having been made to laugh so hard, sort of stop-I'm-killing-me touch. When it was all right again Jenny said:

'Thank you very much, but I don't want to put you to any trouble.' She hoped the cocoa-making would not be turned into a ceremony; she could just see herself pulled on to his knee to be fed cocoa in spoonfuls and be told about Goldilocks, only in this version Papa Bear would turn up by himself at the moment when she started trying out his bed, having seen his wife and child off that morning for a fortnight at Whitley Bay. When Dick, gesturing like an Italian tenor, had said that of course it was no trouble to be of service to such a fair maiden, and had clopped off into the scullery, Jenny sat down in one of the older chairs, drawing her feet up under her and pulling her night-dress into a sack over her knees, so that she was swaddled from the neck down. Apart from the new chair, she could see a couple of the other new things that had so mysteriously begun coming into the house since about Christmas. There was the wood and glass and white-painted-iron room-divider, which was not dividing any rooms at the moment because it was against the wall, but did make the room it was in seem less old. And in the same kind of way there was the nest of tables still in their nest. These bits of wealth had not gone along with any improvement in Thompson cooking. On the contrary, the line started by the lion-house haddock had grown so long that Jenny had lost count: only the cardboard chicken and the dirty-dog mince had stuck in her mind. More and more of her diet was made up of apples and buns and bananas she bought herself and hid in her dressing-table. Martha was evidently doing the minimum these days, wandering off to bed about nine and nearly always letting Jenny wash up in the evenings. She was a deep one, was Martha.

Either making the cocoa had taken it out of him more than usual, or he had been nipping scotch in the scullery, but Dick looked several years older when he came back. He gave her the cup and sank groaning into his chair, head in hands. In a wet-mouthed voice, he said : 'It doesn't agree with me.'

'What, that shepherd's pie we had?' Jenny asked with real surprise. It had not been too bad at all, washed down by a glass of milk and half a bottle of tomato sauce.

'No no no. Drink. Think I'd have more sense. Mixing them like that. Just because it's there. Just because it's free. He's well breeched, mind. Oh, he can afford it all right.'

'Who's this? Where did you go?'

'Oh, you know. Julian's place, over by ... Should see that cellar of his. Whole issue. Stuff from ... all over. What was that yellow muck? With the bloody ... Taxi back, too, cost me fifteen bob. Car's a-mashed up or something. Had to phone for a taxi.'

'I didn't hear you drive up. How long have you been in?'

'Good. Underful. Got him to drop me at the corner. Quiet as a mouse coming in. Don't want Martha down here with a hatchet. Bad press, everything I do. You think I'm all right, though, eh?'

'I thought Julian had gone away.'

'Been married too long. Trouble is, we ... Yeah, bees back now. I was getting worried, but it's just about fixed. Just got to see him once more and that'll be it. He gives you such bloody great drinks, you see. Not a pub measure, not even a double, nothing like that, glug-glug-glug, dirty great tumbler of brandy, not just three-star either. I must go to bed,' he finished off indignantly.

'Will you be all right?'

'Oh, sure.' He got up and stood in front of her, jerking now and then. 'What about kissing me good night?'

'Oh, I don't know that that would be a very good idea, would it? I don't think you're in the state to get the best out of it.'

'Oh yes I am, believe me, just the state. So are you.'

'Eh, that I'm not. I'm out of bed and all mucky.'

'You can say what you like, I don't care what you say like. What you ... say like. I've kept my hands off you all these months and I'm not going to start now. Not ... going to start ...'

He swayed diagonally forward and over her, his hands thudding down on the arms of her chair. His face searched for hers, weaving to and fro like a hungry fish. Jenny folded her arms over her bosom and dug her chin into her shoulder. She could tell now that he had indeed been mixing his drinks, with evidently a bit of coal gas thrown in for good measure. All the time she laughed in the jolliest way she could, searching her memory for all the funny things that had ever happened to her and getting a good ten seconds' worth out of the time the nice-ears boy friend had been helping her on with her topcoat – he was always full of manners – and in putting his hand up at the back to pull her suit coat down had put his hand up her skirt instead (by mistake). She tried to keep up the laughing when Dick found the edge of her mouth and began squirming his own along it, caterpillar-fashion, towards the middle, but laughing into someone else's mouth is hard work, she found, especially when their arms give way and they squash down on your chest. The broad tip of his nose was against hers, too, pushing it far enough round the corner to cut her air-intake by another fifty per cent.

She tried to focus her vision and found an immense eye staring into hers from behind glass like an optician's diagram in 3-D. It was the work of more moments than she thought she could spare to slide an arm out from under him, but having done so she lost no time in unhitching one of the earpieces of his glasses and giving a good twirl. The glasses wheeled sideways, swung from his other ear for an instant, fell on to his upper arm, and then bounced further into the distance as he grabbed and lunged at them. The last lunge, which sent them spinning under the table, took him so far off balance that he rolled off Jenny's lap, bringing the new tables crashing out of their nest for perhaps the first time, and ending up with his face quite dangerously close to the plate-warmer compartment of the stove. Too breathless for any more laughing, Jenny went and gave him a hand, so that he was just about on his feet when the door opened.

Martha Thompson was much too far behind cue to have caught the best of it, but all the same she was in plenty of time to see that something had been going on, and to form a pretty good idea what sort of something, too. 'Aaah,' she said with one of her beams, 'I thought I heard a little *party* assembling, and I see my intuition didn't let me down. How *nice*. So nice to find one's husband isn't entirely neuter, in spite of his convincing performance to the contrary, but *then* ... *well* ... of *course*, with our Miss Bunn so ready to hand, and in her charming dishabille, what more can one –?'

'You've got it all wrong, dear,' Dick said, looking stiff and dazzled. 'There was no harm at all. We didn't – we were just skylarking around, and I –'

'You can tell me all about it later, *dear*. Are those your glasses, cast aside in the heat of passion? Now you take them and run off upstairs like a good boy. Mummy'll be up to kiss you good night when she's had a little chat with Miss Bunn.'

'Look, Martha, you lay off Jenny, you're absolutely up a gum-tree if you think –'

'Come along now, sweetheart, or Mummy'll be cross. Mm. *Very* cross. Off you go and don't forget to clean your teeth and do your ickies. Chop-chop, now. *That's* right.'

'I'm sorry, Jenny.'

'It's okay, Dick.'

'Both the flipping lenses are cracked clear across, it'll be a week at least before –'

The door shut behind him. 'Ah,' Martha said. 'Now if you've got your breath back enough to talk, perhaps we can just ...' Her voice died off and so did her beam. Her chin twitched in a way that made Jenny feel sorry and afraid. 'What's the idea? Aren't you having enough fun as it is? What's the matter with you?'

'It wasn't what you think, we were only just having a g –, a g –'

'I should have thought you were well enough fixed up with what you want without having to bring other people's husbands into it. Why can't you leave people alone? You can collect as many scalps as you like outside this house, that's no affair of mine, but, my God, you might have a bit of discretion, at least, never mind about decency.' Martha was blinking fast now. 'I can't see what you can have hoped to –'

'Dick and I were just fooling around just horseplay that's all and he tripped over and his glasses fell off and went under the table,' Jenny said in one breath. 'And I don't collect –'

'First I knew of it that Dick made 2 a.m. dates for horseplay. You'll have to do better than that.'

'Goodness, is that the time? But it wasn't a date. He just happened to be here when I came down, I didn't know he was here, honestly. I couldn't get to sleep, so I thought I'd –'

'Ah,' Martha said, starting to beam slightly again, 'so your boy friend, I mean of course your regular boy friend, your *chief* boy friend let you down, did he? – couldn't manage to finish off the evening so as to let you sleep the sleep of the *just*, so naturally you found yourself tossing and turning a little, and then what more understandable than that you should . . .'

Jenny had been pulling her dressing-grown round her and huddling as close as possible to the stove. Now she took a step towards Martha, who was leaning forward with her arms on the back of the chair where the kissing-and-glasses session had taken place. 'You don't honestly think I'd make a date with your husband in the kitchen at two o'clock in the morning, do you? Even if he asked me? And do you really think he would ask me, right under everyone's nose like this? And do you think I'd come? Honestly?' She finished this with a tremendous yawn.

'The hot blood of youth,' Martha beamed. Then she dropped her head and said in a conversational voice: 'Why don't you just go and live with him? I would if I were you. I don't see what's stopping you. Go on, what's holding you back?'

'Live with him? You mean –?'

'You know who I mean. Not Dick. It seems the obvious arrangement to me. Bond of common interest and all that. It's not much of an establishment, I grant you, but you'd soon put that right with your old northern know-how and your little housewifely ways, eh? You'd enjoy that.' Martha was moving round the room setting it straight, putting the tables back in their nest, tipping more coals into the stove, plumping the cushions with great thoroughness. Jenny was directly reminded of her mother, who enjoyed sitting down with a cup of tea for ordinary chats, but preferred to give her bits of advice, or at least her considered opinion of the latest boy friend, while she was on something else as well, tidying up, doing the ironing and so on. And anyone would have thought from Martha's tone that she was really trying to help when she went on to say: 'After all, it's common sense, isn't it? Young people like to be together, don't they? At least in the stage you are in at the moment. Gather ye rosebuds while ye may, remember? Or didn't they go into that sort of thing in the Presbyterian High School or wherever you went? Anyway – I'd be into that flat like a shot if I was in your shoes. Think of it: no more of those painful good nights in the –'

'I'll clear out as soon as I can.'

'*That's* the girl.'

'I mean I'll find another room.'

'But you've got another room, dear. All waiting for you. Two of them. I know there's Graham, but being the perfect –'

'You're only pretending, aren't you? I wish you'd stop. You know I'm not like that.'

'Aw ay, tha means tha's not going to stay here and be insoolted, eh, lass? Oop to thee, a course.'

'You are insulting me, but I'm not thinking of that. It's obviously going to be impossible if I –'

'Wait a minute, though.' Martha had straightened everything that could take any straightening and had got down to polishing the chromium towel-rail of the stove with a corner of her dressing-gown, a Chinese affair that had a lot of different-coloured stains on it. 'You don't seriously mean you're not sleeping with him, do you? Because if you're not then you're a bigger fool than I took you for. You won't hold him all that long if you do, but you'll hold him a damn sight less long if you don't. Mind you you'll come to it in the end. But if you're not –'

'What the devil has it got to do with you what I do?' Jenny said indignantly. 'You're as wrong as hell about me and Dick but at least he's your husband. You're like that horrible old woman who lives next door to Patrick who stares at me whenever I go in or out. You're just –'

'Yes, I expect I am. You get like that when you've no life of your own. Living for others, it's called.'

'Oh, I never heard such rubbish. You've got your home and your husband and . . .'

'And? Go on, and what?'

'Lots of women have just got that and they're perfectly happy.'

'How would you know? You think you could handle the whole thing, don't you? – putting on your smart little apron and getting going with your little wet rag and your polishing cloth on the house and Dick until they're both as bright as new pins, just like *Woman's Domain* says they ought to be. And of course a woman with plenty of time on her hands can afford to take up cookery seriously, can't she? – all those exciting new sauces and stocking the herb-cupboard and that marvellous Yugoslav recipe for badger stewed in white wine. Or there's always pottery and weaving, isn't there, and basket-making and flower arrangement? Or learn a language, so that when you go to Torquay in the summer you can talk Spanish to the natives. Or if you happen to be an outdoor type ... Thanks very much. You can leave a list of voluntary organizations and adoption societies on the mantelpiece in the morning. People have got to *do* something about themselves, haven't they?'

During this, which came out at top speed and fairly loud, Jenny hung her head. She had not been really serious when she teased Patrick about Martha being one of his, but no prizes would be offered for seeing that there was something of the sort on Martha's side. It was all part of the marriage and no-children thing, which was much worse. Jenny knew without thinking about it that there was no way of offering Martha sympathy and support. When the other woman had finished she looked up and said: 'I'll look for a new place tomorrow.' She felt inferior and dangerously ignorant.

'Oh, I shouldn't bother, you know.'

'But I've got to, after everything.'

'I thought we'd more or less cleared it all up. Besides, it'd be a bit difficult this time of the year, probably, getting someone in to replace you.' Martha was rubbing parts of her dressing-gown against one another where the stains were.

'I'd pay you a month's money, of course.'

'Now then, Jenny, you're not to *take on* so. You can't go round the place flinging month's moneys away. Whatever would your father think? You modern girls are so impulsive.' The beam had come back part of the way. 'You run along and get a good night's sleep, what's left of it, and everything'll look different in the morning. The thing to do with a problem is to sleep on it. I'm sure you've come across that in your reading, haven't you?'

'But I can't tell whether you believe me that I wasn't doing anything down here, and we weren't up to anything, Dick and me, because we weren't. Do you believe me?'

Martha almost shut her eyes to say: 'Of course I do. Don't you go worrying your little head about that. That's all over – finished and done with, as they say. Let's let bygones be – what is that word? Oh yes: *bygones*.'

It was plain to Jenny that she would never be able to drive Martha off saying everything was all right, not if they chewed the rag until dawn. And she could imagine just how sincerely unbelieving Martha would be if handed a month's money in lieu of notice, tomorrow or any morning. And Jenny did not want to move to a new place, to leave Anna and Dick, whom she had got to know. 'Well, that's nice of you,' she said, then added, because she thought somebody ought to: 'I'm sorry.'

'Granted as soon as asked, no offence intended and none taken I hope. Good night. Sleep well.'

Keeping tight hold of the banister, Jenny trudged upstairs. She felt as if she had just been released from a concentration camp or had spent twenty-four hours doing P.T. with 1A. More than any she could remember, this evening deserved to be over. But before she had finished snuggling down and getting ready to think hard about Patrick again, there was a quiet tap at her door and almost at the same moment she realized that someone was standing beside her bed. She had to work at it a bit before she could managed a proper shriek, because of being so drowsy, but she got there in the end. 'Who's there?' she said. It was what people said.

'Ssshh, it's all right, Jenny darling, it's me, Anna.'

That was another sort of thing that people said. 'What do you want? Oh, it's so late.'

'There was some sort of excitement going on downstairs, wasn't there? I heard things. And then my old friend Dick coming upstairs like a regiment.'

'Nothing to it really. Made a pass at me but he didn't really, and Martha thought he made a pass at me but he didn't really.'

'You were a silly girl to let him. You should have stopped him before he could begin to make a pass.'

'I'd like to have seen you stop him. And I told you he didn't really. He just . . . he didn't really.'

'Jenny, you're so inefficient, my dear. You've no idea how these things are conducted, or ought to be conducted. How terribly young you are. Have you learnt anything at all since you were sixteen?'

'Don't know, haven't thought. Can't remember what I knew when I was sixteen. Don't care.'

'Very little, I'm certain, and you know very little now too. But that's your charm, Jenny.' Anna, who was wearing what Jenny made out as the navy pyjamas sometimes on view at the two ends of the day, sat down heavily on the edge of the bed. 'You haven't grown up, and that makes you my favourite kind of girl.'

That old mercurial thing again. Anna had been at it consistently, if that was the word, all through the winter, had worked away as if she was getting conduct points for it, breaking off the clothes-showing session that had eventually come along with nasty things to say about the Protestant Church, throwing out of the window the bunch of roses she had bought Jenny as a peace-offering (she had said, but to make up for doing what?) after Jenny had put them in water instead of going on hugging and smelling them long enough, making Jenny walk out of a terrific musical at the cinema with her because it was too American, making Jenny stay to the end of a terrible non-musical (it had had all three bad things, being old-fashioned, foreign, and funny) so as to go on watching a chap in the row in front who was necking violently with a very young girl – 'she's mad about him, isn't she?' Anna had whispered, and Jenny had said it was disgusting, he was old enough to be her father, and Anna had said that was who he probably was. If Anna had made up her mind to be mercurial then that was up to her as a general rule, but tonight Jenny felt she simply could not do with anybody at all being mercurial, not this late. She said: 'That's nice of you, but I simply must go to sleep now.'

'Let me comfort you, you're so confused and unhappy.'

'No I'm not, I'm fine, honestly.'

'You're always so brave, but I can tell you're very disturbed.'

'I'm not in the least disturbed, I'm just dog-tired.'

'Being tired is your way of evading reality, you see. And I can't blame you. All that horrible universe of men, it's miraculous how we manage to survive. Just relax. Isn't it amazing how we go on taking things on trust year after year? This squalid business of the man and the woman, like deer in the rutting season, only our season goes on all the time and we don't stay in the same pairs as the deer do. That's right, just let yourself go. And it needn't be like this: ask yourself how we should get on if there were no men. We'd get on very well, let me tell you. What makes us so sure that men and women are basically attracted to each other? We don't know any different, that's all. Men are attracted to men and women to women – you've only to look around you to see this. It's nothing but custom and . . . the crudest biological necessity that stops us from acting on it. That's right, darling. You and your Miss Sinclair – I should like you to know how it sounds when you talk of her. Patrick and that flashy Julian person. Oh, it's so obvious. Let me tell you about the only person I've ever really loved.'

At this point Jenny fell asleep. When she woke up it was still dark and Anna was lying beside her on top of the bed and leaning over her and saying: 'But I've never forgotten her. I couldn't. She was the most wonderful person I've ever known. Gay and witty and wise and sensitive and . . . proud and passionate, so passionate, as you gathered. And so beautiful, with the most tremendous – I can't go into all that again. Whenever I think of her I simply . . . She was the only true free person I've ever met. Ah, these men with their sordid little egos and their great thick bull-necks and their red faces and hands and their pot-bellies and all that *extra* . . . and their huge flabby ears like an elephant or something – what do they know of love? For them, love's what they want to feel about what they want to do. Love, they don't know the meaning of the word. Oh, Geraldine, darling, why did you leave me? Are you awake, Jenny?'

'Er,' Jenny said. 'Look . . . I must . . .'

'I'm sorry, I was carried away, I forgot where I was, in the middle of this dirty ugly old town, I was miles away, somewhere warm and beautiful. She would have adored you, Jenny. I know because I adore you. Oh, how sweet you are. You smell sweet – there's honey along your forehead and at the edge of your hair. Oh, my April love. Do you know that painting, that lovely blonde with the indigo skirt and the sensual hands? She knew what it was all about. And so do you, though you don't realize it yet. So you do. Don't you? Oh ... just ... it'll be so ...'

Jenny took in very little of this lot, as of the previous two lots, because the inside of the bed was like warm mink that had shaped itself to her body, and she hardly noticed it when, still talking, Anna slipped an arm round her shoulders and nuzzled her slightly, but she noticed it very clearly when Anna's other hand started on some funny business with the shoulder-strap of her nightdress and elsewhere in that area. 'Hey, what you doing, what you doing?' she said in a high voice, trying to heave herself up in the bed.

'Oh, Jenny dear, just relax, please, Jenny ...'

'Relax? What for? What have I got to relax for? What are you lying on my bed for? What's all the – what are you fiddling about with me for?'

'Oh, if you only knew how much nicer –'

'Oh, aren't you horrible? Get off me. And how is it *you're* the one who's always on at *me* to be grown-up? What about you, what about you. You're like a horrible little girl. Go on, get *off*.'

'You're a nasty little bourgeois child, prim and prissy and ... I don't know how you can bear to be so –'

'Don't care. Get out now and leave me alone. You're horrible.'

'Nasty, how nasty you are, and you don't realize ...'

'Oh, you're so horrible, the horrible way you –'

'Nasty little creature, nasty little prig, ugh, you just –'

'Oh, why are there so many of you, all being horrible?'

'You nasty –'

'Get *off*.' Jenny had been trying to push Anna off the bed, but she was handicapped by being half-pinned down under the covers, and by the way the mattress sloped down towards the middle, so that getting Anna off was like rolling a beer-barrel up a ramp. 'Go *away*.' She shoved and shoved without making any difference before remembering a good anti-man idea that could always be used once there was no need to worry about his dignity, and what was anti-man ought to go well enough here. Stiffening her fingers and using her nails to the utmost, she gave Anna a tremendous tickling under the ribs, the kind that started hard and went on hard. Anna lay there for a bit, showing that she was against the whole idea of tickling as well as pretending not to be ticklish; then she began jerking and squawking, 'Go on, get off,' Jenny said, her teeth set. As she said it she wondered about her breasts. Why was everyone so interested in them? What was so special about them? They were just ordinary size, after all, if that, and average shape. Why did everyone have to go on as if the word had got round that there were actually three of them?

Anna struggled away. 'You nasty little bitch,' she whispered loudly, sounding really angry, much angrier than over the roses or the too-American musical, and went on to use some words that Jenny had thought were only used by rough drunk men, or rough men, or men. 'What you're holding on to isn't a gold mine, you know,' she said then, a big, all-in wrestler kind of shape against the window; 'but the song-and-dance you make, anybody would think there'd never been a virgin until now. You don't know a thing; you know' – more rough-drunk-men stuff – 'you're so ignorant it isn't true. You wait, you'll come crawling back to me in the end, just you see, you'll be begging for mercy.'

'That'll be the day,' Jenny said, remembering it just in time before the door slammed. She gave a real hippo yawn and snuggled down again, quite surprised in a way not to find Able Seaman Arthur Jackson on one side of her in the mink and the *Here Comes the Bride* expert on the other.

The real part of the evening had ended a long time ago, and it was the most wonderful thing that had ever happened to her by far. But it was not the only thing there was, not in the way she had imagined beforehand it would be the only thing. Her feet wandered slowly down the bed. She thought about Dick and how funny it was that one time you thought all men's mouths were the same and another time they all seemed different. Patrick's and Dick's were as different as an oversized mouse's and a miniature rhinoceros's would probably be, although a scientist would say that one man's mouth was very much like another's. She pulled the bedclothes over her shoulder and put her hand under the pillow. About Martha she now understood the early going to bed. Unhappiness used up energy faster than anything: after Fred told her about Madge Bennett she herself had hardly been able to keep her eyes open as soon as supper was over for weeks and weeks. That was straightforward enough; but where had Anna got all that stuff of hers from? Jenny spread her fingers. She had thought somehow that love with Patrick would make everything stop, but in fact everything seemed to be going on in much the same way as before, to put it no higher. She must be growing up a little to be able to see that and not mind much.

Chapter Seventeen

'What sort of girl is she?'

'Well, you know, old man. She's just a girl really, I suppose. The sort of girl one runs into in London.'

'What sort of girl's that? I'm just asking for information, mind you. I don't seem to run into girls in London.'

'You don't? You should try it some time. Easiest thing in the world. Absolutely nothing to it.'

'If you know where to go,' Patrick said.

'Knowing where not to go's nearer the mark, I'd say. And the old brain-box will see you right on that one. For instance, I've never found Camden Town underground station actually chock-a-block. And I can't say I'd send the questing stranger hot-foot to the House of Commons dining-room. Nor the Oval. Lord's is a different kettle of fish, of course, – try one of the tourist fixtures or the Cambridge match.'

'Thanks, I'll remember that. You were going to tell me about this Joan woman.'

'Was I?' Julian looked puzzled. 'Yes, I suppose I must have been. Well, there she is, you see, very womanly and all that, lots of hair and shoulders and legs and what-have-you. Very jolly creature, you'll like her. Not much background, I'm afraid.

Plenty of foreground, though. You two should get on like a house on fire. Pity you've got to dash off to see this female relative of yours. Joan won't much fancy playing gooseberry. If it comes to that.'

'Oh, I shan't be taking off until very late. My mum'll have a cup of cocoa and a résumé of the last couple of months waiting for me whatever time I arrive.'

'Not that I want to persuade you to stay, you being committed elsewhere and all. I may be old-fashioned but I welcome these monogamous tendencies in the younger generation. Reassuring, somehow.'

'Mono something, anyway. Gamous is putting it a bit high, I'm sorry to say. Oh well. What do these girls do for a living?'

'They sort of model, if you ever heard of such a thing. Oh, I don't mean the 48–18–38 sort people always seem to be reading about in newsagents' windows. Nothing like that about them at all. They model clothes. At least that's what the other one does; Susan. Poor dear's a bit needled at the moment because the types she normally works for have just gone bankrupt. Incidentally, don't ever run away with the idea that bankruptcy's a joke like mothers-in-law and lumbago. Actually they aren't jokes either, come to think of it. I remember the Receiver saying to me, *To what do you attribute your failure?* and I said – oh, two large liqueur brandies and the bill, please. Yes, well I don't want to bore you with all that.'

'You are married, are you?' Patrick asked.

'Rather depends where I am. Think I'm right in saying I'm only unmarried in Mexico. It appears they don't recognize a Mexican divorce in the State of New York, and a Reno divorce doesn't go down all that well in the Motherland, not the kind I had anyway. The D.A. in New York explained the whole thing to me once, but I'm a bit weak on some of the details now. Awfully helpful chap, that D.A. He was going to marry one of my wives so he made it his business to go into all the ramifications. Then there's Italy, of course. I rather fancy I'm a bigamist in Italy, but they don't extradite for it as far as I know.'

'What's our time-table going to be exactly?'

'Well, I thought we might look in at one or two of these joints where the ladies remove their clothing for financial reward, and then we could stroll round to this flat of Susan's and Joan's for drinks and a couple of rubbers of whist.'

'It sounds unbeatable as far as it goes.'

'By the way, I've let it be known that you're a business man, Patty. Joan'll be nicer to you if she thinks you're that. Nicer than if she knew you were a schoolmaster. Of course, she'd be even nicer if she thought you were in films or TV, but I decided you wouldn't know enough about that side of life to carry it off.'

'I don't know anything about business either.'

'Make it up, then. She won't ask you any questions once it's established you can't get her a job or introduce her to someone who can. And for God's sake don't get carried away and say you can, or she'll never leave you alone.'

'I might not mind that.'

'You'd mind the way she wouldn't leave you alone over a thing like that all right. You take my advice and stick to export and import of chemical fertilizers. And furthermore you're not supposed to not mind strange girls not leaving you alone, are you? You're supposed to mind it like hell. Well now, let's throw these down and withdraw. No no, Pat, that's absolutely out of the question. This is my treat. You'll have plenty of chance to be extravagant later on. Not much chance of not being, in fact.'

The afternoon was fine, and where they were going first was only round the corner, Julian said, so they decided to walk. Patrick felt slightly nettled. Here he was, wearing the new dull-green tweed suit and American tie, fresh from a marvellous session at the wheel of the Jaguar and an expensive lunch, on a bright spring day in London. Oh, and in love. And what was he finally going to do with all this? Take it down to mum's on the last tube after an expensive evening with Julian and this Susan and this Joan. There would be nothing left of any of it by the time he reappeared tomorrow evening to pick up Julian, whom some policemen had recently told not to drive for a little while, and take him home. The only point of real interest lay in the impending encounter with this Joan. He hoped that her foreground would indeed prove plentiful, in order that his proposed experiment – seeing how unhappy his internally imposed vow of fidelity to Jenny could make him – might be transacted under conditions of appropriate rigour. He bucked up somewhat at the thought that being in love did not only stop you doing things, it also testified to a certain emotional refinement which, like thrift, courage and veracity, he had often suspected to be foreign to his nature.

His spirits rose further still at the sight of a shop window in which, under the regulation *Books & Magazines* in green neon, were displayed copies of *Kamera, QT, Model, Line and Form,* and other leading journals in the field. Inside, perhaps a dozen browsers were to be seen, looking as various and as respectable as any random sample of London's manhood. Patrick regarded them with understanding and sympathy. Julian paused long enough to shout affably 'Ah, you dirty lot, you dirty lot' through the doorway, an action which alarmed Patrick in the same way as, though more directly than, the other's suggestion during the morning's car-journey that he, Patrick, might like to put on the back of his head the fifth of November mask kept in the glove compartment for just this purpose and drive with his head out of the window: 'quite fascinating for the chaps you overtake.' Patrick hoped with some force that no little stink-bomb or itching-powder japes were scheduled to enliven the evening.

'Shouldn't have done that really, I suppose,' Julian said now, catching him up. 'But I never could resist that sort of thing. Remind me to show you a book I've got at home that absolutely caps the lot in that line. One of these things printed somewhere in South America by types who didn't know English. Full of girls with swelling broasts and firm bollies and exquisite long logs wearing frilly French knockers. Oh yes, and breathing *Oarling* into fellows' ears. Went a bundle on *o* for some reason. Trouble is it rather spoils you for the other stuff when you're trying to take it seriously. Keep being reminded of the old rounded bottocks and such. Here we are. Now let me do all the ordering and paying; we can settle up afterwards.'

They passed between two Sikhs who were gazing at the admirably forthright photographs in the entrance arcade and reached a small uncarpeted foyer where an open book lay on a card-table. Patrick wrote Dick Thompson's name and address in it, noticing that, in general, admission seemed restricted to persons from the industrial north of England. Beyond a flimsy curtain was a squareish, low-ceilinged room with a small stage at the far end. On one side of this a bald man was playing an electric organ, quietly but not quietly enough; on the other a tall depressed-looking Negro was assembling a drum kit. Above a dado of plastic that a drunken or lust-rheumed eye might take for wood in the poor visibility now prevailing, the walls were decorated with pink and purple nudes, large of areola, recalling in their elongation the style favoured by the decorator of the Ivy Bush jazz room. There was a bar. It had red illuminated panels distributed on some random-selection principle between and among its shelves, but bottles too. Julian and Patrick joined the couple of dozen men sitting on folding wooden chairs near the stage. There was a feeling of mild good-fellowship, like that at the start of a motor-coach trip.

A waiter came up to them. The cast in one or other of his eyes made him seem to be interestedly watching both of them at the same time. He gave a smile of fearless candour and said: 'Afternoon, Mr Holmroyd,' or something very like it, without making it clear whether this was a mere phonological variant of Julian's surname or a true alias.

'Good to see you, Percival,' Julian said, giving him a pound note. 'Now what about a nice bottle of scotch, all done up with that funny lead foil stuff they use to seal it with? I promised my grandson I'd collect it for him.'

'Right away, Mr Holmroyd.' With another warm biaxial glance Percival withdrew, swinging his arms a lot.

Julian looked at his watch, which had a sunken, overgrown look among the hairs on his wrist. 'See some action soon,' he said to Patrick. 'There isn't all that much of it, though, none of your donkey acts I'm sorry to say. Don't want to raise your hopes unduly. Ever so decent and British Legion here.' He gave a semicircular nod at the rest of the audience, all of whom, again perhaps in deference to managerial requirement, were wearing dark suits and neat white collars.

'Good,' Patrick said. 'Too much action wouldn't do for me.'

'Ah now, Patty, don't ruin my conception of you by telling me you like to have something left to your imagination.'

'No, for Christ's sake, but there's something basically contradictory about these dos. So I should think, anyway, never having been to one.'

'Try enlarging on that, as the a said to the b. But don't get too basic or you'll leave me behind.'

'Well, it's just that it's no good if they make me want to get up on the stage with them because I wouldn't be allowed to, and if I don't start wanting to get up on the stage with them what do I think I'm doing here?'

'You mustn't be so either-or, Pat. There are all sorts of very jolly in-between states, believe me. Next thing you'll be saying it's immoral for girls not to wear diving-suits in the street if they aren't going to rush up and grab you. What can the stage do but present us with a selective and heightened picture of life? Ah, thank you most awfully, Percy.' Julian handed over much more money. 'And ice too. Whatever is the old place coming to?'

'Why don't they have tables here?' Patrick asked.

'I'm not too sure, but I rather fancy they were more trouble than they were worth. And they weren't worth much trouble. People used to sort of hide behind them, I was told. Percy, is Denise in the show today?'

'Ooh no, why, didn't you know, Mr Holmroyd? She's having a baby.'

'Really? How extraordinary. Simply can't depend on anything any more, can you? Come on now, Patricius, have a nice big drink, it'll buck you up. Just in time, too.'

The lights began to dim in a jerky, uncoordinated manner; a great saccharine growl came from the organ and a slow-motion paradiddle from the drums; a spotlight skidded to a halt at the junction of the curtains, which parted long enough to allow the passage of another bald man and a glimpse of various sections of presumably female flesh. They had a miscellaneous, unorganized look.

Patrick took a long draught of whisky and water. The incrementary bald man fiddled with the standard and flex of his microphone, uttering cries of rebuke, protest, and appeal that, all unamplified as they were, must have carried clearly to every corner of the room. His irritation readily communicated itself to Patrick. What he had seen beyond the curtains, he considered, was much like what one might expect to pick out by swinging an electric torch round a women's public bathroom in Camberwell during a power failure; more like that, at any rate, than what he had been promising himself in the way of warm golden and roseate convexity, softly rounded limbs and so forth. No doubt this Joan bint was going to have an inch-high forehead and a ginger moustache, and so ruin his experiment utterly. At times like the present it often seemed to Patrick that sex was just something that happened in his own mind, no more relevant to anybody else's bedroom habits than a passion for ballistics would be to a man playing cricket. The man with the microphone had started using it to tell a story about a friend of his who had got his finger caught in a mangle. Patrick took another pull of whisky, more angrily than before. The rest of the audience, now somewhat augmented, roared perfunctorily, subsided as the story-teller withdrew and the organ got loose again, settled finally into the judicial seriousness of a W.E.A. class all ready to be told about E. M. Forster. Talk of personnel difficulties and the suitability of arts graduates for technical administration was slowly abandoned.

The curtains were pulled aside and it was all right. The onslaught of so much thigh and midriff and breast, indeed, represented a kind of plunge *in medias res* that was bound to overload a man who, like Patrick, had only experienced female nudity at the price of direct personal involvement. For a minute or two he was happy in an unreflecting, undifferentiating way; then his spirits began to fall, taking their first and biggest knock when he noticed that none of the dozen or so girls could properly be said to be naked at all – wherever he looked there was spangle and sequin and jolly little cone and ever so cunning triangle or in some cases what did triangle's job just as well mind you but was actually star or chinese lantern shape or dirty great question mark hahaha well you might as well make it a bit artistic like while youre about it thats what i say show a bit of imagination if you can and if you cant well whats wrong with a touch of humour after all we arent in church are we.

And why were they all so tall, too tall for their width, as if they had been on the rack, and too tall for women anyway, and rushing to and fro like that as in an octuple game of squash, and singing, and making their singing seem so important to them, and liking that sodding electric organ, and grinning and popping their eyes, and, hey – he realized it for the first time – apparently taking part in some kind of dramatic representation involving *motor-bikes* (a pair of goggles here, an oilcan there, armpit-length gauntlets on one, a black-leather-jacket bolero affair on another)? Mm? Just as he took this in, the singing ended on some definition statement about *my little hot rod*, of all things, the organ went into crescendo, the drums started a fluctuating roll, something happened to the lights and the girls stood relatively still. Perhaps they were all going to ... But then an object slowly came into view at the back of the stage and moved laterally across it. It was a red motor-scooter, looking nice and new, and on it sat a girl, to all appearance nude except for a white crash-helmet and knee-boots. Like all her colleagues, she looked as if she had been sprayed with transparent but matt-finish plastic. The whole thing was fully as exciting as looking up the word *naked* in the *Concise Oxford Dictionary*. Sex dressed up, in all meanings of the phrase, Patrick thought to himself among the applause and the restoration of the house lights and the final obdurate tumult of the organ.

'Drink that up and have another,' Julian said. 'Don't want to sell too much back. Well, what did you think? Very jolly, what?'

'Oh yes, good clean fun.'

'Exactly. That's the whole idea. Wouldn't do at all if it set a pulse beating in your temple and your knuckles whitening under the strain. What a lot of people get out of this sort of caper is a reassurance thing: you know, we saw the lot and there they all were prancing about and we didn't feel a flicker, must be pretty normal kinds of chaps, mustn't we? Same sort of thing goes for Monroe and Bardot and that lot – sexy without being stimulating, so there are all those curves and black stockings and stuff, and all that propaganda, and here we are feeling just cheerful and benevolent, jolly impressive and normal of us, what? Of course, it wouldn't be the thing for most of our fellow-members and guests if there actually were some real nudity here. They want a demonstration of how clean and straightforward and entertaining and part-of-a-spending-spree and good-fun-for-all-concerned sex *really* is, not all those peculiar old other things they're liable to suspect it may possibly be when they read the

News of the World, or pass a girls' school at playtime, or cut across the common last thing at night. Ah, you want to be taken out of yourself when you're on a day out in London, don't you? So don't let's have anything that's going to remind us of anything. That's where all that motor-bike stuff is so frightfully clever. Put those girls in cardigans and wool gloves and nylons and shiny waist-belts and you'd need tear-gas to quieten down this little lot. Here, let me top that up for you.'

'Thanks. I'm not sure I see all that. Surely a lot of these blokes would like a real no-holds-barred nude show.'

'Oh yes, they would if it suddenly happened and at the time. They might even vote for it if the ballot were secret. But it would disturb them no end to set about going to a thing like that in the full knowledge of what they were going to get. I'm talking about the solid citizens, naturally, not city slickers like you and me.'

'Good. What happens next?'

'Oh, they might be cowboys, or space-monsters, or flowers, or cricketers, or fish, or Hawaiians. Pure luck of the draw.'

They were fish. This was a bit better to start with, in that a pair of quite literally half-clad girls were perched on cardboard rocks at the back, being mermaids. Patrick did his best to stare at the better of these, determined to get his, or Julian's, money's worth, but his view was so frequently impeded by girls with lobster-claw gloves, girls with sea-horse hats, girls with sword-fish masks, that he soon just let them all welter reasonlessly before him, like a Sioux at Twickenham. The act was a good deal worse to end with. As before, the girls halted, the music swelled, the lights changed. Then a fat man lumbered abruptly in wearing an aqualung outfit over his pepper-coloured suit and shooting rubber-headed arrows at the girls with an imitation underwater bow. He missed them all. After weaving to and fro for a time and booming inarticulately inside his mask, he came to a halt in front of the curtain and removed his gear, bowing.

'Oof,' he said amid applause. 'Ee, I were getting into right deep water there. Ha ha, never been much good at coming up for the third time, I haven't. See, I'm getting old – when I get in the mood for some fried fish I have to go and buy 'em, ee hee, and wrapped up in newspaper and all. Ha ha, I'm telling you, my bow's no good any more. No, honest, no, I mean it, don't laugh. Ee, it's gone all slack has my bow. Ee, though, I remember when it were new ...'

'I'll arrange for something very unfunny to happen to you on the way back from the show tonight,' Patrick said, draining his glass. He spoke without heat, for with all his deficiencies the fellow had suggested to him a quite new form of Dick-hunt for development with Graham: subaqueous, the huntsman equipped with bows firing arrows with a short point, painful but non-lethal, dipped in some irritant poison, and hounds in the form of barracudas or – for a last great orgiastic jollification – piranhas. He and Graham, or rather he by himself, or rather not by himself, would be floating serenely above the silent tumult and the waterborne clouds of blood, dropping an occasional weary glance at the chase by way of the glass bottom of his craft, but spending more of the time in the embraces of the seagirls who ...

Julian gave the half-empty bottle back to Percy, getting some money in exchange, and they left. They went back to the Jaguar and drove through side-streets encumbered with newspaper vans and mail vans and taxis to a square in which no building was unmistakably occupied. A lot of the windows had names painted in gilt on a green ground. The club, if that was what it was, had no name or anything else at its entrance. Half-way down the stairs there was a cloudy mirror with the legend *Bare Old Jamaica Bum* across it, or so Patrick tremulously thought at first. At the foot of the stairs there was an oldish man who looked like an ex-boxer and redressed the balance of things by turning out really to be one; Patrick entered Dick's name and address in his book and went at once to the lavatory, where a pencilled message warned him that *This Town's women* STINKS WITH MEANNESS. Patrick threw some water over his face, which left it feeling hotter.

Back in the bar, which recalled a non-terminal bus-station café in size and décor, Julian was at the counter drinking whisky in the middle of a crowd of men who had perhaps moved on here immediately after the motor-bike number. Patrick drank whisky too. There was no sign of any stage or curtains or lighting apparatus, indeed of any apparatus at all. Talk of wool and welfare, pension schemes and profit-sharing and price-pegging, argil and zinc, roared away about them, easily drowning the strains of *Tea for Two Cha-cha* from the record-player. Patrick had just decided to wait for death when there was a silence, a man behind the bar shouted some news-item or slogan about a certain Mademoiselle Monique, the player came on at full volume and everybody turned his back on the counter. 'The type of lad you want for area manager,' someone was saying, then fell silent as a near-by door creaked slowly open.

Patrick could have sworn it was the door that led to the Gents and nowhere else, but he dismissed this enigma on taking a look at the young lady who now came sidling and wriggling into the bar, an entry perhaps intentionally given an extra loading of drama and significance by the inoperancy of the record-player, just then between tracks. She was a tall young lady, though without the corresponding attenuation Patrick had noticed in the motor-cyclists: rather the contrary. She shuffled about for a few seconds, smiling cheerfully, until the player got started on some-thing-else cha-cha. With that she began a sort of dance, advancing and retreating a good deal in relation to the men, and every so often flinging one of her many silk scarves over their heads, where it was fielded by the barman. Quite soon she was advancing more than she was retreating, and staying advanced longer, and not retreating so far. When she was down to one silk scarf it was plain that she was wearing only two widely separated garments. There was a lot of laughing going on, especially from the men she came nearest to, each of whom in turn made a ritual pseudo-grab at her. At one stage there was a sort of rip-cord or window-blind effect and the upper garment was abruptly no more. This happened just before she got to Patrick, who tried to put production into his lunge, to make it seem debonair and yet sincere or something. He did not know how he was so certain that she would linger in front of him, her face turning harder and sleepier, especially when in the event her face stayed the same and she retreated sooner and further than for some time. Then it was nearly over: the girl made a decisive with-drawal to the doorway; the ultimate revelation was as decent as it was brief, which was saying a hell of a lot; the lights went out; the door shut; the lights came up; the cha-cha dwindled; everybody about-turned to the bar. 'Yes, we all know an area manager needs drive, but it's the human qualities we're considering at the moment. That's the trend these days.'

'Well, that was more like it, what?'

'Yeah, too true, but what price your solid citizens now?'

'Oh, this is a different bunch altogether.'

'They look the same to me.'

'Well, perhaps some of them are, but they wouldn't find it too different from the other place. It's what you make it, like everything else. We'll just have another sap before we box on. No no, we can settle up tomorrow.'

They came out into brilliant early-evening sunlight that made Patrick groan inwardly. It set his memory spinning with model railways in the garden, sandcastles on the beach, rabbits on the common, lemonade at the corner shop, the band in the park, the cricket, the river, Sunday walks, picnics, blackberrying, mushrooming, Delius, Debussy, always with a girl there or in his mind, it seemed now to have made no difference which. And of course it would not have in those days, before he looked like getting started. What a girl made him think then had as little to do with her as what blackberrying and Delius made him think had to do with them. But that had changed as he grew up, as he began to see living as the art of the possible, began to push the blackberrying-Delius background into the background and treat the mind and body of a girl as the destined, reasonable foreground. No more insolent, incapacitating bewilderment.

Well done. Then why was it that he had to go back to blackberrying-Delius before he could find a time when he had felt all right? – not happy or fulfilled or in tune with things or any of that junk, but simply *all right*: able to sit down to work without yelling with hatred, able to enjoy the sun without worrying about making the emotional and reminiscential and cross-referential most of it, able to talk to a girl without being afraid of missing a chance. It was no use trying to connect Jenny with the sunshine, as he could have done instantly, without trying, if they had both been fourteen. He was in too much of a situation with her – adult, real, mutual, involving conscience, choice, action – for his mind to treat her as it liked. And a good thing too, eh? Hell, who said he had to feel all right, anyway?

Chapter Eighteen

'You never finished that story about the Japanese girl in the Lebanon,' Patrick said to Julian when they were in the car again.

'I didn't? Remiss of me, that. How far had I got?'

'Her manager had just asked you and the American to satisfy yourselves that the eggs being shown round by the maids really were eggs.'

'Oh yes. They were, too; we each cracked one to see. Well, what happened next was quite extraordinary.'

Patrick agreed very warmly when it was described to him, and went on to ask: 'So after that you felt you just couldn't press the matter, I suppose?'

'Well exactly, I mean what sort of chap is it who'd deliberately destroy a national institution? After all, there are standards, even these days, what? Actually before long all was well, because the most delightfully helpful figure came up to old Keeley and me just as we were getting out of the taxi back at the hotel and seemed to know in a *flash* exactly how we were feeling. Uncanny. Almost like a sixth sense.'

'I might have known you'd have fallen on what we'll call your feet in the end, you bastard.'

'One does develop a certain knack, I suppose.'

'I always think luck comes into it a lot. If that'd been me in the Lebanon that chap would have been a nationalist looking for a Westerner to set on fire. Or a tout for a Bible class. But you always get your end away, I expect.'

'Yes, I expect I do. Left at the next traffic light.'

'How many have you had, do you think, about?'

'Oh, I never count them. It's a bad habit, counting them.'

'You're probably right,' Patrick said, hooting to make an attractive back turn round. It had an unattractive front. Was that an omen? 'You know, all this women business often strikes me as being a power thing really.'

'Lot in that, of course. Though I can't help thinking that sex is pretty firmly tied up with it somewhere or other.'

'Sort of trying to prove something to yourself.'

'Succeeding, too, in the more fortunate cases. More and more incontrovertibly every day. It's the last one on the left. We can park just round the corner.'

At first glance there was nothing special about the stone steps leading up to the front door, but when he started the ascent Patrick found a number of unclassifiable anomalies in them, including a reverse-gradient effect that sent him back-pedalling to street level on his first two tries. 'Christ,' he roared.

'What seems to be the trouble?'

'Shouldn't have had that last sap.'

'You drove all right.'

'I was concentrating then.'

'Well, concentrate again now.'

'I was, I am.'

'Not hard enough.'

This time the gradient business turned itself round, so that Patrick found himself at the top of the steps with plenty of kinetic energy in hand, all but enough to take him head first into the door. He heard Julian laugh for the first time since he had met him. 'Ah, what's so bloody funny?'

'Er-er-er-er-er-er. You er-er-er-er-er-er.'

'Belt up, can't you?'

'*Her.* Just thinking of Joan's escort arriving for the evening, one of the rising young architects of Britain's post-war er-er-er-er-er-er.'

'Give it a rest, for Christ's sake.'

'Certainly sweep her off her feet if you can manage to point yourself in the right direction. *Her.*'

This went on while they ascended in the lift, which was so small as to render sexual assault virtually binding on passengers of opposite sexes, Patrick considered, and – this being London – not all that unbinding on guy-guy and girl-girl duos, too. They reached the relevant floor without offence but in varying humours.

The door of the flat was opened by a tall pretty woman in her early thirties wearing a grey woollen dress and holding a glass.

'Here you are at last, then,' she said loudly; 'we thought you must have fallen by the wayside. Julian, darling, it's lovely to see you, oh, how long is it?' She gave him a warm hug, carefully keeping her glass level. 'And you must be Patrick – that's right, isn't it? Now I'm going to kiss you too just to show you we – mm – we don't stand on ceremony here. Of course Joanie and I have been at the bottle already, getting the party spirit going, but honestly we've been so miserable, and *bored*, you wouldn't believe : do you know we actually got down to gin-rummy last night, can you imagine?' She lowered her voice and pointed with her shapely dark head to a closed door. 'Of course you know how she is – she can be very . . .' Her eye fell on Patrick and she went loud again. '*Patrick*; does that mean you're from the owled Emerald Oil, begorra?'

'Not me personally; my mother was.'

'Oh. *Does yah mother come from Oireland, cars there's* . . . Come on now, you boys, you've got some catching up to do. You're way behind the party.'

'I wouldn't say that, would you?' Julian asked Patrick.

'Oh, you've been knocking them back already, have you? I might have known. Some gilded haunt of sin, I bet. Well – Julian, there's just – could you come out to the kitchen a minute? – I just want to . . . Patrick dear, would you like to go and make yourself agreeable to Joan just for a minute? In there. Mind you help yourself to a drink. Excuse us, won't you?'

It was with feelings mixed to a fine *purée* that Patrick Standish, M.A.(Lond.), winner of the E. Alun Roberts Medal for Latin Verse Composition, threw open what was presumably the sitting-room door and entered, but he soon forgot all about that on apprehending that the mere collation of sense-data was going to use up all his attention indefinitely. The task of shutting the door behind him seemed to dislodge his brain to the point where it fell with a plop into a tank of neat whisky. His vision had darkened. Then he saw that there were venetian blinds on all the windows. He could make out white armchairs and couch with pink-striped cushions, light-coloured-wood tables and things, a television set which nattered and chirruped feebly while men in archaic costume twitched about on its screen; but he had no resources to spare for sociological observation. A girl was sitting looking at a magazine with her back partly turned towards him; she appeared large rather than small; she was wearing a black dress; she had blonde hair piled up at the back and top of her head. He made his brain swallow down these findings. When it could do no more with them he made his legs carry him towards her. On the way he came to the edge of a rug, which he surmounted as one might step over a sleeping Great Dane. At this point she looked up, and he saw that her foreground was more than adequate for his experiment.

'Hallo, I parry stashed a nowhere hermes peck humour speech own,' he heard himself say. 'June I haggle unction when donned ring gone oh swear.'

'Pardon? What did you say?'

He made a great effort, which was considerably helped by the fear roused in him by her appearance: nobly high forehead (he had been dead wrong in his forecast about that), wide-set blue eyes, firm straight mouth, decisive chin, delicate pink ears. She was staring at him with a contained haughtiness that sent his mind plodding back to what Susan had said and made him feel that he too knew how she was and could make a decent guess at the thing that she could be very. She looked like a brilliantly catty novelist and reviewer with a Ph.D. on Wittgenstein, and yet not quite, because no such person would have had a skin like that, a bosom like that, a dress like that. And not just not quite: not at all, because nobody with the whole lot like that would have dreamed of bothering with novels or Wittgenstein. It was worse than anything he could have imagined. He said aloud: 'I'm sorry, I can do better than that as a rule. Why don't we start with you being Patrick and me being Joan?'

'Eh? How do you mean? I don't like the sound of that.'

'Oh God. You know what I mean. I'm Patrick.'

'Pleased to meet you. I say, you do look queer.'

'I'll be fine in a few minutes.'

'Been drinking, have you?'

'A little, yes. Can I get you a drink?'

'Gin and italian, please. Over at the cocktail cabinet. With two cherries on a stick.'

While he saw to this she went back to reading her magazine,

or rather to looking at it, for no more seemed possible in such twilight. 'I hope that glass isn't too big for you,' he said.

'Oh, it'll do. What have you got yourself? Lime juice? Well, I hope it makes you feel better.'

'It will, don't you worry. I'll be like a tiger later on.'

'Yeah, big deal.' She dropped her head to her magazine, showing a converging pair of snowy partings among the fine gold.

'Jolly nice place you've got here.'

'Oh, it's all right.'

'Must cost a packet to keep up.'

'Quite a bit, I expect.' After a moment, she added: 'I don't have anything to do with that. My husband pays for the flat and Susan's husband pays for everything else, see? So I don't know what anything costs. I'm nothing to do with that side of it.'

'I see. You're divorced, are you?'

'Susan is, I'm not, not properly. Separated, though.'

'Is he anywhere around?'

'Who?'

'Your husband.'

'No,' she said, with contempt for his ignorance, 'he's in the States, went there last year. Couldn't stand it here, he said.'

And he knew what he was talking about, didn't he? Patrick thought. Christ, what next? 'I hope that car'll be all right.'

'Where is it?'

'Just round the corner.'

'Oh, it'll be all right. They don't bother much round here.' Then, reluctantly, she said: 'What sort is it?'

'It's a Jaguar.'

'Which? The Mark Nine?'

'I don't know, I'm afraid.'

'Oh, isn't it yours, then? It's the other fellow's, is it, Julian's? What sort have you got?'

'It's . . . a Sunbeam-Talbot.'

'Oh. Do you have it on the firm?'

'No, it's my own.'

'Most of my friends have them on the firm,' she said, with the sort of lift of the old proud head that he could hardly believe had not accompanied a limiting judgement on Villiers de l'Isle Adam.

'Well, of course,' he said with a laugh, 'the firm bought it and pay all the bills, but it's mine to do as I like with.'

'I see. That's having it on the firm really, isn't it?'

'Yes, I suppose so.'

'Do you have a chauffeur?'

'No, I like to drive myself.'

'Are you to do with films or TV or anything like that?'

'No,' he said, preparing to enjoy himself. 'I'm to do with export and import. Chemical fertilizers. Disinfectants. Pest sprays. Sheep dip. Cattle dip. Goat dip. Horse dip. Pig dip. Donkey dip. Mule dip. Camel dip. Elephant dip. Llama dip. Buffalo dip. Er . . .'

'Come on, there can't be elephant dip. How could you dip an elephant?' she asked vigilantly. 'An elephant's too big to be dipped.'

'Well, you don't actually dip him, you see, that's just the term we use in the trade for it. You more sort of hose him.'

'What's it for, the way you hose him?'

'To get out all the parasites and ticks and things.'

'Oh.' She turned a page as a ghostly chuckle came from the TV set. When she spoke again, he fancied it was with slightly less absolute composure than she had so far shown. 'Do you know Billy Bolton? He's in some export and import thing, he said, I think it was.'

'I'm afraid not,' he said, grinning buoyantly. In this girl's world a Billy-Bolton-type gambit, with all its risks of self-revelation, surely amounted to an offer of friendship. He repented a little of the dip anthology. Striving with almost complete success to keep his knees below crotch-level he marched to the window and heaved savagely about until he had disposed of the blinds, turned the television off with a flourish, snatched up Joan's half-empty glass and bore it away.

'Here, what are you doing?' she asked several times.

'Come on now, Joan, forget about that magazine and let's you and me get acquainted, huh? We're having a party, remember?' He dredged his brain for more of Sheila's idioms, feeling strongly tempted to throw in a go at the accent as well, but reasoned that Joan might well notice the difference: she had not let the elephant dip pass her by. 'I'll fix you another drink – you could use one, that's for sure. Here. Now you just come over and sit by me.'

'I'm quite all right where I am, thank you.'

'Come on, relax, will you? I want to talk to you about where to go for dinner tonight. Somewhere really good – you'll know.'

She rose to her feet and he saw with renewed alarm how powerful her hips were, how long and stately her legs. When she came over to him she increased in apparent size more than could be accounted for by the provisions of the laws of perspective. 'Got a light?' she asked. He stood up and gave her one, ordering a thrill of desire to pass through him. It failed to do so, which was annoying in a way, but then she sat down beside him on the white couch with no air of reluctance, nor of concession; not immovable after all, just on the line of least resistance. 'Do you know the Caprice?' she asked. 'It's nice there.'

'Isn't it?' He tried to visualize the contents of his wallet.

'Or there's that place, you go downstairs to it and there are big red candles. I've forgotten what it's called, but the man gives all the ladies a flower. He comes round with them.'

'I know where you mean. We'll go there instead if you like.'

'I don't really mind where we go. As long as I haven't got to have any of that foreign muck with all fat and things, and sauces.'

Coming as it did out of that austere, authoritative mouth, this observation pierced him with its acuteness and finality. As well go on respecting Robinson Ellis after Housman had finished with him as ever again see any virtue in foreign muck. 'That's right,' he said.

'I can't see why they have to mess about with decent food.'

'Spoils it, doesn't it?'

'They just mess it up.'

'Covering it with all those sauces and muck.'

'You don't know what you're eating any more.'

'All you can taste is the sauce and muck.'

'It all tastes the same.'

He was strongly reminded of the yokel game he played with Jenny. Another pang went through him, this time of boredom, pure, keen, and authentic as a boy's first love. The thought of Jenny was still there at the end of it. He remembered that he had an experiment to perform. The line on this was to model himself in the image, so far as this could be glimpsed, of Billy Bolton. 'Did anybody ever tell you how beautiful you are?' It was unlikely that nobody had thought to do so, he considered, looking at the elegant neck, the long sensitive fingers, the lavishly arched eyebrows. 'You're wonderful.'

Her eyes met his squarely for the first time and his brain slithered back into the retort of scotch from which it had been laboriously crawling. When she said 'Thank you, kind sir' he just managed to trap the thought that from some points of view he might as well have said '*Dies* in the singular Common we decline. But its plural cases are Always masculine' but that at any rate he had brought off (1) P – K4 without upsetting the board. Then things began getting out of hand again. There was a kiss of some sort, or an attempt at one. It was not repeated. While the rest of them – for Susan and Julian, whom he had not thought of for a long time, were in the room now – operated at 78 r.p.m. he struggled along at 16⅔, and with a good deal of mains-frequency fluctuation, too. At different times he had a drink, some coffee, some aspirins, a drink, something like aspirins but not them, a glass of milk, some coffee. At one stage he was lying down on a big bed with his head on a circular pillow, at another he was in a taxi. Things he noticed Julian saying included 'I sold out a bit sharpish when I heard who was making the bid', 'Oh, he's had a long day', and 'Criminal law's the stuff if you've got simple tastes.' He noticed Susan saying 'He looks terribly white' and 'Do you think he'll be all right when he's got some food in him?' 'Big deal' was all he noticed Joan saying. Then it was different: he was in a restaurant and beginning to feel better. He danced with Joan until she said everyone was looking, so they sat down and he told her all about the South African situation, his eyes filling with tears from time to time. In the taxi home he held Joan's hand and stared at the moonlit buildings wheeling by and felt all right. He knew that someone, either Julian or a waiter or himself, had telephoned his mother. In the lift he kissed Joan, but it was rather like kissing somebody over a garden wall. By toothbrush time he was telling himself he was pretty sober.

He lay in bed and watched her undress. As she finished

arranging her clothes and turned towards him he saw all of her for a moment, her slenderness and fullness, strength and grace. 'Let me look at you,' he said.

'You've looked.' She got into bed and turned out the light. 'What do you want to go and stare at me for?'

Her beauty made him want to cry, and that was all. 'Oh darling,' he said now and then. 'You're so lovely. Sorry about this. Do you think you could . . .?'

'You give your orders.'

'There, that's right, isn't it?'

'No.'

'Darling, I'm so sorry,' he said frequently. 'I love you so much, I wouldn't have had this happen for anything.'

'Let's forget about it, I'm tired.'

'Wait a minute, I think . . .'

'Oh, pack it up, I want to go to sleep. Why did you want to keep on at me to come back here if you're in this state?'

'How's that?'

'No good. Look, I said pack it up.'

'Oh Christ,' he said nearly all the time.

'Stop swearing, can't you? What was all this about you being sober now? Big deal. Now leave me alone.'

'Darling Joan, I'm sorry. Remember I love you, dearest.'

'Don't worry, you'll make some nice man a wonderful wife one of these days, I shouldn't wonder.'

Patrick spent an hour or two telling himself it was relevant to wonder where she got that from.

Chapter Nineteen

HE felt like an old book: spine defective, covers dull, slight foxing, fly missing, rather shaken copy. The colour from his cheeks, he saw from the bathroom mirror, appeared to have drained into the whites of his eyes. Shame, remorse, self-contempt, self-boredom surrounded him, deployed in depth. He forbore to analyse them: a survivor has other things to think about than the gross tonnage, secondary armament, and date of commissioning of the cruiser that has just sunk him. Of much more moment is the condition of his lifebelt. And as to that, Patrick decided, things were far from bad just now. Even an alcoholic cloud may turn out to have a silver lining if taken in time. He scrubbed his tongue with soap until it shone like a brisket of beef, cleaned his teeth a second time and hurried back into the bedroom. He got in beside Joan and turned her gently round to face him.

She awoke slowly, her eyes opening like a winter morning, her pink dry lips parted, the whole of her warm, ample, sleek, unfriendly. 'Ah, beat it, can't you?' she said with all her majesty about her. 'What do you want to go and wake me up for?'

He started kissing her. Her mouth was as sweet as fresh herbs.

'You'll be just like last night, and I couldn't stand another of them, I don't mind telling you, so lay off.'

He went on kissing her.

'All right, but I'll have to go to the bathroom first.'

'No you won't.'

'Don't you tell me, fellow.'

'Don't be long, then.'

'I'll be back when I'm quite ready, thank you very much.'

She kept her word, to the temporary detriment of Patrick's lifebelt, but in the end honour was satisfied, rather more thoroughly than he was, in fact.

'I'm getting up now,' she said after a minimal pause.

'Oh, don't go yet. It's so nice here.'

'You stay if you want, I'm going to have a bath.'

'I'll come and have a shave and talk to you.'

'You will not. There are times when I like to be alone.'

Patrick was nearly dressed when she came back wrapped in a big fluffy white towel. With much decorum she put on clean underclothes, black silk pyjamas and a rich-looking dressing-gown. He went up and kissed the nape of her neck, clouded with fine fair hair. 'Thank you,' he said. 'You're beautiful.'

She half-turned and smiled at him, tying the cord; then her face took on more than its usual weight of immaculate serious-ness. 'I hope Susan's getting up. I don't want to have to sit round half the morning waiting for breakfast. I'm hungry.' She went out.

While he shaved, Patrick thought about that smile. The addition of a look of sweetness to a look of intellect and to beauty was overwhelming. *'What Lola wants,'* he sang to himself, *'Lola gets.'* It made no difference to point out that the sweetness was as adventitious as the intellect, because the beauty was not. Beauty was not of an order of being in which it made sense to talk of adventitiousness. *'What Lola goes through the motions of wanting and oughtn't to have, Lola all too often gets.'* You could not have beauty that had a look of sourness or stupidity; we didn't call that beauty. Beauty without *real* sweetness or *real* mind was as beautiful as beauty with. It was only when it came to dealing with the two sorts that you saw a difference. Did you? Did he? In two or three years would there be much to choose between his relations with Joan if he were Mr Joan and with Jenny if he were Mr Jenny? *'What Lola imagines she might be thought original and interesting if she pretended to want, Lola will use her sex on some poor bloody fool to see that she gets.'* He wondered if he could persuade Joan that a nice lie-down after lunch would do her good. He could not go to his mother's now.

There being two bathrooms in the flat, Susan had had time to get herself ready to prepare breakfast before Joan could do much more than start to have to sit around waiting for it. Patrick found Susan, who was wearing a kind of skiing outfit without the skis, in the kitchen getting out crockery while Frank Sinatra sang with strings in the sitting-room. Susan looked up at Patrick, then grinned. 'You made a come-back, I see,' she said. 'I was afraid you were too far gone. Our Joanie wouldn't have liked that. Not after being talked into letting you stay.'

'I shouldn't think our anybody would have liked it any time.'

'Check, but the madam would have had more to say about it than most. You should hear poor old Billy Bolton go on about that side of her character. You know him, don't you?'

'Never even heard of him until yesterday. Can I do anything?'

'No, it's all done, really. I thought you were in the same line, you and Billy.'

'It's a big line, you know. Why don't you get Joan to give you a hand with this stuff?'

'Ha-a, listen to him. You've known her quite long enough not to have to ask that. Our Joanie likes to have things the way she likes to have them, and one of the ways she doesn't like to have them is to have to do anything. You ought to see her with a kid. My sister brings hers here sometimes, a real education that is. He peed on her handbag and gloves once, you never saw such a carry-on, trying to make Mary give him a good thrashing, going on about the gloves being irreplaceable because she got them in Rome, asking for ten quid to make it good, the lot. I'd have paid up like a shot and given him ten quid for himself as well, bless his heart. And bloody ridiculous, what kids drink, it doesn't stain, you'd need a magnifying glass. That's the madam for you, I'm afraid.'

'I don't know why you put up with it.'

'Well, you see, she pays the flat, her old man does rather, and then she's away a lot, Austria for the skiing, you know, and Spain or something in the spring, and week-ends in Paris and that. Oh, she's not so bad. One thing she does do, she'll always do you a facial or a set or a manicure any time, I'll give her that. That used to be her line, beauty, till she found she hadn't got to work.'

'Doesn't she do anything now?'

'Not what you'd call do anything, no.'

'Doesn't she get bored?'

'Are you kidding? It gives me the screaming hab-dabs just to see her sitting on her backside hour after hour – it's a good back-side all right, even I can see that – sitting in that chair, specially made for her of course, some poor bastard in the design line had it run up to her measurements, supposed to minimize fatigue they called it. She had a bed the same, only she got rid of that because the headboard wasn't right, cheap wood she said. He had to come and get it taken away, nearest he ever got to it with her around, poor sod. Oh yes, she's like that – *that man thinks he's only got to give me a few presents and I'll do what he wants, the cheek of it*, I've heard her. You were in luck, my lad, building yourself up from scratch in that state. I told Julian I quite expected to find you on the couch this morning, especially after your lost-week-end act. He said it would be all right, but I wondered. It must be your bonny blue eyes, though I never thought she cared much for the old one two, you know, sort of

227

for itself. All she likes as a rule is having lots of money spent on her and being promised she's going on films or TV. Perhaps she cottoned on to you because you don't look rich – no offence, dear – and you can't get her on films or anything. Well, we live and learn.'

'I'm surprised she hasn't got on already.'

'Well I know, it does seem extraordinary, but what it is, you see, it's the waiting about she can't stand. She's had boy friends who can jump the queue for her, but then there's still a lot to be gone through after that, tests and rehearsals and the rest of it, and she doesn't like that. She was all set for a walk-on in one of these historical crinoline things, one of the guests at a ball, nothing much but that's how you get started, and then she found she had to wait for half an hour to see the casting director, so she came home. Can you beat it? *The cheek of that man*, she kept saying. *Who does he think he is?* she wanted to know. I like that, don't you? Who does *he* think *he* is? What it is, she doesn't want to be *made into* a star, she wants to *be* a star, just like that. With all of them running round with her bag and her lighter and chocolates and gin-and-its with two cherries on sticks, and if the madam's out of sorts, sorry boys, hard luck, no shooting today. And she's twenty-nine, you know, that's getting on a bit to be making a start in that game.'

'But she lets these fellows go on promising to get her in?'

'Oh yes, *this* time it'll be different, *this* time it'll be the real thing, the chap can get her to the top first go. Of course he never can, but she thinks it's bound to come off in the end, because that's the way she wants it, she'll be a top actress right off. That's the real yell, the acting part. I went along with her once, she was going to do a bit of commercial for TV, only one line, something about *I love Scrunchy-Lunch*. Oh, you should have been there. Funniest thing you ever saw in your life. They took her through it about nineteen hundred times and it was the same every bloody time: *I ... lav .., Scranchy-Lanch*. Christ, I can hear her now. There was one of these little Jew boys there trying to get her to do it properly, tearing his hair and jumping up and down and screaming at her. She never took a blind bit of notice. She walked off after a bit, of course; she hadn't come there to be shouted at by a nasty little Jew boy. Who did he think he was? Oh, it was the killingest thing you ever saw. *Actress*. That'll be the day. Really, I don't know what I'd do without her for laughs, you've got to hand her that. Now, I think that's everything.'

While she talked she had efficiently assembled fruit juice, cereal, bacon, eggs, sausages, toast, tea, and coffee. 'It certainly looks like everything,' Patrick said.

'One thing you can do is to go and get the bold bad baron out of bed, if you would. And on the way back you can tell your light of love that *brairkfahst aweets her leedyship's plairzhah.*'

Julian was sitting up in bed reading the Sunday papers. His dark colouring and his bare chest, which was extravagantly hairy but far from podgy, made him look a good deal like an oil sheikh, one of the second-generation kind with a private gymnasium and a welfare scheme. 'Princess Alexandra has a slight cold,' he said. 'Thank God you've come, old boy. I was afraid I might die of excitement in here.'

'Susan says breakfast's ready.'

'Less bad. I think I'll just sit and meditate a moment longer.'

'I hope I wasn't too much of a nuisance last night.'

'As to that I couldn't say. We parted before seeking our couches, as you may recall. But the way, I hope you didn't literally have to seek a couch. Susan seemed to think it might come to that.'

'No, it was okay, thanks. Actually I meant earlier on.'

'Oh, you were fine. You did seem somewhat keen on letting the company know you were a schoolmaster and taught Latin. I had to sit on that one a bit slickish. The way Joan was looking the least thing might have got you on to that couch. I explained it was all a guilt thing from making too much money: you had a fantasy life where you slept in a garret and sweated your guts out for humanity. I had to go on rather because you kept reciting a poem you said was by Martial or some gagster.'

'Christ, did I do all that?'

'You were delivering babies in the East End the last time you got tight, I told them. You seemed to catch on at that stage and went into a long guffaw-laden saga about preserving the headmaster's daughter from ruin. Jolly affecting, I thought. The only time I sensed a slight strain was when you kept insisting about ringing up your mater. Got our Joanna frightfully tight-lipped, that bit.'

'Why the hell was that?'

'Well, as far as I could gather she thought you were insulting her intelligence, which would have been no mean feat, what? She didn't believe you had a mother, or if you had she was safely tucked up in her shack in Ballyhooly – which I may say you had rather led us to suspect from all your spalpeen and colleen and shebeen and poteen line, not that –'

'Oh Christ, not the Irish lot too.'

'It didn't last long. I saw to that. Anyway, as I was saying, I deduced that what was bugging Joan was having all this mum stuff and last trains and hiring cars and phone calls played out note for note in front of her, when it was perfectly clear that you'd never had the remotest intention of proceeding mumwards right from the start. She wanted to know who you thought you were fooling. I felt like telling her it was something of a compliment to be charaded like a vicar's daughter, but then I decided against it.'

'But,' Patrick said, 'but you believe I had arranged to go on home last thing, don't you?'

'Let's just say that was how you seemed to want to play it yesterday afternoon and points earlier. It wasn't for me not to go along with the act.'

'There was no act, honestly. I really intended – I'd written –'

'Easy now, Pat, nobody'd dream of blaming you for wanting to run your eye over mum's rival first. You could have taken my word for it, but *caveat emptor* is what I always say, and with your grounding in the dead tongues you doubtless say it too. Now throw me that robe thing, will you, behind you? Ta. Well, everything turned out for the best in the end, eh? Though mum-distracted and booze-bemused, Standish brings home the bacon, none the worse apart from half a *crêpe suzette* on the left kneecap. Sheer grit and guts and nerve. Well, this does the heart good, what? Not to speak of points south.'

While Julian seated himself at the kitchen table Patrick went to fetch Joan. 'About time too,' she said definitely. 'I'm starving. Where's the *Sunday Express*?'

To his amazement Patrick found that he was fetching it from

Susan's room, muttering to himself. Joan took it without a word or look, folded it up small beside her breakfast plate and read it at a speed that suggested she was committing it to memory. Only Patrick had no paper. He read the cereal packet instead. As the food began to penetrate, his hangover, which had re- treated to a distant speck, returned to the charge with uneasi- ness in close support. He hoped that if he ever saw himself as a bastard, instead of just seeing himself as seeing himself as a bastard, he would be drunk or in bed with a woman at the time. What price his experiment now? He read some more of the cereal packet. From assuming a hidden, malign significance the exhortations and recipes began to take on the appearance of a translation from some French experimental work or other. To immerse himself further in the state of the inside of his head, to marvel anew at its august authority, he lit a cigarette. Joan beat the smoke away with her hand, her eyes still on the *Express*. He blew some more in her direction.

'Very jolly,' Julian said in his warmest tone, rising to his feet. Patrick leant across in the sure expectation of being regaled by a starlet pictured in at most a bathing suit, but encountered only a report that a satellite Communist politician of hitherto irre- proachable savagery was now facing charges of Westernization. Although he wondered thoroughly about this while he helped Susan wash up, enlightenment remained at a distance. In the sitting-room he found Julian on the phone.

'Well, would you speak to Miss Calcott when she comes in and ask her to get in touch with me? She knows where. Yes, she'll understand. Thank you.' He dialled again, looking very dedicated, like a general or a gangster. The new call involved operators, and perfunctory gallantry towards these. 'Ah, thank you, sweetheart . . . Too perfect of you . . . Hallo? Hallo, darling, this is Julian. In London. Oh, just some chums, you know. No, this is someone quite different. Well, that's very sweet of you, and of course I'd adore to after all this time, but it would be rather awkward. Oh dear. Oh, I'm sorry to hear that. Yes, of course. Well, I know what you mean about him. And I've got some news for you, too. In person would be better. Let's think again, then. The trouble is I've got someone with me. No, a young man. Yes, but not that versatile. I could indeed, thank you. I think you could call him that, yes. All right then, perfect. Cheers.'

He came over to where Patrick was looking through the terrible pile of LPs: not only Sinatras but operatic pops and music from musicals. 'Sorry to have to tell you this, Patty, but you and I have got to go out to dinner tonight. Some old chums of mine. Bevvy and scoff more than adequate, but in other respects rather a bind for you, I fear. Quite a stretch, too: out beyond that R.A.F. Station we passed on the way in.'

'Oh, that'll be quite handy for getting home, anyway.'

'That's true,' Julian said abstractedly. 'Not worth taking a chance on driving out myself, rules being rules.'

'Don't you worry, I'll be pleased to take you. No trouble.'

Julian stared at him, grinning, then began to sing slow rising notes in a wordless falsetto. 'You deserve a better celestial choir than that, old man, but it's all I can manage, there only being the one of me. Now I think a crafty shave and shampoo and such and it'll be getting on for time for a stroll across the park and a glass of beer.'

For a few minutes Patrick helped Susan tidy up the flat, not because he wanted to or thought he should but as a way of not going to see what Joan was up to. Then, just about the time it seemed that he might have to vacuum the sitting-room carpet, he decided it was silly not to see what Joan was up to. It would not do at all to have behaved towards her with anything less than condign voracity. He went into the bedroom. In the distance the buzzing of Julian's razor dropped in pitch, became laboured as the mechanism took up the extra load at some denser patch of bristle.

'Just remember to knock in future if you don't mind.' Joan was lying on the bed in her pyjamas. Her face was covered with a thick layer of what appeared to be cement. She spoke indistinctly.

'Sorry. What the hell is all that stuff on your face?'

'Pack, of course. I'm not supposed to talk.'

'I see. Must be a strain for you.' He wondered whether to find some way of disorganizing the pack by sending her into fits of laughter or screaming, but soon resolved not to. After that he stood meditating for a time. All he came up with was the perception that the whiteness of the cement made little difference to the whiteness of her teeth or the whites of her eyes. Finally he said: 'We thought we'd go out for a walk soon, and have a drink. Would you like to come?'

'I can't, I'm going out to lunch.'

'I see. What time do you think you'll be back?'

'I really couldn't say.'

'Because Julian and I'll have to be off before five, I expect.' He put in some more meditation, a shorter passage this time. Not to have to say *I see* again as much as anything, and reasoning that *You're beautiful* would not do just now, he moved off. 'Well, have a nice lunch.'

'Here a minute,' she called when he was outside the room.

This was it. *I can't let you go without ... Darling, I just want to say ... Remember, if you're ever ...* He leant against the doorjamb. 'Yes, Joan?'

'Get the *Woman's Mirror* off Susan, will you? She's had it long enough, must have finished by now.'

When they left, Joan was in the bathroom again, perhaps having another bath to judge by the rumble of water, and there was a valediction of sorts through the closed door. 'Cheero, Joan ... Cheero, Joan.' 'What?' 'Cheero, Joan.' 'Cheero.' 'And thanks for everything.' 'What?' And when they got back after the tripartite stroll and drink and snack lunch, she was of course not there. Before setting off with Julian, Patrick took a final look round the bedroom. 'And every attempt is a wholly new start,' he muttered to himself, 'and a different kind of failure. Yeah. A raid on the inarticulate – my Christ – with shabby equipment always deteriorating – thanks for *that*.'

The bedroom contained nothing but furniture, clothes, and beauty aids; none of those handy little speculation-generators like old group photographs, teddy-bears, snowstorm globes, the odd rosary, not even the expensive male handkerchief forgotten in a corner. No engagement diary, because there would always be reminders. And, naturally, nothing locked up. Joan did without possessions – without, at least, those which might define or differentiate her – to an extent that must be rare outside nunneries and jails. Her life was all inward, if anywhere. It piqued him that he had not begun to find it nor been able to make any mark upon it. That was no doubt why he had not liked her going out to lunch, over and above just not liking her not to be there, why he had not liked hearing the inevitable facts of her Austrian and Spanish and Parisian activities. What message should he leave, gouged into the woodwork preferably, to notify Joan of his existence?

He tore a page from his pocket diary and wrote on it: *Dearest Joan, It was*. Then he crumpled it up and threw it into the waste-paper basket among the empty shampoo cartons and bits of cotton wool.

Chapter Twenty

SUSAN kissed Patrick good-bye warmly. 'I hope we'll be seeing you again, old boy, now you know the way. I could tell you made quite a hit with our Joanie. If she hadn't liked you she'd have taken her breakfast into her room. Anyway, good luck, and try and keep Sir Jasper in order, won't you?'

As he took the Jaguar along Bayswater Patrick was feeling not too bad at all. The sun and the touches of greenery and the almost deserted look of things made him view with favour the notion of spending eternity like this, with frequent halts for refreshment and recreation, of course.

'Very jolly pair, what?' Julian said, lighting a cigarette from the gadget in the dashboard. 'That Susan is an absolute archangel. Almost feel I could marry the girl sometimes, but I've done enough of that already to last me for the next half-century or so. And that Mexico feature on top of everything.'

'Known her some time, have you?'

'On and off, yes. Moving as all hell to see how you and mistress Joan latched on to each other, by the way. Wouldn't mind a tilt at her myself, only I know a nice clean doorstep when I see one. Much more your kind of personage than mine, anyway.'

'Don't see how you make that out.'

'Don't you? Don't you see how I make that out? I think you and the fair Joan have got heaps in common.'

'Oh, thanks a whole lot.'

'Take it easy, china, I only meant you were both beautiful. I can quite see it's a bit sort of cat-sat-on-the-mat talking to her, or did you get her going on her stamp collection?'

'No, but I didn't mind that. In fact, not having to be talked to was the second best thing about her,' Patrick said, conscious of the merits of this new idea.

'Oh, I thought you were a great one for a chin-wag.'

'Yes, as long as it's a something-else-wag as well. I've been wagging my chin so fast these last months it'll seize up soon.'

'The old waiting game getting you down, eh?'

'Hard. I'm not going to stand it much longer. You know, I'd almost forgotten what it was like to sleep with a girl. How nice it is. And how little fuss there need be. Christ, it's not as if she's better-looking than Joan, is it? Or more sought after?'

'Nicer, though. Detectably nicer. So much must be allowed Miss B.'

'Miss B. can keep it. I'm a steady now, do you realize that? A swain. A suitor. A young man. I'm courting, see? They'll be jeering at me in the street if I let it go on. Tamed. Corralled.'

'You don't sound very corralled.'

'I won't look it, either, soon. There'll be some changes made. I'll even change the number hanging on my flat. I'll probably have to. Ah, because nobody loves you when you're old and grey.'

'Come on, Pat, why don't you marry the girl? It'll buck you up.'

'Have you gone out of your mind? Who wants to be bucked up? Do you honestly think I'm going to get drawn into that huge historical bloody confidence-trick? Actually it's not even that, though, really, is it? What is it about everyone? Can you imagine the chap saying *According to a lot of people this brick isn't gold at all?*'

'Calm down, Patty. You'll get married all right. Everybody who likes sex does (plus a lot of chaps who don't, of course). Once you've resigned yourself to it you can take a lot of the sting out of it by grabbing one of the really good ones as she comes past. That's what you ought to be working on. Then all you have to guard against is grabbing a subsequent good one. The second marriage is the one to avoid, not the first. That's if you're a man, anyway, and you're one of those, aren't you?'

'Sometimes I'm not so sure.'

During the next half-hour, the background of Patrick's consciousness went on with its propaganda-ministry job on the events of the last eighteen hours. His experiment had turned out curiously, but it had been love, as well as drink, that had rendered him incapable. His eventual capability belonged elsewhere, far away from Jenny or anything into which she entered or could enter – belonged to the image of himself – a rakehell, but with heart, but a rakehell – that he had been trying so long and so staunchly to manhandle across the threshold of reality. With that settled, he was free to start being in love with Jenny again, and managed to get off a couple of remarks in her favour before they arrived, to remove any impression that he might have been less than fair to her.

This concern distracted him from giving full attention to the length of time that elapsed between their entry at a tall stone gateway and their arrival in front of a long stone house. On alighting, Patrick found that for some reason he was in the middle of a fair-sized estate, or park. He abruptly modified the kind of charm in his smile on becoming aware that the person who opened the door to them was not their host but a man-servant, in all probability a butler. Their next encounter was with a white-haired character of pensionable age in a kind of jacket-length dressing-gown. Besides being old Archie Edgerstoune, which was what he had been in Julian's earlier remarks about him, he turned out to be called Lord Edgerstoune as well. He shook hands in a conciliatory, bewildered way, as if Patrick were just one more feature of the modernity he spent most of his time trying to come to terms with. 'Do sit down, Mr Standish,' he said pleadingly. 'Julian, do you think you could possibly see to the drinks?'

Patrick made up his mind to be as nice as possible to Lord Edgerstoune. It was up to him to show the old boy that he for one was not given over to any unworthy prejudice; after all, nobody could help being an aristocrat, could they? This particular seigneur seemed to have little to say for himself, doing no more than nod at unpredictable intervals while a long monologue, replete with Nigel and St Tropez and Vanessa and Claridge's and Francis and Glyndebourne and Mildred and Bognor (what was that doing there?) and Paul and Cape Cod and Sonia and St Tropez and Nigel, issued from Julian with perhaps excessive *élan* : tolerance and even respect for that type of stuff was all very well, but although it had to be granted that there was good and bad in every breed the world over it was no use pretending we were all made the same way because we were not. When conversational conditions should change and the last be heard of Bognor and Vanessa, it was not going to be easy to think what to say to the viscount or baron now on view. A casual query about the tenants or the leads on the orangery might be just the thing to unchoke an obsessional conduit; alternatively, it might prove to be rather worse than asking a Venetian gourmet if he had many chums in the hokey-pokey racket. Well, he would have to cross that bridge when and if he came to it.

A dose of sherry – it reached about two-thirds of the way up a cut-glass tumbler dating no doubt from a year or two after Hastings – was passed to him. Patrick liked thinking and knowing about drinks as well as drinking them, and he collected wine pamphlets and so on much as another might sjambok-catalogues, but after last night and the pints of lunchtime bitter his palate was in no condition for any of that amontillado and manzanilla jazz. It was sherry and he drank it, so much so that he had drunk another couple before anything fresh happened. The innovation consisted of the entry of a fairly fat but just for the time being still attractive woman in her early forties. Her dress and demeanour were quiet enough to make Patrick wonder whether this might not be an additional servant, and he had another spot of trouble shuffling his two grades of charm. The energy with which Julian and the woman embraced, however, removed all real doubt that here was Lady Edgerstoune. When he was introduced, Patrick decided he had never seen anyone who more clearly bore the marks of multiple marriage – something about the eyebrows, was it, or the vertical hair-do? She gave him a queenly, sensitive look, as if to assure him that not all her time, nor all her significance, was exhausted by oscillation between the states of marriage, divorcement, and widowhood. (That last one was there all right, somewhere in face or hands.)

While Julian got her a drink, she said in a friendly tone: 'Let's see, I don't think we've met, have we? I'm so bad at names. And faces too nowadays. I can't see them properly, you know. Archie wants me to be measured for glasses, but I won't go. I feel I should really be admitting I was getting on if I did. Doesn't that sound silly? Because of course one is getting on, glasses or no glasses, isn't one? Do you have to wear them at all? – not that you're getting on, absolutely not, I can still see well enough for that, but do you?'

Patrick, though far from being prepared to agree that he was not getting on – there had been enough hairs in his comb that morning to stuff a fairly luxurious doll's-cushion – said apologetically that as yet he had never worn glasses.

'Perhaps you don't have very much close work to do. Does your job take you out of doors? I think one's so lucky nowadays if it does.'

'No, I'm a schoolteacher.' It seemed to him non-U to say *schoolmaster* here, like *perspiration* instead of *sweat*. 'If I look healthy at all it's just the old alcoholic flush getting going.'

'How wonderful,' she said, doubtless in answer to his first observation. 'How wonderful.' Two sorts of wonderful were possible in this context: the wonderful that a test pilot was for being a test pilot, and the wonderful that an octogenarian widow was for walking three miles each morning to fetch scraps for her cat. Both were here. 'But isn't it simply exhausting, looking after all those children?'

'Very. It's only things like this that keep me going.'

'Ah, that is sweet of you, darling.' Rather as before, this referred not to his last remark, but to the arrival of Julian with a drink. 'Your nice friend has been telling me he's a schoolteacher. Would you get him another drink, Julian? I must tell Archie. Archie, Julian's friend is a schoolteacher.'

'What's that, Dot?'

'Julian's friend is a schoolteacher.'

By this time it had the bleak authority of a sentence for English-Latin translation. Its delivery, however, retained the blurred quality Patrick had noticed in the countess's earlier utterances and, since in his experience it was being drunk that made people sound drunk, had put down to drink. But the way she handled her current drink, putting it aside after one sip, was not that of a drink-fancier. No no no – of course, sounding drunk was an aristocratic thing, like the Welsh sing-song and foreigners making a mess of the *th* sound. The theory that TV aristocrats sounded as drunk as they did because they really were drunk was soon knocked on the head by observing how well they and their colleagues carried on with their jobs. How could they keep going year after year with such unflagging devotion, pluckily working away at Cowes and Goodwood and Ascot and Eton *v*. Harrow and Henley and the hunting and the shooting and all the London balls, if they were chronically as drunk as was suggested by the pretty random sample of them to be seen and heard on television? The idea was ridiculous. Try making all the Jews in London drunk and see how long Pass-over and the Feast of Tabernacles would carry on. The whole thing would just fold up.

His being a schoolteacher tided them over nicely. He enjoyed himself, bringing out all his best horror-stories about the declining educational standard, fading up the test-pilot sort of way he was wonderful and damping down the octogenarian cat-cherishing sort, conscious of simultaneously spreading the gospel about school problems in a fresh social group and bringing two members of that group news of how life was lived in the world at large. He was quite sorry for all their sakes when the doors at the end of the room opened – there were two of them, like doors at the side-exit of a cinema – and the butler came in to an-nounce dinner, but cheered up at once, felt like an Indiana-politan at the Trooping the Colour, when the announcement turned out to be that *dinner was served*. He was sorry again to be leaving the *library*, with its many leather-bound books, its sturdy, canvas-like wallpaper, its freehand pictures with their remarkable range of sizes, but similarly remembered that later he would be permitted to view the *drawing-room*, where after the typical port-and-cigar observances they would presumably be *joining the lady*.

Here he was mistaken. At the end of the meal there was a brief exchange between Julian and Lady Edgerstoune, who said: 'I must talk to you about that frightful little man who came to see me – now what on earth was his name?'

Julian said: 'Perhaps we could run an eye over the documents at the same time. Only take a few minutes.'

'There wasn't a single thing he saw that he didn't say we wouldn't get much for it. He hated everything on sight.'

'Where are the papers? In that den of yours, no doubt.'

'He behaved as if he intended to buy everything himself. And the way he laughed when I said what I thought the pictures were worth. The most dreadful laugh, like a rook cawing.'

'Shall we just pop up now and have a quick gander?'

'He was pleased by the whole idea, you know. I felt like one of those poor ladies in Russia when the Bolsheviks came.'

'I'm sure these lads will entertain each other adequately.'

'And he worked so hard at his accent, but as soon as he got excited he was really quite refined. Oh yes, of course. Well, we shan't be very long. Do excuse us, er, both of you. Archie, Julian and I are going to have a look at the papers. You'll be all right here, won't you?'

'What do you say, Dot?'

'The papers, Archie. Julian and I are going to have a look at them. Now you mustn't talk Julian's young friend under the table. Let him say something too, dear, from time to time.'

'All right, Dot.'

When he and the old patrician were alone, Patrick thought to himself that that final caution had been rather unjust, seeing that his own conversational offerings had so far exceeded the other's by something like 1,000:1. There was silence for a space, while Patrick's brain moved on from tenants and orangery leads to farmers and parish councils, fishing rights and vicars. It was more efficient on arrival there than would have been possible for it an hour earlier, for despite the great quantity of wine the butler had given him he had eaten enough to take care of it and to neutralize some part of the sherry, too. He now felt less like an anthropologist who had struck it rich than a shagged-out schoolmaster (or schoolteacher) in whose brain the self-winding mechanism that expounded conditional sentences in *oratio obliqua* must be in position at nine-fifteen the following morning. The silence was broken, technically at least, by the *pianissimo* rumbling of the port-decanter as the margrave pushed it towards him over the polished wood. He helped himself sparingly. A more substantial diversion was afforded soon afterwards when the butler arrived for the *nunc dimittis* ritual. This was enacted without recourse to the *will that be all, my lord?* formula Patrick had been on the alert for, but when a dialogue about locking up came as postlude he was as much moved as if Graham had assured him categorically that it was a braw bricht moonlicht nicht the nicht.

The butler's departure seemed to relax things. Old Archie played about a little longer with the two or three pairs of half-lenses which, in flat contradiction to his wife's views on optical aids, he had had near him throughout; then, fixing on his nose what must have been the easiest ones to see over, he said in his irresolute tones: 'I had hoped to have some younger company along tonight, but my nephew and his wife had to go back to London after tea.'

'What a pity. But I mean it's been very –'

'He's in the Treasury.' The heyduck gave this time to sink in by filling and lighting his pipe, which had a mouthpiece adapted for the use of those with false teeth. Puffing urgently, he continued: 'I was sorry to see him go, more especially because he took his wife with him.' He paused again, as he was often to do during what followed, with an air of partial finality that left Patrick in doubt whether to respond with gratitude for what he had had or expectation of more of the same. 'Which it was perfectly natural for him to do. But I was sorry, as I said, although in one way I suppose I should have been glad. She's one of those little wispy things with big eyes. I've always been rather susceptible to that type. I'm afraid I pawed her from time to time. Quite harmlessly, of course. It was totally unconnected with their early departure. But I wish I hadn't pawed her at all, because I'd told myself I wasn't going to this time. I'd asked myself what good it could do. And I don't just mean that as a competitor with Robin, or almost any other man living, I'm in a grotesque position.'

What he did mean remained unuttered for so long that Patrick felt it might never leave the womb of time. He felt too that eventually he could reconcile himself to that prospect. Somewhere overhead a door shut, faint but clear, as across a vast empty hall. He poured himself another small dose of port.

'When we were boys,' his host ventured, 'we were always fooling about with electric torches. We used to have a way of testing to see whether there was any guts left in a battery. What we did was to lay our tongues on the little brass strip things at the business end. If there was any juice remaining, then we used to get a tingling feeling in our tongues. A little, faint tingling that showed there was still some life in the thing. We could have tried it on a bulb, I suppose, but that would have been too easy. We liked to know in advance what the effect was going to be when we put the battery in a torch and pressed the button. Well, now. When I put my arm round Nancy's waist and give her a little kiss on the ear, or something like that, I'm testing for a tingling, that's all. Seeing if there's any juice left.'

Patrick wanted to applaud the skill and foresight that, evoking some major feat of literary symbolism, had after about an hour and a quarter brought together comparison and thing compared. 'I see,' he said.

'There never is, of course, but I can't seem to break the habit. I remember with the batteries, we'd try the old ones time after time. Even when we were quite sure they were as dead as a doornail. I suppose we thought they might somehow have recovered in the meantime. Hope springing eternal, that's what it is. When nothing else does.

'I must have reached this stage a little earlier than some men. It certainly hadn't arrived when I married Dot, nine years ago. I was a very very young sixty-odd then. A little slow off the mark, perhaps, but perfectly reliable, no different from when I was a man of forty. And then, quite suddenly, almost from one day to the next, everything changed. Or rather, one thing changed, and everything else was exactly the same as before. Not intensified, thank heaven. The same. The same when I see them and the same when I don't see them, when I merely think about them. And when I talk to them, or have drinks with them, or sit in the car with them, or ... Until I touch them. Then it's different. But part of it stays the same, what I think, what I feel. So much so I can't believe it isn't all the same. It's all in the mind. It's as if one's right hand had suddenly ceased to function. There it is, it's still a part of one, of course it can pick things up, it can open doors, it can hold a pen, it can pour a drink, it can tie a shoelace. Until one tries. Then it can't. Then it's useless. And it isn't going to get better. That's the thing one can't ever quite believe, I suppose. And what would one do if one did manage to believe it, all the time? That's the really fascinating question.'

This had been delivered intermittently enough for Patrick to have poured and drunk one very large glass of port and poured and half drunk another before it finally and unmistakably ended. He got to his feet and said: 'Do you think I could ... ?'

There was a slow focusing of attention, then a quick reaction. 'Of course, my dear fellow, how shockingly remiss of me. Let me just indicate. Oh, you know your way. Oh yes, you ...'

Patrick did what he had to do at great speed and without noticing anything, like a man about to catch a train. Almost immediately afterwards he found an outside door and left the house. He did not want to see Lord Edgerstoune for a while or ever again be told anything by him. It was very dark, and he stumbled several times before coming to a level stretch of grass. A couple of hundred yards away, down what he sensed as a slope, the wind was rising in some trees. Near by there was a strip of illumination from an upper window. Shivering, he went and stood in this, so that he could see parts of himself. After a moment he heard a mumble of voices above his head, followed by a man's laughter: Julian's. This at once calmed him. On the edge of the lighted patch there was a long flower-bed running off into the darkness, with some begonias or azaleas or whatever the hell they were. Patrick went over and stooped down by them.

'There you are then, you silly little things,' he muttered. 'How are you getting on? Plenty of nitrates and Christ knows what? That's the spirit. Just you go on sucking them up. Probably be stacks of sun tomorrow for you to make with the old photo-synthesis. Well done. You funny little things.'

After that he thought about Jenny for a bit, and then about how odd it was that what you did when people were not there turned out afterwards to be as important as what you did when they were there. 'Never again,' he said. 'I know now.' He walked a few yards into the darkness. 'I'm sorry, I know I'm a bastard, but I'm trying not to be. But you know all that. That's your job, isn't it? You may not be much good at anything else but you're scholarship standard on that one. But I'm not trying to get credit with you by saying I know I'm a bastard. Nor by saying I'm not trying to get credit. Nor by saying I'm not trying to by saying ... trying ... you know what I mean. Nor by saying that. Nor by saying that.'

He broke off this familiar regressive series and spent some time trying to see the future as real, to visualize himself, for example, going in to bat for the Masters against the College on Wednesday next, turning up at the gigantic party Julian was planning for the Saturday following. This effort succeeded only in part, but by now he felt that there was nothing in particular to keep him away from the world of men, and women, so he said good night to the flowers. He found old Archie back in the library looking at one of his own leather-bound books. It had to do with early smoking habits and materials, on which old Archie was evidently by way of being an expert. A whisky and water in his hand, Patrick let himself be told about early smoking habits and materials. By the time Julian reappeared, Patrick was nearly as much of an expert on them as old Archie was.

'Papers all in order,' Julian said. 'Now we really must be going.' In the car he looked at his watch. 'If we take it steadily we can be back at the scene of action by one-thirty.'

'What? But I thought we were –'

'Where's your fighting spirit, soldier? It's an easy run back in the morning. What time do you function? Ah, nothing to it.'

'But surely they'll be –'

'Very late birds, those two. Oh, I'm not guessing. You don't think I would over a thing like that, do you? Had Susan on the blower just now while old Dot was powdering her nose. The two young misses are all agog, believe me. Come on, Patty, handbrake off. Not like you to disappoint a lady, what?'

Chapter Twenty-One

'Do I look the part?' Jenny asked.

Patrick took his time running his eyes over her new full-skirted summer dress, which she had not thought had any details that needed working out. 'Oh yes,' he said. 'I don't know which part you mean quite, but you look it, rest assured of that.'

'I meant I wondered whether I ought to have worn a hat and lace gloves and things to a do like this.'

'Seeing you in a hat would have been fine, but there's no need. I'll buy you one for the big match at the end of term when all the parents come.'

'Oh, how lovely, darling. Isn't this a big match, then? Look, there's someone wearing a hat.'

Patrick glanced over towards the sports pavilion, on the low balcony of which a woman of about fifty was standing. Some of the bright sunlight was reflected from her cherry-coloured dress, which with its topcoat-type lapels and flying panels had obviously used up more material and labour than Jenny's pink check gingham. A triple row of pearls went with the cherry-coloured effort to give a vague Royal-Family effect. On the woman's head there was a kind of shallow yellow fez with what looked like desiccated coco-nut thrown over it. After a quick but thorough glance round the cricket field, evidently to make sure that everything was as it ought to be, she turned and spoke to a hunched-up boy in white flannels who was just putting a whole round chocolate biscuit into his mouth.

'Christ,' Patrick said in a groaning whisper. 'You want to steer well clear of her. She's called Mrs Charlton, the College secretary's wife. Powerful shags, the pair of them. That's their son with her. Puny shag. The Eleven's a bit below par this season, else he'd never have got in. I hit him for two fours in his first over – pity you weren't here to see that. Right off the middle of the bat to the mid-off boundary, same place each time. As good as sex. Sorry. And it wasn't really. Then I was out straight after that, in the next over.'

'Oh, I am wild at missing you wearing your pads.'

'If we want to hear this orchestra we'd better stroll over. What? Why did you want to see me in my pads?'

'It'd be a new view of the little legs, in the little pads. Have you got special short ones made? Or do you get a lend from one of the juniors?'

'What do you mean? I haven't got little legs.'

Jenny looked down at them, walking along beside her in their neatly creased white trousers, and giggled. 'Yes you have. They're nice, though. They're sweet little legs.'

'What are you talking about?' He stopped by a row of vacant deck-chairs and glared at her. 'What makes you say things like that? Why do you keep trying to make me feel ridiculous? Christ.'

'I don't, darling. You aren't a bit ridiculous and I don't mean you're not wonderful and attractive and everything. You're beautiful. But you have got funny little stumpy legs.'

'I've got ... What the hell am I supposed to do about it?'

'Not much you can, is there, love? You're saddled with 'em.'

'Why, you cheeky little bitch. Sometimes I wonder why I ...' His voice died off and so did his glare. 'I'd hate to think you didn't take me seriously.'

'Oh, Patrick, I do, you know that, surely, but that doesn't mean I can't laugh at you sometimes, does it?'

'That's what everyone says but I'm not so sure. Stumpy legs, eh? Well now ...' He looked her up and down as they started walking again. 'Your thorax is too short.'

'What do you mean? I'm not a beetle.'

'The part between your neck and your waist, that's your thorax. And it's too short.'

'Nonsense, you're just jealous of my lovely long racehorse legs. Now give me a kiss.'

'Don't be ridiculous, Jenny, I can't here. They'll all see.'

'Don't care. Anyway not many of them will. Go on.' She moved round and began walking backwards in front of him. 'They're not looking. Go on.'

He took hold of her so that his arms seemed to go round her about twice and his chest to be creeping round on both sides of hers like a sort of big warm bony jellyfish. Both their faces turned into all mouth and cheeks. That was what it felt like outside; inside it was as if someone had fired off a small pistol somewhere about her middle. The smell of cut grass mingled with his breath and the sun beat down on the nape of her neck; she was wearing her hair up because he had said it made her look more sophisticated.

'Oh, Jenny, I do love you so much,' he said in a hurt, despairing way as they walked on.

'Oh, I love you, Patrick.'

'And I want you so much.'

'And I want you.'

'Not as much as I want you.'

'I couldn't want you any more than I do, dearest.'

'Jenny, let's go for a little holiday together in the summer, you and me, Cornwall or somewhere, or if my old woman's done well out of the Italian dresses I might get enough out of her to take us to France for a week or so. Would you like that?'

'Oh God,' she said, 'I'd hate it like poison, you bet I would. Oh darling, could we really?'

'It's only up to you to fix it with your parents. Would they let you go, do you think?'

'Oh, sure to.' She was going to add that her parents were pretty free and easy, but realized she no longer quite thought of them in that way. 'I'll manage it all right. They both like you.'

'I always thought they were a sensible pair.'

'Separate rooms, Patrick.' She said it quickly before she could have a chance of saying it in the wrong way by thinking about it, and saw his mouth straighten and his eyes go inattentive for a second. Whenever this kind of thing happened between them, she had a tiny feeling of sort of *auntie*, as if just for the time being she had become somebody who always insisted on a stone hot-water-bottle in her bed from 1 November to 30 April and carried round in her bag a packet of her own special brand of tea for when she had a cup somewhere out. The auntie idea had never heard of records and new clothes and cars and going dancing and make-up, or if it had it was only because a stooge and/or dud curate with black shiners and wide trousers had explained to it that the youth of today had the right to enjoy itself in its own way and that God was on the side of high spirits and gaiety always provided that, etc. and afterwards there will be a short prayer meeting for those who wish to stay.

Patrick's face had gone nearly all the way back to what it had been before she mentioned the separate bedrooms but, as always, not quite. At the same time the difference was small enough for her to be able to tell he was not doing it deliberately. These days he hardly ever did that sort of thing deliberately. He said: 'You have it the way you want it. I'd go on any terms.'

'Darling ...' She forgot about auntie and the curate.

'It'll be wonderful away from the bastards. They'll try and prevent it, of course. But they won't succeed. They couldn't stop that kiss. Nice one, wasn't it?'

As she felt now she could have let Mr Burrage tell her twice over all his stories about when he was in business and asked him for more, lived for a week on Auntie Minnie's brick-red tea and pliable ginger-biscuits. She looked ahead to where the thin stream of boys and masters and wives and so on was arriving at a fat brown building at one corner of the field. Here and there the sunlight was pale where there was haze, and the air smelt of dusty paths and hot greenery. The bits of the town that could be seen from here – a spire or two, a lock-keeper's cottage – had a villagey look. A stocky man in shirtsleeves with a leather waistcoat and leggings moved parallel to them along the top of a near-by slope, needing only a straw between his teeth to have stepped straight out of a television serial, one of the Sunday-evening sort with flood disasters and cruel fathers. Several people were hanging about on the asphalt strip in front of the brown building, from which the sound of instruments tuning up could be heard. Jenny recognized the Sheila girl from the Ivy Bush and excitedly caught Patrick's arm. 'Ooh, look who's here, it's that –'

'Sshh,' he went, quietly but violently, then called out 'Hallo' to a tall thin man who was standing near Sheila. 'This is the headmaster ... Well, how's it going?'

The man's mouth turned down at the corners. 'Can you explain to me why we have to have this second dose? Isn't this supposed to be a cricket match? Wasn't that great slice of overture and folk tune they gave us after lunch enough for them? It's Horse again. Look at this damned programme: *Two move-*

ments from Symphonie Espagnole – *Lalo. Solo violin, L. J. Levy.*
All right, when's he going to start on painting and take over the senior staff common room for his first one-man show? It's becoming . . . oh, sorry.'

'This is Mr Torkington, Jenny. Jenny Bunn.'

'Oh, how do you do, so you're the . . . I suppose you might as well meet my daughter. Come along, Sheila. This is Sheila.'

'We met, remember?' Sheila said to Jenny with a glare just like the first time. 'Why, hallo, Mr Standish.' This was said with a completely different type of glare, though the actual state of the features did not alter much. Jenny compared father and daughter, wishing she could ask whether Mrs Torkington was the same as both of these two or not. If not, what was the idea of having these two the same?

'Sheila's broadening out,' her father said. 'Watching cricket. Listening to music. She'll be reading a book next.'

'Oh, I just like to keep in touch with what goes on,' Sheila said.

'There's somebody else who likes to do that,' her father said, looking over to where the flying-panel woman was arriving, her eyes moving about as if she was counting those present. With her was her son and a stout man in a grey suit. 'I must just have a word with Charlton, it'll save seeing him properly. You three go in.'

'Well, and how's love's young dream?' Sheila asked Jenny. 'Aren't you the lucky girl? My, but you look just radiant.'

'Wah, that's mahta fahn a you all, Miss Sheila,' Patrick cut in, 'to take a heed a little old us, but we just plain folks, we knows our place. Mm *hm*. And that's inside right now. Our place, I mean. Come on, Jenny, we might as well get a seat.'

Entering the brown building was hard. Nearly everybody else had decided to do it then, several young boys with red grinning faces had decided to leave instead, and a tall boy with thin wrists was dodging in front of people every so often in his efforts to undo the top bolt of half a double door. It was no wonder that Jenny and Patrick got separated. In the main hall part she ran into Graham, who took her off to one side so as to be able to explain to her better about the badge on his blazer and the way the school orchestra was run, and to introduce her to the famous

Thackeray. She had already, just after arriving, caught a glimpse of Thackeray on the field, or two glimpses really, once when he walked out to the wicket and again immediately afterwards when he walked back. Seen close to, he did not look different enough from anyone else to measure up to the great mass of mentions of him she had heard in the last few months. Over his cricket gear he wore a bright green sports jacket that looked almost new and had a big heart-shaped cigarette burn near the top pocket. She could tell he did not want her to sympathize with him about this. 'We'd best get ourselves seated,' Graham said. 'I should suggest near the back. The acoustics of this place leave a great deal to be desired.'

'Why do they have the music here, then?'

'No doubt they feel they must find some use for it. This is the Old Gymnasium, so called because ... Nowadays it fulfils no real function. I think these two will do,' he said, obviously not believing they would. 'Come along, Thackeray, there's another here.'

'How did you do in the batting, Graham?' Jenny asked, looking everywhere for Patrick. Then she saw him sitting with Sheila, some rows further forward and to the side. He saw her at the same moment and made a crying face. She recognized it as genuine, not a difficult job with him the most inefficient person at being deceitful she had ever met, and waved and grinned. She had to wonder a little about him not having told her who Sheila was. It was very odd that the girl was the headmaster's daughter, but surely no more than that. Probably he had mentioned it to her when she was daydreaming.

'I held out for a good long time,' Graham was saying. 'I helped to wear down the bowling though I only scored six runs. Do you understand cricket at all, Jenny?'

'Robbie, that's my young brother, he's taught me a bit about it.'

'Good. Eh, but what about Dick Thompson playing? Isn't that the funniest thing you ever heard?'

'Dick playing? I didn't know that. How? He's not a master.'

'Did Patrick not tell you? Well, we were one short on the team, you see, and he was the only ... I'll explain later.'

The music had evidently been going on for some time, but too quietly for those not at the front to notice. Then more and more people got the idea until it was only the ones at the back who were still talking and shuffling and moving chairs. When the Head and the fat man in grey, Mr Flying-Panel, had walked up the aisle and sat down, the fat man making more noise on tiptoe than the Head on the flat of his shoes, things were quiet, except to some extent the music. This relied chiefly on long single notes from the wind instruments with deep soft groanings from the two double-basses at the back. After a while the two big serious boys playing these plucked the strings instead of bowing them, but it was not at all like the noise Bill Stokes got out of his bass. In Jenny's reckoning this was the second-best sort of classical music, the film-music sort: although not as good as the tunes sort, it was better than Bach-and-Handel, which was goey but stayed in the same place all the time. Graham nudged her and showed her a part of the programme which said: *Tone Poem*, The Enchanted Lake – *Liadov*. Then he looked at her to see how she was taking it. There seemed no point in disagreeing, so she nodded.

After that she lost herself in the music, but not for long, because it had barely stopped starting before it started stopping. Some of those sitting near her, the younger ones especially, evidently felt that making them come had been a dirty trick on someone's part; others had a bullied, insulted expression that showed they were following carefully. This gradually changed, as the music got quieter and had fewer notes and more gaps in it, into anxiety about missing the end and clapping at the wrong time. But the conductor, a tall big-eared boy who moved his arms in a stiff way that made it very likely he was a stooge, gave everyone the nod by sort of saying cheero for now to the orchestra and suddenly whipping round on the audience. There was a lot of clapping and the usual competition to see who would be the one to give the last clap. A funny little creature with no neck sitting near them won.

'Quite an interesting piece,' Graham said. 'Slight, but cleverly orchestrated.'

Jenny nodded again. That remark, and the watchful look that went with it, had in it what she now saw as the thing that ruined his chances far more than any amount of face could: a heaviness that would make *Alice in Wonderland* sound like something by Sir Walter Scott or one of those, a way of talking about everything so as to make it as important as everything else and fit in with everything else. Did it come with the face or because of it or just by chance?

As if set on leaving her in no doubt that, wherever it came from, he had it, Graham added: 'Late nineteenth-century, one of the nationalist school. Ah, here's young Levy now. I think he can be trusted to give a good account of himself.'

There was more clapping while a boy with a violin came round the edge of the cellos and got ready. He did look like a horse, but a nice dreamy sugar-eating horse with big brown eyes. He played well, too, as far as Jenny could judge. So did the orchestra, though she wished the boy on flute could have got more of his breath into the flute instead of round the sides of it. It was the tunes kind of stuff this time, with complications every now and then to prove that it was a classical and not just out of a musical or anything. But Jenny enjoyed the liveliness of it. These days she did not need things to be sad as she had once done, music or books or stories or films; she no longer wanted to, she could not, snuggle down in the idea of being someone who had sacrificed her whole life for an ideal, or had renounced a selfish dream of happiness with everyone else taking notice of her doing it.

Before the end, her attention wandered. She gazed at the hooks in the ceiling from which ropes had no doubt hung, years and years ago, at a section of wall-bars nobody had bothered to remove, at some mahogany plaques informing her in dirty gold lettering that somebody called E. R. W. Titmuss had been gymnastics champion in 1911. After A. I. Mackenzie-Smith in 1937 it seemed that nobody had been that unless, as was likely, they were it in a New Gymnasium somewhere. The sunlight streamed in through the windows high in the walls and, during a quiet part of the music, Jenny heard a boy's shout from outside and the popping of a motor-mower. She had never been more pleased to be where she was, but nowadays she felt like this pretty well all the time. When the violin went into a gypsy tune she wanted to do a dance, and thought it was a pity that, even if she could have done it properly and the audience and orchestra would have sat by and let her, dancing on your own was so daft and full of all-watch-me.

Through a gap in the heads and necks she saw that the Sheila girl had squirmed herself up pretty close to Patrick, as if he was on the phone and she wanted to hear what the other person was saying. She had one hand on the back of his chair, near his shoulder. As Jenny watched, just out of interest, Sheila moved her face sideways towards Patrick's; he moved his away the same amount. After a moment the two faces shifted back together to where they had been. Then Jenny saw that the Charlton boy, who was right at the side a couple of rows behind the other two, was peering at them round the edge of someone's hat. His mother, rocking herself to and fro in her chair, was trying to get a look too. Jenny realized that being a schoolmaster, especially one that was also an attractive chap, carried heavy responsibilities outside just the teaching. It was doubly awkward to have a girl like Sheila so obviously interested in you, actually trebly in this case with Sheila being the Head's daughter. In a town like this you were a public figure and it was up to you to set an example to the community. Of course, if you had a good wife ... Jenny started concentrating hard on the music.

It ended soon after that. Graham said it had been interesting but rather shallow, though melodic. Thackeray slipped and banged his knee hard on some woodwork, moving off sideways in a huddled position immediately afterwards, perhaps to prevent Jenny from rubbing the place for him if she had been so inclined. Going out took even longer than coming in. The first person Jenny recognized outside was the boy who had been playing the violin. He was gazing over to where another boy of about his age, but more sporty-looking and in cricketing clothes, was chatting and laughing with a very handsome younger boy. The violinist's face was sad, but that went with being artistic.

Patrick, without Sheila, was waiting for her. 'You survived, then,' he said. 'I thought old Horse did quite well in that dago thing, didn't you? Not that I'm any judge, thank God.'

'Yes, it was lovely. Look, what's all this about Dick playing in the match? I shouldn't have thought you'd let him.'

'I know, but it couldn't be helped. He was down here before

the start, never having any work to do, and when we got word that Gammon couldn't make it because his wife's ill in bed – my guess is he just wanted to get in there with her, but anyway, at that stage Dick was the only non-boy in sight who was able-bodied, or not too unable-bodied. I put him in early so as to make sure their fast bowler got a crack at him, and even then he scored a run. Bloody terrible. If Skinner gets going – that's the College wicket-keeper, he hits like hell – I might give Dick a bowl at him, he's already asked me if he can have a bowl. Old Skinner would hit him over the pavilion every time.'

'You never know, perhaps he can bowl all right.'

'What, that? That bowl all right?'

He nodded in the direction of Dick who, looking frailer than usual in his borrowed whites, was cawing away with Graham and Thackeray. Jenny looked up at Patrick and laughed. How beautiful he was, his cricket clothes neat but not fussy, his crop of brown hair nice and long and a little untidy, his lips firm, his grey eyes fixed on hers with an effect of completely understanding her, and only her. There was no need for him to have been beautiful, she would have loved him anyway, but it was a marvellous extra, given away free with him so to speak, that he was. They went on staring at each other; it was a terrific moment really.

'Standish. Over here a minute, do you mind? I want to have a word with you.'

Chapter Twenty-Two

THE speaker, who spoke in a chewy voice, was the fat man, Charlton, who had evidently just sent his wife and son off towards the pavilion. The College, Jenny realized, was part of the adult world, a big elaborate organization where people were having words with each other all the time. This particular word, as far as she could tell from a few yards off, was a fairly serious one, going by the emphatic way the fat man was speaking and Patrick's worried face. Perhaps the College was in debt and someone was going to foreclose on something. But then the fat man raised his voice to say: 'That's one thing you seem to have overlooked, my lad. Now: if that boy's name isn't on that list first thing tomorrow morning you know what course of action I shall take. Right?' Patrick's face went more worried then. He half turned and caught her eye and said he would see her over by the pavilion in a couple of minutes.

He did, and he had time to joke with her before leading his team on to the field, but she could tell he was still worried, so that she missed a chance of enjoying being the captain's girl-friend. She hoped he would tell her later what was bothering him. He was so conscientious that it was sure to turn out to be something quite small.

Play began. The Masters had only scored 88, which Patrick said the College ought to knock off in about an hour. But with the very first ball there was a great roar from Graham behind the stumps and the batsman turned and came back to the pavilion.

'What happened?' a la-di-da voice called to him from the balcony.

'The ball hit my bat and then a man caught it before it touched the ground,' the batsman called back in the same voice. Another one passed him in the opposite direction, not looking at him.

Jenny was pleased for Graham, who looked very dangerous in his wicket-keeper's pads and gloves. She had known he would be as good at stumping as trying could make you. He was much freer in his movements on the field than he ever was off it, making great jumps at balls he had no hope of reaching, clapping his gloves together to encourage fielders to throw to him, leaving his arms up in the air for a quarter of a minute when once he missed a ball and it went to the boundary behind him. He went on roaring at intervals, and after one of the roars another batsman came out, though the spectators agreed that it was l.b.w. Graham was easily the outstanding player on the fielding side, not Patrick, who stayed as one of a group near the wicket and bent down when the rest did. But she could have picked him out from a mile off.

The new batsman turned his body sideways and whacked the ball towards Jenny. It bounced once and fizzed past her through the air to crack up against the pavilion wall. Soon afterwards he did the same thing again and some people in deck-chairs had to scatter, but the next ball made a mess of his wicket. Jenny looked up to see what they were changing the scoreboard to: 23 for 3, last man 9. The Masters were doing well.

Just then the Head and Sheila came and sat down on either side of her. Sheila did not say anything, and kept giving her inquisitive, unbelieving looks out of the corner of her eye, as if Jenny, while staying the same in every other way, had met a famous sex-murderer and got away with it. But the Head said a lot, mainly about the College and what it was like being head of it. He did it well, though, never going off on his own with it, and asking her questions about her own work, and listening to her replies. She had never seen a man get and stay so animated without the old I'm-available-girlie sign turning itself on in his eyes. While he was saying: 'We like to keep the damned parents out of the way as far as we can on this fixture,' there was a loud knock of bat on ball and she glanced up to see Dick running backwards with his face lifted in the air. The ball finally thumped on the ground some yards in front of him, just about where he had originally been standing. Jenny could tell by Patrick's movements what he was thinking, even though he was a hundred yards away. The scoreboard read: 39-4-11. A couple of minutes later some sort of argument at the pitch ended with a batsman coming in. 'Our mentors have evidently decided that no holds are barred, sport being an analogue of war,' the la-di-da voice said. 'You don't run out a batsman who's backing up without warning him first, do you? So I seem to remember from when I played this game, anyway.'

'This is the celebrated Skinner,' the Head said, gesturing towards a short cruel-looking boy with broad shoulders who was coming down the steps. 'I'm afraid this is the end for Patrick's chaps.'

There was a roar from Graham at each of the first two balls bowled to Skinner. 'Mac aims at setting up an association-pattern whereby to make a stroke at a ball is linked with hearing a disagreeable noise and so to be avoided,' the la-di-da voice said.

Skinner hit the next ball into some trees on the far side of the field. 'See what I mean?' the Head said. But before Skinner

256

could get another chance two more boys were out. The Head lit a cigarette excitedly. 'That's Lawrence, the gym master, did that. He's been off the beer for a month, I'm told. But it's remarkable all the same. Forty-eight for seven. I can't believe it. Now if young Skinner can only keep the bowling . . .'

As soon as it was Skinner's turn he hit the ball into the trees again, and after that he hit one that bounced twice before crashing into the wire on some tennis courts. The batsman at the other end seemed to be settling down and even hit a boundary himself. Now and then one or the other of them hit the ball ordinarily and they ran between the wickets. When Skinner hit one on to the pavilion roof Patrick put a new bowler on. Skinner ran down the pitch to him and hit him over the tennis courts. The last ball of that over he hit nearly to the boundary, but took only one run off it. The idea of this – Jenny was pleased with herself for getting one of the finer points – was to arrange that he, and not his partner, should be up against Lawrence. There was almost complete silence as Lawrence ran up for the first ball of his over. By the end of it Skinner, try as he would, had not managed to hit the ball further than the fielders standing near the wicket. People clapped. 'A maiden against Skinner,' the voice on the balcony said. 'Our David Herbert has enough dark male wisdom for two.'

A pause developed on the field of play. From the way Dick was standing by the stumps and getting the fielders to move about, it was plain that he was about to bowl. Patrick explained to Jenny later that he had wanted to round the match off nicely (it was already as good as lost) by the public humiliation of Dick, whom either Skinner or his partner seemed capable of hitting into the canal at will. Dick paced out his run and came tottering and skipping up to the wicket and bowled as if throwing a bomb while being shot at. The ball bounced several times and rolled to a stop a yard or two to one side of Graham, who threw it back. The next one was faster. It passed the batsman about shoulder high and Graham caught it by hurling himself as far sideways as before but in the opposite direction. Jenny read the enjoyment in Patrick's movements and felt a little sorry for Dick. The third ball looked normal enough, apart from being very slow. Skinner's partner hit it hard and high into the air, but not far enough, because a man who might have been Lawrence separated himself from a group of fielders, ran like an idiot for about fifty yards and caught the ball in one outstretched hand. Everybody clapped. Dick could be seen giving a serious thank-you wave, which also got in a hint that this had all been prearranged, in the direction of Lawrence, now on his feet again and massaging his elbow.

'Well, that was a surprise,' the Head said. 'It must have been a better ball than it looked. That friend of Patrick's bowling, isn't it? – the chap they brought in at the last minute. He didn't look much like a cricketer earlier on. Afraid of the damned ball, I'd have said. Oh well. That's what? eighty-one for eight, last man five. I suppose there is just a faint chance . . .'

'I'm taking off now, Daddy.' Sheila, who had been watching her father's keenness and Jenny's interest with increasing irritation, got up with a lady-discus-thrower movement. 'I just can't stand to sit here any longer and have these jerks pitch themselves around.'

'Ah, come along, dear, it'll be over in a moment and we can drive down. Two minutes. Excuse me, Miss Bunn. Sheila . . . look . . . it'll only . . .' He went after her round the corner of the pavilion.

Jenny thought to herself that here she was, nearly twenty-one, and instead of having been a teenager all she had managed to do was spend a certain amount of time getting from the age of twelve to the age of twenty. She had believed herself lucky to miss all the gang and vice and fighting and in need of care and protection and delinquency you read about and saw on TV, but if that was really a part of life instead of just something that happened somewhere else, could someone who had missed it claim to know much about things in general? But surely to understand about delinquency you would have to *be* a delinquent? She gave it up and looked back at the cricket.

She was in time to see the ball being thrown back from the far boundary, where the new batsman had evidently hit it. Getting it safely back into Dick's hands turned out to be troublesome, with a sort of pig-in-the-middle touch when the fielders on either side of him threw it to and fro in the hope that sooner or later he would catch it. Finally he did, and bowled again. The batsman skipped out to meet the ball and gave a great swipe at it, but missed. It was a faster one than before. Graham caught it near the ground before it had bounced and knocked the stumps down with it, roaring, while the batsman was still in mid-air on his way back. Through the noise that followed Jenny heard a car starting up and a moment later the Head, with Sheila next to him, drove slowly out from behind the pavilion and down the cinder-track to the gate. Jenny saw him gazing over at the cricket-pitch for a moment before driving on round the corner of the hedge.

'All right, Horace,' a different la-di-da voice said. 'All we want from you is a forcing knock of nought not out. Last ball of the over, if you recall.'

Jenny was quite surprised to see the son of fatty buster and flying panel plodding towards the field of play. It had not really occurred to her that he would be thought capable of batting in an actual match. She felt full of hope that Patrick's team would win as she watched Dick, who had no doubt been praising Graham for his cooperation, walk back to his place. His body was tilted further over than she had ever seen it since the first day they met, but he had been carrying her zip bag then. Did he not know about it, or did he know about it and not care?

The umpire showed Horace where to hold his bat and Horace tapped it on the ground once or twice. Dick hurtled up to the wicket, his arms and legs going in all directions, and bowled. Something went wrong with his stride at the last minute, or perhaps he slipped. Anyway, this time he gave an imitation of a man being shot while throwing a bomb. The ball travelled very fast and high towards Horace, who seemed uncertain whether to make a stroke at it or duck out of the way. In the event he did neither; before he could come to a decision the ball hit him loudly on the head and laid him out full length beside his wicket. He was up and about again almost at once, rubbing away at the injured part while the fielders came crowding round, and Jenny could see Dick apologizing, but there was no getting away from the fact that some part of Horace or his equipment had knocked one of his stumps over to one side. Jenny gathered from those near her that this was something called *hit wicket* and that the Masters had therefore beaten the College by three runs. 'Three for four in one over,' one of the voices said. 'A pretty devastating spell, you might say.'

The players began to come in. The last to move was Skinner, who had been standing like a statue, hand on hip and leaning on his bat, while all these things he could do nothing about went on. Some of the spectators went out to meet the cricketers, Horace's mother in the lead. He told her, several times and loudly, to leave him alone, so she went on to being queenly over Dick's apologies. Skinner walked through without taking any notice of those who congratulated him on his innings and clumped off into the dressing-room. Patrick came up, grinning. 'All right, eh? A pity about Dick seeming to have done so well, but the Horace thing nearly makes up for it.'

'For shame, Patrick, you're not pleased about that, are you?'

'Oh yes I am, it'll do him good. Show no mercy to bastards, for they will show you none. You see if I'm not right.' Then he frowned. 'Actually it doesn't make up for the Dick thing, any-where near. We'll never hear the end of this. Old Eat-All-Sup-All-Pay-Nowt'll be reminiscing about it as long as we know him.' He lit a cigarette. 'But we needn't go on doing that, need we? Why don't you move out of that bloody rat-hole, fast?'

'Oh, it's not so bad, it's cheap and I know them.'

'Who wants to know them? Anyway, I thought Mrs T. had been coming the acid rather.'

'She's all right again now. She's quite sweet.'

'Sweet, my royal Irish . . . We'll talk about it later. I'm going to change. Won't take me a minute.'

Jenny talked to Graham for a moment, telling him how well he had done behind the stumps and being told in return that yes, his dismissal of the captain of the Eleven off the first ball of the innings had been a blow in morale and material from which the College team could fairly be said never to have recovered. Dick, although still concerned about laying Horace out, was so thrilled with himself that Jenny would not have had the heart not to congratulate him even if she had wanted not to. Then one of the older boys came up and started explaining how much free time he got, how easy it was for him to get out of College in the evenings and how very fetching, if he might say so, she looked in that dress. The way he got from 'Hallo' to 'One *can* enjoy oneself in this town if one knows where to go' before the end of the first sentence certainly showed how ones of this age were coming on, though of course it was a different class. The only thing was that he arrived just that little bit too quickly at explaining about the short cut back to the High Street he could show her, and she was not sorry when Patrick reappeared and the boy said he was afraid he must be getting back to his House. Patrick hung about for a moment to call out remarks to various mates, which she liked seeing, because men together was always pleasant. It showed that they could feel genuine friendliness when sex was not in question, which went some way to suggest that they also felt it when sex was, and again it helped to knock on the head (unless they were all very good actors) the fantasy she occasionally had at difficult times, that the whole bunch of them had ganged up in an anti-virginity conspiracy which filled in every spare minute.

Patrick took her arm and walked her over to the 110. 'Graham'll be a few minutes yet,' he said. 'He hadn't started discussing the College batting when I left.' He put his bag in the car and led her down a short path towards a shed by the hedge. Near it there was something that looked like the ribs of a small boat mounted on a frame. Jenny knew from Robbie that it was a machine used for catching practice. A dozen yards away cars were moving slowly along the cinder-track among strolling, chatting groups of boys and adults, but Jenny paid no attention to any of them. She was with Patrick. That meant that this small corner by the hedge had a light and colour as striking as if she had just stepped into it out of a darkened room, and yet being here was so full of different things to think and feel that it affected her like something already in the past, like one of those flashes from a summer holiday or a Saturday evening walk years ago which would suddenly come back to her for a moment with all its flavour intact, the exact shade of sunlight and the air on her skin and herself in her own body, before it faded and left her trying to visualize and remember. France, she thought, France. She looked down at a tiny stream that ran along the hedge, and it was as if she was looking down from an aeroplane on a river far from civilization, complete with rapids and stony banks and thick greenery overhanging the water.

Patrick stopped by the catching-machine and said: 'I've got something to tell you.'

It was going to be bad but honest; his expression told her that. She tried to get herself ready. 'Yes?' she said.

'I'm doing it now because I'm not kissing you or anything, I can't here with these people, and it isn't late at night or romantic or anything. Anyway.' She saw him bite the tip of his tongue. 'Darling . . . I can't carry on any longer as we are. I've tried but it's too much of a strain. I love you and I want to sleep with you. I can't go on seeing you and not. I couldn't go to France with you and not. I shouldn't have mentioned France to you. I shan't be able to stop sleeping with anyone much longer. Then I couldn't tell you about it because that'd muck everything up, only you'd know, and if I did tell you it'd be the same. So I'm saying this first, before it happens. It isn't blackmail, this, what I'm saying, just how things are, that's all. Isn't it?'

She nodded. 'Yes,' she said, wondering why he seemed to be trying to comfort her. She waited for him to go on.

'There's no sense wrapping this up. If you, you know, feel you can, then come round and see me, come round to the flat on Saturday afternoon. It's Julian's party in the evening. We could go on there later. Come round about two.'

'You mean come round and be made love to, don't you, all the way?'

'Yes.'

'I see. What happens if I don't come?'

'Well, then that's the –'

'All right, I'll come.'

'Good. I'm sorry I mentioned France when I did.'

'Oh, that's all right.'

'About two on Saturday, then.'

'All right.'

They got into the car as if they had agreed to part, not go to bed together. Patrick said: 'I'll run you up and then I'm going off to have a few beers with Graham and Thackeray and Lawrence and one or two of the others. I thought it would be easier for us both if we didn't see each other this evening; or until Saturday.'

'Yes.' That last bit was in the comforting style again.

Graham and Thackeray turned up with their cricket bags. Sometime after they had started off, Jenny heard Graham say to Thackeray in the back seat: 'Let's see that finger. Mm, nasty, you'll have a nail off there, I should say. At the pace Skinner hits them it's unwise to try to stop them unless you know you can get your whole hand to them.' That was all she remembered of the short car-journey to the Thompsons', from the moment she got out and walked up the path.

She lay on her bed, gathering the energy to go down to the kitchen and see exactly how dry her supper had become. There was a faint chance that she would be able to make her own, if this was one of Martha's absolute dormouse lazy evenings. The household was short on energy these days and seemed to have shrunk, as if all sorts of people who used to be living there had come into money and gone off and bought posh houses in London. Dick and Anna treated her with a very similar mixture of resentment and embarrassment, plus just about enough sub-normal ordinariness to make life bearable; Martha, who was chiefly to be seen shuffling along to her bedroom or the bath-room or the front room with a book and a bag of sweets, treated her as a senior guest would treat a junior in a boarding-house. This evening particularly, Jenny was sorry she had never bought herself a kitten as she had planned at the start. But she could not have given it the run of the house, and to keep it shut up in her room would have been cruel, with her out so much of the time. They had to have company.

She was surprised to realize that she had not thought about Patrick and the rest of it since they had talked at the sports field. Each time she tried to imagine what it would be like on Saturday afternoon her mind went blank. Mostly she thought she felt frightened, in the way of someone who had done a bad thing that might be found out at any moment. What had happened to those beliefs of hers, the broad one that said Saturday afternoon would be wrong and the personal one that said it was not her way of going on? They were still there, but they had a thin, sort of last-year's feel to them. The trouble with them was that they did not bring other people in, only herself and that there were not enough of them. There could not be; how could there be a rule for everything you did from one second to the next, and for how you were to feel about it? If you were given a scout compass and told to use it to find a certain building in a strange city, you would probably never get there, and if you did you would not have found out anything about the city.

She curled up on the bed and fell asleep. She dreamt that she had found out the best way of taming tigers: you gave them a lot of green apples to eat and then a lot of ice-water to drink. Then when their stomach-aches got really terrible you rubbed their stomachs for them, which they could not do themselves, and after that they would do anything for you. At a big banquet they gave in her honour the head one got up and said that nobody had done more than Miss Bunn to bring about a better mutual understanding and to improve tiger-people relations.

A door slammed – Martha's? – and the banqueting tigers collapsed like burst balloons. Jenny sat up and yawned. For a moment she thought of putting a call through to Trixie; but that would not do any good. She would go round and see Elsie Carter instead. Not that she would discuss anything with her. She was getting tired of being told authoritatively that she was a fool for doing or not doing what she intended to do or not do. Her eye fell on the yellow-berried plant, and she felt guilty for not having watered it for so long. She really must give it a drink soon, leaves and all. But not just yet.

Chapter Twenty-Three

PATRICK's chief administrative difficulty on the Saturday turned out to be the disposal of Graham. His normal fee for absenting himself from their flat was an account from Patrick of what had taken place there. In the present instance Patrick was unwilling to meet this, especially since a really serious sexual passage on his part would entail the delivery of a fuller communiqué than usual, one richer in innuendo. Further, Graham was opposed to the seduction of virgins in general, unmoved by Patrick's plea that after all someone had got to do it, and could be relied on to upbraid him sharply every few hours until the end of term for the seduction of this virgin in particular. In the present state of Patrick's conscience this was a daunting prospect. And without revealing the full magnitude of Saturday's operation it would be impossible to impress on Graham, who was given to terminating his absences unexpectedly early about one time in fifteen, the utter necessity of his staying out of the picture for a full six hours. The thing was, then, to cajole him into doing something which would keep him at a safe distance but which could be represented as beneficial to him. Yes. But what? Mm?

After much self-communing, Patrick decided that the key to the problem lay in cricket. Somehow he must build up in Graham a deep conviction that to miss the first day's play in the impending match between the M.C.C. and the touring team would rank as a crippling deprivation. Accordingly he went through the Masters v. College game repeatedly and from all possible angles, laying stress on Graham's own contribution (which had been real enough). He discussed the M.C.C. team individually, as a unit, in and for itself, as a preview of England's Test side, examined the tourists' record in their previous home season, against their Pakistani visitors of the preceding year, at last week's charity fixture with the Hon. Ansley Coale's Eleven. Throughout he dwelt on the sad inferiority of a TV view of Saturday's proceedings as compared with attendance in person. On the Friday morning he struck. Feigning some trouble with his watch, he got himself and Graham out of bed a full half-hour earlier than usual, and used the extra time to read aloud every word of both the *Guardian* and the *Express* accounts for tomorrow's prospects. 'Well, what do you think?' he said. 'Shall we drive up in the morning and have a look at them?'

'Ah, we might, though it seems an awful long trip for a few hours' cricket.'

'Oh no, it shouldn't take us more than an hour either way. I must say I'm very keen to see this new fast bowler of theirs. The chap in the *Express* the other day compared him with the young Larwood.'

'Parking's going to be a great headache.'

'Oh, they make special arrangements for that. Did you see he took seven for twenty-three in the last Test against Pakistan?'

'You told me. The weather doesn't look too bright. Let me see . . .'

'These chaps aren't used to sticky wickets. If there is a spot of rain the M.C.C. spinners ought to –'

'Here we are. *A belt of depression will spread . . . showers in southern districts . . . further rain likely . . .* Mm. It doesn't sound very healthy.'

'They're always way off on these long-range forecasts,' Patrick said, pouring Graham more coffee and wishing it was whisky.

'Well, we'll see. I thought you'd have been out with Jenny on a Saturday afternoon.'

'She's taking some kids out somewhere, I gather.' The kids' outing was destined to fall through at about noon the next day.

'We'll make up our minds tomorrow morning.'

Patrick spent an hour and a half that evening looking over the 110 to make sure nothing was imminently going to go wrong with it. Once it had done its job of taking Graham as far as the metropolis the thing could blow up for all he cared, but a flat tyre or a choked petrol-feed in the first few miles would be undesirable. It was a labour of love to clean the plugs and top up the battery.

There was rain during the night, and more in the morning. *The weeping Pleiads wester*, Patrick said to himself, *and I lie down alone*. He said lots of other things to himself. By eleven the rain had petered out; by twelve there were feeble bursts of sun, though the air remained cold; by twelve-thirty Patrick had got Graham into the George and was explaining about Jenny's kids' outing. The George was important because it had no wireless or TV from which Graham might think to get information about the state of affairs at Lord's. Patrick got Graham a double scotch, explaining that he had had a cheque from his mother that morning, and went into a tragic monologue about not being able to see the M.C.C. spinners at work in conditions that might have been made to order for them. Graham listened attentively and said: 'I don't think I'll bother on my own, Standish.'

'Oh, you'd be a fool to miss a situation like this, chum. I wish to Christ I could ditch –'

'It's probably raining in London while we sit here.'

'Stuff that, it's all part of the same geographical area. If the M.C.C. win the toss they'll put them in, of course. By tea-time –'

'Nothing more depressing than hanging about at a cricket ground.'

'One reason I'm sorry to miss it,' Patick said abstractedly, 'is that according to Julian Ormerod it's one of the occasions in the year when half the point in going is to see what you can pick up. They all turn out in force, apparently. Might have been fun, but –'

'You're not serious. At Lord's cricket ground, the headquarters of the Marylebone Cricket Club? Girls waiting to be picked up?'

'I'm perfectly serious. Julian was. I gathered it was an understood thing. Of course, they wouldn't be pick-ups in the crude sense. Just, you know, decent girls seeing what's available.'

'I see. It still sounds fantastic.'

'I know, I thought just the same. But old Julian knows what he's talking about on that subject.'

'He does indeed. The sun seems a little stronger now. Yes, there's some blue sky over the heath there. Well – what have I got to lose?'

Five minutes later Patrick was standing outside the flat watching the 110 descend towards the London road and anxiously noting the amount of oil it was burning. But hell, he had done all man could. And how beautiful and important everything looked. Through gaps in the buildings he could see, more than half a mile off, part of a chain of barges moving along the canal; further off still a red van was moving up the road to the common; nearer at hand a man on a mobile gantry was doing something to a street-lamp. For once in its life the old place was doing its best to act up to a town's God-given, cinematic role of serving as background, relevant in its irrelevance, to some major human act. Nothing short of a hydrogen missile on the capital, he now felt, could interfere with this afternoon. He went in, took the street door off its latch and turned on the TV set in the sitting-room.

Before the vision came on a voice said to Patrick as if it loved him: '... not what one might have hoped. However, the umpires are making another inspection of the pitch at two-fifteen, and I should say that it would be premature, quite definitely premature, to say categorically *at this stage* that there will be no play at all today. Don't you think so, John?' John said that that was what he thought. 'We shall be back with you at two-fifteen, and in the meantime, after one more look round the ground, we shall return you to the studio. So for the moment it's good-bye from all of us at Lord's, or shall I say – *au revoir*?'

'Yeah, you say that, boy,' Patrick said, as the camera tracked from one thinly-occupied block of seats to the next. An occasional umbrella was up, whether because its owner had died of rage under it or because rain was actually falling could not be established. There were some views of great heaps of ragged newspaper, then a long shot of the pitch with the covers on it. Finally a card saying *M.C.C. v. Tourists' XI* NO PLAY YET came up. Patrick switched off, making a short speech to the Creator, ironical in tone and tendency, for having made it rain today when there was no reason why it should not have been fine.

Well, there was no point in not going ahead. It was one o'clock. He removed a handful of Oxford texts from the shelf and took out the half-bottle of gin that had been patiently waiting there since Thursday. He drank some of it, mixed with about the same quantity of tonic water. Putting clean sheets on the bed and getting through the bathroom part took him until one-forty. Then he had another drink. While he did this he topped up two half-empty tonic bottles with an ounce or two of gin. Getting drink into Jenny was usually like getting blood into a stone, but this afternoon was something of a special occasion, after all, and he owed it to her to see that she got more than she was prepared to give herself. He took a small white box from his pocket and looked at the pair of earrings inside. He knew she would like them; he had always been good at choosing presents. The memory of how long it had taken him to decide against giving her an engagement ring instead almost made him grab the bottle of gin and run out of the building. With delight and anticipatory gratitude he visualized arriving at Julian's party with an earringed and radiant Jenny. He could not visualize their love-making. At least his imagination could not, but something else could; anyway, parts of his stomach seemed to be missing, or present only in a sketchy, token fashion, a phenomenon he had not experienced since facing his first College class, and his heart was going at clock-tick speed. He poured himself a small drink, sat down gently and drank it gently: it would never do to have the old coronary do its stuff at a time like this.

He took down *Bonjour Tristesse* and started reading it. Abandoning this after about fifty seconds, he got up and went over to the horrible pallid cupboard, liberally ringed with heat-marks and fluted with cigarette-burns, in which Jenny had been trying to make him keep his gramophone records. One of these, having a curious title and an irrelevant but real-stuff girl on the coloured wrapper, he divested of its coverings and laid on the turntable of the player that Graham had more or less built for him. Graham liked record-players, regarding records as things that showed off record-players. Patrick only liked record-players as things that played records. Every couple of weeks Graham found out some new way of reducing distortion or filtering off surface noise or eliminating wow, took the player to pieces and kept it so. The only way of making him put it together again was to buy a new record, for he recognized as just and reason-able the desire to hear such a record without delay. If he moved into an energetic phase, such as the fancied prospect of sexual success often brought on, keeping the player entire could cost a lot of money. Patrick felt there was a lot to be said for the pristine kind of gramophone being gazed at by a degenerate-looking dog on the label of the present record.

The music played. It was East Coast stuff, carphology in sound. After a frugal tune had twice been announced in unison, an alto saxophone offered a sixty-four bar contribution to the permanent overthrow of melody. Just when it seemed that the musician must break out into verbal abuse, a trumpet began to rave. Several kinds of drum and cymbal continued a self-renew-ing frenzy in what had at one time been called the background, while underneath it all the string bass plodded metrically on as if undismayed. And the thing had got four stars in *Jazz Monthly*. An idea entered Patrick's head and he searched along the bookshelf at his side for something to write on. A couple of battered sheets of typescript came to hand: what the hell was this? He unfolded them with foreboding and read:

more recent editors, but first advanced by Otto, that we have here a short lacuna. *Although Otto's views are always worthy of respect, on this occasion he appears to have reached out too eagerly for the traditional versus nonnullos excidisse credo life-belt. Further, he was not aware, as we are, that MS G is not derived from M via A, but descends from the authoritative P.*

Retention of the G and A reading admittedly involves us in a form of anacoluthon to which elegiac verse affords no exact parallel. However, we read at Metamorphoses oh christ why has thackeray still got my copy cant he get one of his own why cant he learn the mean sodding calibans deathmask of a

There was still room on one of the sheets for what he had been intending ever since picking up a book called *Twelve Bad Men* at Susan's and Joan's. It had proved not to be a work on Conservative prime ministers or classical scholars or Dixieland musicians, but an anthology of famous trials for fraud of various kinds – he had half expected to see a younger Julian grinning up at him from the photographic section. He took out his ballpoint and wrote off at a creditable speed:

> *1. Sir Malcolm Sargent*
> *2. Cicero*
> *3. Dick Thompson* *
> *4. John Coltrane*
> *5. Milton*
> *6. Sir John Gielgud*
> *7. Charlton*
> *8. Selwyn Lloyd †*
> *9. Charlie Crosland*
> *10. Rimbaud*
> *11. Billy Bolton*
> *12th man: Beethoven*

* *Denotes captain*   † *Denotes wicket-keeper*

Patrick stubbed out his cigarette on the underside of a bookshelf and dropped it into the waste-paper basket, feeling the glow of artistic endeavour fade into a question about what had happened to the Patrick who had at any rate got started on a textual note and used to read a book occasionally. At that moment a sharp uneasiness started up somewhere inside him. His breathing quickened and deepened as at the onset of sexual excitement, but this was not his condition. He felt his heart speeding up again and becoming irregular, like a bird making shorter and longer hops. There was a faint, hollow rolling and grinding in his ears, while a tepid prickling spread over his skin from a point midway between his shoulderblades. Nothing in his thoughts or his situation accounted for these symptoms which, the accompaniments of terror, stirred in him more than one kind of terror, as they had recently been doing every other night or so while he lay awake in bed. This was the first time they had come on in the day. He tried to control his breathing and bit his lips to stifle a moan. His heart struck at the inside of his chest, then paused, while his body in its chair appeared to be gliding sideways on the arc of a circle or spiral, accelerating as the bird, seemingly in mid-air now, broke laboriously into flight. At this point his own vision of death, refined and extended nightly for years, was directly before him. To the accompaniment of a buzzing sound, the chair would slowly tilt backwards until his body dropped off head first, but face up, into completely dark water that filled his lungs and disposed of everything but the struggle to breathe, giving place some time later to thick water, then thin mud, then thick mud, just mud and the struggle to breathe, a gradual loss of consciousness followed by dreams of water and mud and the struggle to breathe, dreams superseded by identical dreams, a death prolonged for ever.

The bird alighted, the chair stopped its apparent motion. He lay back, thinking of nothing but that he seemed to be still there, until he was sure he was on the far side of the thing. He did some deep breathing for a minute or so, then walked with all the steadiness he could manage to the window, intent on seeing a human figure, and was rewarded by the sight of a lorry-load of booze moving majestically up the hill in the direction of the country club. These chaps worked a long week, but then they were performing a vital service. At once he felt much better, almost as much better as the sight of a lorry-load of the real stuff would have made him feel. Which reminded him: it was now two-fifteen. Well, he had said *about* two. For Jenny to have arrived on the dot would have been too much like a salmon's leap taking it full toss into the creel.

The Jazz Research Team on the record-player had gone into

an unlyrical ballad in an attempt to make a single 32-bar chorus last five minutes. He examined their faces on the back of the sleeve: solemn, horn-rimmed, bearded. Someone had told them that they were creative artists, and they had believed him. 'Why is the jass music,' he asked them, 'and therefore the jass band?' He shut them off in the middle of a long arhythmic bicycle-bell cadenza, poured himself another drink in celebration of having been taken off Charon's quota for the day, and switched on the TV.

Music. That was bad. And there was an added sting in its being one of those galop or cotillon or strathspey things. The NO PLAY YET card flashed into visibility. After a moment the galop receded slightly and a formal voice said: 'The news from Lord's: the umpires have just inspected the pitch and have announced that, if there is no further rain, play will commence at three o'clock.' Just then there was a slight noise from the window as a handful of small drops blew against it. Swearing in a pedestrian, uninventive vein, Patrick switched off. He wished he knew more about things climatic, but it was clearly too late for serious hyetographical inquiry. That fright of his, he was now in a position to reason, had been of no particular significance and was certainly not based on cardiac nonsense or anything of that kind. All that type of stuff, dying and so on, was a long way off, not such a long way off as it had once been, admitted, and no doubt the time when it wouldn't be such a long way off as all that wasn't such a long way off as all that, but still. Still what? Well, in the meantime, this cardiac business of his was obviously psychogenic, or – what the hell was that other -genic one? – neurogenic, recalling in inverted form that schizophrenic thing he had thought was brewing up four or five years previously. That lot was long since written off as somatogenic, to do with late nights and his liver and so on, rather as the present lot was to do with insecurity and remorse and feeling guilty about Jenny and so on.

Not that that last bit could be laughed off with any efficiency, least of all at a time – two twenty-five – when the girl was conceivably about to deny him substantial cause to feel guilty about her. She was a good person, a factor which, as a convinced moralist, he imagined he set a high value upon, but to be prevented from, instead of voluntarily deciding against, altering her from what she was and should go on being had no relish of salvation in it. He went and looked out of the window again. It was raining in a chary, furtive fashion, trying to pass off sharp saturated gusts as mere wafts of cold damp air. The houses opposite had shifted from massive indifference to their usual complacent nullity. Was tragic dignity or *c'est-la-vie* sophistication to be the prepared position on which he ought soon to be thinking about falling back? Another drink would strengthen either. And it would have the added advantage of finally sluicing down some remote spiritual cloaca those scruples about what he thought he was up to, or still hoped to get the chance of being up to. He had his other drink. Then, thinking about what tremendous, pride-engendering and – his obligations having been what they were – morally unimpugnable fun that second night with Joan had been, he had another other drink. Then, as a revenge on something, he played to himself the whole of a recording of *Concerto No. 3 in C major*, op. 26, for pianoforte and orchestra, by Serge Prokofiev (1891–1953), the property of Graham. Then, after scanning himself for any fragments of edification that might have lodged in him, he turned on the wireless (the next TV visit to Lord's was not until four-thirty) and heard a trustworthy country voice saying: '. . . in what I would call a most inspiring way. But at the moment it makes a melancholy picture, that can't be denied: the brooding grey sky that promises more rain to come, the little forlorn knots of spectators, or would-be spectators – I can see one of them now, a stocky blond raincoated figure just underneath me here, sadly opening a last bottle of stout – all of them hoping without any real confidence that when the umpires make what must surely be their last inspection of the pitch at four o'clock, the verdict may –'

Patrick cut him off before he could see another of the would-be spectators, an ill-built mouse-haired nose-twitching figure, sadly thrusting his hand into the bosom of some better-built figure. For a moment he felt ashamed at having dropped that girl-finding project so thoroughly, before recollecting the duty of physicians to heal themselves. He went to the phone and dialled the Thompsons' number, replacing the receiver immediately after the last digit. When he had done that he thought he would try a gin and tonic. He did, reading some book or other the while. The gin and tonic turned out to be very nice, and so did its successor. He was holding the bottle up to what light there was and wondering what had become of so much of its contents when he heard the street-door slam and footsteps start coming up the stairs. He smoothed his hair back, set his mouth at the *sensitive* position (it needed some tugging), and threw open the door, uttering a welcoming 'Ah' which went up by about a diminished fifth when he saw that his visitor was not Jenny but Sheila.

Chapter Twenty-Four

'I was just passing this way, so I thought I'd drop up,' she said. He shut the door and motioned into the drinking area. 'Well done. Like a gin and tonic?'

'That's a great idea. What is this, a party?'

'That kind of thing,' he assured her, picking up the gin-and-tonic bottle.

'What happened to your room-mate?'

'He's in London.'

'Is that right? He's a real odd-ball.'

'He's . . .? Oh, an odd-ball. Yes, he is, isn't he?'

'He was around me all the chance he got at that cricket game. You don't have ice, do you?'

'I'm afraid I don't, I mean I haven't. Graham was around you, you say? But that's ex –'

'He's quite a guy, isn't he?'

'In a sense, yes, he is.'

'But let's not talk about him; the great thing is he's out of the way.' She was looking at him. More than that, she was looking at him with the look she used to indicate availability, which given her history was rather like an executioner with mask, tights and axe wearing a placard round his neck that said I KILL PEOPLE. 'I've got you by myself at last.'

'So you have.'

'Are you free just now?'

'I'm not going anywhere.'

'Great.' She moved nearer. 'You and I have got some unfinished business to get through together.'

'Do you really think so?'

'Sure I do. Do I have to draw you a picture?'

'That might be fun.' He saw that she had stepped up the availability look to the extreme phase, one that set the sophisticated mind running on thoughts of approved schools and corrective training, while the less worldly might have taken it as stark terror or even religious awe. Her crimson coarse-weave cardigan was a great advance on those quite unnecessarily mannish striped shirts she used to wear, and her chin seemed to have shrunk slightly in the last three days, as if she had been rubbing it with bust-reducing cream, a commodity that in other respects she could have had little use for. Further, she was wearing a lot of scent. He liked scent. It reminded him of sex.

'Aw, why pretend, lover? Let's lay it on the line, shall we? If you want me to spell it out I will. You can do anything you like with me, as of right now.'

Patrick set his glass down carefully on the pallid cupboard and clasped his hands behind him. First clearing his throat, he said: 'Now listen, Sheila. I don't think you quite understand everything that's involved here. This isn't the kind of thing one can just leap into without looking ahead. There are lots of things you seem to have forgotten. First of all, you're very young, only just over seventeen, too young to be getting mixed up with – any of that kind of thing. And it's not as if I'm that sort of age myself, either. I'm an older man, not quite old enough to be your father but certainly old enough to know better, old enough to have acquired some sort of sense of responsibility, of duty towards other people. It's my job to set you an example, to do what I can to restrain you from any foolish or immoral behaviour, not to encourage you in it and above all not to, er, participate in it with you. Quite apart from all that, I stand to you in a special position of trust on account of my situation in relation to your father. I'm accountable to him in all my dealings with you. It's a simple, straightforward question of *loyalty*, Sheila. There is such a thing as faith, after all, and decency. I don't think you've considered any of those arguments, have you?'

She took a quick sip from her drink. 'I guess I didn't.'

'I rather imagined not. After you leave here I want you to promise me to weigh them up carefully and try to understand them. The whole point is this: you should never have come here at all. However, since you've taken the trouble to turn up . . .'

About an hour later he noticed that she was crying. Closer scrutiny showed that her chin had reverted to its accustomed size, but this gave her a look of pathos. And the code said always to be nice to them when they cried, other things being equal. He kissed her shoulder and murmured: 'Ah, what's the matter, honey? Come on, tell me about it.'

'Oh, I couldn't, it's too terrible. Oh, I wish I was dead.'

He gave her the it-can't-be-as-bad-as-that treatment, more kisses, etc.

'I'm in the most awful trouble,' she said finally, sobbing.

'What? Not as soon as this? How can you tell? You can't be.'

'No, silly, not you, someone else.'

He felt slightly dashed to find that she was not crying over anything that he had done, but went on manfully: 'Who is he? If I'm going to be able to help I've got to know who he is.'

'You can't help, nobody can. There's nothing anybody can do. It's too late. Oh, poor old Dad.'

'Sheila, how old is it? Talk sensibly, now, there's a good girl.'

She wiped her cheeks on the sheet. 'Well, it's nearly three weeks now since I was supposed to.'

'Was that the first one you've missed?'

'Yes.'

'Then we're all right.' It would mean a heavy inroad on the old *potabile aurum*, but he had survived that before. 'Don't worry about it. But who is he? Is he married?'

'No.'

'Who is he?'

'Oh, I can't . . . I wasn't to . . . he's . . . it's . . .'

'Who is he?'

'Horace Charlton.'

Patrick managed to stifle his laughter. 'I thought you didn't like him,' he said.

'Oh, I don't, I was such a goof, but he kept on at me, and I'd got lonely, you know how you do, and so ...'

'Yes, I know. Now I'm just going downstairs to fix you up. I'll only be about ten minutes. Don't go away.'

In the sitting-room, a dressing-gown about him, he started by having another drink. Then he removed from the outside of the door a notice that said he had gone to the pictures and substituted one that said he had gone to the George (it was now nearly six o'clock). Then he made two phone calls. Then, wincing loudly, praying for a boom in the clothing business, he wrote out a cheque. Then he turned on the television. The card said *M.C.C. v. Tourists' XI* NO PLAY TODAY. 'That's all you know, brother,' he said.

Upstairs again, he handed Sheila a sheet of paper. 'It's all fixed,' he told her. 'That's the address. That's the time of the appointment. That's your name. That's your age. That's who recommended you. That's the reason why you can't have it. That's the lot. Oh, there's this too. Cash it at a branch in London.'

'Oh, Patrick, can you afford it?'

'No, so you tell Horace he's got to sell everything he can lay his hands on and give you the money to give to me. He can flog some of his old man's suits for a start. There's another message I want you to pass on to Horace, but we won't worry about that for the moment. What you must do is stop worrying. This man's very good and very kind and very clean and very safe. He was in Harley Street at one stage. You can rely on him absolutely.'

'Oh, Patrick, you are marvellous, I do love you. Come over here where I can thank you properly.'

Thanking him properly took another half-hour or so. Afterwards they sat and had a drink. Patrick said: 'This is the other thing I want you to tell Horace. His old man knows I've, well, run into you now and then and he keeps threatening to tell your father. Old Charlton gets a lot of his dope from Horace. I've stalled Charlton off for a bit by putting Horace's name on the scholarship list, which I'd threatened not to do. But that won't hold him off for ever. Now you tell Horace to tell his old man that he was dead wrong about me and you. All a misunderstanding. I just about know you to speak to and that's it. Tell him that if I ever do find myself up in front of your dad he'll find himself there too and you'll tell everyone what he's been up to. Have you got all that?'

'Yes.'

'Will you do it?'

'Yes.'

'Can you make Horace do his part of it?'

'Yes.'

'I hope to God you can. He has impulses, that lad. To behave stupidly and talk piss. Now about the other business. It's absolutely vital that you keep that appointment and you'll have to stay around at the place for a day or two afterwards. Can you manage that?'

'Sure, it's a push-over. Nothing easier. One of my girl friends'll cover up for me.'

'That's everything, then. You're nicely fixed up. Christ, I wish I felt I was. Are you sure Horace'll play? When will you know?'

'He's meeting me right after I get out of here to . . .'

The old midatlantic tones faded. He gazed at her. A blush mantled her burly face. 'To hear how you got on,' he supplied.

'Oh, I feel just awful, after you've been so –'

'That's all right, doll. No complaints.'

'I'd like for you to know that even if I hadn't wanted anything from you I'd still've –'

'Yes, I know you'd still've. I believe you, mate. What interests me is when you'll be able to make me feel easier in my mind about Horace's part of the bargain.'

'He'll do anything I tell him, I promise you. But if you're anxious I could call you later, when I'm through talking with him.'

'Yes, you could ring me up when you've finished talking to him. At this number.' He wrote it down on the sheet of operation instructions. 'Don't lose this or you're cooked.'

'I'll be going now. You're a wonderful guy. I'll never be able to thank you.'

'You already have. Now don't worry. This chap's marvellous,

I'm told, very skilful and very kind. He won't ask you any nasty questions or anything. No trouble at all.'

'Funny, when I came in here I was just the unhappiest girl in the world and now I'm just walking on air.'

'All part of the service,' he said, shutting the door after her brawny figure before she could say: 'Thanks – for believing in me, Mr Blake,' before the music swelled and the credits rolled up, before, above all, he could be further struck by the very great disparity in attraction between the said brawny figure and its allotrope of half an hour ago. He was tired and hungry, but not the eating sort of hungry. To deal with both these conditions he finished the gin. Other troublesome symptoms – feeling more ashamed and humiliated than he had ever felt in his life, for example – would yield less readily to treatment of this kind. The commercial aspect of Sheila's dealings with him was trifling; it was outweighed a hundred times over by his brilliant conversion of the business into an anti-Charlton screen. What got him down was what he had actually done to Sheila. It was his worst thing so far, he thought as he phoned for a taxi, but plenty of time, no doubt, for worse yet. Wherever Jenny had got to, there was not much left of that elaborate structure of love and obligation and restraint which the two of them had been struggling to assemble and which he had begun to believe was bastard-proof. The enemy had been within the gates, he intoned over the two fingers of scotch – gorilla's fingers – he had found in the kitchen.

When the taxi came he wondered why it was not the 110, but got into it all the same and gave Julian's address. Yes, where was Graham? Still at Lord's making sure of a decent seat for Monday morning, or sitting in the Savoy cocktail lounge with some animate pin-up who had asked him to share her umbrella on the mid-wicket boundary? Ah, screw that. Screw *all* that. He rang Julian's bell as the taxi, presumably paid and tipped, drove off.

'Oh, it's you, Patty. You're a little early, about three hours, in fact, but never mind, come on in.'

'I want to lie down.'

'So I see. Are you always like this these days, or only when I happen to be around? Well now, won't take an instant to fix you up. You'll be meeting one or two old pals tonight, so you'll want to be in roaring form. Mind those steps – often have trouble there, don't you? Er er er er er er. Afraid this isn't much and the light won't work for some reason, but you won't be needing one, will you? *Her*. Just wander towards the talk and the laughter when you feel strong enough.'

Led, as one might lead a bear, into some dressing-room or other, Patrick drew the curtains and lay down on a divan he found. He dreamt he was walking round a large city square slashing people's clothes with a razor-blade. Nobody took any notice, which irritated him. Then some other people picked him up and carried him into a large building of classical design that occupied the whole of one side of the square. On the pediment there was an inscription. It read:

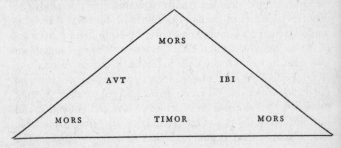

MORS

AVT   IBI

MORS   TIMOR   MORS

He tried to rearrange this to make sense, but he was soon across the threshold and placed on a couch, where heavy rugs were thrown over him. Men in white coats approached through the gloom, talking about him. They were surgeons. 'Not enough rugs,' they said. More rugs were brought and spread on him, heavier ones than before. One of them fell across his face and restricted his breathing until he managed to throw it off. This was difficult, because of the rugs covering his arms. 'Still not enough rugs.' The third lot of rugs were not spread over him, merely dropped in heaps. One landed on his feet, weighing them down, another on his face. It took him a long time to get that one off, and when he did his breathing was still laboured. 'More rugs for his face.' It had got darker, but he made out, walking away down a corridor, the figure of a woman. She was tall and slender, with long black hair reaching to her shoulders, and beneath a tight white skirt her hips and thighs moved in the way he knew and loved. He fought to sit up, throwing off the rugs with arms that seemed loaded down even when free, and ran after the woman, stumbling at every step over the rug at his feet, which he had not been able to remove. He caught her up quite soon, however, and she turned to face him. From the front she was a surgeon, with false hair stuck to the white skull-cap, looking at him over half-lenses. As he screamed, a rug was thrown over his head and among its folds he heard his own thin whimpering. Then he was borne down on to some other couch-like surface and tightly strapped in place. The straps were heavier than the rugs had been. The ones on his face and chest made it almost impossible to breathe. Soon he was conscious of nothing but darkness and the struggle to breathe. Finally, there was a buzzing sound and what he was lying on began slowly tilting downwards at the end where his head was.

He found that his arms and legs were struggling and that something had altered: it was real now. But what was all this hot suffocating heaviness that covered him, that yielded as he pushed and heaved, then fell back on him? He writhed, rolled over and fell on the floor. There was air; he screeched, fought, rolled over again, was free. Moaning and blubbering, he lay on his face for a moment. Then a door creaked open and some light came in. Somebody clicked a switch up and down with no result. 'What on earth's the matter?' a frightened voice asked: Jenny's voice.

'Oh, Jenny . . .'

'Patrick, love, what's been happening to you? Are you ill? See, it's me. You're all right, aren't you? What was all that noise about?'

He heaved himself up and her bare arms went round him, her face next to his with her fresh breath, all her slender body close to him and her warm clean young smell. 'Oh, I had such a nightmare,' he said. 'Such a horrible nightmare.'

'Well, it's all over now, sweet, all finished and done with. Just a silly old dream. There, it's all right now. Hey, what are all these things on the floor?'

A voice Patrick half-recognized called from the doorway: 'Darling, what was that most incredible row like somebody having about fifteen pink fits or something? Oh sorry, am I barging in?'

'What's going on?' a man's voice asked.

'It's all right,' Jenny called back, 'he's had a nightmare but he's all right now.'

'Nightmare? Why isn't there a light in here? I say, this is where I told all the chaps to dump their stuff.'

'They must have thrown their coats over the poor fellow's recumbent form,' Julian's voice said. 'All unknowing, as it were. Not too hard to work up a spot of the old *cauchemar* under half a ton or so of camel-hair and West of England. Deepest regrets, Patty. I should have told Tony here where you were, but somehow you slipped my mind, or where I'd put you did. Can I get you a drink?'

'I'll be all right.'

'Says he'll be all right.'

'He's in good hands.'

'Better leave him.'

'Oh, you poor pet,' Jenny murmured, stroking his hair. 'What did they do to you? Never mind, then.'

Patrick's afternoon returned with a rush. He drew free of Jenny and stood up, feeling for a cigarette. That however-since-you've-taken-the-trouble-to-turn-up routine with Sheila had been a real scream, hadn't it? Mm? He said angrily: 'And just where the hell were you at two o'clock, eh?'

Chapter Twenty-Five

'Oh, I'm so sorry, darling, I know it was awful of me, but when it came to it I found I just couldn't; I know I should have rung –'

'Oh, you know that, do you? and you know it was awful, but you did it just the same, or rather you didn't do it. You realize what you sound like? Like a bloody woman. *I know it's bad, but.* I thought you were supposed to be a cut above all that.'

'Patrick, listen, I did mean to, I got all ready, I spent I don't know how long, I kept telling myself I'd be off in a minute and

282

then I kept putting it off from one minute to the next, until in the end it seemed too late, but all the time up until then I meant to come.'

'Why didn't you, then? Actually I don't know why I'm bothering to ask. You found out when you came to it you couldn't. Couldn't break out of the dear old Methodist bloody youth club.'

'All right, if you like. But you ought to try and realize what it means, on an ordinary Saturday afternoon after corned beef and mashed potatoes, with Dick doing some hammering somewhere upstairs and Anna popping in to borrow a match and the geyser rumbling away, and then you're meant to just titivate yourself up a bit and slip your coat on and tootle round the corner and walk in and say here I am, then, come to be made an ex-virgin of, nice weather we're having for the time of year. It's no excuse, mind, I can see that, I'm just telling you how it happened, in case you're interested.'

'But you said you'd come, you'd made your decision.'

'But then I found I had to make it all over again, you see. And I didn't want to do that. That's really why I didn't ring, I suppose. I wanted to go on pretending I still might come right up until it was too late to. I was half-hoping you might come round and fetch me, too. Why didn't you do that?'

'I didn't know where you were.'

'Oh no, I might have been at the pictures or feeding the ducks or anywhere, mightn't I? If you'd've been there all the time, or if you'd've come round, well then, probably we –'

'You mean kissing and fondling you and persuading you and the rest of it?'

'Yes, then I wouldn't've had to –'

'Christ, you can't win at this bloody game, can you? I deliberately *didn't* do it like that, I went out of my way to pick the most unromantic circumstances I could so as you wouldn't feel you were being dragged into anything when you were all excited and couldn't be clear-headed about it. Now I'm told I should have done a straightforward sort of seduction job with drinks and soft lights and cushions and I-love-you and all the rest of the bloody circus.'

'You might have done better for yourself if you had.'

'That's good, that is. Here I go trying to be fair to you and all

283

that happens is I find I ought to have been unfair. Well, where the hell do you go after that?'

'I've no quarrel with you being fair to me, don't think that. Even if the one you were really after being fair to was you, so you wouldn't feel bad afterwards because it was all fifty-fifty, like. I'm only saying what your best policy was to get me into bed with you. And being unfair was that, every time. With most girls, what gets them into bed is the chap being unfair to them like that. The first chap, anyway. That's one of the reasons I'm against it.'

He puffed at his cigarette in the half light. 'So I gather. Where do we stand now, then?'

'Where we were, I expect.'

'Where's that? Where we were when? When I popped the question on that sort of cabbage patch on College field, or at two o'clock this afternoon?'

'They're the same, can't you see? You know, you've messed things up properly, you have. Saying I'll have a cup of coffee with you now'll be like saying I'm ready for bed. And you're a funny kind of lover, aren't you? Nobody'd think to hear you talk you were supposed to be trying to turn me into your mistress or whatever it is you call it. You remind me so much of that first time you took me out and you found I wouldn't do what you wanted right off. I'm beginning to wonder which is the real you.'

'Fine, wonder away and welcome.' He started towards the door. 'I'm going to get a drink.'

'Patrick, darling, I only just meant if you'd just be a little more ... And you're still all upset after your ... I shouldn't have ...'

She chased him as far as the head of the stairs, but he cantered down them much too fast for her stiletto heels to follow. When she got to the main room where the party was, he was over by the drinks table already talking hard to a tall dark woman in grey called Susan, whom Jenny had met earlier. She wandered slowly in the same direction through the crowds of people, who seemed to have doubled in numbers since she rushed upstairs to Patrick. The new ones had perhaps had a long way to come, and that would have been understandable, because you could hardly hope to get together fifty people of so much the same sort, and the sort they were, just from round about. They were all throwing themselves into enjoying themselves, both sexes with half-closed eyes and half-open mouths, but the women with their mouths in something like smiles, the men with theirs in a loose O that brought the lower lip a little forward, as in pictures of men who knew the Royal Family. The way they held their drinks and cigarettes was different, too: the women had their hands apart as if they had just finished a French shrug, the men in the position of a boxer whose guard has begun to drop. But the enjoyment thing was the same with both, reminding Jenny of TV commercials that showed how frantic a party could get on prune juice or chocolate biscuits, only these people would have been a bit old for anything like that.

She moved between the last two groups, the men getting out of her way when they did not need to, the women not doing so when they did, and arrived at the table. On the white cloth of this, apart from a large damp purple stain and several plain damp ones, and in addition to the big silver punch-bowl and the bottles with foreign labels, were a few puzzle objects: a key big enough to open a castle but which she had already seen being used for just opening bottles of tonic water, a round biscuit smeared with pink paste and a black cigar struck through the hole in the middle of it to make a sort of rich-child's top, a woman's hat with a prawn in the veil so as to give a miniature trawling effect. Near this was a silver cigarette-box – a lot of things must have been brought out of the cabinet for tonight's occasion – on which an inscription said: *To Orm the Norm from all the Shower at 956 Squadron Christmas 1940*. What was *Norm*? Perhaps an extra way of saying *Norman*, like *Asian* and *Asiatic*. Just then the man who was obviously *Orm* arrived on the far side of the table and started opening bottles at a great rate. 'Hallo, beautiful,' he said, waggling his eyes in the way he had. 'Got a drink to irrigate that bewitching throat?'

'Not at the moment, no.'

'We'll soon fix that. Just let me make up some more of this punch.' He did this by pouring two bottles of Somebody's Gin and two of Nuits Somebody into the bowl, followed by a two-thirds-full bottle of Something Cognac. As an afterthought he threw in two slices of orange from a plate at his side. 'Here, this'll fix you.'

'It'll be awfully strong with all that gin and things.'

'Nonsense, angel, it's only a bit of old fruit cup, bursting with vitamins. Help you to see in the dark, which may turn out to be a valuable accomplishment in an hour or two. Henry, brandy and soda was yours, wasn't it? I'm afraid we've run out of soda so I'll fill it up with brandy.'

'This is a lot of work for you,' Jenny said. 'Where are those two people who work for you, what are they, the . . .?'

'The Foots – I've given them the night off. Mrs has got a bit too much of a bias against this kind of thing. And Mr hasn't got quite enough of one.'

'But what about all the clearing up and everything?'

'Oh, I haven't given them any of tomorrow off. They'll be prowling round the place at first light, doing good. Well, a bit after then, preferably. Ah, my duck, how's it going? Glad to see you've found yourself a nice young man.'

Susan, the tall woman in grey, turned round with a smile, not the half-shut-eye sort. She said: 'I've just been giving him the low-down on our Joanie.'

'Sterling work,' Julian put in, 'but I'd much rather hear about this new musical caper at the –'

'Yes, of course the Joan stuff can't be very interesting to any-body who doesn't –'

'Keep right on going,' Patrick said. 'You've got me inter-ested.'

Susan looked quickly round the group and puffed at her cigarette. 'Well, there isn't any more, really. She had just this one line to say, supposed to be in front of this oil place that's on fire. This is the girl who shares the flat with me in London,' she explained to Jenny; 'beautiful as all hell, you've got to admit it, but *dumb*? – a complete zombie. Anyway, the madam was sup-posed to be staring up at these bloody great flames and clouds of smoke – actually that part's on a film but you don't see that – and she says, *My God, my Jim's in there, can't somebody do something?* And of course, out it came as flat as a pancake – a fellow I know was there doing the lighting, he told me – you know, *My Gud my Jim's in thuh can't sambody do samthing.*

Real sleepwalking stuff. And they all went overboard about it. *Dazed with shock,* they said. *Too much for her to take in.* They were wild about it. She's got another one coming up next week now. Dazed with her own –'

'I was really more interested in that business about Billy Bolton,' Patrick said, glancing at Jenny. 'Is he really going to marry her after all? I must say I can well understand –'

'Now who, I wonder,' Julian said, 'can this newcomer be?' He took Jenny's arm and led her towards the window, where a flicker of headlights was swinging across the curtains. 'Go and let them in, would you, Jennifer, like a sweetheart? That catch is always slipping out and denying entry.'

Jenny got the door open without difficulty as a thickly built man was climbing the few steps to the Greek-temple porch. His movements were weary and she heard him sigh. When the light from the hall fell on his face he blinked furiously. 'Graham,' Jenny said. 'Everyone was expecting you hours ago. What have you been up to?'

'Being made a fool of,' he replied in a rapid, businesslike tone. 'I wanted to go to bed but I made myself come here. I need company.'

'Graham, what happened? You sound awful. Are you all right? Here, let me take that coat.'

'Thanks, if I can just hang it somewhere.'

'It's upstairs, I'll show you. Who's been making a fool of you, Graham?'

'As you might expect, Jenny, a girl. No doubt Patrick told you I went up to Lord's cricket ground to see the first day's play in the match between the M.C.C. and the touring team. Not a single ball was bowled from first to last, but they were unable to make up their minds finally until quite late on. In the tavern there I got in with a crowd of youngish people from south-west London somewhere – a bit flashy, some of the men, and their accents were appalling, but they seemed friendly enough. And generous. Ah, shall I just throw it down here? Good. Well, when the party broke up there was a girl left over. Nothing out of the way for looks, but quite pleasant, or so I then thought, and very ready to talk. Now where's the lavatory?'

'Over there. I'll wait for you.' Jenny looked for a moment at a picture in the passage, of a woman in historical clothes whose eyes and mouth had got as far away from her nose as possible, then listened to the roar of the party below. It would not have made a bad imitation of an Albert Road playtime if put on tape and speeded up. The thought of Patrick nagged at her: she would need all her tact and confidence to get him on his own and try to win him back. Another drink might help.

Graham reappeared, blowing his nose with a vengeance. 'So when the announcement that there would be no play finally came,' he said briskly as they went down together, 'I invited her to have a drink with me. We went to a place she said she knew and drank champagne. It was very expensive, the champagne, and not very good. Then we went to a restaurant somewhere off Piccadilly and had dinner. That was very expensive, too. I wasn't in the mood to count the pennies. Jenny, could you maybe go in and get me a drink? I don't just fancy talking to anyone else for a wee while. Thank you,' he said when she came back with a glass of the punch for him and one for herself. 'At ten minutes to nine she said she had a telephone call to make and would I excuse her. I sat there for precisely an hour with the confounded Italian waiters grinning at me, then, at ten minutes to ten, I came away. Oh, I'd been had for a sucker, as the expression goes. And she seemed too nice, too . . . ordinary to be a gold-digger.'

'Ooh, the bitch,' Jenny said, 'just let me get my hands on her. That's real immoral, is that. Ooh, if only I could get hold of her, I'd . . . They get us girls a bad name, they do, bitches like that.'

'Then on the way back, just by that reservoir, I had a flat tyre. And I found the spare was flat, too; Patrick must have forgotten to take it in. That pretty well put the tin lid on things. I don't know what I'd have done but for a young fellow coming up to me, just an ordinary working lad he was, and saying there was a friend of his living just round the corner who worked in a garage, and he would take me to him. The pair of them had me fixed up inside half an hour. Ah, you can say what you like, there are some decent people still left in the world. I gave them a ten-shilling note apiece for their trouble on top of what I paid for the job.'

'Ooh, that bloody bitch, I can't get her out of my head. Ooh . . .'

Graham smiled at her, a lovely smile she had not seen before. Oh God, she thought vaguely, smasher's looks and dud's morals, what wouldn't I do for you? 'You're getting into bad habits with all that bad language,' he said, like a big rough old dog trying to play.

'I know, swearing and smoking and drinking and speaking to men, whatever will I be getting up to next?' It was one of Patrick's she had taken over.

'I'm afraid I've been running on about myself again.'

'Well, I should think so.'

'It's you lending your pretty little ear in sympathy that does it . . . Well, what about you? How was your afternoon?'

'Oh, terrible,' she said without thinking.

'Why, what happened? I understand your children's outing was cancelled and you went out with Patrick.'

'Oh, oh yes, it was quite nice really. I was thinking more of the weather. Depressing, wasn't it? Mucky.'

'Most unpleasant, I agree. No trace of that sun we had midweek. Chill and dank. What the Scots call –' He never said what, because just then the phone started ringing. 'Ah now, I suppose I should answer that.' He went to where it stood on a polished wooden pedestal with ridges and scrolls. 'Hallo, yes? It is. Yes, he is, I'll have him brought to the telephone.' He covered the mouthpiece with his hand. 'It's for Patrick. Whereabouts is he?'

'I'll get him.' He was roughly where she had last seen him, but more dishevelled and moving about on his feet more, telling a story to Susan and that Wendy, the blondeish busty one from the shooting day. 'Patrick, you're wanted on the telephone.'

'What?' he began irritably, then his expression changed and he hurried past her. 'Thanks, I'll be right there.'

She followed slowly, not out of inquisitiveness but because she did not want Graham to feel left, and arrived to get an unfriendly grinning stare from Patrick. Except at one point he kept his eyes on her while he talked.

'Hallo, *Sheila*? And? He did? That's tremendous. You're

quite sure? Oh, wonderful. I knew I could rely on you. Hey, where are you speaking from? Well, good God ...' That was when he took his eyes off Jenny. 'I *told* you ... Oh, are they? Both of them? Snoring? Thank Christ for that. You clever little creature. Listen, you've still got that bit of paper, I hope, the vital one? Good. Ah, not at all. Any time. Only keep them to a minimum in future, eh? Of course I will. Yes, okay. Cheers, doll.'

Soon after that began Jenny tried to lead Graham away, but he kept his head bent and shushed her. Then when she said she would see him inside he did the same. Finally she retreated as far as possible and waited to catch Patrick when he finished. Instead of ringing off he gave the receiver back to Graham. As Patrick went to stride past her she put her hand on his arm. He looked at her as if he just remembered her from an evening in the George about Christmas time.

'Patrick, I want to say I'm sorry –'

'Don't bother, you're not spoiling my evening.'

Graham said into the phone : 'Well, when are you free?'

'Oh, darling, please don't be hard like that, I'll do anything to make you see –'

'Will you? Do anything? Anything?'

'Well, you know what I mean, I –'

'Yes, I know what you mean all right. Too bloody well. Now I'm going to be as fair to you as I know how. So fair you'll never believe it. Are you ready?'

'Thursday sounds fine. Excuse me just while I consult my diary.'

'Oh, please, Patrick.'

'Here it is. We're finished. Even if you walked in on me naked I wouldn't touch you. I just couldn't stand all the sodding inquests and fairness and unfairness and your rights and my rights and who's to blame and what shall I tell my parents and your duty and my duty and ... So there we are. I'm fed up with you and your bloody little small-town conscience. See you around in the Bible class.'

'Seven-thirty it is. Good-bye now.' Graham rang off and came confidently towards her, but went less confident almost at once. 'You look a wee bit under the weather, Jenny. Are you sure that drink's not too strong for you? Ormerod's a real demon when he comes to handing out the liquor.'

'No, it's all right. A bit hot in here, don't you think?'

'I do. Well, if you're sure you're all right let's plunge into the maelstrom. I feel much better now.'

Inside the room again – half of it, she realized now, was where they had had the drinks that Sunday and the rest of it had been revealed by some folding doors being folded – she emptied her glass of punch. The wine part of it was not bad, and she could have stood the whole thing quite well but for that hot chemical-works taste of the spirits. Puffing straight away at a cigarette covered some of it up. Anyway, she was going to have another. It would help her to believe what she was telling herself, that Patrick had not meant the bit about not touching her if she was naked, and that the look he had given her after the Bible-class bit showed it was mostly an act. The drink after that would be the one to use on what she felt about his phone call from Sheila Torkington.

Turning away from the punch-bowl she was run into by someone who was coming towards it full steam ahead. 'Hallo, Jenny.' It was Dick. He had a long-term smile going which split his face into two roughly equal halves. 'Gosh, you're looking stunning. Excuse me while I replenish. Well, this is worth a bus-ride and a hike, eh? Pretty lavish, old Julian, isn't he?'

'Yes – how are we going to get back?'

'Oh, someone'll be going our way to drop us off, sure to. You keep your ears open and I'll do the same, and we'll maintain contact, okay? Don't want to start making tracks yet awhile, though, do we? This is too good to miss. Look at it all.'

'Hallo, Dick, how are you, old boy?' Patrick had come over, but kept himself separate from Jenny. 'What a show, eh? Monte Carlo isn't in it. Here, you don't want to waste your time on that muck, that's for the outer circle. Let me mix you one of Julian's specials. It's a sort of long cocktail – he got the formula off a barman in Marrakesh or some-bloody-where. Won't take me a moment.'

'Here, Patrick, I've been caught with Julian's drinks before, I want to know what's in this surprise packet.'

'Don't you worry, it's a vermouth base, special stuff from Sicily. Nothing lethal. You talk to Jenny.'

'A pity Martha didn't feel up to it tonight,' Jenny said.

Dick interrupted his smile for a moment with a screwed-together face. 'Well,' he said, making it last about a quarter of a minute, 'she does get awfully tired. It's, you know, a woman's thing, connected with ... I expect you've gathered we can't have a child.'

'Yes, I had. I am sorry.' Past Dick's seesawing arm she could see Patrick pouring a chartreuse-coloured drink into a beerglass. It looked like the stuff people had after dinner out of much smaller glasses. 'And you'd have loved one, wouldn't you, the both of you?'

'Oh yes, we would, there's no turning a blind eye to that one. But, well,' he said as before, 'you can get used to a lot, you know, with time. But it is a pity she doesn't come out more.' With a very absent-minded expression he took a cigarette straight from his pocket and put it in his mouth. 'She used to, mind, but then about the year Anna came ... Where's she, by the way? I haven't set eyes on her for a good hour. Oh ho, then she was really holding 'em spellbound, half a dozen of these London characters, she was going on about the Welfare State, had 'em eating out of her hand. Not that I agree with her attitude, not in the least, but these French, you've got to hand it to them, they know how to enjoy themselves. Oh, there's no one can touch 'em for gaiety.' He lit his cigarette and coughed a good deal, after which he took another drag and did some more coughing. To pull himself round from the second lot of coughing he took a deeper drag still. He coughed more still. Jenny wondered if she ought to explain to him that it was the cigarette that was making him cough.

'Here we are, Dick. This'll do you good.'

'Ah, thanks, Patrick. Phew, this looks a real witches' brew, doesn't it, Jenny?'

'Now a long pull and a strong pull, Dick, none of your vicarage-tea-party sips. This is supposed to be a cooler. I know, we'll drink to the Thompson bowling performance against the College. Bit of luck for us you were available. Haven't seen you since to congratulate you properly. Cheers.'

Dick drank deeply and coughed his best yet. 'Wow,' he said as soon as he could, 'what's in this concoction, nitro-glycerine? I notice you're not risking your neck.'

During the last coughing Patrick had glanced at Jenny in a way she knew meant he was going to wink at her, but he remembered just in time that he was not doing any more of that with her. Now he said to Dick: 'Ah, that's the secret ingredient – ginger cordial, hot but harmless. No, I'm on something stronger. The second go'll be better, throat gets sort of anaesthetized. You try.'

Dick tried. 'No better,' he gasped, wiping his mouth on the back of his hand. 'I suppose I could get used to it in time, but it'd be a fight. Well, I'd better replenish these pots and take 'em back. That's what I'm supposed to be here for.'

'Knock that heeltap back before you go.'

'Might as well, eh? Wow. Flipping murder. Be seeing you.'

While Jenny stood on her own for a moment, for Patrick had turned away as soon as Dick, three near-by men swivelled round in her direction at once. Then she saw Julian waving to her from where he stood by a pretty Chinese screen of ochre silk. She filled her glass at the punch-bowl and went over. Julian introduced the plump woman he was with as Lady Edgerstoune.

'Oh, how do you do,' Jenny said, fighting off *pleased to meet you* and *your ladyship*, together with the little curtsy her knees were trying to do. The last *Woman's Domain* she had read, two or three weeks back, had had an article on how to meet the aristocracy. It had said that really they were just like everyone else, only of course you could not expect to treat them as if they were.

'How do you do, my dear. How pretty you are, aren't you? And what a beautiful dress. You know, Julian, I never see lovely dresses like that anywhere. It's so gorgeously plain. The ones I see are like battlefields, you know. Yes, with pockets and plackets and pleats and yokes and – what are those ghastly streamer affairs?'

'Flying panels,' Jenny suggested.

'*Yes*. Now fancy you knowing about flying panels. I'd as soon have expected you to know about open buses and the General Strike and that sort of thing. I was only a mite then myself, of course, I mustn't overdo this grandmammy act of mine. Anyhow, that's a lovely dress, and you look very nice in it, and now that I've said that again perhaps you won't mind too much if I go on to say that that man you were talking to just now is easily the ghastliest man here.'

'Which one do you mean?' Jenny asked.

'I'm sure he can't be your husband or anything. The one who always leans over and has that laugh.'

'Oh, Dick Thompson. How funny you knowing him, Lady Edgerstoune.'

'He was going to sell our house and furniture for us. My husband and I are going to live abroad, you know. I think our lawyer must have been dishonest in the way he arranged it. He's a new man in the firm. I didn't like the look of your Mr Thing at all. So I got Julian here to find out about him. Why I didn't ask you to arrange it all for me in the first place I don't know.'

'I was away, Dot, if you remember. And then I had to go away again, otherwise everything would have been fixed up long since.'

'Of course, I knew there had to be a reason, darling. And you were so good. He went to no end of trouble on our behalf, my dear. He simply slaved at it.'

'Oh, Dotty dear, it was huge fun dressing up as a lawyer looking for a crooked auctioneer. And finding one. And becoming pally with good old Dick put me in touch with all sorts of charming characters I shouldn't have come across otherwise.'

'I'm glad. I would so love to tell that Mr Thing that he won't be selling our property for us after all. That should make him lean over all right.'

'Now, Dot, the fellow does appear to be my guest, after all.'

'Yes, I was going to ask you how that had come about.'

'Bit of a teaser, I confess. He must have heard about it somehow and felt he simply had to arrange to turn up, him and me being such chums and about to become partners in crime, but especially such chums. Penalty one pays for bringing sentiment into business.'

'I'm afraid he must have found out from me,' Jenny said. 'But as soon as I mentioned it he seemed to know all about it.'

'That old professional acumen at work. What an extraordinary figure it is, to be sure. Ah, still on your feet, Nigel? Sorry about that. Sonia, your place is at my side, to put it at its lowest. And as for you ... Why have you thrown all that drink over yourself?'

'Is your husband here tonight, Lady Edgerstoune?'

'I'm afraid not, my dear, and he would have loved it so. Julian, wouldn't Archie have loved this party?'

'Oh, right up his ...' He paused and looked at Jenny. 'Well, perhaps he might have felt ...'

Lady Edgerstoune looked at Jenny too. 'Yes, he might have found it a little ...'

'Strenuous for him. He does get rather ...'

'Overtired at any large gathering. It's his age and his ...'

'Temperament tells against him. He's far better off ...'

'In bed reading. A new book on hubble-bubbles came this morning.'

Jenny met, probably for the first time, Nigel and Sonia, and, almost certainly not for the first time, some other people with names like that. They were all fairly alike to start with, and a tired feeling in her head made the differences less easy to pick out. One called Tony took her glass away and refilled it. When he came back after refilling some others hers was empty again, so he took it away and refilled it again. The nasty part of drinking the punch came a few moments after swallowing now instead of straight away, and that made it easier.

Chapter Twenty-Six

Suddenly it was later. Jenny could tell this by the way the stiffening seemed to have been taken out of people's faces, so that they looked second-hand instead of new. Although some of them, including a couple or two embracing in the passage or on the stairs, had quietened down a lot from how they had been, and others had evidently gone altogether, there was more noise than before, much of it coming from outside the house. She went in search of it half-heartedly and found herself in a smallish room, perhaps near the kitchen. From here an open glass door gave on to a conservatory, beyond which there were shifting lights and the sound of shouts and laughter. Perhaps Patrick was out there, but she no longer intended to find him and get him on his own.

'Ah, there you are, darling, come and join the circle.' It was Wendy, lying sideways across an armchair with her shoes off. 'Susan and I having a little quiet girls' get-together while those maniacs outside set each other alight or whatever the silly shits are trying to do. Little Anna's a teeny bit under the weather with all the talking she's had to do so we dumped her on there and told her to snore away and not mind us. And this sweet Susan's been keeping me in absolute fits about this mad boy friend of yours. Darling, I don't want to alarm you or anything but he's been upstairs for about nine hours with some red-haired creature with some name like Veronica or Victoria or something.'

'Vanessa and that painter chap were about the first to leave, as a matter of fact.' Susan was sitting on a small oval table with her feet on a dining-chair. 'And Patrick's been outside with the others for I don't know how long. Sit down, dear, and tell us a tale.'

'All right, Susan, there's no need to get all British all of a sudden. Jenny knows what she's up against, don't you, darling? And what have you been doing all the evening? My sweet Tony's got his eye on you all right hasn't he? I could see him absolutely stripping you stark naked with his eyes, you know, slavering like some enormous great beast. Honestly, aren't they revolting? Of course you're his type, he loves that sort of gazelle touch. The way he keeps on at me to get my weight down. I think he'd like me to wear one of those steel corset affairs and lace myself up so I couldn't breathe. Some of them go for that don't they? Like high heels and rubber macs and these little chariots. I wonder how they decide that that's what they like.'

Jenny had sat down at the table with her elbows on it and her hands on her cheeks. 'Thought you were supposed to be in New Zealand.'

'She *couldn't* stand it there, she told me,' Susan said. 'So naturally they *had* to come back.'

'I'll say we *had* to come back. Of course we did. Bloody cheek you've got, Susan. You go and live down under and see how you like it. You think it's terribly funny when you go to your first party and find it's all bus-conductors and railway porters and plumbers all dressed up in fifty-guinea suits and talking about trade cycles and price spirals. Then you find everyone's a bus-conductor. And the wives are all charladies and fish-and-chip women.'

'I'm going to get another drink,' Susan said. 'Anybody else want one?'

'Brandy for me, darling. Out of that funny bottle – you know.'

'I'll have some more of that punch out of the bowl if there's any left,' Jenny said. 'Thank you.'

When Susan had gone, Jenny heard a man shout from out-side: 'Disqualify him. Bring him back. Start again.' With her eyes fixed on a glass bowl of fruit in front of her, she said: 'Why do people make a fuss about virginity?' She found parts of it difficult to say.

'About *virginity*? Darling, I didn't know they did. Are you sure they do? There was never any fuss about mine. Well no, actually there was starting to be very early on, so I got rid of it as soon as I could and put it out of my mind. Why? Is someone fussing about yours? You are clever to still have it.'

'Why do people bother so much about it? What good's it do you?'

'I told you, it's no use asking me. I thought it was all to do with arranged marriages and betrothals and dowries and purdah and all that. I thought the whole thing had more or less blown over.'

'Do you think it's right to give up your principles for some-body you're in love with?'

'I say, we are getting down to the eternal verities, aren't we? I don't know, darling; why are you asking me all this? I don't know anything about principles. They just make life harder don't they? Susan, Jenny's got a problem. All about virginity and principles.'

Susan gave out the drinks, a cigarette burning in her mouth. 'What? About virginity? What about it?'

'Patrick wants her to give him hers and she isn't sure whether she ought to let him have it.'

'Well, an old hand like me, it's not easy for me to say. But I don't know, I should have thought if you like someone enough, then all that solves itself, doesn't it? I don't think you ought to make a fuss about it, anyway. As far as I can see that always makes things worse, making a fuss about anything to do with sex. People weren't made for just the one other person and we might as well face it, don't you reckon? Oh, I was the same, I used to think a lot about meeting Mr Right and the rest of it, but the way I look at it nowadays, I'm lucky if I can hold on to Mr Not-too-bad. Don't want to depress you or anything. Anyway, don't take any notice of me: I'm dead cynical. The voice of doom, that's me.'

'Nobody knows what they want,' Anna said from her couch. She beat at the hair that had fallen over her face, but it seemed to make her eyes roll too much and she stopped. 'How solemn you all are, you English women. But I ... I feel sick.'

'Oh Christ I'm going out, I can't bear people being sick in front of me,' Wendy said, struggling up.

'Come on, Anna, I'll take you to the bathroom. Can you get up? That's the spirit. It's only a little way.'

'Want any help, Jenny?' Susan asked.

'No, we'll be fine.'

'I can walk, thank you.'

Jenny helped Anna to be sick, holding her hair back with one hand and putting the other on her forehead, so that Anna would have something to push against. 'You'll feel better in a minute.'

'Thanks a lot,' Anna said after a moment, gasping and wiping her eyes. 'Why did I drink all that muck? Must be off my head. I'm as bad as that fool Dick. He was heaving his heart up in the garden the last I saw of him. You could hear him for miles.'

Jenny looked at her in amazement. 'But you're ...'

'That's right, love. I'm no more French than you are. Way back, perhaps; I come from Guernsey. My father's got a tomato business there. Of course, I know France quite well. Not well enough for one of the women here this evening, however. I'm surprised it hasn't happened before.'

'But why did you pretend, put on this act? All these months ...'

'Playing a part's the only thing left these days, it shows you won't deal with society in the way it wants you to. But I've got sick of this one. It was too much effort; I had to be on my guard all the time. I started it when I got on the train to come here without really realizing I could never drop it as long as I stayed. I'll try something less demanding for my next one.'

'But how can you? I mean, people will notice.'

'Oh, I'm moving on. The time's come for that. In this civilization you can't stay for long in one place without rusting. Attachment to an environment or a set of people – that's bad. I'm off first thing on Monday morning.'

'Where to?'

'I haven't thought yet. Ireland, perhaps; not London.'

Jenny gazed at her. Anna's face had gone smooth, almost comfortable, and her big brown eyes had an inquisitive look. She reminded Jenny of a woman in a corner sweet-shop at home who had dealt out the lollies and the chocolate lunches to the school kids. 'Oh, Anna, I shall miss you.'

'I can't think why. All I ever did was make a pass at you and scare you. That wasn't part of the act, by the way. I'd still love to have slept with you – I never have with a girl, you know, only wanted to. If I hadn't been playing my part I should never have dared to touch you. That's what it does for you, it liberates you, and we all need that in this mass society of ours. But then in another way you find you can't have some things you'd like. Oh, Jenny, I did want you to be my friend.'

'But I am your friend, love.'

'Not to the extent I wanted. Oh, I don't mean sleeping together, though I'd have loved that too. But none of it would have been any good. I'm not nearly nice enough for you.'

'That you are, I think you're sweet.' Jenny did not move when Anna stroked the back of her head.

'You don't know me, I take good care nobody does. You think that if people are nice to you, then they're nice. That's your great weakness, Jenny darling.'

'Anna, what do you think I ought to do about Patrick?'

'Stay with him. It'd be the right thing for you. It wouldn't for me – I mustn't stay with people. I rust away if I do. Go back to the party, Jenny, I shall be all right.'

'You'll drop me a line from wherever you go, won't you?'

'A beautiful picture postcard. But I'll see you before I leave. Now you run along. I think I'm going to be sick again.'

Jenny got up from where she had been sitting, Anna kneeling, on the bathroom mat. Somebody was chasing somebody else up the higher staircase as she reached the lower one. She thought for a second that it was funny how Anna managed to be even more like the part she had played after she stopped playing it. But she did not want to think about Anna not being French, or Dick being a crook, or Julian being whatever he was. Nor did she want to think about Patrick. With some difficulty she found her way back to the room she had just left. It was empty. She held her nose and drank down the glass of punch Susan had brought her. Then she spent some time finding a cigarette and longer finding a match. She sat down and had smoked half of it before she noticed that the walls and furniture seemed to be softening and twisting slightly, like sheets and sticks of gelatine. She went through the conservatory, where the tops of some plants were silhouetted against a mixture of lights outside. When she got into the open the cold air hit her in the face and made her gasp. She walked along a gravel path, through a stone gateway, stumbling at the threshold, and into the stable yard. At one end of this a fire had been built on the cobbles. Some of the people were standing still, others moving about. She could not recognize any of them nor identify their voices. They were all male voices.

'Give me a hand over here.' 'This any good to anyone?' 'What are all these bloody signs doing in here?' 'I think I saw one in the kitchen.' 'Let's have a look.' 'Francis. Anyone seen Francis?' 'My tank's pretty full, we can siphon some out.' '*Road Under Water*, *Diversion*, *Yacht Races*.' 'No, we tried that.' 'Have a care, you can go too far.' 'I said two of you, not a bloody platoon.' 'Ten miles there and back, not more.' 'No, better leave that.' 'Mildred. Where the hell has that bitch got to?' 'You'll have to smash it up.' 'All these bloody danger lamps.' 'Watch it, you clown.' 'Right, here she goes.' 'Put that cigarette out.' 'Better go back for some more.' 'You bloody fool.'

Leaning on the gatepost, shivering and half attending, Jenny could not understand what they were all doing. When she closed her eyes there was a cold sensation. The gatepost, where her bare arm touched it, was damp and gritty; she pushed herself upright and rubbed at her skin with her hand. The heat from the fire was rumpling the outlines of the buildings and trees and bushes and other objects above and around it, but the same thing seemed to be happening to things that were not near the fire. Jenny's earlier feelings had changed to bewilderment, or had been overcome by it. When she tried to think about Patrick it was as if she could not reach quite as far as that part of her mind, and indeed she no longer knew what she thought or felt about anything. Everything she cared about had merged into everything else, and nothing stood out as in any way special. When a man who was probably Tony asked her to come inside with him out of the cold she came. 'Have a drink.' She had a drink. 'Have a cigarette.' She had a cigarette. 'Give me a kiss.' She gave him a kiss. 'Say something.' She said something. Then he said something. It was: 'What about you and me slipping upstairs for a bit?'

She looked for and found his face. It had a moustache, and two other things of the same size and shape and colour; they were eyebrows and were completely straight. 'No,' she said. That was what you said when men asked you about you and them slipping upstairs. She noticed that they were at the end of a large room, where it was nearly dark. Further off it was lighter and some people were standing about.

'All right, we'll carry on here for a bit and have another think later.' He held her wrists with one hand and did things with the other. She struggled as hard as she could, but that was not very hard. She did not feel worried, because she was sure that any moment he would realize she was not particularly enjoying herself and stop. Her head slipped off the edge of the window-seat where they were and she felt her hair come loose and trail down away from her head.

'What the blazes do you think you're doing, sir?' somebody

said indignantly. 'Can't you see the girl's drunk? Take your hands off her this instant.'

The man moved away. 'What's it got to do with you, Jock? This is a private party over here.'

'To hell with that. You take yourself off, sir. You're a positive disgrace.'

'What are you, the Watch Committee or something?'

'Never mind who I am. Leave the room immediately.'

Jenny had sat up and rearranged herself. 'Graham.'

'I soon sent him packing. Soon sent him about his business. Now, would you like to go and lie down for a while?'

'Graham ... but I couldn't even ...'

'I'll get one of the women to put you to bed somewhere. You'd have thought a man of that education would have had more decency.'

She tried to say: 'Did I hear you fixing up a date with Sheila Torkington earlier on?' but not much of it came out as intended.

'I'm afraid your speech is rather indistinct, Jenny.' The jovial grin he gave with this did the usual comedian thing to his face, this time one of the red-nosed sort.

'Sheila. Have date?'

'There's an old saying about beggars and choosers you may have heard, but this is neither the time nor the place to explore the matter. But don't worry about me, I'm not utterly irresponsible. Now just you stay there a minute.'

Jenny stayed there over five seconds and under five hours. The things around her were much more extraordinary, and yet much less interesting, than she remembered things being usually. During them, Graham and Susan came over to her. Instead of coming over to her on a diagonal, which they must have had to do to move from the door to her, they appeared to be moving directly sideways while getting bigger all the time, like cars she remembered once having looked at through Robbie's telescope. 'Come along now, princess,' Susan said. 'Let's get you bedded down and off to the land of nod.'

'Sorry to be such a ...'

'Can you manage her?'

'Oh, she's as light as a feather.'

In the hall a lot of people were standing about drinking out of mugs that had steam rising from them. A telephone was ringing.

'Gangway, chaps, another casualty.' 'Answer that bloody phone.' 'In the end room, angel – the bed's made up.' 'You'll have to shout, there's a hell of a row going on here.' 'Darling you can cope can't you?' 'Up the wooden hill.' 'Miss Bunn, is she supposed to be here?' 'Why's a woman doing a man's job?' 'That's Miss Bunn there, the centre of attraction.' 'She obviously can't take a call now.' 'Jenny, someone on the phone for you.' 'Some joker, no doubt.' 'Get the name.' 'Quiet, everybody.' 'Fine bloody time to be ringing a girl up, what?' 'Whicker or Widdicombe or something.' 'Jenny, you know anybody called Widdicombe?' 'Some joker.' 'Tom Pearce, Tom Pearce, lend me your grey mare.' 'Shut up, can't you?' 'Tell 'em to get stuffed.' 'You bloody fool.' 'The morning'll do.'

It all faded away. Time went by in the same queer speedless way as before. Then Patrick was with her. He had been there for some minutes or hours when she first realized he was, and again was in bed with her without seeming to have got there. What he did was off by itself and nothing to do with her. All the same, she wanted him to stop, but her movements were all the wrong ones for that and he was kissing her too much for her to try to tell him. She thought he would stop anyway as soon as he realized how much off on his own he was. But he did not, and did not stop, so she put her arms round him and tried to be with him, only there was no way of doing it and nothing to feel. Then there was another interval, after which he told her he loved her and would never leave her now. She said she loved him too, and asked him if it had been nice. He said it had been wonderful, and went on to talk about France.

While he was on that, the light came on and Julian's voice was in the room with them. He and Patrick talked loudly to each other over by the door. She did not understand parts of what they said, and there were other parts she missed altogether.

'Well, not as drunk as all that.'

'Not too drunk for you, anyway.'

'Had to get it done somehow.'

'And it didn't much matter how, eh?'

'Life was becoming absolutely impossible as it was.'

'Do you know what I'd sooner do?'

'Oh, for Christ's sake.'

'That's what I'd sooner do.'

'Snooping around.'

'Blankets in here, if you're interested.'

'I thought you were supposed to be in favour of all this kind of thing.'

'Most of it, Patty, yes. But fairness.'

'I'm tired of fairness.'

'Clearly.'

'Asking me to get out of the house in a minute.'

'Yes, I would, old chum, if this were anything to do with me. But as it is.'

'Lovely party.'

'You're welcome, Pattikins.'

After more time, Jenny heard Patrick say: 'Who does he think he is?' and then, in a crying voice: 'Oh Christ. Oh Christ. I am a bastard. Oh Christ. Right, this is your lot, Jack.' She tried to turn over towards him, but the door slammed.

Before Jenny fell asleep she heard a loud bang in the distance, and then shouting. It was nothing to do with her. She put her hand under the pillow and spread the fingers.

Chapter Twenty-Seven

'HERE's some breakfast. Don't feel you've got to eat it, though.'

Getting away from sleep and towards the voice was like crawling up a long burrow. On arrival, Jenny started to sit up, then found she was wearing only her stockings and lay down again. 'Oh, you are an angel, Susan,' she said. Speaking was hard; it used up air.

'But try and eat something. Don't worry about the time, dear. I brought your bag up – it is yours, isn't it? The bathroom's next door on the left.' Susan went out.

Then Jenny did sit up. She tried to look round for her clothes, but kept forgetting she was doing it. Her dress was on a hanger that was hooked to a dark-coloured wardrobe. Part of the skirt had a purplish stain, as if she had been paddling in punch and a wave had come up too high. Her pants, rolled into a ball, were in bed with her. So was her waist-pettie. Eventually she found her suspender belt and her bra on the floor by the bed. The last of these she put on, taking some time over it, because her arms and hands seemed badly made this morning. She felt so awful from the stomach to the head, both ends inclusive, that for the time being she had to ignore everything else.

She drank the cup of tea Susan had brought her; it went down well, but managed to do so without touching her mouth or throat. Afterwards her teeth still felt large and disused. Eating two pieces of toast altered her a little for the better at first, then very much for the worse, so much so that she jumped out of bed, ran into the bathroom and was sick, hurling herself forward like a rugger-player on TV scoring a try. Do what she might, she had never been able to be sick quietly; she heard her own monkey yells ringing round the room and along the passage. She got them down to groans eventually and went and locked the door. Then she had a bath, which was nice, but after a few minutes' soaking she had to do a smart side-vault out of it in order to be sick into it. It happened a third time about a quarter of an hour later, when she threw herself off the bed and just managed to get her chin over the edge of a cardboard box that had on it in green letters: THIS CONTAINER REMAINS THE PROPERTY OF THE SPEEDEE LAUNDRY CO. The laundry's property was in a pretty soggy state by the time she had finished washing it out, but she thought, or thought she thought, that it might be angry if it never got its property back at all. So she scattered a lot of talcum powder into the box and put it back where she had found it.

Feeling tired, but not as tired as she was of lying on the bed, she got up and dressed. She was very sorry that it would not have done to clean her teeth with the bathroom nailbrush, and gazed at it with longing before working vigorously away with her fingers instead. When she came to make up her face she found that, so far from looking like the ghost with a tummy upset she felt like, her eyes were as bright and her cheeks as glowing as if she had just come back from a fortnight at Redcar.

Her hair was the only trouble; it had gone stiff and thatchy and kept falling over her eyes, but it would have to wait until she got back to her room and her shampoos. She picked up her tray and went downstairs, where things still had a feel of awful energy about them, as if everybody had just bolted out of the front door, filled glasses and burning cigarettes in their hands, when they heard her coming. A middle-aged woman in a blue overall, no doubt Mrs Foot, told her that Mr Ormerod was out at the back before throwing a broken glass into a bin half full of others like it.

Julian was sitting up to the table in the kitchen she remembered from that Sunday. Among plates on the shelves there was an old-fashioned wall-clock that said twenty to eleven. He put his paper down when she came in. 'Saw nude body, phoned police,' he muttered, then went on more loudly: 'Appetizing as ever, my lovely. How do you feel?'

'Terrible. I've never felt so bad in all my life.'

'The old heave-ho, eh? Yes, I can remember what it used to be like. Cup of coffee?'

'Ooh, I'd love one. Where are the cups?'

'There's one here – you sit down.' He moved used crockery about; there was a good deal of it. Either people had had lots of breakfast, or lots of people had had breakfast. 'Here. There's plenty more. Well, you're probably in better shape than our stretcher case.'

'Stretcher case? Whatever happened?'

'Dick Thompson was shot last night, or rather in the small hours.'

'You mean he's dead?'

'Far from it, I'm sorry to say. Just a flesh wound in the left buttock, enough to keep him on his face for a day or two. I phoned the house just now and spoke to Anna. The physician had paid him a visit and pronounced himself satisfied. Oh, it was great fun getting him into Nigel's car; he could walk but he couldn't sit or bend. I'd have got my own sawbones up here to him, but he insisted on getting home to his wife. Who took one look at him and went and slept on the couch downstairs, according to Anna. Old Anna showed up to great effect, incidentally. Looked after him like a mum.'

'But how did it happen? Who did it?'

'It appears old Ricardo had been voiding the contents of his upper alimentary tract in the rhododendron patch and then threw himself with abandon into the sort of revel, or *rag*, that was brewing up round the stables there. Incredible resilience in one so lacking in physical endowment – sort of chap they can't hang. So resilient was he that I rather fancy it was he who kindled most of that fire in the yard. Innocent little caper, that. Nigel and I saved most of the small garage from going up – only got the doors and a corner of the roof.'

'How disgusting. They must have been mad drunk.'

'Oh, nothing to it. Bit of good management on my part to get them out of the house. Last year a piano went. They enjoy enjoying themselves. Well, during the firefighting some anonymous jester wandered into my gun-room, which I blame myself for having omitted to lock, and picked up a fowling-piece, which he proceeded to discharge in the general direction of the Thompson arse. Nearly missed him, but not quite. Must have got him out of one of the gun-room windows; they run just along there. Jolly mordant bit of wit, what?'

'What a thing to have done. They get like animals, don't they, some of them, when they've had a few? They might have killed him. And you don't know who it was?'

'Hard to be sure. Several people were departing about that time, including your friend Tony, who's always been a great wag in that kind of way. But there are other possibilities. Yes, Mrs Foot?'

'There's a gentleman at the door, Mr Ormerod, I can't seem to make out what he wants.'

'Ah, sounds like one of last night's guests. Excuse me a minute, dear girl. Have a butcher's at the *News of the World* and be thankful you're a normal young lady with lots of nice normal friends. Well, normal friends. Fairly normal, anyway.'

Jenny decided reading would be too much for her. She smoked a cigarette until her insides felt as if they were getting as far away from the middle of her as they could. Then she put it out. But even with that big hollow in her interior she was recovering enough to start getting the first edge of thought. For it to have gone like that, almost without her noticing. At that she rebuked herself, sitting up straight in her chair. What was so special about her that it should have happened to her in the way she had imagined it, alone with a man in a country cottage surrounded by beautiful scenery, with the owls suddenly waking her up in the early hours and him putting his arms round her and soothing her, and then in the morning the birds singing and the horses neighing, and her frying eggs and bacon and spreading a wholemeal loaf with thick farm butter? A lot of sentimental rubbish, that was – she would be asking for roses and violins next. Much better be sensible, think herself lucky it had not gone for her as it did for some, sordid and frightening and painful and with someone you hated or hardly knew. That was happening every day.

'That was good old Patrick,' Julian said, coming to the doorway. 'He decided he'd wait in the garden. Lots of air out there.'

'Oh? What does he want?'

'He's come to give you a lift home, I gathered.'

'I see.'

'If you feel you'd rather hang on for a bit, pigeon, just breathe the word and I'll run you down later myself. Be delighted to.'

'That's very kind of you, Julian, and thank you very much, but I'll have to see him and I might as well do it straight away.'

'Surely. I'll get your coat.'

At the front door she said: 'There, I think I've got everything. Thank you for a lovely party, and it was ever so kind of you to put me up, all at such short notice like that.'

'An overmastering pleasure, divine one.' He put his hand on the latch, then took it off again. 'I'm very sorry if you had any sort of a rough time last night. I feel responsible.'

'Don't you give it a thought. See you again soon, I hope.'

'Alas, not so soon as I would wish. I'm off abroad in a couple of days for quite a spell. But I shall be back in this area towards the end of the year. We might get together then.'

'I would like that. Good-bye, Julian, and have a nice trip. Oh, and say good-bye to Susan for me, will you, and thank her for being so kind?'

'I'll do that diminutive thing,' he said, and kissed her en-

thusiastically. 'Mm, very jolly. Great pity you aren't the maison-
nette type. If you ever decide you are, be sure to let me know.'

'You bet I will. Cheero, love.'

'Cheers, Jenny. And good luck.'

He opened the door and she went out. The sunlight made her
blink. The sky was a light blue, faintly milky in places. The
trees seemed to have an extra lot of leaves on them. Patrick threw
his cigarette away and came towards her, smiling as if he had
been told to. He was wearing the green jacket and drill trousers
he had been wearing that Sunday. 'What sort of hangover have
you got?' he said. 'I've been wondering which of the Seven
dwarfs I've got most in common with. Sleepy, certainly. Doc in
the sense of advanced age. And Gropey – Christ –' He burst
out laughing. 'I mean ... sort of portmanteau ...' He laughed
some more, then stopped. 'What about you?'

'I'm not too bad, thank you.'

He moved to take her hand; she let him. 'Jenny, I'm sorry. I
was a bastard. It shouldn't have happened to you like that. Anyone else, but not you. But I couldn't help myself. And I'm glad
it happened, in one way. We're together now. I've got you and
you've got me. Oh, it'll be such a marvellous –'

'Patrick, will you stop talking and drive me home?'

He made a clicking noise with his tongue. 'All right.'

The road went between fields, along the marshy part where
Julian had fired his shot over their heads, through the woods.
Jenny took no interest in any of it. When they stopped outside
Carshalton Beeches, part of the town was spread out below
them, but she did not look at it. She got out, noticing another
car, a small green saloon, parked a few yards further down the
hill : the doctor's, perhaps.

'Surely you're going to say something before you go off?'
Patrick asked from the driver's seat, taking out his cigarettes.

'Yes, I am. I don't want to see you again. And this is no act,
son. You were right about one thing : I spent too much time
looking after my honour. It prevented me taking enough notice
of the kind of man you are. If you are a man, *lover boy*. It's not
what you did I object to; it would probably have happened anyway, sooner or later. But to do it like that.'

He looked down. 'Yes, that was bad.'

'*But*. It was bad, *but*. I've got another name for you, better than Georgie Porgie. It's one you gave poor old Dick, but it fits you much better. Mr Eat-All-Sup-All-Pay-Nowt. Remember?'

'This is what they call good-bye, then, is it?'

'That's right. But not quite yet, surely?'

'How do you mean?'

'Aren't you coming in to see how your victim's doing?'

'Sorry, I'm not with you.'

'You haven't forgotten shooting Dick, have you?'

'What? I was nothing to do with that.'

'Oh no, not *much*. If there'd been a million people there last night I'd still have known who got up to that little lark. It was only like throwing stones at the hens, wasn't it, or Horace getting knocked on the head? Do them good. It's a pity nobody does you a bit of good. You had two goes at Dick, once at the cricket and then that drink, and neither of them came off, so you decided to shoot him. What a laugh for the boys in the George, eh? A real scream. I'll give him your love.'

'I'll come back when you've cooled off a bit.'

'I shan't be in,' she shouted after him.

Going upstairs to her room she met Martha with a suitcase in each hand. 'Ah, I did hope I'd see you before I left,' she said, beaming. 'Nicely timed.'

'Where are you going?'

'Away. I'm leaving my husband. Shocking, isn't it?'

'But why? What's he done?'

'Well, it seems he had a little business deal all fixed up, whereby he was going to make a nice fat killing – hence all the lovely new bits and pieces we started having on hire-purchase. But now we find the deal isn't on after all, according to what somebody called Lady Edgerstoune told him last night, and so all the new stuff'll have to go back, and we shall be just as we were before, only slightly more so. I decided I couldn't stand that. And so I'm not going to.'

'But when he's like this, laid up . . .'

Martha laughed loudly. 'Oh yes, isn't that wonderful? That was the finishing touch. On top of everything else he has to go and get himself shot up the bum. There's Richard Haines Thompson for you.'

'But this is just the sort of time when he needs –'

'When he's at his most intolerable. Have you ever seen him when he's ill? No? What a picture – caption, *They can't do this to me*. Oh God, it's unbelievable until you see it. I'm afraid you'll have to see it, at least for today. His sister'll be here in the morning. She's a nice, comfortable, motherly, cheerful sort of body. You and she'll get on like a house on fire. I'm sure that with Anna to lend a hand you'll be able to *carry on* until Laura gets here. It'll be a little adventure for you, won't it? – buckling to and seeing it through. Don't forget to feed the hens. Well, mustn't stand here yarning all the morning. I've got a train to catch, and you've got some visitors. You are having an exciting day.'

'Visitors? Who are they?'

'I'm afraid I don't know. I asked them to wait downstairs, but they said they wanted to see you in private. Sounds awfully sinister, doesn't it? I said you'd be back any minute – that was about half an hour ago. You don't look in much of a state to receive them, but Sunday's an informal sort of day, isn't it?'

'I must go and see what they want. Good-bye, Martha. I'm sorry if I –'

'Ah, but you're not the sort of girl who does things she's sorry for, are you? Good-bye, dear, and remember to always wear wool next your skin.'

In Jenny's room three people were sitting. They were Miss Sinclair, Elsie Carter, and a young man Jenny had never seen before. She wondered how much of her conversation with Martha had penetrated into here. The man got quickly to his feet when Jenny came in. He was thin and dark with a small head, wearing a well-pressed navy suit and looking uncomfortable.

'Ah, good morning, Miss Bunn,' Miss Sinclair said. She was looking very neat in her grey suit with the watch at the lapel. 'I'm sorry we're lying in wait for you like this, but we did want to get hold of you rather urgently. Oh, I don't think you've met Mr Whittaker, have you?'

'No, I –'

'But we've heard a lot about you at home, of course, Miss

Bunn,' the man said, shaking hands with a quick up-and-down movement.

Jenny looked at Elsie, whose face had an expression of warning or sympathy on it, then at Miss Sinclair, who said pleasantly: 'Mr Whittaker is John Whittaker's father. One of your pupils, Miss Bunn.'

'Oh, how is John, Mr Whittaker?'

'That's really why we're here,' Miss Sinclair said. 'Because of how John is. Let me just explain the position to you. Now, yesterday evening John was out playing with his friends in an old ruined cottage on the edge of the woods up here. We're not quite sure what happened, but at one point John fell off the top of a wall and sprained his ankle rather severely.'

'Oh, poor little lad,' Jenny said. 'I do hope there were no bones broken or anything.'

'No bones broken, fortunately,' Miss Sinclair went on. 'But there was another sort of complication. By the time John had his fall, all the other children had gone, except one. The one who was still there was Michael Primrose – another of your pupils, Miss Bunn. One of your favourites, I believe.'

Jenny nodded. While she talked, Miss Sinclair had been looking her up and down from thatchy hair to muddy shoes, with wine-splashed dress playing an important part in between. Now that her eyes were back on Jenny's there was no friendliness in them, although her tone stayed bright.

'An attractive child, no doubt, but spoilt and self-willed. Being so indulged by his parents he should, perhaps, have been treated with a little less leniency at school. He's a strong lad for his age, I should say, strong enough to have tried to help John out of this cottage and as far as the nearest house, if no further. But Michael decided he couldn't manage that unassisted. He went off and left John, saying he would bring help. Well, for one reason or another, the help didn't arrive – I shall be asking Michael one or two questions about that part of it tomorrow. So John was left by himself. He might have been able to hop out of the cottage on his own – I don't know the place – but if that entered his head he was too demoralized to try it, by the time he realized that no help was forthcoming. So he just lay there and shouted, he said. Eventually the man at the end house, nearest the cottage, went out into his garden for something and heard him. By which time it was nearly dark, and John was in a rather hysterical state.'

'Oh, how awful.'

'Isn't it? This man finally got John's address out of him and drove him home. The doctor was fetched, the ankle attended to and a sedative was ... administered. John slept quite soundly, it seems, until – what time was it, Mr Whittaker?'

'About half-eleven. And then he ...'

'Yes, go on, Mr Whittaker.'

'Well,' the man said unwillingly, glancing round at them, 'then he woke up with a jump and started crying. After a bit he was in a real state. I was for telephoning the doctor to come back, but Mrs Whittaker, she wouldn't have it. She doesn't like the doctor. All push and no real care, she says. Then John starts on about wanting to see Miss Bunn. I told him it's late at night, Miss Bunn's in bed and asleep, but that won't hold him, he's only a kid, got no sense of time. Anyway, he keeps on at it, he's got to see Miss Bunn. Well, we're not sure where you're living, Miss Bunn, so we're held up until Mrs Whittaker thinks of telephoning you, Miss Sinclair, and you give me Miss Bunn's telephone number, and I can't get you, Miss Bunn, but the lady I speak to gives me *another* number where you are. I'm afraid this is getting rather complicated, isn't it?'

'Well, when we get that far I'm for packing up for the night, it's getting really late, but Mrs Whittaker keeps on about you always being so kind to John, Miss Bunn, and how you'd want to come if you knew, and so it lands up she won't give me any peace till I've telephoned this other number. So I try, but I can't seem to get no sense out of the gentleman I speak to, and I thought there was some kind of disturbance going on where he was – I hope nobody was having any trouble there, Miss Bunn?'

Jenny's cheeks were hot by now, and there appeared to be less of her insides left than at any earlier time that morning. 'No, it was just a party and some of them had got up to some silly horseplay.'

'Ah, I see, that's all right, then. Well, after that Mrs Whittaker gets me to fetch Mrs Carter up, she's only just down the street from us. Not that I like doing it. Then between us we get John off all right. And that's the whole of it.'

'Except that John was asking for Miss Bunn again this morning, wasn't he?'

'That's right, Miss Sinclair, but not really agitated, not like last night. More just thinking it would be nice to see her, kind of. He was all right when we left, wasn't he, Mrs Carter?'

'At any rate, Miss Bunn,' Miss Sinclair said, 'I called in this morning to see how John was, and we thought it would be a good idea if we came and picked you up here and took you along to see John. We thought like Mrs Whittaker, that you'd want to be with him. But we seem to have chosen an inconvenient time.'

'Oh, not a bit,' Jenny said, getting up from the bed, 'I'm ready. Let's go there now.'

'Oh, it's good of you, Miss Bunn,' Mr Whittaker said, 'but we don't want to trouble you, with you just come in from staying the night and all. I told them, John's quite –'

'It's no trouble,' Jenny said. 'I want to see him.'

Miss Sinclair got up too and brushed her skirt down with her hand. 'On second thoughts,' she said, 'I'm inclined to agree with Mr Whittaker. There would be no point in disturbing John if he's settled down. I'm sorry to seem so changeable, but I hadn't taken that into account before. I'm afraid we've come here and bothered you for no very good reason, Miss Bunn. Well, we musn't take up any more of your time.'

Jenny said urgently: 'Please let me come, Miss Sinclair.'

The two exchanged looks, Miss Sinclair's saying that she knew the kind of girl Jenny was and at the same time that she did not understand Jenny's look, which said that she was not that kind of girl. Then Miss Sinclair said: 'There's no need to put yourself out, Miss Bunn. I'm sure you must have lots of things to do.' She gave Jenny the up-and-down treatment in a shortened form, then finished: 'Good-bye. Are you coming with us, Mrs Carter? I can drop you when I take Mr Whittaker.'

'I'll catch you up, Miss Sinclair,' Elsie said, speaking for the first time since Jenny's arrival. 'I just want to have a word with Jenny a minute.'

'Sorry to trouble you, Miss Bunn,' Mr Whittaker said as he went out, glancing at her in an apologetic, wondering way.

'I'd like to stay, love,' Elsie said when they were alone, 'but you know how Ted is when he doesn't get his dinner. That was a real going over you got, wasn't it? The old bitch. You're not to take any notice of her.'

'She's not a bitch. She was quite right.'

'She came round specially to do that. There wasn't any need. Whittaker wouldn't have come, not without her and his wife pushing him into it. The kid's all right, believe me, right as rain. He's forgotten all about it by now, just said he wanted you this morning so as to make a bit of a fuss and draw attention.'

'But it was different last night, he really wanted me then.'

'Jenny, you're human, you can't be at everybody's beck and call. Your free time's your free time, for God's sake. Of course, she's been gunning for you, you realize that.'

'What for? I haven't done anything to her.'

'I saw that type in the A.T.S. in the war. They're always down on the ones that look as if they're having a good time. You put it out of your mind, love, it's not worth bothering about. Just jealousy.'

'I'll go up there after dinner, to the Whittakers'.'

'Well yes, it'd look kind, wouldn't it? Now I really must fly, else I'll be in the hat for keeping her waiting. Pop in on your way this afternoon and we'll have a cup of tea and a good old palaver. Ted'll be on the allotment, so we can really put our feet up. Was it a thick night? You look a bit peaky. You can tell me all the sordid details this afternoon. Bye-bye for now, Jen. And don't you worry about her.'

Jenny stared at the wall until she heard the front door shut, and for a little longer. The car drove away. She pulled herself up and went to the table-with-railings, from which she took a box containing a teddy bear (the sort with a nice face) that she was sending to her nephew, Trixie's baby, for his second birthday. She took some brown paper out of a drawer and wrapped the box up with a *You're 2 today* card inside, but then found she had no string and was pretty sure there was none in the kitchen, so she put the parcel down again. Then she lay on her bed and cried for about half an hour. She was just thinking she ought to be seeing about Dick's dinner when she heard another car drive up, one whose noise she recognized. She peeped out of the window and saw Patrick getting out of the 110. She wiped her eyes and blew her nose vigorously, squaring her shoulders and telling herself she would not give in, but when he knocked and came into the room she went up to him and put her arms round his neck and started crying again. He held her tight and said nothing but endearments and nice things until she had it under control. Then he said: 'I've been sitting in the car for an hour just round the corner. Couldn't get any further. Look, is all this me or is there something else as well?'

'Oh, I did the most awful thing ...' She told him about John Whittaker and Miss Sinclair and the rest of it.

'Guilt is hell,' he said when she finished. 'And your Sinclair woman's evidently one of those neurotics who spend their time working on other people to give them cause to feel guilt. And you're ideal for that role – it's got to be someone with a strong moral sense, they're the ones for that lark.'

Jenny still had her arms round his neck. 'I haven't much right to a moral sense now, have I?'

'Oh, what absolute rubbish. Do you think that sort of thing can be blotted out by just one incident, and one you didn't have any part in, as far as actually doing a positive action went? You're still the same girl. What people do doesn't change their nature.'

She shook her head. She would never be able to explain to him what it meant to her not to have gone to John Whittaker when he needed her. And at almost the same time she was wishing she could be sure that she had resisted Patrick as hard as she could have done when he got into bed with her early that morning. 'What they do is their nature,' she said.

'Up to a point, perhaps. Anyway, what I'm going to do next is certainly my nature. It's taking you off to Charlie Crosland's establishment and buying you a bloody good lunch. I shall have one myself too, naturally. I'm just feeling the benefit of those two demi-tasses of bicarbonate I had for breakfast. Oh, I was going to give you these yesterday, but somehow they slipped my mind.'

In the plain white box was a pair of lovely earrings, and of course that set the blessed waterworks going a third time.

'Come on, darling, there's nothing to cry about.'

She shook her head again, but this time meaning that she agreed. She knew more or less what their future would be like, and how different it would be from what she had hoped, but she felt now that there had been something selfish in that hope, that a lot of the time she had been pursuing not what was right but what she wanted. And she could hardly pretend that what she had got was not worth having at all. She must learn to take the rough with the smooth, just like everybody else.

'I thought we might come back here this afternoon,' he said.

'I've got to see John this afternoon.'

'That won't take all the afternoon.'

'And I've got to get Dick's dinner.'

'Open a tin.'

'I could.'

He sighed. 'I didn't mean to hurt him. I got carried away by all those other mad sods. And I thought I hadn't got you. But now I have, I'll never need to do that sort of thing again. I'll be helping blind men across the street and taking stones out of horses' hooves.'

'I can't wait to see that.'

'I'll be altogether different.'

'You know, Patrick Standish, I should really never have met you. Or I should have got rid of you while I still had the chance. But I couldn't think how to. And it's a bit late for that now, isn't it? I'll just change my dress. Well, those old Bible-class ideas have certainly taken a knocking, haven't they?'

'They were bound to, you know, darling, with a girl like you. It was inevitable.'

'Oh yes, I expect it was. But I can't help feeling it's rather a pity.'

MORE ABOUT PENGUINS

Penguinews, which appears every month, contains details of all the new books issued by Penguins as they are published. From time to time it is supplemented by *Penguins in Print*, which is a complete list of all books published by Penguins which are in print. (There are well over three thousand of these.)

A specimen copy of *Penguinews* will be sent to you free on request, and you can become a subscriber for the price of the postage. For a year's issues (including the complete lists) please send 30p if you live in the United Kingdom, or 60p if you live elsewhere. Just write to Dept EP, Penguin Books Ltd, Harmondsworth, Middlesex, enclosing a cheque or postal order, and your name will be added to the mailing list.

Note: *Penguinews* and *Penguins in Print* are not available in the U.S.A. or Canada